To Helen,

Merry Christmas.
Hope you enjoy as
much as i did!

Lots of Love,

Heather
xxx

Chasing Daisy

Also by Paige Toon

Lucy in the Sky

Johnny Be Good

Paige Toon

Chasing Daisy

POCKET BOOKS

LONDON • SYDNEY • NEW YORK • TORONTO

First published in Great Britain by Pocket Books UK, 2009
An imprint of Simon & Schuster UK Ltd
A CBS COMPANY

3 5 7 9 10 8 6 4

Simon & Schuster UK Ltd
1st floor
222 Gray's Inn Road
London WC1X 8HB

Simon & Schuster Australia
Sydney

www.simonandschuster.co.uk

A CIP catalogue record for this book is available from the British Library

ISBN 978-1-84739-390-6

Typeset by M Rules
Printed by CPI Cox & Wyman, Reading, Berkshire RG1 8EX

For inspiring me, for encouraging me, for believing in me . . .

This one's for you, Dad

Prologue

'YOU SON OF A . . . *Figlio di puttana*!' That jerk in a yellow Ferrari just cut me up! 'Yeah, that's right, you heard me, you *testa di cazzo*!' I shout at him as he pulls into the petrol station opposite me. His window slides down.

'What the hell are you saying to me, you crazy bitch?'

How dare he! He nearly squished my scooter and me to a pulp with his fancy car!

'You nearly ran into me, you *coglione*!'

He gets out of his car, looking cross. 'Cogli-*what*?'

'*Coglione*! Dickhead!' I shout at him from across the street.

'Why don't you speak in English?' he shouts back.

'Because we're in BRAZIL, *cretino*!'

'*I'm* Brazilian! And that's no language I know!' He throws his hands up in the air.

Well, okay, it's Italian, if he's going to be fussy about it. I always swear in Italian. But that's beside the point.

Oh no, he's coming over here.

'You almost ran over me, you arsehole!' I plaster my angry face back on.

'That's better,' he says sarcastically. 'At least I can understand what you're saying to me, now.'

It's then that I notice he's quite good-looking. Olive skin, black hair, dark-brown eyes . . . Don't get distracted, Daisy. Remember where you're at. And where I'm at is mightily annoyed.

'You almost killed me!'

'I didn't almost kill you,' he scoffs. 'Anyway, you didn't put your indicator on. How was I supposed to know you wanted to go over there?' He points to the petrol station.

'I did SO have it on! *Va fanculo*!'

'What?'

'*Va fanculo*!'

'Did you just tell me to fuck off?' He looks incredulous.

'Ah, so you *do* speak Italian?'

'Hardly any, but I know what that means. *Va se lixar*!'

'What?'

'Piss off!' he says, angrily, and starts to cross the road to get back to his car.

'Piss off? Is that the best you can do?'

He casts a look over his shoulder that implies he thinks I'm seriously deranged and then opens the door to his Ferrari.

'Hey! You!' I shout. 'I haven't finished!'

'I have,' he calls.

'Get back here and give me an apology!'

'An apology?' He laughs. 'You owe *me* an apology. You almost scratched my car.' He gets into his Ferrari and slams the door. 'Silly woman driver!' he shouts through the still-open window.

'How dare you! You, you, you, *STRONSO*!' Translation: bastard. 'I hope you run out of petrol and get car-jacked!' I scream after him, cleverly realising he didn't fill his Ferrari with juice. But he can't hear me. He's long gone.

Some people. Argh!

How dare he imply I can't drive! I'm still angry. Not angry enough to forgo my hotdog, mind. I pull out of the lay-by and cross the road to the petrol station, ignoring the stares from onlookers who witnessed our altercation.

Stupid five-star hotel . . . It doesn't *do* junk food, so I borrowed one of the team's scooters and sneaked out.

I shouldn't have to sneak out, but I work in hospitality and catering for a Formula 1 team, and we don't *do* junk food either. I'm supposed to be setting an example, but I'm American, for Christ's sake. How can I live without it?

Partly American, in any case. I was actually born in England. As for the rest of me, that's hot-blooded Italian. That's the side you just witnessed, there.

I arrive at the hotel fifteen minutes later and my friend and colleague Holly is waiting on the front steps. She hisses at me to hurry.

'Sorry!' I hiss back. 'Had to run an urgent errand!'

'Doesn't matter!' She beckons me towards her.

It's then that I catch a glimpse of yellow in the car park. Yellow Ferrari. Oh, no.

'Quick!' she urges, as my heart sinks.

I knew I recognised him from somewhere. He's a driver. A racing driver.

'The rumours must be true,' she says, gleefully pushing me into the lobby.

And at that moment, I see the Ferrari Fucker walking in the direction of the hotel bar with the team boss.

'Luis Castro is signing with the team!' Holly squeaks as I dive behind a potted palm tree.

Shit, damn, fuck, tits.

Not even Italian is going to cut it this time.

Chapter 1

'Don't you dare,' Holly warns, as I suppress an unbearable urge to crawl under the nearest table.

We're in Melbourne, Australia, for the start of the season, and Luis Castro has just walked into the hospitality area. I'm desperately hoping he will have forgotten all about me during the last five months, because until early November when we end up back in Brazil for his home-town race, we'll be seeing a LOT of each other.

There's no getting away from it – I'm going to have to face him sometime – but just not now. Please, not now.

'Daisy!' Frederick barks. 'I need you to run an errand.'

My boss! My saviour! Thank you, thank you, thank you!

'The look of relief on your face,' Holly comments with wry amusement as I scuttle away in the direction of the kitchen.

'Where are you going?' Frederick asks in bewilderment as I duck under the arm he was resting against the doorframe.

'Just in here!' I reply brightly, waving my hands around to denote the kitchen, which is excellently out of Luis's line of vision.

Frederick looks perplexed, but continues. 'Catalina wants some popcorn. And I don't have any goddamn popcorn. Go and get some from one of the stands.' He hands me some money.

'Yes, boss!' I beam.

He gives me an odd look as I hurry out of the kitchen and back through the hospitality area with my head down.

Catalina is Simon's wife. Simon Andrews is the big boss and he owns the team. But Frederick – Frederick Vogel – is my immediate boss. He's the head chef.

Frederick is German, by the way. And Catalina is Spanish. Simon is English and Holly, while we're at it, is Scottish. What a multi-national bunch we are.

The Australian Grand Prix takes place in Albert Park, and yesterday I spotted a popcorn stand being set up on the other side of the shimmering green lake. I grab one of the team scooters and start it up.

It's Friday, two days before race day, but the track is still packed with spectators, here to watch the practice sessions. I drive carefully, breathing in the fresh, sunny air. It's the end of March, and unlike Europe and America which are swinging into spring, Australia is well into autumn. We've been told to expect rain this weekend, but right now there's barely a cloud in the sky. Melbourne's city skyscrapers soar up in the distance ahead of me, and behind me, I picture the ocean sparkling cool and blue.

I can smell the popcorn stand before I see it, salt and butter wafting towards me on a light breeze. Mmm, junk food . . . I wonder if I could also squeeze some for myself in the scooter's storage box? I consider it while the guy behind the counter scoops the fluffy, white kernels into a bag, but eventually decide it's a no-go.

I pay for the popcorn and stuff Frederick's change into my pocket, then unlock the box under my seat. Hmm, this popcorn is going to spill out – the bag's full to the brim and I need to be able to fold the top over. I suppose I could ask for another bag to wrap over the top . . . Or . . . I could eat some! Yes, that's the only logical conclusion.

I lean up against the scooter and delve in. The guy at the popcorn stand is watching me with amusement. What the hell are you staring at, buster? My glare wards off his gaze, but he's still grinning. I stuff another handful into my mouth. It's so warm and so . . . perfectly popped. I've probably eaten enough, now. Maybe just a little more . . . Right, that's it. Stop, now. Now! Regretfully I close the bag and store it under my seat, then start up the scooter.

If there are this many people here now, it's going to be packed on race day, I think to myself as I swerve around a group of slow-walking pedestrians. All of a sudden I spot two men wearing our team's overalls up ahead, and just as I go to turn a corner in front of a set of grandstands, I realise they're racing drivers, one of whom is Luis.

My back wheel catches some grit and slides out from under me as I take the corner. Suddenly the whole scooter is skidding and I can hear the grandstand half-full of spectators gasp in unison as I shoot across the gravel in front of them.

'Whoa!' Will Trust – the team's other driver – jumps out of the way, but Luis stays put, frozen in a crouch as though expecting to catch me.

'JESUS CHRIST!' I hear an Australian woman cry as my bike comes to a stop right in front of him. 'She almost ran over Luis Castro!'

She pronounces the name, 'Lewis', not 'Lew-eesh', as she's supposed to. I may not like the jackass, but it still bugs me when people can't say his name properly.

'That'll make a nice change from him running over me, then,' I snap, getting to my feet.

I immediately realise my mistake. That woman's mispronunciation error distracted me and I've idiotically just reminded him about our altercation. Maybe he wasn't paying attention. I quickly brush myself off as I feel his eyes boring into me.

'You,' Luis says.

Darn.

'You. The girl on the scooter.'

'Er, not anymore,' I say sarcastically, indicating the fallen vehicle. I bend down to try to stand it up.

'Hang on, let me get it.' Will Trust appears by my side and lifts up the scooter. 'Are you alright?' he asks, clear blue eyes looking searchingly into mine.

I almost jump backwards. 'Yes, yes, I'm fine,' I reply, blushing furiously. Actually, I'm not fine. My right hand is stinging like crazy from where I put it down on the gravel, and my knee feels horribly tender beneath the black pants of my black, white and gold team uniform.

'Let me see that.' Will takes my hand in his, pressing down on my fingers with his thumb to straighten my palm. He leans in and studies the graze and I feel jittery as I, in turn, study him. His light blond hair is falling just across his eye-line. I have a strong compulsion to reach over and push it off his face . . .

'It *is* you,' Luis says again.

Is he still here? Bummer.

I look around to see that quite a crowd has gathered to watch me and revel in my embarrassment. At least they're more interested in the drivers than me. Speaking of which . . .

'The girl in Brazil. The petrol station,' Luis continues.

Will lets me go and looks at us, questioningly. 'You know each other?'

I flex my hand. The feel of him is still there.

'Yeah, she almost crashed into my Ferrari in São Paulo last year,' Luis says.

'*I* almost crashed into *YOUR* Ferrari?' I come back to my senses, outraged. 'You nearly killed me!'

'Ha!' He laughs in my face. 'You're ridiculous. *And* you can't drive. I said you were a silly woman driver at the time and now you've just proved me right.'

'You, you, you . . .' I glare at him, lost for words.

'You're not going to call me a *coglione* again, are you?'

'No, but you are a *testa di cazzo*,' I mutter under my breath. It means the same thing. Literally, 'head of dick'. I smirk.

'What did you say?' Luis demands. 'What did she say?' he asks Will.

Will shrugs in amusement and bends down to dust off the scooter. I suddenly remember what I've done.

'I haven't scratched it, have I?' I bend down beside him and scrutinise the bike.

'It's not too bad,' Will says.

'I hope Simon doesn't fire me . . .'

'Simon won't notice. He's got too much else on his mind.'

'Simon notices everything,' Luis helpfully interjects.

Will rolls his eyes at me and my heart flutters, despite my fear of being axed.

'Will, are you coming or what?' Luis butts in.

'Sure, yeah. Will you be okay, er . . .' He looks at the name embroidered in gold on the front of my white team shirt.

'Daisy,' I say before he does. 'Yes, don't worry about me, I'll be fine.'

'I've seen you around. You're a front-of-house girl, right?' he checks. 'You help out with the catering?'

'Jesus, that's all we need,' Luis grumbles.

Will and I look at him in confusion.

'She'll probably give me food poisoning,' he points out.

'Don't flatter yourself,' I can't help but say. 'I wouldn't go to the trouble of trying.'

I spot a so-tanned-he's-orange marshal running over to us. 'Are you okay, miss?' he asks in an Australian accent.

'We'll leave you to it,' Will says, winking at me. I feel my face heat up again so I quickly turn my attention to the marshal.

Orange Man eventually deems I'm not a danger to myself or others and lets me go on my way, so I carefully drive back to our hospitality area, resisting the urge to speed. I've been gone ages.

I park up and locate the, well, it's not really a bag *full* of popcorn anymore, and go inside to look for Catalina. I scan my eyes around the room. There are a fair few people here today, considering it's only Friday. The tables are peppered with guests: sponsors, wives or girlfriends and the occasional friend or family member of someone in the team. Bigger teams than ours often invite the odd celebrity, too, but Simon doesn't seem to know anyone famous.

Aah, there she is.

Catalina is sitting at a table next to a skinny, tanned brunette, with medium-length, wavy hair. They look alike and, as I approach, I realise they're speaking Spanish. I wonder if they're sisters. Holly will know. Holly knows everything.

'Hi, Catalina, Frederick said you wanted this?' I offer it to her.

'What is it?' Her tone is as horrible as the look she gives me. 'Oh, popcorn,' she says, spying the crumpled packaging. 'Where's the rest of it?' she demands to know.

'Um, I couldn't fit it in my—'

'Have you been *eating* it?'

'I couldn't fit it—'

'Put it there,' she huffily interrupts, pointing to the tabletop in front of her.

The catering here is excellent, so why she's demanding popcorn in the first place is beyond me. Actually, I take that back. Nothing beats popcorn. But unlike her, if the rumours are to be believed, I won't be throwing it up in the toilets later.

I finally return to the kitchen.

'Where the hell have you been?' Frederick shouts.

'I had a bit of an accident,' I explain.

'You smell like you've been eating . . .' He leans towards me and gives a single loud sniff through his extremely large nostrils. 'Popcorn!'

He looks like a cartoon gangster, Frederick. Big nose, greasy black hair. And he's very tall and extremely lanky. I glance back at him to see him eyeing me suspiciously.

'Um, do I?' I ask innocently. He has an annoyingly good sense of smell. I guess it's useful if you're a chef, but in situations like these . . .

'What sort of accident?' he snaps.

I anxiously lead him outside to the scooter.

'It could be worse,' he grumpily concludes after he's inspected the damage.

'What happened?' Holly appears around the corner, full of

concern when she sees us kneeling on the floor studying the scratches.

I fill her in, her eyes widening when I tell her who my audience was.

'Right, enough,' Frederick interrupts. 'Back to work. There are three bags of potatoes for you to peel, Daisy.'

I notice that Holly gets to decorate a cake. I always get the shittiest jobs.

'Hey,' Holly says later, when Frederick pops out of the kitchen. I've been watching her distractedly for the last ten minutes as she's cut a sponge cake into large cubes and plastered them with chocolate icing. 'A few of the lads have been talking about going out tonight. Fancy it?'

'Sure, where?'

'St Kilda,' she says, dipping one of the chocolate-covered cubes into desiccated coconut.

'What the hell are you doing?' Curiosity gets the better of me.

'What?'

'With that cake.' I nod at the furry-looking cube.

'Lamingtons,' she explains. 'They're Aussie cakes.'

We always try to cater according to the country we're in and it sometimes makes for an 'interesting' menu.

'Anyway, back to tonight . . .' She leans against the counter and wipes the coconut off her hands.

'Where's St Kilda?' I ask.

'It's a really cool suburb on the other side of the park.'

'Will we be able to get away in time?'

'Yeah, should be fine. We did the early shift and half the team is going to that sponsorship event anyway so we don't really need to be around after eight thirty. I'm gagging for a drink.' She puts her hands up to her head and tightens her high, bleached-blonde ponytail.

'I need a drink, too. Especially after earlier . . .'

'I still need to hear all about that,' she says. 'Not now, though,' she adds, as Frederick walks back in, so we both put our heads down and crack on.

'You called him a dickhead again? In front of Will?' Holly claps her hand over her mouth in wide-eyed shock, then starts laughing through her fingers.

The air is hot and humid and we're seated outside a pub in St Kilda. We walked here straight from the track, along Fitzroy Street's dozens of cafés, restaurants and bars, all spilling out onto the pavement with rowdy revellers.

'He deserved it,' I say flippantly.

'Who deserved what?' Pete, one of the mechanics, plonks himself down on a recently vacated chair next to us. A few of the 'lads', as Holly likes to call them, have joined us for a drink. It's ten o'clock at night and they've only just come from the track, although they swear they're heading back to the hotel by midnight. Last time they said this, we were in Shanghai towards the end of the season, and they were out on the town until three a.m. When Simon got wind of it, he was not happy.

'She crashed one of the team scooters in front of Will and Luis earlier,' Holly tells him.

'Holly!' I erupt. She's had a few too many beers.

'They're going to find out sooner or later,' she says to me, giggling at Pete.

'Oh, I've already heard about that,' he says dismissively.

'You've heard about it?' I ask, humiliated.

'Yeah, yeah, Luis was going on about it earlier. Said you could have broken his legs.'

'Broken his legs?' I explode, humiliation swiftly transforming into irritation. '*Figlio di puttana*!'

'Son of a bitch,' Holly casually explains to Pete. She knows as many Italian swear words as I do. One of the undeniable bonuses of working with me.

'Actually, it literally translates to "son of a whore",' I point out pedantically, before continuing with my rant. 'I can't believe that!'

Pete just laughs and raises his eyebrows, taking a swig from his beer bottle.

'Don't worry about it,' Holly soothes. 'No one will remember it by tomorrow.'

'*Eeeeeeeeeeeee* . . . BOOM!' Another mechanic makes a loud crashing sound as he pulls up a chair and joins us at the table. 'Way to go, Daisy!' he laughs.

'Thanks, Dan. Appreciate your support,' I answer, glumly.

Dan is quite short compared to Pete, who's enormous at six foot four, but both are broad and muscular, unlike Luis and Will who are about six foot and slim-built. You have to be to fit in those Formula 1 cars.

Two more mechanics zoom past the table, pretending to screech to a stop.

'Haven't you guys got anything better to do?' I call after them.

I lean back in my seat and watch as a group of gorgeous girls in their late teens strut by. I feel old, and I'm only twenty-six. I know I look older. People tell me it's the way I carry myself. I think it's because of the size of my heels. I'm five foot nine, but I never go out in less than three inches. Well, that was back in America. I've started wearing flats since I got this job. I'm on my feet all the time and I'm not really a massive fan of torture. Plus, Holly is tiny at five foot one and I look enough like a giant next to her as it is.

'Wicked!' Dan interrupts my thoughts. He's looking down at his mobile phone. 'Luis is coming by for a drink. He's just left that event.'

Oh, for God's sake. I was enjoying myself. Now we'll have to find another venue to drink at and everywhere is so busy around here.

'Staying true to form, then,' Holly comments.

What she means by that is, Luis has a reputation for being a hard-partying ladies' man. This is his first year in Formula 1. Prior to that he raced in the American IRL – Indy Racing League – series and won the infamous Indy 500 three times in a row, which is why I vaguely recognised him – not that I've ever been that interested in racing before. Anyway, everyone speculated that he would have to calm down his wild ways and slot into the fold once he started working for Serious Simon, but he's clearly sticking his fingers up at that idea.

'I thought you guys were having an early night?' I say.

'He's a driver.' Dan shrugs. 'I can't blow him out. Another round?'

'Er . . .' I'm about to make our excuses about moving on, but Holly's response is too quick.

'Sure!' She lifts up her glass of beer dregs. 'Same again!'

'What did you go and do that for?' I complain as soon as Dan and Pete have left the table. 'I don't want to stay here if he's coming.'

'Aw, come on, Daisy, we're having fun. Maybe it'll do you good to get to know Luis socially.'

'I don't want to get to know him socially. He's a dick. I want to go somewhere else.'

'Just one drink? I wonder if Will might join him,' she muses.

A strange shiver goes through me at the sound of Will's name.

'I doubt it,' I answer, albeit slightly hesitantly. 'Isn't he a bit too committed to go out drinking the night before qualifying?'

'Maybe. But perhaps he'll take some time off for a change. Have a few beers with the lads, you know, good for team morale . . .'

A tiny glimmer of hope starts to flicker inside me. Dan returns with our drinks and then goes off to chat to Pete and the other mechanics standing on the pavement.

Unusually for a racing team, our previous drivers both retired at the end of last year, so we started this season with two newbies. Will, unlike Luis, has been in Formula 1 for a couple of years. The British have gone bananas over him, because he's young, good-looking *and* talented, so it was a quite a coup for Simon to scoop him up. I've seen him around the track a bit in the past, but have never been in close proximity to him. Until yesterday.

'Do you ever see him at team headquarters?' I turn back to Holly.

'Who?' she asks.

'Will.'

'Oh. Yeah, occasionally, yes. He's been in to use the simulator a few times.'

'Simulator?'

'It's like a car-sized PlayStation racing game. They use it to learn the different track layouts. It's wicked, actually. Pete let me have a go on it a few weeks ago.'

'Aah, right.'

'Why are you asking about Will?' She remembers my initial question.

'Um, no reason . . .'

'You fancy him, don't you?' She slams her hand down on the table.

'No!' I deny.

'You bloody do! You've gone all red!'

'I have not!'

'You have! I thought you were sworn off men?'

'I am,' I respond.

'Are you ever going to tell me why?'

I shake my head and take a sip of my drink.

'Why not?' she asks for about the zillionth time. At least, that's what it feels like to me.

'I can't,' I reply.

'Why? Are you worried your ex will hunt you down and kick your arse?'

I don't answer.

She looks stricken. 'That's not it, is it? Oh God, Daisy, I'm so sorry if it is. I would never make fun of—'

'I'm not a victim of domestic violence,' I wearily interject. 'I just don't want to discuss it.'

'Huh. Fine.' She looks put out, then she adds, 'Well, Will's got a girlfriend anyway, so he's off-limits.'

'Does he?' I try to keep my voice light, but the disappointment is immense.

'Of course he does. How can you not know that? They're always in the tabloids together.'

'I don't read the papers.'

'Still, how can you have missed them?'

'Why? What's their story?'

'Childhood sweethearts.'

My heart sinks.

Holly carries on, oblivious to my pain. 'They grew up in the same village together. The press back home love it how Will has stayed with her through thick and thin and has never been tempted by all the bimbos on the racing scene.'

This is getting worse.

'She works for a children's charity.'

'Are you making this up?' I look at Holly, incredulous.

She laughs. 'No, it's true. Sorry.'

'Well, like you say, I'm sworn off men.'

And yes, I am. I had my heart broken in America and felt like I had to leave the goddamn country because I couldn't go anywhere without bumping into the bastard.

Repeat: I am okay on my own. I am okay on my own. I am okay on my own.

And I am sure as hell not going to chase after someone who has a girlfriend. That's not my style.

I notice Holly wiping some of the lipgloss off her beer glass and smudging it back onto her lips.

'That is such a good look,' I say.

'You are really quite sarcastic for an American, aren't you?' she answers wryly, as Pete plonks himself back down at the table.

'I was born in England,' I remind her.

My mother is Italian and my father is British, but when I was six, he moved the whole family to America. I'd been there for almost twenty years when I relocated to the UK and secured a job working as a waitress for Frederick and his wife Ingrid's catering company in London. Then last October, Frederick asked me if I'd like to come along to the final three races as a front-of-house girl. That title means working in hospitality and making sure the team and its guests are looked after, but I also help out in the kitchen whenever it's required. Opportunities like this – to see the world and get paid for it – don't come along very often, so naturally I jumped at the chance.

Holly and I hit it off immediately. When we're not racing, she works in the canteen at the team's headquarters in Berkshire, England. I say canteen, but it's actually more like a Michelin-starred restaurant. We met for the first time in Japan last year where we got through several jugs of sake in the hotel bar one night. The jugs are only tiny, but boy is rice wine strong. We were shit-faced by ten p.m, and you don't even want to know what we consumed a week later in China.

After Brazil, Frederick asked me to stay on for another year to do a full season. I don't know what came over him, but yay!

Holly has been rummaging around in her bag for ages and now she finally emerges with a tube of pink lipgloss. She reapplies some, giving me an overtly smug look.

I could do with some of that, actually. Just in case Will does deign to join us. What am I thinking? No, no, NO!

Damn it. 'Can I have some?' I have very little willpower. I slick some over my lips, then tuck my long, dark hair behind my ears and wait.

A few minutes later, a taxi pulls up outside the pub and the high-heel-clad feet of a woman gracefully step out of it onto the pavement.

I recognise her. It's the woman Catalina was talking to in the grandstand . . . Her sister?

Then Luis climbs out of the car behind her. I crane my neck, but there's no Will. I feel momentarily crushed, but firmly tell myself it's for the best.

'Oi, oi, oi!' I hear a few of the lads behind us shout. Luis grins at them.

'Who's that he's with?' I ask Holly.

'Alberta. Catalina's cousin,' Holly answers.

Sister . . . Cousin . . . Close enough.

'Getting in with the boss's family, is he?' My tone is wry as I watch Luis put his hand on the woman's lower back to steer her through the crowd.

'Clearly,' Holly replies.

He reaches our gathering and is enthusiastically welcomed by the mechanics, most of whom are standing on the pavement behind our table. Holly and I remain seated, while Pete stands up and leans across us to clap Luis on the back. Holly smiles and lifts her hand in a half-wave of hello, but I can't bear to look at him so I busy myself pretending to pick a fly out of my wine glass.

'*Hello!*' I hear him pointedly say in my direction.

'Oh, hello!' I reply, as though becoming aware of his presence for the first time.

'Written off any scooters lately?'

The boys around him crack up laughing and a couple of them make loud crashing noises.

'Ha ha,' I reply sarcastically and turn back to the imaginary insect in my glass.

One of the lads lifts a chair over the heads of the people drinking at the table next to us and plonks it down beside me, waving his hand with a flourish to Alberta. Pete immediately offers his chair to Luis.

'No, it's okay,' Luis says. 'I'm happy to stand.'

'It's alright, I'm going back to the bar,' Pete says. 'What are you having?'

Luis produces a wad of notes. 'My round,' he says.

'That's too much, mate!' Pete waves Luis's money away.

'No, no, take it!' Luis insists. 'Put it in the, what do you call it? Kitty?'

Pete eyes it sceptically.

'Take it!' Luis forces it into his hand.

'Do you want a bottle of champers?' Pete asks Luis.

'No, no, a beer for me.'

'Saving the champagne for race day . . .' Alberta comments in a husky voice.

Luis just laughs. 'Will you have some?' he asks her.

'I wouldn't mind,' she replies, sexily.

'Go on then, Pete, get a bottle. Do you need some more?' He reaches for his wallet.

'No, mate, no!' Pete practically shouts, holding up the wad in his hand. 'I've got enough here to buy a house! Girls? Same again?'

'I'm fine, thank y—'

'We'll help out with the champers!' Holly shouts. 'Daisy, stop being such a lame-arse,' she whispers to me when Pete has departed.

'So Frederick let you come out to play?' Luis looks straight at me.

I nod. 'Uh-huh.'

I feel Alberta's chocolate-brown eyes fall on me and am taken aback by how cool her gaze is, considering her eye colour is so warm. It's the same with her sister. Cousin, I mean. Whatever. The silly Bs are related, that's all I need to know.

'I heard he's a ball-breaker . . .' Luis continues.

I don't answer.

'I'm Holly!' Holly puts a stop to the awkwardness and offers her hand to Alberta, followed by Luis.

'Do you work with this one?' Luis asks Holly, nodding my way.

'As a front-of-house girl, yes.' She smiles warmly, cutting short whatever sarcastic comment I'm certain Luis was about to make. 'How was the sponsorship event?' she asks, her tone bubbling over with friendliness. I don't know how she does it.

'Boring,' Luis answers.

'Oh, thank you very much.' Alberta pretends to be upset.

'With the exception of the present company, of course.'

I'm about to put my fingers down my throat and make gagging noises when I notice her hand on his leg and am rendered speechless.

Pete returns with a tray full of drinks for the lads, plus glasses, champagne and an ice bucket. Holly and I help him unload it before he heads back to the bar to return the tray.

I hear a cork pop as Luis deftly pours champagne into three glasses, handing one to each of us girls.

'No, thank you,' I say, fingering the stem of my wine glass. I still have a few sips of Shiraz in there somewhere.

'Don't waste it,' Luis states.

'I'll drink yours, Daisy,' Holly offers, so I push it across the table to her.

'There's plenty to go around.' Luis pushes the glass back in my direction and turns to Alberta.

I give him a look of such distaste that he must surely feel my eyes branding the back of his skull, then I inadvertently glance down and am greeted with the sight of Alberta sliding her hand in the direction of Luis's crotch. Dirty cow! I look at Holly in shock. A split second later I hear the sound of a chair scraping on the pavement and turn back to see Luis standing up.

'Where are you going?' Alberta asks, her brow furrowed with annoyance.

'The men's room,' Luis tells her.

'I wouldn't mind going, too,' she says silkily, making me feel as invisible as that fly in my drink.

'I need a *piss*,' Luis says firmly, putting to a halt whatever naughty things Alberta had planned for their cubicle excursion. She slumps back in her seat and watches his departing backside.

'Have you been to a Grand Prix before?' Holly tactfully changes the subject.

'Of course,' Alberta answers dismissively.

'Do you enjoy the racing?'

'That's not what I'm here for.'

'Oh. What are you here for?'

'The fun! The glamour!' She casts her arms around her in an extravagant manner.

Glamour? I decide against pointing out the wasted youth who has just vomited on the kerb.

She takes a huge mouthful of champagne and reaches for the bottle.

'Let me do that for you,' Holly offers, making use of her hospitality skills. Alberta takes the refilled glass without so much as a thank you and sits back in her seat, crossing her legs so her mini skirt rides even further up her thighs.

I look away, bored and unable to play the game like my friend, and see Luis emerge from the pub doors. Alberta sits back up in her seat, but is visibly deflated when Luis stops to chat to the lads.

I know how she feels. I'd give anything to be able to gossip freely with Holly instead of watching my words in front of this beacon of bitchiness.

'Have you been Catalina's cousin for long?' Holly asks, in all innocence.

I look at her and crack up with laughter. She realises what she's said and joins me in hysterics.

'I've had too much to drink!' she squeals, lifting up her champagne glass in one hand and her beer glass in the other.

Alberta glares at us both before standing up, plucking the champagne bottle out of the ice bucket and going to join Luis.

'Come on, Holly, please can we go somewhere else, now?'

'Yeah, okay,' she agrees, knocking back first her beer, followed by her champagne and then rising to her feet.

We wind our way out towards the pavement, squeezing past the revellers already swarming to occupy our recently vacated chairs.

'We're off! See ya, lads!' Holly calls to the group of mechanics.

'Lightweights!' Pete shouts.

'We're not going back to the hotel, we're going partying, you pussy!' Holly shouts, and I pull on her arm, laughingly trying to ignore Luis's dark-eyed stare as we back away from the crowd.

Chapter 2

'I feel like a porcupine has rolled onto my eyelids,' Holly moans.

'I feel like a porcupine has lifted up my eyelid and stuck one of his spiky pine things into my retina,' I reply.

'I feel like a porcupine has lifted one of my eyelids and scraped *five* of his SPINES, I think you'll find they're called, into my—'

'Girls!' Frederick barks.

We abruptly fall silent. The pain is worth it – we had such a laugh last night. We bumped into a couple of girls who work in hospitality for another team and they talked us into going on the rickety little rollercoaster in Luna Park, St Kilda's oceanfront amusement park. It was seriously scary – I thought we were going to come off the rails – but damn, it was funny. Then they wanted to go to the beach to go night swimming, but Holly and I thought we'd better get to bed as we were only going to get three hours' sleep as it was.

Right now it's the ludicrous time of five a.m. and we're already at the track prepping food for the day's menu. Holly's mixing muesli with a variety of fruit and nuts, while I'm trimming bacon fat. I told you I always get the crappiest jobs.

'I wonder how Luis is feeling this morning,' I muse, when Frederick leaves us alone for a moment to harass a couple of other front-of-house staff, a husband and wife team from Germany called Klaus and Gertrude. They're weird as hell when you chat to them socially, but scarily efficient at their jobs.

'Concerned for Luis's welfare now, are you?' Holly raises one eyebrow at me.

'No,' I answer, annoyed.

'I imagine he's feeling on top of the world after his shag last night,' she says.

'You reckon they did the dirty deed?' I struggle to keep my tone light.

'I *know* they did the dirty deed,' she says, ominously. 'Alberta came out of Luis's room at three o'clock this morning looking very much like the cat that got the cream.'

'How do you *know* these things?' I shake my head in awe.

She just smiles secretively. 'Never give away my sources. Anyway, Luis will be in for a tough time with Simon if he doesn't pull out all the stops in qualifying today.'

'Haven't you finished yet?' Frederick snaps, coming back over to us.

'Yes, Chef!' we chorus.

'Then get outside to the serving table, both of you!'

Ten minutes later, I'm trying not to let the smell of frying bacon turn my stomach when a dishevelled-looking Luis walks through the hospitality doors. He's unshaven and wearing sunglasses, and everyone knows Simon likes his drivers to be well turned out.

He comes straight over to us.

'What can I get you?' Holly asks, ever-chirpy.

'Just a coffee. Strong,' he adds.

'Get lucky last night, did you?' I give him a dry look.

'You have got such a mouth on you,' he answers, not amused.

I should be careful, actually. I shouldn't really speak to a 'revered' driver like this, but when it comes to Luis, I just can't help myself.

'You look a bit worse for wear yourself,' he adds, still staring at me.

'Why, thank you very much, sir. You sure know how to please a lady.'

'That's what I was told last night.'

I look at him, open-mouthed. He takes his coffee and wanders off, nonchalantly.

'Did you hear what he just said?' My voice has risen an octave.

'Yes, yes, I heard it. You don't half ask for it, though.' Holly rolls her eyes.

'I knew Alberta was a Screwdriver the minute I clapped eyes on her,' I say hotly.

A 'Screwdriver' is a term we use in the business for women who chase after racing drivers. Or, to put it another way, for women who *screw* drivers. Nice, huh?

'Why should you care, anyway?' Holly asks. 'You can't stand the guy.'

'He's a jerk,' I respond, just to reaffirm my feelings if they were at all unclear.

'Freakishly good-looking though,' she says.

'Good-looking?' I scoff. 'How can you say that?'

She just laughs. 'Ooh, look, it's Prince Charming.' She nods towards the door and I glance up to see Will walk in.

He heads over to the serving table, looking different to how I remembered him. I could have sworn his face was rounder.

'Alright?' he says.

Holly gives me a discreet shove when I don't immediately find my voice. 'Hello! What can I get you?' I ask him sweetly, coming to life.

'That looks good,' he says, eyeing up the bacon. 'But I'd better go for some of that.' He points to Holly's muesli instead.

I feel dejected as I watch her serve him.

'Out last night with the lads?' Will looks straight at me.

'How did you know . . . Oh, looking a bit rough, am I?'

'No, I just heard from a couple of the guys that you were out on the town. Good night?'

'Great,' I respond, delighted from the top of my head down to the tips of my rose-coloured toenails. He was talking about me!

'Where did you go?'

'St Kilda. It's just on the other side of the—'

'I know it.'

'Skimmed, semi or full fat?' Holly interrupts, indicating the silver milk jugs.

'Semi.'

She pours some milk into his bowl and he takes it from her.

'Would you like a coffee or anything to drink?' I ask.

'An orange juice, thanks.'

I pass him a glass, my hand shaking ever so slightly.

He grins and nods at it. 'Is that a result of your scooter accident or alcohol withdrawal?'

Actually it's because I'm so nervous about being this close to you. But I lie and tell him it's probably alcohol related.

'You should have come out with us!' Holly gushes.

'Nah,' he replies.

'Too dedicated.' I smile at him warmly. I can see Holly out of the corner of my eye and just *know* she's on the brink of cracking up.

He raises his eyebrows in amusement and backs away, holding up his bowl of muesli and glass of juice. 'Better get this down me. See you later.'

'Absolutely.' I beam at him.

'Way too OTT, Daisy!' Holly exclaims when he's gone.

'Was not,' I grumble.

The hospitality area is situated directly behind the team garages, otherwise known as the pits, so later, when qualifying is already in full swing, Frederick allows us time out to go and take a look.

The garage is a hive of activity. Mechanics in black, white and gold overalls are swarming all over Luis's car. I think I can spot Dan hovering over the front wing, but it's hard to tell. All the mechanics have to wear protective clothing from head to toe, so you can barely tell one from the other. But Dan sees me watching him and gives me a wave, before busily getting back to work.

Will is out on the track at the moment, so we stand at the back of his garage and watch from every angle as six television screens broadcast the action.

'Hey!'

I glance up to see a big, tall mechanic looking down at me. He's wearing a helmet so I peer into it and realise it's Pete. He's the chief mechanic on Will's car.

'How's it going?' I shout over the thunderous noise of the cars zooming down the straight on the other side of the pit wall.

'Great guns!' he shouts back. 'WHOA!'

His exclamation is mirrored by several other mechanics watching the TV screens. I glance up to see Will has taken first place, known in the industry as pole position.

'Cool!' I shout.

'Got a little way to go yet,' he shouts back, then to the lads, 'He's coming in!'

They all swarm outside to the pit lane.

As Will pulls up, Luis's car zooms out of the garage next to us.

The on-car camera is riding with Luis, and we watch as he speeds around the corners, car bumping over the kerbs as he takes the fastest racing line.

Usually the drivers stay inside their cars for the duration of qualifying and watch the on-track action on a television stationed above their heads, but today Pete asks Will to climb out so they can make some adjustments. I stop watching Luis's lap for the moment to focus on him. He takes off his helmet, a navy blue and silver design, and then tugs off his fireproof balaclava. His blond hair is damp with sweat, and as he pushes it back off his face, I'm hit by an image of him in bed with me.

I shake my head involuntarily and force my gaze back up to the screens. Luis's helmet is bright green, and I have to admit it does stand out, gaudy though it is.

I feel someone's presence beside me and turn to see Will standing there. Warmth radiates from him and the arm of his overall brushes against my elbow, freezing me to the spot. I watch him out of the corner of my eye as he studies the TV screens. His jaw is rigid with tension, then he seems to relax. I look back up and notice Luis is currently in fifth place on the grid, but the positions are changing all the time, and suddenly another driver takes pole position.

'We should go back,' Holly says.

Will glances down and acknowledges us with a nod, before checking the screens again to see he's currently in third place for the start tomorrow.

'Will!' one of the mechanics calls.

'Daisy . . .' Holly urges as I distractedly watch Will return to his car and pull on his helmet before climbing back in. 'Frederick won't let us watch the race if we take the piss too much.'

'Okay, okay, I'm coming.' I desperately want to stay and see if Will can win back pole position when he next goes out, but I guess we'll have to wait for news after the event.

Frederick isn't even in the kitchen when we return and I can't help but feel grumpy. I wasn't that bothered about the racing last season, so it's funny how much more riveting it's become since Will joined the team. Holly ignores my mood and gets on with loading canapés onto a silver tray.

'Are you coming?' she asks me, raising a perfectly plucked eyebrow. 'You know you can watch it while you work, yeah?'

I completely forgot about the big screen in the hospitality area. I hurriedly load up my own tray with kangaroo kebabs and mini burgers.

As we approach the overexcited guests we realise that Luis has just scored pole position and Will is out on the track completing his last lap. I can't hold the tray steady and no one's interested in food at the moment anyway, so I pull back and focus on Will as he speeds around the final corner on to the pit straight. Can he do it?

YES!

Everyone cheers as he swipes pole back from under his teammate's wheels, leaving us with a one/two start tomorrow. For two new drivers and a team that usually ranks fourth or fifth in the championship, this result is outstanding.

I'm on edge as I wait for the drivers and team to return to the hospitality area. Frederick has instructed us to make sure champagne flows freely throughout the afternoon and evening and I'm just hoping that Will is going to join us for the celebrations. I soon spot him outside talking to the press along with Luis and Simon, but then I'm distracted with work and when I look back, all three of them have gone.

'Off for a post-qualifying meeting, I guess,' Holly says, reading my mind.

I plaster a smile on my face and carry on with work, while waiting for them to return. When Luis emerges my heart lifts, but there's no sign of his team-mate, and hours later when we finally call it quits for the night, I go to bed feeling oddly flat.

Chapter 3

'That was Kylie Minogue!' Holly excitedly points outside the garages.

'Come on, let's stalk her!'

It's race day and the buzz is electrifying. All our most important sponsors are in the pits and Frederick has allowed some of his crew to watch the start. The build-up is just as exciting as the actual race because there are gazillions of celebrities and camera crews traipsing around. Holly and I really want to see who else we can spot aside from Kylie, so we squeeze our way through all the people to get to the pit wall. The drivers and their cars are already lined up in their positions on the starting grid, but earlier they took part in a parade around the track on the back of a truck, and we could hear horns and whistles blowing from far away as they passed thousands of cheering spectators in the grandstands.

I look for Will, but only catch a glimpse of his car at the very front. Luis's bright green helmet comes into view and I realise he's surrounded by grid girls having their picture taken with him. What an idiot. Grid girls – or brolly dollies – are the models who stand on the grid holding umbrellas to keep the drivers out of the sun. Sometimes they just hold placards with the start numbers on them. It doesn't surprise me that Luis is lapping up all the attention he can get from them; most of the drivers do. I spot Emilio Rizzo, an Italian driver in his mid-thirties, pretending to grab one of the girl's boobs.

'That'll be nice for his wife,' Holly comments, seeing what I'm seeing. 'Crazy flirt, that one.'

Most of the drivers have got wives or girlfriends. I've seen a fair few since I've been working here. Some of them are supermodel-stunning – in fact, Benni Fischer from Germany is going out with quite a famous actress – but others are just nice, normal girls. Almost all of them attend the races to support their boys.

I wonder if Will misses *his* girlfriend . . .

'If she loved him that much she would be here, wouldn't she?'

'If who loved who?' Holly asks, confused.

'Will's girlfriend.'

Holly whacks me on the arm. 'Stop it, you. Anyway, I think Laura is organising a charity ball in London this weekend.'

Laura. So that's her name. 'Have you seen them together? You know, in person?'

'Er, yeah, she came to the British Grand Prix last year. His parents were there too, actually. Very cold and aloof. His dad is high up in banking or something, and his mother is a society wife.'

'Oh, right. What's Laura like? Is she aloof, too?'

Holly gives me a look. 'No. She seemed really nice. Blonde. Sweet. Very pretty, too.'

'Okay, okay! Enough!'

She grins and looks away.

It's overcast today. It rained this morning, but the weather is supposed to hold out for the race. There's little need for the Factor 30

I applied this morning. Yeah, yeah, I know UV rays can still get you and all that, especially down here where the ozone layer is so thin, but I'm just pleased Simon doesn't make us wear hats.

Today our uniform is skirts, not trousers. All the teams have uniforms created by top fashion designers, and different outfits are provided for different days. When we're travelling we have to wear black and gold trouser suits, on Friday practice days we wear black trousers and white shirts, and on Saturdays and Sundays we wear black skirts with white trim and gold silk shirts. The outfits look better than they sound. And if you lose an item of clothing or sell it on eBay, you're in serious trouble. In fact, one girl last year got the sack for it.

The other things you must absolutely not lose are your race credentials. They're a bit like ski passes. They hang around your neck and you have to swipe them to get through the security gates into the paddock area. The paddock is where the hospitality suites and garages are situated – areas which are strictly forbidden to the general public – but our passes are access-all-areas. They're like gold dust – each team only gets a certain number of passes like this, so I know how lucky I am.

The people on the grid are thinning out because it's almost time for the race to start. I take one last look at Will's car and manage to spot his navy blue and silver helmet in the cockpit. He's already strapped in. Holly and I hurry back to the garages along with swarms of team members vacating the starting grid and stand in front of the television screens. The sound of the engines is deafening as the twenty-odd drivers set off on the warm-up lap, zigzagging from side to side along the straights to heat up their tyres. Finally they file around the last corner onto the pit straight and take their positions on the grid. The atmosphere is tense as the five traffic lights above the starting line glow red, red, red, red, red, then they go out and it's GO!

Will has a good start and takes the first corner without too much trouble, but the driver in fourth place – a Canadian called Kit Bryson – nips up the inside and swipes second place from under Luis's nose, relegating him down to third. Over the next few laps, Will starts to pull away from the pack, but then there's an accident halfway down the field and the safety car is brought out as a cautionary measure. The safety car slows the drivers down so the track can be cleared of crash debris and consequently the gap between Will and Kit Bryson is closed as the pack tightens up. When the flag goes green and the racing kicks into gear again, Will manages to keep his lead, but there's a problem a few laps later. Smoke is coming from the back of Will's car and the sight of it makes several of our mechanics curse. They hurry outside to the pit lane, but Will doesn't even make it around the last corner before his engine gives up. He pulls into one of the gravel pits – designed to slow down the cars that have run off the track – and we watch on the screens as he gets out of the car and track marshals swarm over it.

Simon is sitting at the control desk on the pit wall in front of a bank of computers and one of the television cameras zooms in on the side of his stony face. Another screen shows Will starting the trek to the pits.

Holly tugs on my sleeve. 'We'd better get back,' she says, ever the professional.

I follow her reluctantly, wishing I could be there when Will arrives.

Twenty minutes go by in the hospitality area and Holly and I are kept busy serving drinks and canapés to the guests watching the race on the big screens. Luis hasn't managed to overtake Kit, but he's given it a good shot a couple of times. I'm standing there watching the action when Will walks in. The crowd applauds him and he waves his acknowledgement, then makes his way towards his private room.

He's all alone. No girlfriend, not even his parents to comfort him.

I wonder if he needs anything?

My feet are walking in the direction of his room before I can properly stop to think about it. Even when I start to doubt my actions they just keep moving and finally I'm outside his door and my hand is lifting up to knock . . .

What am I doing?

The door opens and he's standing there, his overalls stripped down to his waist and his naked chest gleaming with sweat.

'Er, hi.' He regards me warily.

'Sorry to bother you,' I quickly tell him, the words stumbling out of my mouth. 'I was just wondering if you wanted me to get anything for you. A drink, some food, some clean clothes . . .'

'Actually, I can't find my team shirt. There was a whole stack of them here, somewhere.' He glances around his room.

'Shall I take a look?' I ask.

He stands aside and waves me in. The drivers' rooms at the various tracks around the world are not big, but they're big enough for the drivers to relax in and get some peace and quiet.

My fingers tremble as I open drawers in a small cupboard and hunt out Will's shirts. There's a small black team carry case identical to mine sitting at the bottom of one cupboard.

'Could they be in here?'

He shrugs, so I pull it out and unzip it. It's full of team clothing.

'Aha!' he says. 'I hadn't got that far, yet.'

'Such a boy,' I tut. I unpack the shirt he should be wearing today and hand it over. 'What about your pants?'

He tugs on the elastic of his boxer shorts, poking out from beneath his overalls. 'What about them?'

My face immediately starts to burn. 'I meant your trousers! We call them pants in the US . . .'

He chuckles. 'I know, I'm only teasing. Don't worry, I can take it from here.'

'Okay, well, good.' I back out of the room, trying to regain my composure. 'Is there anything else I can get for you? A drink? Something to eat?' Yes, that was good, Daisy. Keep it professional!

'Nah.' His face becomes serious again. 'I should probably get out there and show my face to the sponsors.' He points his thumb in the direction of the hospitality area.

'Okay, then.' I turn and make a run for it.

'Thanks!' he calls after me.

'Where have you been?' Holly asks when I reappear. 'Have you just been in Will's room?' She looks at me with disbelief.

'Er, yes.'

'What were you doing?'

'Don't get excited, I was just helping him find his team shirt.' She casts her eyes heavenwards as I hasten to explain. 'You know, since Jennifer got the sack, the drivers don't have a dedicated person on hand to look after them.'

Jennifer was the front-of-house girl assigned to look after Sandro and Marcus last year – Will and Luis's predecessors. She's the *cretina* who sold her stuff on eBay.

'Hmm,' Holly says, jokily suspicious. 'Fair enough.'

'Better attend to that lot.' I hurry to the kitchen and load up another tray of canapés.

A few people clap as I approach them watching the race on the big screens. I'm confused for a moment because they can't be *that* hungry and then I realise Will has come out of his room behind me. That could have been *way* embarrassing; I almost smiled and curtsied. I stand back and let him shake hands with the sponsors, and the air is full of the sound of their commiserations. A bullish American man turns to me and shouts, 'Give the man something to eat, for Christ's sake!' before cracking up laughing at his own non-wit. Will smirks at me as he relieves my tray of a prawn skewer.

The laps count down towards the finish and Luis is still running in second place, although Kit has managed to put some distance between them. The pit stops have come and gone, but Luis hasn't managed to close the gap and it looks like he – and the team – will walk away from Australia with eight championship points. We would have received ten for a win, and as it is, Will gets nothing.

I pause for a break to watch the cars go round the last few laps. It must be hard for Will to sit here and watch his team-mate walk away with the glory. It's Luis's first year in Formula 1 and this result is going to create a real buzz around him.

Will stands up in front of me. Most of the spectators turn to stare at him.

'I'd better go join the team in the pits,' he says.

The most important sponsors are in the garages already, so the majority of people stay put in their seats, looking sorrowful at the sight of the team's most famous driver departing. He spins around and comes face to face with me.

'Daisy, are you coming to the pits?' I hear Holly call, and look over my shoulder to see she's just come from the kitchen, which means Frederick has given us the go-ahead.

'Er, yeah, sure!' I call back, distractedly side-stepping to let Will past. But he calmly indicates for me to go first, so I nervously lead the way out of the hospitality area. The three of us walk across the grass and asphalt to the pits while I desperately try to think of something to say. The garage looms just metres away and I want to kick myself because nothing comes to mind.

He. Has. A. Girlfriend.

Yes, yes, apart from that. Too late, we're here.

A few mechanics call Will over to the television screens. Holly and I tag along to watch the last couple of laps. Finally the black and white chequered flag waves to denote the finish and everyone in Luis's side of the garage cheers and embraces, delighted with their second-place result. Will's side of the garage is more restrained, but they all clap politely.

We run outside to watch the victory lap and wait for Luis to pull in. He leaps out of the car and bounds over to the waiting mechanics for a massive group hug. I'm in the middle of the throng, getting pulled this way and that, and it's easy to get swept away in the mood of the moment. The thought occurs to me that if Luis hadn't messed up his start, he would have won. Maybe he should cut out the late nights and partying . . . I wonder if Simon is also thinking the same thing.

We go excitedly en masse to witness the handing out of the trophies and Holly and I squeal as the drivers on the podium spray champagne over us and the crowd below. Finally they file inside for the press conference. I look around but can't see Will, then I notice him being interviewed by a camera crew. He looks serious.

Professional. At that moment he glances my way, and as our eyes meet, he seems to falter for a split-second. He quickly turns back to the interviewer and continues, but as Holly and I return to the garages to watch the press conference on the TV screens, I'm too caught up in my thoughts to concentrate.

Hours later, when we're in the middle of a mass clear-up session, Simon calls me in to the directors' suite. Holly and Frederick look at me in alarm as I hurry after him, terrified he's going to fire me for damaging one of the scooters. Inside the suite, he motions for me to sit down on the sofa as he takes the one opposite.

'How are you finding things?' he asks, blue-grey eyes studying me. He's quite attractive, Simon. In his mid-forties, with a tanned, weathered face and short, sandy-blond hair.

'Fine, fine,' I stutter.

'Not planning on jumping ship anytime soon?'

'No, no, of course not.'

'Good,' he says brusquely. 'Daisy, as you know, last year we had Jen to look after the boys.' He means Jennifer, the girl I mentioned earlier. I nod, both intrigued and relieved this is not about my scooter crash. 'This year I was after a more hands-on approach with everyone helping out.'

'Yes?'

'But one of the boys has asked if we can revert to last year's set-up.'

One of the boys?

'Right . . .'

'I'm wondering if you'd be up for doing the job.'

I'm speechless with surprise. Will asked for me? It can't have been Luis.

'It's the same sort of thing you're doing now,' he continues. 'Helping out Frederick and looking after the rest of the team as usual, but you'd also have more direct contact with Will and Luis – and me, if I need help with anything. Does that sound okay?'

He doesn't expect me to say no.

'Yes! That sounds great!'

'Good.' He stands up and it's clear our meeting is over.

I walk back into the kitchen and Holly and Frederick know right away that I haven't been fired.

'What is it?' Holly asks, smiling.

'I've got Jennifer's job,' I reply, still feeling a little dazed.

'Jen's job?' she checks suspiciously.

'Yes. Looking after Will, Luis and Simon . . .'

'Oh!' She seems surprised. 'Well, good for you,' she says, and carries on cleaning down the surfaces.

I was expecting her to be happier for me than that, but perhaps it's because Frederick is around.

Speaking of whom. 'You're not above washing the dishes,' Frederick says gruffly, pointing to the sink.

But as my promotion sinks in, not even the Eiffel Tower of plates in front of me can wipe the smile off my face.

Chapter 4

I can't remember what Will looks like. I've had intense crushes before, when the same thing has happened. It's been this way ever since I was a teenager.

I concentrate hard and try to focus on Will's face in my mind. Those blue eyes . . . Yes! There he is! And almost as suddenly he's gone again.

I switch on my bedside lamp and climb out of bed. On the dressing table there's a pile of magazines and I riffle through them until I come to an old issue from a few weeks ago. Will's face graces the front cover, but no, it doesn't look right. Something's missing.

'Daisy, switch off the bloody light!'

I quickly put down the magazine and climb back into bed, doing as Holly says.

'Sorry!' I whisper.

She just groans and pushes the sheet off her body in the bed next to me.

It's so hot and humid here. We're in Kuala Lumpur and it's been four days since I last saw Will. Holly and I flew straight here on Monday afternoon and we're sticking around after the race for a week's holiday on the island of Langkawi. Pristine beaches, crystal-clear water and palm trees galore . . . When you're coming to a location as beautiful as Malaysia, it would be stupid not to make the most of it.

A couple of days ago we met up with Frederick to help source local produce and set up the hospitality facilities at the track. The mechanics arrived yesterday, and today the drivers do. I can't sleep from the anticipation of seeing Will again. It's only three thirty in the morning and we have to be at the track for five. I'm going to look a right state, but there's nothing I can do about it.

Will has been in Kuala Lumpur himself for the last few days with his personal trainer, acclimatising himself to the environment. I've been on tenterhooks in case I bump into him, but it's unlikely in a city as big as this. He's staying in a different hotel along with Simon and the directors. And Luis, of course.

Eventually, Holly switches the light back on.

'Can't sleep?' I ask.

'No thanks to you,' she grumbles.

'It's too hot here,' I say, for want of an explanation that doesn't involve a certain racing driver.

'Well, why did you switch off the damn air-conditioning in the middle of the night?'

'It was too cold, then,' I reply innocently.

She just humphs and gets out of bed, heading in the direction of the shower.

An hour later we arrive at the track and I'm jumpy with adrenalin.

'Have you been drinking too much coffee?' Holly asks, when

I jolt at the sight of a team member entering the white-tented hospitality suite.

I walk back into the kitchen and she follows. I'm about to ask Frederick what needs doing when someone calls my name from the door. Holly and I both turn to see Simon standing there. He beckons for me to go over to him.

'Hi, Simon, what can I get for you?'

'Nothing at the moment, but Daisy, it's no good if you're not staying in the same hotel as us. We'll have to get that sorted for the next race.'

'Okay . . .'

'Speak to Ally,' he calls over his shoulder as he walks off.

Ally is Simon's PA back in the UK. She liaises with the team's travel agent among many, many other things.

'What was that about?' Holly is immediately on my case.

I fill her in.

'Oh. That means we won't be able to share a room.'

'It's only for Bahrain. We're all staying in the same hotels once we hit Europe, right?'

'I guess so.'

'It'll be okay.'

'At least you'll be happy.' She gives me a small smile.

'I'd rather be with you, actually.'

'Yeah, right!' she exclaims. 'You'll be well within stalking distance of Prince Charming.'

'Shh!' I warn. 'Anyway, *stalking* distance?' I ask huffily.

'I saw the magazine you were looking at in the middle of the night . . .'

'It wasn't the middle of the night; it was this morning. Will you quit teasing me?'

'Sorry.' Then she whispers, 'Consider yourself lucky. I'll probably have to share with Klaus and Gertrude.' She glances at the German couple diligently working away at one of the counters. Klaus is de-heading fresh prawns and passing them to Gertrude to finish shelling before he hands her the next.

I give Holly an 'aren't they weird?' look before adding, 'Threesome?'

She groans distastefully and swipes me on the arm with a wet tea towel.

'Ow!' I shout.

'DAISY!' Frederick snaps, so I wipe the smile off my face.

I head out to the serving table just in time to see a black-haired, olive-skinned figure walk in.

'Hi, Luis, what can I get you?' I ask in a deliberately bored-sounding voice.

'Black coffee.'

I glance over at Frederick, who's just about to sit down for a meeting with Tarquin, Will's nutritionist/personal trainer. Luis looks over his shoulder and spots the scene before glancing back at me with amusement.

'And I'll have some bacon and eggs, too,' he says.

'Shouldn't you have a nutritionist?' I ask, serving up the greasy food onto a plate.

'Don't need one,' he says, taking the coffee and blowing on it, his dark eyes watching me over the rim of his cup.

I raise my eyebrows disapprovingly and hand him his plate.

'So,' he says, not taking his plate from me. 'I hear you're our designated bun tart?'

'Your *what?*' I splutter.

'Bun tart. Haven't you heard that term before? That's what we call you girls.'

'You call us bun tarts?' I ask in horror.

'Sure.' He shrugs. 'Don't shoot the messenger,' he adds calmly.

'Hey, Luis.' Holly comes out of the kitchen. 'Whoa, you must be hungry.' She looks at the plate I'm still holding. 'I can't believe you're not going for some of my nice muesli.'

He glances at it. 'Hmm,' he decides. 'Maybe I will have some.'

'So you don't want this?' I interrupt, nodding at the plate in my hand.

'No, thanks.' He actually has the audacity to wink at me.

I irritably spin around and sweep the bacon and eggs from his plate into the bin behind the serving table. When I turn back, Holly is spooning muesli into a bowl.

'Extra nuts?' she asks.

Luis nods pleasantly.

'Did you hear what he just called me? Us?' My voice sounds squeaky with annoyance.

'No, what?' Holly flashes Luis an apologetic smile.

'Bun tarts!' I explode.

She laughs. 'That's our nickname, Daisy.'

'What, yours and mine?' I'm now very unpleasantly surprised.

'No,' she waves her hand dismissively. 'All of us. All of the front-of-house girls. It's the same in every team. It's a term of affection.'

'Well, I don't know about that,' Luis mutters.

Holly hands him a bowl filled to the brim. 'Do you want a protein shake to go with that?' she asks.

Luis glances down at his coffee and then cocks his head to one side. 'Go on, then.'

I stand there and glare at him.

'What?' he asks innocently.

At that moment Will walks into the hospitality area and my expression must have changed dramatically because Luis sharply spins around to see who has caught my attention. I quickly try to cover up by tidying the serving table in front of me as I notice Will taking a seat with Tarquin and Frederick. I glance back at Luis and see a twinkle in his eye.

Later that afternoon, I'm hard at work when I hear someone shout.

'Oi, Daisy!' Pete pops his head around the door.

'What do you want?' I shout back cheekily.

'Are you coming out tonight?'

'Why, what's the plan?'

He looks comically from side to side to make sure no one is within earshot. 'We're going for a piss-up in the city.'

'Another one? Shouldn't you be setting an example?' I joke. 'You're the chief mechanic.'

'Yeah, well, you're the chief bun tart.' He grins at me and I notice a couple of catering staff surreptitiously smirk at each other.

'What is it with that term?' I explode. 'I heard it for the first time today and now everyone's saying it!'

Pete cracks up laughing. 'Yeah, Luis told me your face was such a picture this morning.'

Him again.

'He's not coming out, is he?'

'Nah, he's got some sponsorship event to attend.'

'*Another* one?'

'Yeah. All the bloody time. He hates them.'

'Too bad for him. I'll come, then,' I say, snootily. 'As long as *he's* not coming.'

'I can't guarantee he won't turn up later . . .'

We're staying at a hotel in the city – all the mechanics are in the same one as us so we arrange to meet at the hotel bar later. Once again, Holly and I did the early shift, so Frederick lets us leave soon after we've helped out with dinner. Luckily, Klaus and Gertrude are not really party animals so that works out just fine.

We go to a bar with a perfect view of the soaring Petronas Twin Towers, glowing white in the night. Even after an hour, I'm finding it hard to tear my eyes away from the strange Islamic-looking skyscrapers with their interlinking bridge, but when Dan gets a text from Luis demanding to know where we are, my attention is immediately diverted.

'Don't tell him!' I beg.

He just laughs while typing out a reply. 'Why don't you like him?' he asks afterwards.

'I don't know how anyone *can* like him!'

'What's he ever done to you?' he persists.

'He almost ran over me and then called me a silly woman driver, for one thing.'

'He's only teasing . . .'

'He is not!' I respond hotly.

'Okay, okay.' Dan gives up.

Later, when Luis emerges, I'm still in a mood. I don't see the person behind him until he's almost at our table.

'Will!' Pete shouts.

I feel dazed, jittery, sick with excitement. While the lads all jump up to shake the drivers' hands, I flash a glance at Holly. She rolls her eyes at me.

'Budge over, will you.'

I look up to see Luis standing by my side. I must have a delayed reaction because he pushes my arm and indicates the chair next to me. I reluctantly move across to it.

'How's it going, bun tart?' he asks, when he's seated.

I glare at him. 'You really expect me to answer?'

He leans back in his chair and grins at me, smile sparkling in the low-level lighting.

'You don't like me, do you?' he asks.

'Where on earth did you get that idea?' I reply sarcastically, flashing a look at Will amongst all the mechanics.

Luis glances up at him and then leans towards me and whispers conspiratorially, 'But you like him, don't you?' He laughs when he sees my horrified face. 'Don't worry, your secret's safe with me.'

'*Fottiti*!' I hiss at him.

'Now, what does that mean?' He's still smiling and I want to slap him.

'It means go fuck yourself!'

'*Nossa Senhora* . . .' Luis looks disturbed and leans back in his seat again.

I don't speak Portuguese – the language of Brazil – but I recognise his words as being simply, 'Our Lady', as in the virgin mother.

'You really are a piece of work, aren't you?' he adds.

I instantly regret being so snappy. The look on his face tells me he really was only teasing and I've just been a complete bitch, but I still can't help folding my arms in defiance.

Luis taps his fingers on the table and stares across at Holly, unsmiling.

'Is she talking dirty to you again?' Holly calls, trying to clear the air.

'If she were talking dirty, I wouldn't mind,' Luis calls back.

I should apologise, but the words just won't come. A few seconds later, Luis stands up.

'I need a drink,' he says unhappily, heading over to a few of the lads at the bar.

Holly gives me a disapproving look.

'I know, I know,' I say crossly.

She lets it drop, but the jittery sickness I felt earlier has been replaced with another kind of sickness, and it's not pleasant.

I glance at Will again, and at that moment, he catches my eye and joins us at the table.

'Alright?' he asks.

'Hi!' I immediately perk up.

'Can I get you a drink?' He looks from Holly to me.

'Um . . .' Holly considers his question.

'No, no, we're fine!' I interject. Sorry, Holly, but I don't want him to go off again. 'Have a seat!' I point to the one recently vacated by Luis.

'We don't usually see you out and about,' Holly says as he sits down.

'Mmm, Tarquin wouldn't be too impressed,' he replies wryly. 'Luis dragged me along. Promised me we'd just stay for the one . . .' He looks down at his watch, then casts his eyes over to Luis and the lads at the bar.

'What are you drinking?' I ask, just out of curiosity.

'Water,' he replies, holding it up. 'Got to keep my fluids up in this heat.'

'It was like, 70 per cent humidity today, wasn't it?' I grimace.

'Something like that,' he replies.

'Do you ever drink alcohol?' Holly chips in.

He grins. 'Sometimes.'

'Just champagne on the podium?' I ask, then inwardly cringe when I remember Alberta said a similar thing to Luis in Melbourne last week.

'I might pop to the bar after all,' Holly interrupts, distracting Will from the look of mortification on my face.

'I'll go.' Will joins Holly on her feet, but Holly shoots him down.

'No, *I* will,' she insists. 'I'm a feminist. I don't like men to buy me drinks.'

Which is utter rubbish, but it does the trick.

Will settles himself back in his seat. An awkward silence ensues where I'm completely lost for words, but finally he speaks.

'You're not staying at our hotel, are you?'

'No,' I reply. 'I will be in Bahrain, though.'

'Cool.'

Why is it cool? Do you want me there? Why?

Girlfriend, Daisy, remember his girlfriend!

'Is your . . . *Laura* coming out this weekend?' Her name almost sticks on my tongue, but I manage to say it.

'No, she's attending some do in London.'

'A charity event?'

'That's right.'

'Do you miss her?'

'Course.' He eyes me steadily. 'It's been like this for years, though, so we're pretty used to it.'

I look away uncomfortably.

'Have you got a boyfriend?' he asks offhandedly.

'Er, no, not me.'

'Really?' He looks surprised.

'Why? Should I?' Did that sound too defensive?

'Not if you don't want one, no.'

'I mean, I could get one if I wanted one . . .'

'I'm sure you could.' He sounds amused.

'But I don't want one.' Will you shut up, Daisy?

'Fair enough.' He glances at his watch again. *Cazzo*, I'm really messing this up.

'Do your parents come to many races?' I ask quickly. I don't want to do small talk. There's not enough time.

'No. They don't.' His reply is blunt.

'Why is that?' I *so* want to get to the bottom of him . . .

He rests his heel up on the edge of his chair and casually wraps one arm around his knee. When he doesn't immediately answer, I start to regret my line of questioning, but then he speaks.

'We're not that close.' He rubs away some of the condensation that has formed on the outside of his glass.

'Has it always been like that?' I swivel to face him, willing him to look at me.

'Pretty much,' he replies, glancing my way. 'Ever since I was a kid and they sent me off to boarding school.' He pauses. 'Aah, there were moments . . .' His voice trails off.

'Like what?' I prompt.

'Oh, I was just remembering how one of our horses broke free and almost trampled me when I was very little. My mother was nice to me, then.' I hold my breath because I can't believe he's opening up to me about this. But then his voice hardens. 'On the whole, though, she kept me at a distance. My father has always done that.' He takes a sip of his water.

'That's sad,' I murmur, staring at him.

'It's okay,' he says flippantly, putting his foot back down on the floor. 'You come to terms with it.'

'No, you don't,' I reply firmly. 'You never come to terms with it.'

He meets my eyes for a long moment. The hurt on his face is hurting me too, but I can't look away. 'They must be proud of you now,' I say hurriedly. I want to make it better.

His expression turns to confusion and he shakes his head slightly then turns away and laughs a brittle laugh. 'I don't know why I'm telling you this.'

I fall silent. He looks over at the bar again. 'I should hunt out Luis.' He starts to get up.

'He's probably picked up a screwdriver somewhere,' I say bluntly.

Will chuckles. 'I'll tell him you said that.'

'No, don't,' I plead. 'He hates me enough as it is.'

He smiles, clearly thinking I'm joking. 'Are you coming?' he asks, pointing towards the bar. 'I don't want to leave you here on your own.'

I look over and spot Holly doing shots with Pete.

'Sure.' Holly has left her handbag on her chair so I pick it up and we go to join the team.

'Daisy!' Dan shouts. 'Come and do a shot with us!'

'I've got to be up in a few hours!' I laugh. 'So do you for that matter.'

'Where's Will?' Holly yells.

Where is Will, actually?

I look around frantically, but he's nowhere to be seen. I feel out of it, separated from the crowd. If Will's not here, I don't want to be here. Where is he? Has he really—

'He's gone.' Luis interrupts my thoughts and it's like a shotgun has gone off in my head.

I don't look at him.

'It's alright, bun tart, you'll see him tomorrow.'

'STOP CALLING ME THAT!' I shout at the top of my voice. Everyone turns to look at me.

'Daisy!' Holly jumps in surprise.

'That's it, I'm off!' And with a look that could surely kill everyone around me, I storm out of the room.

Chapter 5

Luis appears first for breakfast. I refuse to look at him so Holly takes over.

'What can I get you?' she asks warmly.

'Muesli. And a couple of hash browns.'

Nice, healthy mix there, Luis. I don't vocalise my thoughts.

'Coffee? Juice? Shake?' Holly enquires.

'Juice. Thanks.'

And that's it. He walks off. I watch his departing back with confusion.

'What?' Holly asks me.

'He didn't say anything to me.'

'Are you surprised after the way you spoke to him last night?'

Hmm. I go into the kitchen to bring out some more toast and have a quick tidy up and when I return, Will is walking away from the serving table. I look after him in dismay. Holly, thankfully, doesn't make a point of noticing.

The next time I see him is after I've clawed my way through the humidity to get to the pits. I have to stock up the food supplies for the team members too busy to take a break. There's a drivers' room in the garages at Kuala Lumpur's Sepang circuit and as I'm about to return to the hospitality area, Will comes out of it, wearing his racing overalls.

'Good time last night?'

'Great!' Until you did your disappearing act, that is. 'All set for qualifying?' I ask the obvious question.

'Yep.' He pats the helmet under his arm.

'Good.' What else to say, what else to say?

At that moment Luis emerges from the drivers' room behind him. He glances in our direction, but quickly looks away again, heading over to his car on the other side of the garage. My eyes follow him distractedly.

'Catch you later,' I hear Will say.

I quickly return my attention to him. 'Of course, yes. Good luck!'

He doesn't reply and I hurry back through the outside heat to the blissfully air-conditioned hospitality area, heart pounding ever so slightly faster than it was before.

In Melbourne, Will and Luis qualified on the front row of the grid, a result which surprised everyone in the industry. So all eyes are on our team today. Can Will swipe pole position again? Will Luis beat him to it?

Luis does end up in the running for pole, but against another driver, Nils Broden from Sweden. Luis comes second in the end, followed by Kit Bryson in third, while Will only just manages to pull fourth out of the bag. It's still a good result, but not good enough for Will it seems. He leaves the track early on Saturday afternoon, while Luis sits around, happily chatting to the sponsors in the hospitality area.

Holly and I don't go out that night. Her hangover is still raging inside her head so she persuades me to stay in our hotel room and watch a movie. I don't take much persuading, to be honest. I know Will won't be out on the town again and I'm quite happy to avoid Luis or any teasing that might come, probably quite rightly, from the mechanics.

The Malaysian Grand Prix the following day passes by with barely any incidents. Will has a good start, managing to overtake Kit Bryson to nab third place, while Luis keeps his second-place position, and this is pretty much how it stays until the end. With both drivers taking home trophies, we're once again the centre of attention. But Luis is the driver most people are talking about. He now leads the championship – an impressive feat for someone in his first ever season. Will, on the other hand, has been in Formula 1 for two years and is yet to win a race.

I wonder how he feels seeing team boss Simon give Luis a pat on the back following the press conference. Even *I* feel quite bizarrely like I want to congratulate Luis, but he's always surrounded by people, and I'm too afraid he might snub me after my behaviour on Friday night.

Early that evening as we're well into the swing of tidy-up mode, I come out of the kitchen to see Simon chatting to the team's technical and financial directors. Will and Luis are talking behind him, with Will making swerving motions with his hands as though describing a manoeuvre he made during the race.

Simon turns around and sees me. 'Ah, Daisy. We're off, now.'

I presume he means to Bahrain. It's two weeks until the next race, but the drivers once again need to acclimatise themselves to the hot conditions.

'Did you speak to Ally?'

He's talking about his PA.

'Yes, I did. She managed to switch my hotel.' I'm aware that Will and Luis have finished their conversation and are now listening to this exchange. It's making me nervous.

'And when do you arrive?'

'Um, on the Wednesday before the race. Is that okay?'

'Not really, no. I think we'll need you out there before then. Does that interfere with your plans?' His tone is brusque.

It does, actually. Holly and I were going to Langkawi this week.

'When were you thinking?' I ask, my heart sinking as the image of us drinking cocktails together on white, sandy beaches slips away.

'Later this week would be better.'

'Okay,' I reply a touch hesitantly. At least I'll be able to spend a couple of days with my friend. 'I'll speak to Ally again.'

'Good.'

Still, she's not going to be pleased. But as Will flashes me a smile, suddenly Holly is no longer at the forefront of my thoughts.

Chapter 6

That's it, I am officially bored. Don't get me wrong, it is *beautiful* here. Warm, sunny days . . . A five-star hotel overlooking the sparkling waters of Manama Bay . . . Our own private beach and palm trees aplenty by a stunning outdoor pool. I know I shouldn't complain, but dammit! I miss Holly!

I flew in straight from Kuala Lumpur and instead of the usual fun I'd have on the plane in business class luxury with my pal, I had to sit next to Frederick. Holly and I spend most of our flights gossiping and knocking back free drinks, but my boss slept most of the way and I could hear his snores even through my headphones. Aeroplane films just don't have the same impact when the sound of a chainsaw is going off in the background.

At first I didn't realise Frederick was coming too, and since I've been here, my days have been spent with him, preparing the drivers' and core crew members' meals in the penthouse suite of our über posh hotel, after which I scuttle back down to my room a couple of floors below. Will and Luis, on the other hand, spend the majority of their time with their personal trainers, Tarquin and João – Luis flew João in from Brazil on Simon's insistence.

I've barely seen Will. Luis is being mildly pleasant, but on the whole acts like I don't exist, and I'm sick to death of Catalina's demands. In fact, anyone would think I'm her slave. 'Get this! Get that! I need water! WATER!'

Urgh.

I can't wait for Holly to get here in a couple of days so we can check out the souks in Manama City. I haven't had anyone to sightsee with and I'm dying to see the Al Fateh Mosque, plus, apparently, there's this crazy tree, all alone in the middle of the desert, which is kept alive by an underwater spring! It's called the Tree of Life, or something.

Yes, I've had a lot of time to read the travel brochures in my hotel room, can you tell?

By day five, though, I've had enough, and head down to the hotel bar for a change of scenery. Alcohol may not be illegal in Bahrain – unlike neighbouring Saudi Arabia – but I haven't had anyone to drink with here, anyway. Will's practically tee-total and Luis, well, Luis is Luis. But after several lonely evenings by the pool followed by solitary television viewing in my room, tonight I've decided I'll get drunk on my own if I have to. Call me an alcoholic if you must.

The bar overlooks the swimming pool and blue ocean beyond. I stand and look out at it for a moment while slurping my cocktail through a straw. And then I notice a dark-haired man sitting alone at a table by the window. Luis.

The wave of relief is enough to make me bite the bullet and take my drink over to his table. It occurs to me as I reach it that perhaps he's meeting a woman, but it's too late to turn back. He's seen me.

'Hello, bun tart,' he says.

I take a seat, too much in need of company to mind.

'Hello, *testa di cazzo*,' I reply with a smile.

'Dickhead?'

'You're learning.'

'Fair enough. Cheers.' He leans across and chinks my glass.

'What are you drinking?' I ask.

'Vodka tonic.'

'Does your personal trainer know about this?' I raise one eyebrow.

'Not unless you plan to tell him.'

'I'll see how I feel later.'

He grins at me and I relax back into my chair.

'So what are you doing down here?' he asks, swirling the ice around in his glass.

'Bored.'

'No one to play with?'

'No. I miss Holly.'

'You'll just have to play with me instead.'

'I think you've got more than enough women to play with.'

'Not tonight, though, bun tart.'

'Piss off. Or how do you say it? *Va se lixar*?'

'Well remembered. Do you speak any Portuguese?'

'Afraid not. Just Italian.'

'How's that, then?'

'My mother is Italian,' I explain. 'Although I've spent most of my life in America.'

'So you grew up bilingual?'

'Funnily enough, no. My mother never spoke to me in Italian. I learned it when I was a teenager.'

'Wanted to get back to your roots?'

'That's right.' Hmm. Actually quite perceptive. For an idiot. 'My grandparents on my mother's side live in Italy and I went to stay with them one summer when I was eleven. They didn't speak much English so I started to teach myself Italian with books. Then I studied it at school when I returned to the States. Sorry, this is really boring.'

'Far from it,' he says. 'What about your name? Daisy Rogers doesn't sound very Italian.'

'No. That's my father for you. My middle names sound more Italian: Paola Giuseppe. I was named Paola after my grandmother. Giuseppe is my mother's maiden name.'

'Paola. There's something feisty about Paola. I think it suits you more than Daisy.'

It's not the first time I've heard such words and I shudder as a memory comes back to me.

'And where did you learn to swear in Italian?'

I laugh. 'Well, that was from an Italian boy I went out with.'

'Aha! I see.'

'Much to my father's disgust,' I add.

He leans forward with interest. 'That's a bit hypocritical considering he married your mother.'

'You don't have to tell me my father's a hypocrite,' I reply. Hang on, why am I opening up to him about all of this?

'What about you?' I change the subject. 'Do you get along with your family?'

'There are a lot of us, but yes.'

'A lot of you?'

'Mum, dad, three sisters and four brothers.'

'No way, that's humungous!'

'Thirteen cousins, five uncles and four aunties.'

'Grandparents?'

'Alive and well.'

I sigh. 'Wow. I'm jealous.'

He leans back in his chair again. I lean back in mine and rest the tips of my silver-grey ballet pumps on the low table.

'Do you want another?' Luis motions towards my drink and clicks his fingers for service.

'Sure.'

A waiter comes over and takes our order. A few minutes later he returns with our drinks.

'So,' Luis says, crossing one leg over the other so that his ankle rests on the opposite knee. He's wearing a red T-shirt and dark-denim jeans. 'What's going on with you and Will?'

'What do you mean, what's going on? Nothing's going on!' I can feel my face heating up.

'You can tell me, I won't tell anyone.'

'Oh, sure,' I reply sarcastically. 'Just like you didn't tell anyone I nearly broke your legs.'

He cracks up laughing and almost spills his drink. 'I was only joking.' He waves his hand dismissively.

'If Simon had heard you say that, I could have been fired,' I point out, pedantically.

'Simon did hear me say it.'

'*WHAT?*'

'Keep your bra on, bun tart, I didn't know he was behind me.'

'Keep my *bra* on? You are such a chauvinistic pig!'

'Thanks.' He flashes me a grin with his annoyingly white teeth.

'How did he react?' I push.

'He just asked me if I was alright, if I'd been hurt, and I laughed and said of course not, you weren't trying hard enough.'

'Please tell me you're joking . . . Oh my God, I can't believe he hasn't fired me.'

'Far from it. You got a promotion.'

'No thanks to you!' I snipe.

'Actually . . .'

'What do you mean?'

'What, you thought Will had requested you?' he asks, smirking.

The disappointment is crushing. I look down at the table.

'God, you crack me up. Have you met his girlfriend?' he asks.

'No. Have you?' Now, I'm curious.

'Yeah, at a do in London before the season started. Pretty.'

I fall silent and study my drink.

'Not as pretty as you, though,' he adds. I look up at him and there's a familiar twinkle in his eye.

'Shut up.' But I smile at his teasing. 'What about you? Have you got a girlfriend?'

'No. It would be cruel to limit myself to just one girl. I need to share myself around.'

I shake my head at him in mock disgust. 'How old are you?'

'Twenty-six. Why?'

'That's the same age as me!' I exclaim. I was about to tell him he's immature, but I'm easily distracted.

'And Will,' he adds.

'No shit? What a coincidence!'

'Yes, what a coincidence.' He's being mildly sarcastic. He knocks back his drink and holds up his empty. 'Another?' I nod and he raises his hand for service.

'Can we get a bottle of champagne, please?' he asks the waiter who has just arrived at our table.

'Certainly, sir,' the waiter replies.

I start to protest, but Luis interrupts. 'As soon as possible, thanks.'

'I thought you didn't drink champagne?' I'm confused as I watch the waiter rush away.

'I don't, but I want to freak Will out.'

'*Will?*'

'Don't look!' Luis hushes me, but I'm already sitting up in my chair like a hare in the headlights. 'You are so obvious,' he chides, half hiding his face with his hand.

'Where is he?' I demand to know.

'Shh!'

'*Where?*' I can't bear the thought of him going upstairs to his room without seeing me.

The waiter comes out from behind the bar area with a bottle of champagne and at that point, Luis stands up.

'Will!' he calls.

I still can't see him, but I don't have a clear line of vision towards the reception desk.

'He's coming.' Luis grins at me as he sits down.

'Are you winding me up?' I ask, as the waiter pops the cork and starts to pour the fizzing liquid into two tall flutes. I can't see now because he's blocking my view.

'That's fine, thanks,' Luis says to the waiter. He leans across the table and hands me a glass.

'Hi!' Will appears at our table and my heart flips. 'Oh, hello!' he says in surprise, looking down at me. His eyes flit from Luis to me and I have a horrible feeling that he's getting completely the wrong idea.

'Hi!' I say warmly, trying to undo the damage. 'Sit down, sit down! Can we get another glass?' I call after the departing waiter. My voice sounds slightly unhinged.

'No, no,' Will brushes me off.

'Oh, that's right, you don't drink.' I start to giggle. It's my nerves – and the fact that a few days without alcohol means it's gone straight to my head.

'I was just off to bed,' Will says.

'Don't! Stay!' I stand up and try to drag one of the really quite deceptively heavy chairs over to our table.

'I don't want to gatecrash,' he says.

'You're not gatecrashing!' I insist. 'Is he, Luis? He's not gatecrashing?'

'Hmm?' Luis calmly lazes back in his chair and sips his drink.

'Tell him to sit down!' Okay, now I'm sounding a bit scary.

'Sure, take a seat.'

He does, and I immediately adjust my body language so I'm leaning forward to talk to him. 'Where have you been?'

'Training.'

'You're working late,' I comment, impressed.

'Yeah, I'm knackered.'

'Just have one drink with us,' I plead. 'I've been bored shitless here.'

A waiter comes over with another glass. 'I'll just have a soda water,' Will tells him. He's wearing a baseball cap with one of the team sponsors' logos on the front and when he takes it off, his blond hair has a slight dent in it. 'So why have you been bored?' He looks at me. 'Are we not keeping you busy enough?'

'No,' I reply.

'We might have to rectify that situation,' Luis chips in.

'You seem to be rectifying it now,' Will tells him. Am I imagining the frosty tone in his voice?

'I'm doing what I can,' Luis replies.

'Have you been out today?' Will asks him.

'Couldn't be arsed.'

Will raises his eyebrows. But Luis did go out! I saw him leave with his personal trainer earlier.

'You—' I start, but Luis interrupts me.

'Top up?' His dark eyes look like they're warning me. I shut my mouth again and obediently hold up my glass.

'Thanks,' Will says to the waiter returning with his drink.

Now I can't think of anything to say. At the moment, Luis knows more about me than Will does. It's strange how the people you care about least, sometimes know you the best. You let your guard down with them because you don't mind that they see you, warts and all. If your personality malfunctions scare them, so what?

But I don't want to waste this opportunity to get to know Will. I just don't feel comfortable talking in front of his team-mate. We need a subject that's safe. I know! I look across at Luis and smirk. 'So where's Alberta this weekend?'

Luis shrugs. 'No idea.'

'What, you didn't call?' I ask, mock innocently. 'You didn't write? You didn't text? That's not very boyfriendly of you.'

'Boyfriend!' He stiffens in horror.

'I can't believe you'd treat the boss's sister-in-law with such disdain.'

'She got what she wanted,' Luis replies, with a wink.

'I doubt that,' I scoff, looking him up and down.

He chuckles good-naturedly. 'She used and abused me. Then ran back to her husband in Spain.'

'She's married?' I interrupt, looking at Luis in shock.

Luis laughs. 'I'm joking. I would never steal another man's girl.' He gives me a sly look that says, 'Unlike you.'

'Neither would I!' I reply crossly.

'Isn't she Catalina's cousin?' Will asks, seemingly oblivious to whatever's going on between Luis and me.

'Oh, yeah,' Luis says.

'Who cares?' I ask.

Luis laughs. Will leans back in his chair and stretches his legs out under the table. He runs his hands through his blond hair and yawns.

'Are we keeping you up?' Luis asks.

'I should probably hit the sack,' Will replies, making to stand up.

No! 'Have another drink,' I plead.

'No, really,' he says, rising to his feet.

'Got to run off and call his girlfriend,' Luis says.

Will winks at him and smiles at me. 'See you in the morning.'

I slump back down against the soft leather as I dejectedly watch him walk away.

Luis whistles low under his breath. I follow his gaze and see that two leggy blondes have just pulled up stools at the bar. I look back at Luis, but he's still staring in their direction. My eye catches something on Will's chair.

'Hey, Will left his cap here.' I reach across and pick it up. I could take it to him before he settles in his room.

'Hmm?' Luis asks, distracted.

'I'm going to bed.' I get to my feet.

He looks up at me. 'You're going to bed?'

'Yes.' I hide the cap behind my back.

'Okay. I might go to the bar.' He stands up lazily and I roll my eyes at him. 'After you,' he says.

'No, after you,' I reply. I don't want him to see what I'm holding in my hands. He shrugs and leads the way out. 'Night,' I call, quickly moving the cap to my front as I turn away.

'Bye,' he calls back, but doesn't even look in my direction as I walk up to the lifts and push the call button. Inside, I watch the numbers above the lift door glow red as we pass each floor. Finally we reach my destination as it comes to a smooth stop. The doors swish open and Will is standing on the landing.

'Hi!' he says in surprise.

'Hi!' I reply with equal surprise. I step out. 'I brought you your cap.'

'Aah, thanks.' He reaches out and takes it from me, turning it over in his hands. 'I was just debating whether to come back down for it.'

'I saved you the trouble. Why were you debating? Too tired to make the long journey?' I ask, jokily.

He puts his cap back on and leans against the wall, crossing his arms. 'Er, no, I didn't know if I should interrupt you and Luis again.'

'Ha! You've got to be joking, you'd hardly be interrupting anything.'

His face is dark under his cap, but I can see him watching me in amusement.

'Seriously,' I hurry on to explain. 'I was bored out of my brains. That's the only reason I'd go drinking with that moron.'

He laughs. 'That's a relief,' he says.

'Is it? Why?'

'I thought I was going to have to warn you off him, big brother-style.'

I ignore the use of 'brother'. 'You don't have to warn me about him. I know what he's like. I think he's just pulled a couple of Screwdrivers at the bar, actually.'

He grins. 'Well, you're welcome to come and watch a movie with me next time you're bored.'

'Really?' My heart starts to pound faster.

'Sure.'

I want to ask when, but don't want to seem desperate. Now? Please, God, please, now.

'Tomorrow if you like,' he says, pushing himself away from the wall and standing up straight.

That'll do! I'm a bit trashed at the moment anyway.

'It's a date!' I tell him enthusiastically. 'I mean, it's not a date, but, oh you know what I'm saying.'

He laughs.

'What shall we watch?' I change tack. 'It better not be a war movie.'

'I can't promise anything,' he says as he sets off down the corridor to his suite. 'But as long as you don't make me watch any of that chick-flick crap, we'll be alright.'

'Okay!' I call after him.

'Thanks for my cap,' he calls back, sliding his electronic key card into the slot and going inside.

'Sure thing!' But the door has already closed behind him.

Chapter 7

The next evening at eight o'clock on the dot, I nervously knock on Will's door. He seems a little flustered when he answers it.

'Come in,' he says, waving me inside.

'Is this a bad time?' I ask, warily.

'No, it's fine.' He shuts the door behind me. It's then that I notice he's still wearing one of his team T-shirts and it looks more than a little sweaty.

'Have you only just got back from your training session?' I ask.

'Yeah, Tarquin kept me out later today.'

'Oh, I'm sorry, I should let you shower and eat and stuff.' I stand by the door, hesitantly.

'No, don't worry. Well,' he says, looking down at his T-shirt, 'I could probably do with a shower.'

'I'll come back, then?'

'Or just wait in front of the telly if you like? I'll be quick.'

'As is your forte!' I quip, before groaning inwardly. He looks at me like he doesn't get my dodgy fast-driving joke. I'm not about to explain it so I point towards what I assume is the living room area.

'Yeah, go right through.' He, in turn, heads into the bathroom.

His suite is enormous and furnished with modern furniture. There are two grey suede-covered sofas facing a giant flatscreen television and I can see a huge super-kingsize bed in the bedroom behind the living room. Nice.

I sit down on a sofa and put my feet up on the coffee table, then take them down again, crossing my legs instead and folding my arms. I hear the shower switch on in the bathroom. Sigh . . .

I lean forward and pick up the complicated-looking remote. How do I work this thing? I point it at the television and press the red button. It buzzes into life.

Oh my freaking God, he's on the porn channel! Quick! Quick! Change it before he gets out here! I rapidly push buttons as I hear the shower turn off, but the numbers I'm pressing come up on the screen while the channel remains the same. *Cazzo*! What do I do? In a panic I study the remote control and spy an 'Enter' button. I try again, pressing a couple of digits, followed by 'Enter'. The channel changes just as the bathroom door opens and Will emerges along with a cloud of steam.

'Yes, my name is Iggle Piggle . . .'

I hear a song coming from the television. A quick glance in its direction tells me I'm watching kiddie TV. A quick glance back at Will tells me he's not wearing anything under that little white towel. Argh!

'Forgot to take clean clothes in with me.' He apologises for his attire – or lack of it – as he wanders past the sofas into the bedroom. He turns to pull on the huge sliding doors that separate his room from the living room, but doesn't quite manage to close them. I twist my body around to take a quick peek and nearly have a heart attack when I spot his naked bum. In light-headed shock I return my focus to the strange blue creature dancing about on the television. I could attempt to change the channel again, but it's a bit risky. Moments later, Will reappears.

'*In the Night Garden*?' He grins and nods at the television.

'Is that what it's called?' I ask.

'Yeah. My niece is a big fan.'

'How old is your niece?'

'Three.' He slumps down on the other sofa.

'Brother or sister's child?' I ask, then immediately wonder if said child is one of Laura's siblings' offspring. Are they that close for him to be considered an uncle?

'Sister,' he replies, putting his bare feet up on the coffee table.

'Your sister?'

'Yes,' he says cautiously, as though he thinks I might be a little bit stupid.

'I meant, was it *your* sister or Laura's sister,' I explain, then want to kick myself for bringing up his girlfriend.

'Oh, I *see*,' he says. 'My sister. Laura is an only child.'

'Aah, okay. I empathise. I am, too.'

'Are you?'

'Yes. Always wanted a brother. Or a sister. Or even a cat would have done. Hell, I would have made do with a goldfish.'

He laughs and pushes his still-wet hair off his face, before casually resting one toned arm on the back of the sofa. 'Lonely, were you?'

'Just a bit. Was Laura?'

'Nah. She had me.' He grins.

Hmm. 'You grew up together, didn't you?'

'Yeah, her parents ran the farm next to my house.'

'Were you always over there, romping in the haystacks?' Oh my Lordy, Lord. What am I saying?

He looks amused. 'I was a good boy.'

And *that's* why you were watching the porn channel, hey pal?

'What?' Will asks, seeing the sneaky look on my face.

'I bet you're not as nice as you seem.' It's out of my mouth almost before I have a chance to think it.

'Oh, really?' His eyes widen in surprise. He folds his arms. 'What makes you think that?'

Now I've gone and done it. 'No reason.'

'No way, missy, now you've started something, you're going to have to finish it.' He raises one eyebrow. I would say flirtatiously, but he's got a girlfriend.

'Shall we watch this movie?' I ask.

'I don't think so.'

'I don't know how to work the remote control,' I say, holding it up.

'Pass it over.' He takes his feet off the table and leans across to me. I hand it to him, a little surprised and relieved that I managed to get out of that one. And then he points the control at the telly and turns it off. Oh.

'What are you doing?' I ask, all innocent.

He puts his feet back on the table.

'Would Laura say you're a nice boy?' I ask, head swimming a little, now.

He raises one eyebrow at me. 'You'd have to ask her that.'

'I would do, but she never comes to any of the races.'

He purses his lips at me, thoughtfully. Then he points the remote at the telly and switches it back on. I hear the sound of the porn channel before I see it.

'Jesus, this bloody TV,' he mutters, hastily pointing it again and changing the channel.

I burst out laughing.

'What?' he asks. Then it clicks. 'Did that just happen to you?' He lifts up the remote control. 'Is that why you think I'm not a nice boy?' He's grinning.

I nod, unable to speak.

He starts to laugh, too. 'So if I watch porn, it means I'm a bastard?'

'Well . . .' I consider his question.

'What if I'm lonely?' he interrupts. 'Seeing as, like you say, my girlfriend doesn't come to any races . . .'

'Whatever takes your fancy, Will,' I say, flippantly, and he stares at me with those beautiful blue eyes.

'What?' I ask, when he doesn't look away. It makes me feel jittery.

'Nothing.' He presses a few buttons on the remote control to bring up a menu. 'Now, what shall we watch?'

'*Debbie Does Dallas*? *Deep Throat*?' I crack up laughing again.

'Now, how would a nice girl like *you* know the names of porn movies?'

I immediately hit him back with, 'How would a nice boy like you know that I'm talking about porn movies?'

He gives me a sly look. 'I bet *you're* not a nice girl.'

Want to find out? No! Girlfriend! Girlfriend! Girlfriend!

'Is Laura a nice girl?'

He glances away at the TV. 'Of course she is.' My stomach falls flat. 'Right, then,' he continues. 'What shall we watch? *The Bridge On the River Kwai*?'

'Are you joking?' That's a war movie!

'*The Great Escape*?'

Another one! I give him a comedy glare and he leans over

and drops the remote control on the sofa next to me. 'You choose.'

Forty-five minutes later, my viewing of *When Harry Met Sally* is disturbed by the gentle sound of Will's breathing. I look over and see that he's asleep. I watch him for a moment, the rise and fall of his chest almost hypnotic, his face so peaceful. Finally I tear my eyes away, turn off the television and quietly leave his suite. I've seen this movie a thousand times anyway, and if I don't leave now, I might do something stupid like climb into his arms.

Chapter 8

'I waited for you in the bar last night, bun tart. Where the hell were you?'

'Good morning, Luis. How are you on this fine, sunny day?'

'Is it sunny again? I hadn't noticed.'

'Maybe you should take your dark glasses off, then,' I tell him. 'Too much to drink?'

'Had to drown my sorrows all on my own.'

'Yeah, right. Sorrows? What sorrows? Anyway, I bet you picked up a girl, eventually.'

We're waiting in the hotel lobby with a few other team members and we're about to head off to the track for the first time since we got here. I'm excited about seeing Holly again.

'Hey . . .' I hear footsteps behind me and turn around to see Will, looking fresh as a daisy in comparison to his team-mate.

'Hello!' I chirp.

He comes over to us and taps me on my elbow. 'First you make me watch that crap, and then you go and leave before the end! Bad girl.'

I start to laugh. 'You fell asleep!'

'What crap?' Luis butts in.

'*When Harry Met Sally*. We watched it in Will's room,' I tell him distractedly. Simon has just emerged from the lift and Will goes over to him. Catalina isn't with him, so I presume she's having a lie-in. Nothing new there, then.

'You blew me out for *When Harry Met Sally*?'

I ignore Luis and wave my acknowledgement at Simon and Frederick, who has also just appeared.

'Let's get this show on the road.' Simon claps his hands and the group of us start to follow him out of the lobby to the two black people carriers waiting at the bottom of the steps.

'I would never fall asleep in your company, bun tart,' I hear someone say in my ear as I climb into one of the cars. I whip around to see Luis wink at me as he climbs into the other one.

Holly is already at the track when we arrive and I run over to greet her.

'Hello! How are you?' She's breathless from the force of my hug.

'I missed you!' I complain.

She beams at me, warmly. 'I missed you, too. I had to make friends with some backpackers after you left.'

'Any hotties?'

She turns her nose up. 'Sadly, no. *And* I almost got bitten by a monkey.'

'Seriously?'

Langkawi's mangrove swamps are home to plenty of monkeys. We saw a few in the two days I was there, but they kept their distance.

'Yep. Little fucker,' she mutters.

'What did you do? Provoke it?'

'I just wanted a wee photo . . .' Her voice trails off wistfully before she snaps back into action. 'Come on.' She grabs my hand and pulls me towards the kitchen. 'What's been going on with you? Tell me everything!'

'Honestly, it's been sooooo dull without you. Until the last couple of nights I haven't known what to do with myself.'

'Last couple of nights? Explain.'

'Last night I watched a film with Will in his room . . .'

'No way!'

I fill her in on the details.

'And the night before that I just got pissed with Luis.'

'With *Luis*?' she exclaims. 'I thought you couldn't stand him!'

'Will was there, too. Briefly.'

'Will doesn't drink, does he?'

'No.'

'But you got pissed?'

'Yes.'

'With Luis?'

'Yes.'

'The guy you hate?'

'He's not that bad.'

'AHA!' She points at me. 'I told you!'

'Yeah, yeah.'

It's thirty-two degrees today and there's a dust haze covering the track. Bahrain's Sakhir circuit is situated in the desert, unlike our hotel, which is right by the sea. The facilities here are nice and new: the raised-up purpose-built hospitality buildings are glass-fronted and modern, with balconies out the front and outside stairs leading down to ground level. Several guests are currently sitting at tables in the sunshine. It's quite a contrast to the weather they're experiencing in England at the moment. In fact, if it keeps up this weekend, we'll be flying back to a snow-covered country on Monday. I hope our flight isn't delayed.

'Daisy!' Frederick calls. 'Can you come here, please?'

'Sure.' I give Holly a look and head out of the kitchen to see my boss.

'I want you to sit in on my meeting with Tarquin and João.'

'Okay,' I say, pleasantly surprised that I'm being involved in the discussion about the drivers' nutrition.

For the rest of the weekend, I liaise with the two nutritionists about Will's and Luis's diets and it's up to me to ensure they're served the right things at the right times. Luis messes with me a little bit, opting for falafel instead of lean chicken and vegetables, but on the whole behaves himself and sticks to the menu designed for him. Will is as good as gold, as expected.

On Sunday, just before the race, I go to check on Will and Luis in their private rooms.

Yesterday's qualifying session was interesting. Luis only managed to swipe fifth position, whereas Will came a more respectable third. This time it was the Brazilian who made himself scarce afterwards while Will chilled out on the balcony in the sun, chatting to sponsors.

'Luis, are you okay? Is there anything I can do for you?' I ask, after knocking tentatively on his door.

'Wow, bun tart, that's so nice of you. I drive much better after sex.'

I narrow my eyes at him and close the door on his laughter before knocking on Will's door.

'Are you alright?' I ask when he calls for me to enter.

'Yeah, I'm fine.' He's sitting on a chair in his room, resting his elbows on his knees. 'Somebody's cheered up.' He gives me a wry look and nods towards Luis's room. 'What's he laughing about?'

I roll my eyes. 'Just making another lewd joke about me.'

'Want me to break his legs for you?'

I laugh. 'That would probably suit both of us quite nicely . . .'

He grins and stands up. 'Nah, I'll be able to knock him off the top of the championship without resorting to that.' He's already kitted out in his racing overalls, minus his helmet, which is resting on the low table. I pick it up and hand it to him.

'Cheers.' He goes to the door and opens it for me to go through. 'You coming to watch the race?'

'If Frederick will let me, definitely,' I tell him over my shoulder as he follows me back into the hospitality area.

'See you later, then,' he says, tailing off in the direction of the pits.

'Bye! Good luck!'

I'm in charge of the catering in the garages, but Holly joins me in time to watch the race. Yesterday's dust haze has cleared, so the driving conditions are much safer, although we're still not expecting big things for the team today.

All that changes when both Will and Luis manage to climb a place each during the start. Luis takes another position during a pit stop when a mechanic for Emilio Rizzo in third place has a problem with the refuelling rig. By the time Holly and I reluctantly return to the hospitality area, Will and Luis are running second and third. There's a real buzz amongst the team and its guests, and Holly and I keep stopping to watch the action on the big screen. At one point, Luis is hot on Will's tail – they're only a second apart according to the commentators.

'Whoa!' one of the commentators says suddenly as Luis

attempts an overtaking manoeuvre. Luis pulls back into line behind Will, but a moment later, he's at it again. This time he outbreaks Will into a corner and swipes second place from under his wheels. There's a collective gasp around me.

'And he's done it!' I hear one of the commentators cry. 'That was spectacular, wasn't it?'

'Indeed it was. I don't think I've ever seen anyone attempt an overtaking manoeuvre on that corner before, much less succeeded.'

'Trust won't be happy about that,' he says of Will.

'Oh, no, he most definitely won't. Luis Castro is shaping up to be quite some driver, wouldn't you say?'

'Absolutely. If he— OH MY GOD, HE'S AT IT AGAIN!'

Luis is right behind Kit Bryson in the lead and I watch as he zips out from behind him and once again, outbreaks him into a corner.

'Incredible!' one of the commentators cries as the guests in the hospitality area break into applause and some leap out of their seats in astonishment. Amongst the mayhem, I try to zone in on what the commentators are saying.

'Absolutely! As I was about to say, if Castro manages to keep his second position, he'll be leading the championship by quite some distance.'

'This is looking like his first victory, at this rate. There was something quite "Ayrton Senna" about that move, wasn't there?'

'Let's not get ahead of ourselves . . .'

Ayrton Senna was one of the greatest drivers of his time before he was killed during a race. He crashed when he was leading the 1994 San Marino Grand Prix in Italy and I still remember it well, because I was staying with my grandparents at the time. I wasn't big into racing, but my grandfather was, and the news of Senna's death was everywhere. He was Brazilian, like Luis, and it's not the first time I've heard them being compared.

Standing there, seeing the looks of admiration on people's faces, I can't help but feel a strange sense of respect for Luis. I don't know why, but it makes me feel oddly uneasy. Perhaps it's because I'm disappointed for Will, but I can't dwell on that now because it's time to return to work. I glance back at the television screen one more time to see the camera following Luis as he speeds off into the Sakhir desert.

Chapter 9

My mobile rings and I snatch it up. 'Yes?'

'Your taxi's here.'

Cazzo! Is it that time already?

'Okay, I'll be down in a few minutes,' I tell the woman on the other end of the line.

I'm at home in my tiny rented studio flat on Camden Road in north London. I've been back in the UK for two weeks and have been helping out Frederick and Ingrid with various catering functions, so I haven't seen Holly at all. Her home is in Berkshire, near team HQ, and she adores living in the country. Me, I'm a city girl, through and through. But back to the present. I haven't even finished ironing my trousers and my car has arrived to take me to the airport. I quickly whip the iron round, turn it off, and then put on the trousers and their matching suit jacket.

I throw the last couple of things into my team carry case and zip it up, then lug it down two flights of stairs to the pavement below, where I scan the road for my taxi before realising it's in the car park behind the flat. The recent snowfall has given way to rain, rain and more rain, so I hold my handbag over my head to keep my hair dry as I stumble to the car.

Heathrow is bustling as always, but it doesn't take me long to find the rest of the hospitality crew because they're all wearing identical outfits to mine: black trouser suits and gold shirts. It's our travelling attire, and as I've already mentioned, Simon likes us to be well turned out at all times.

We're on our way to Barcelona in Spain for the first of the European races and I'm excited about seeing our new hospitality area. I've only ever been to flyaways before – the races that the team has to fly to, such as Australia, Malaysia and Japan. In those countries, we use the facilities provided for us at each of the tracks, but for the European races and the ones certain team members can travel to by truck, we bring our own facilities with us.

The flight is only short compared to the ones we've been taking recently, but Holly and I have just about enough time to chow down a couple of tubes of Pringles and catch up with each other after our time apart. We don't drink, because we're going straight to the track from the airport, and anyway, we're staying in a five-star hotel in the centre of Barcelona so we'll be making the most of the nightlife there during the course of the next few days.

We arrive at the Circuit de Catalunya, where the motorhomes have already been constructed by the truck drivers who got here on Sunday. I say motorhomes, but that's a ridiculous term. It refers to the old days when the teams had big, comfy buses, but now the motorhomes are portable, hi-tech buildings. I look up at ours in awe. It's shiny black and gold and is two storeys' high. A quick tour reveals that upstairs we have a directors' suite and private rooms each for Luis and Will, while downstairs there's a fully equipped kitchen and a massive hospitality area. It's air-conditioned and the directors even have a balcony on the top floor.

Two days in and that's where I find myself. Catalina is being bossier than ever and has called me up to the blissfully sun-drenched balcony to take down a list of things she needs – including tampons, and I have no idea where I'm going to find them here. She's in her element – it's her home race and she clearly feels she has a right to act like more of a queen than ever. Her whole family is going to be here for the weekend. I'm dreading it. It's not my job to be at her beck and call, but I can't really do anything about it.

'Have you got all that?' she asks me frostily, as I scribble away madly on my pad.

'Yes, I think so.'

'Think so or know so?' I know her eyes are glaring at me behind her dark sunglasses. She's sunbathing on a sunlounger while I'm standing in front of her like an obedient puppy.

'Yes, I've got it.'

'Good.' She rests her head back on her pillow so I walk away.

'I hate that bitch!' I explode to Holly when I get back to the kitchen.

'I don't know how you deal with her the way you do,' Holly empathises.

'Neither do I. She treats me like I'm a little ant that she can tread on. It's like she thinks all I'm ever going to be is a waitress in a car park, but I've got plans. I won't be here forever!'

Holly looks at me, amused. 'Where are you going, then?'

'Maybe I'll set up my own catering company, I don't know.'

So okay, I don't know. I don't really have any plans. I'm kind of just going with the flow for the moment, but Holly, thankfully, doesn't take me to task over it.

Later that afternoon, Catalina is at it again. I only hear the clicking at first, but when I turn around, I see her at the kitchen door, making the sound with her fingers.

'You. Come here.'

I project my unhappiness at Frederick, who looks a little perturbed by the sight of the boss's wife in his kitchen.

'You,' Catalina says again. 'Dahlia.'

'Daisy,' I correct her.

'Whatever,' she replies. 'I need you.'

'Daisy can't come right now,' Frederick interrupts. 'She's preparing Will and Luis's dinner.'

Yes! Ha ha! I avert my gaze so the bitch can't see my look of glee. It would only come back to bite me, knowing her.

'Then, you!' she spits. I look around to see her pointing at Holly, who in turn, is glaring at Frederick. He shrugs, helpless, because Holly has finished her chores for the moment and has been leaning against the counter taking a break.

'Come on!' Catalina snaps. Holly reluctantly follows her out of the kitchen.

Later, when she returns, she's in a foul mood.

'I am not doing that again!' she says angrily.

'What did she make you do?' I ask.

'Oh, she only bloody well wanted me to make her and her posse tortillas in Simon's room. But it's not that, that's easy, it's the fact that we prepare all this lovely food – even paella is on the menu today! – but none of it is good enough for her! I'm telling you, that's it. Next time I'm saying no.'

'How will you get out of it?' I ask worriedly. 'She's the boss's wife.'

'So speak to the boss,' Frederick interrupts calmly.

'Speak to Simon?' I scoff.

'Yes,' he replies.

'Do you know what,' Holly says, still cross. 'That's exactly what I'm going to do.' And she storms off in a huff.

'Holly!' I call after her in alarm, but she pays no notice.

'Chef!' I exclaim. 'What if Simon fires her?'

'He won't fire her,' Frederick rebuffs me. 'Simon likes people who stand up for themselves. You should have done it long ago.'

The minutes tick by until, finally, Holly re-emerges, looking haughty.

'Did you speak to him?' I whisper loudly.

'I can still hear you,' Frederick says wearily. 'But go on, tell us all.' He indicates Klaus and Gertrude and the other catering staff in the room who were hanging on to our every word a short while ago.

'Yes, I did,' Holly replies. 'And it won't happen again.'

'No way!'

'Yes way.'

'What do you mean? What did you say to him?' I persist.

'I told him we weren't Catalina's pets, we had our own jobs to do and that if she needs a personal assistant, maybe he should hire one for her. He's got enough money.'

'You didn't say that last part!' I'm horrified.

'I absolutely did,' she replies, firmly.

'How did he take it?'

'He took it,' she says simply.

'He *took* it?'

'Yes. That's it. We won't be bothered by her again.'

I've never seen Holly in this light before. It's freaking me out a bit.

'So, let me get this straight, Simon is going to hire a personal assistant for his wife because you told him to?'

'I don't know if he'll go as far as that, or if he'll just tell the stupid cow to make her own frigging tortillas.'

Frederick laughs. I look at him in shock. He never laughs. Certainly not when he's in the kitchen.

'Good for you!' he bellows at Holly.

She grins at him. 'Thanks.'

'Now, Daisy,' he barks at me, back to his old self. 'Have you finished stringing those beans? We haven't got all day.'

'Yes, Chef.' Along with the rest of the staff in the kitchen I look at Holly in awe and then turn back to my chores.

That evening, Holly and I are scrubbing down the worktops when Pete and Dan clamber into the kitchen.

'Is it true?' Dan asks eagerly. 'Did you tell Catalina to go fuck herself?'

Holly laughs. 'Blimey, doesn't news travel fast. Why? What have you heard?'

'She and Simon had a massive barney earlier. Curtis heard it.' Curtis is one of the engineers: a short, plump, bald man with an even bigger appetite for gossip than he has for food.

'Really?' I ask. 'What happened?'

'Well, Luis said—'

'Luis? What's he got to do with it?' I interrupt.

'Curtis told Luis about it and he told us.'

'God, it's like Chinese whispers,' I mutter, starting to feel a little dirty about the whole thing.

'Shut up, Daisy, let them get a word in.' Holly flicks me on my arm.

'He was just going on about you girls not being there at her beck and call and—'

'REALLY?' Holly and I interrupt.

'—and to stop bothering you because you've got your own jobs to do.'

'Seriously?' I exclaim.

'Yeah, it was nuts. She was screaming at him, apparently.'

'Serves her right,' Holly says tautly.

'She's not going to like us very much after this,' I say.

'Like she liked us anyway.' Holly turns her nose up.

'Hmm . . .'

'Daisy! Stop being a misery guts. This is brilliant news. We'll never be bugged by that silly old tart again!'

'Are you girls coming out tonight?' Pete changes the subject.

'Bit late, isn't it?' I ask, getting wry looks from all concerned. 'I'm joking! Where are you going?'

'Thought we'd go to the tapas bars on Las Ramblas,' Pete answers.

'Sounds good.'

By the time race day comes around, my belly is so full of Sangria that I don't know how I haven't turned into a giant jug. I'm in the kitchen absent-mindedly fingering a packet of rice when Frederick barks at me.

'Why aren't you outside doing breakfast?'

'Sorry, Chef,' I say, gingerly placing the rice packet on the countertop.

'Get with it! Are you hungover again?'

'No, no, I'm on it,' I fib, willing my feet to take me out of the kitchen. They come to an automatic stop when I see who's standing at the serving table.

'There you are,' Will says.

'Sorry,' I reply, kick-starting myself into action again. I hurry behind the table. 'Have you been waiting long?'

'Only a minute.'

'What can I get you?' I gaze up at him and try not to jolt at the sight of his blue eyes. They still surprise me every time I look at them.

'Did you go out last night?' he asks me.

'Yeah. To a bar in the old town.'

'Nice?'

'Brilliant, you should've come.' I know I've said this before, but I just can't help myself. 'Luis popped in for a couple. Oh, here he is now.'

Will turns around in time to see Luis join us at the serving table. 'Alright?' he says.

'Yep,' Luis answers bluntly, looking at me. 'Good morning, Daisy.'

My mouth falls open.

'What?' Luis asks.

'You just called me Daisy.'

'Isn't that your name?' He sounds wary.

'Yes, but . . . Oh, never mind.' I shake my head. 'What are you having?'

I get on with Luis's order before noticing Will tapping his foot impatiently.

'Oh, sorry, Will,' I apologise, awkwardly realising I should have served him first.

'He can wait,' Luis chips in. 'He's used to coming second.' Luis winks at me, but when I glance at Will, he's not looking amused. Luis qualified on pole yesterday. Will, brilliantly, although clearly not brilliantly enough for him, qualified second.

'Sorry about that,' I say to Will as Luis heads off and plonks himself down at a table next to one of the team's engineers. 'What can I get you?'

He gives me a hard stare before answering. 'Same.'

It's then that I realise Luis opted for a rare healthy breakfast, right down to Will's favourite choice of protein shake.

Flustered, I hurry up and put Will's order together.

Luis shouts, 'Snap!' as Will walks past his table, but Will ignores him, heading towards the stairs to retreat to his room.

I sigh, deflated, and start to tidy up the serving table.

'Get me some bacon and eggs, will you, bun tart?' I look up to see Luis there, his bowl still half-full of muesli. 'And you can take this crap, too.' He passes over his glass. 'I don't know how Will drinks it.'

'It doesn't do his racing any harm,' I comment.

'It doesn't do it any good, either,' Luis says. 'Coffee, black.' He nods at the jug. I pour him one and hand it over. 'Mmm, that's better,' he says, slurping some. At that moment his personal trainer walks through the doors.

'Oh, *merda*!' I think that means 'shit'. 'Shake! Shake!' Luis waves his hands at me for the glass of liquid I'm just about to dispose of. 'Whoops, sorry,' I say innocently, pouring it down the drain. I try not to laugh as João spies Luis's bacon and starts going off on one in Portuguese.

Half an hour later I dismiss myself and head upstairs to Will's room. I knock on the door.

'Yep?' Will calls.

'Hi,' I say, poking my head around the door. 'Can I clear those away?' I point to the breakfast plates on the table.

'Sure.' He gets up and hands them to me.

'Sorry about that earlier,' I say uneasily, as he sits back down on his chair.

'What? Oh, Luis,' he says. 'Don't worry about it.'

'He's just trying to psyche you out before the race.'

'I know. He's a bit of a prick like that.'

I laugh and his face breaks into a smile. 'Do you want to sit down a minute?' He indicates the chair next to him. I pause, then put his breakfast plates down again on the table.

He's wearing a white short-sleeve team shirt and not for the first time I notice how tanned his arms are, presumably from all that working out in the sun in the last three countries we've been to.

'Are you staying on tonight?' he asks.

'Yes. We fly out tomorrow afternoon. You?'

'Supposed to be going back straight after the race.'

'Supposed to be?'

'Mmm.'

'You don't sound too sure?' He doesn't look too sure, either. He sighs. 'You sound fed up, Will.'

He slides down and rests his head on the back of the chair, looking at me through half-closed eyes. 'I am a bit,' he answers, truthfully.

'Why?'

'I could do with a night off.'

I sit up in my seat. 'So why don't you change your flight? Stay another night? Come out with us after the race?'

He doesn't answer, just continues to regard me, calmly. I look away.

'Might do.' He leans forward and rests his elbows on his knees.

I try to focus. 'How are you feeling about today? Is the car performing well?'

He raises one eyebrow in amusement, but I attempt to look professional, so his answer is straightforward. 'It still had a bit of understeer in practice this morning, but hopefully we've sorted that out.'

'Mmmhmm.' I nod, keeping my face serious.

He grins. 'You have absolutely no idea what I'm talking about, do you?'

I shake my head resolutely. 'No.'

'Didn't think so.'

'But the intent was there.' I smile back at him. 'I know nothing about cars, I'm afraid.'

'Can you drive?'

'Just about.'

'You don't sound too confident.'

'I'm not.' I laugh. 'I can drive a scooter, though.'

'Oh, yeah.' He rolls his eyes. 'I've seen you drive a scooter.'

'Oi! Now, you're sounding as bad as Luis!'

'We can't have that.'

'No, we can't have that.'

We smile at each other for a moment, before he looks away and stands up. 'Right, I'd better get ready.'

'Of course, yes.' I get quickly to my feet and pick up his breakfast plates again. 'So will you change your flight?'

'Don't know.' He looks distracted.

'Okay, well, have a good race.' I pause by the door.

'Cheers.' He bends down and starts searching through his carry case.

'Do you need help finding anything?' I ask hesitantly.

'No, I'm fine. Thanks, Daisy,' he says brusquely. He doesn't look at me as I walk through the door.

Red, red, red, red, red, GO! The cars scream away from the starting grid. Will almost takes Luis at the first corner, but his team-mate manages to keep pole position and now Will is hot on his tail. Argh! I'm so tense! A quick glance around the garage tells me everyone else is feeling the same. I glue my eyes back to the television screens above. Will is still right behind Luis. Can he take him? Go on, Will!

You should have seen his face before the race. Holly and I went for a wander down the pit lane and I have never seen anyone look so focussed or determined in my life. He was standing by the wall under an umbrella and he gave us a brief nod, but wouldn't speak to the press. Luis was doing the complete opposite. When he wasn't chatting to camera crews, he was chatting up skimpily dressed brolly dollies.

'Oh, Jesus, I hope he doesn't take him out,' Holly says beside me.

Will has just attempted another overtaking manoeuvre. He's all over Luis like a rash.

'Surely Simon's going to tell him to back off,' Holly says.

The team boss can speak to the drivers over the radio.

'Why?' I snap. 'If Will can take him, Simon should tell Luis to let him past. He's obviously quicker.'

I don't know if that's what happens, but a second later, Will overtakes Luis on a corner and I have to stop myself from cheering out loud. Will is now in the lead, but the tension inside me doesn't dissipate, even when Will starts to put some distance between himself and his team-mate. In fact, as the race goes on, my throat starts to feel more and more constricted and my stomach feels gripped in the clutch of something. I don't want to leave Will's garage, but it's actually quite a relief when Holly drags me away and I have something other than the race to concentrate on.

We return to the pits for the last few laps and the countdown to the chequered flag feels like it goes on forever, but when Will crosses the line and we see him punch the air with joy, all the anxiety inside me evaporates. This is his first Formula 1 victory and I know this will be a moment that will stay with him forever. A few minutes later, he's climbing out of his car and is running to his cheering mechanics waiting behind the fence. Holly and I are right there amongst them, and even though I only get the briefest hug from Will, and even though he's all wet with sweat and probably doesn't even register that it's me, I feel – quite bizarrely – like I'm in the middle of one of the happiest moments of my life.

Luis arrives soon afterwards, his expression far from ecstatic, but his reception from his team-mates is just as joyous. The driver in third place, a Spaniard called Antonio Aranda, also receives rapturous applause from his home-town crowd.

Later, when we're all back in the hospitality area, Holly and I are run off our feet making sure everyone has a full glass of champagne. I'm on edge because I can't see Will anywhere. I know he has interviews to do, but Luis arrived back ten minutes ago and I'll be devastated if Will goes home to England without saying goodbye. The next race is in Istanbul in two weeks' time and that feels like a lifetime away.

When Will finally makes an appearance to the sound of rapturous applause, I can't keep the smile from my face or the spring from my step. My heart is soaring, and then I'm distracted because everywhere I go I'm acutely aware of Will's presence in the room as he mingles with the sponsors and the rest of the team. I keep trying to manoeuvre myself in his direction, but there's always another glass to fill and, in the interim, he moves off.

At one point, I find myself amongst Catalina and her Spanish posse. She holds out her glass for me to top up, but doesn't acknowledge me or say thank you. She's barely come out of the directors' suite all weekend. I notice Alberta beside her and attend to her glass, too. I didn't realise she was here. My champagne bottle is almost empty so I hurry back into the kitchen and return to the hospitality area with a fresh one.

'Fill her up, bun tart.'

I almost bump into Luis standing just outside the kitchen. He's changed out of his racing overalls into jeans and a T-shirt.

'I see your girlfriend's here,' I say wryly, pouring fizzing liquid into his glass.

He raises one eyebrow at me. 'She's ignored me all weekend.'

'Oh dear,' I reply. 'It's not really your day today, is it? What with losing to Will and all that . . . How did that happen, anyway?'

'Were you asleep?' he asks.

'No, I watched most of it.'

'Well, he had a much better car today. Simple as that.'

'What was wrong with yours?'

'Too much oversteer.'

'Oversteer? Is that the same as understeer?'

'Er, no, otherwise it would be called understeer, wouldn't it.'

'She's not talking cars again, is she?'

I spin around at the sound of Will's voice. I feel light-headed as he grins, his blue eyes sparkling.

'Want me to help you with that?' He points at the almost-full bottle of champagne I'm wielding.

'Do you want some?' I check.

'Please.' He holds out his glass and I tilt the bottle, willing my hands to keep steady as the fluid hits the flute. The bubbles threaten to spill over the top and I hold my breath, but they subside again so I top up the glass with a little more.

'I'm gonna switch to beer.' Luis excuses himself, nudging me as he goes past. I look back at Will. He'll leave, too, now. I just know it.

And he does. He walks away without saying a word. Dammit!

Hang on, he's coming back again. With a champagne glass!

'What's that?' I ask.

'It's called a glass. They come in quite useful if you work in catering.'

I smack him on his arm and smile. 'I know that, you jerk. What are you doing with it?'

He hands me his almost-full glass. 'Hold that.' I do as he says. Then he takes the bottle of champagne from me and tops up the empty flute. He puts the champagne bottle down on a nearby tabletop and hands me the fresh glass, removing the other one I'm holding.

'Cheers.' He takes a sip and leans back on the tabletop.

'Cheers,' I say warily, before adding, 'I can't really stand here, drinking.'

'Why not?'

'I should be working.'

'There are enough of you. God,' he says, looking around the room, 'it's like a beehive in here.'

I cast my eyes around the room and see all of the front-of-house staff, and even a couple of caterers, hard at work. The guests can barely walk two feet without coming face to face with a bottle of champagne or a tray of canapés.

'Well done, by the way. Congratulations,' I say.

'Thanks.'

'You managed to sort out that understeer problem, then.'

He smirks at me. 'So where are we going tonight?'

'Tonight?' My eyes widen. 'Did you change your flight?'

He nods.

'Brilliant!' Oh my God, I'm so happy I could hug him! Calm down, Daisy, otherwise he might get a restraining order. 'Well, I think we're heading to Las Ramblas again.' I try to keep a straight face.

'Cool. What time?'

'We have to finish cleaning up here, so maybe eight o'clock? Are you going back to the hotel, soon?'

'Yeah, in half an hour or so.'

'I'll come and get you if you like?'

'Okay.' He takes a sip of his drink and looks around the room.

'I should get back to work.' I pick up the champagne bottle and put my half-full glass down on the table.

'See you later, then.'

'Bye . . .'

Two hours later, the hospitality area has finally cleared out and we're hard at work, scrubbing down the kitchen. I glance at my watch. It's already seven thirty.

'What time did you tell him?' Holly asks me.

I look at her, worriedly. 'Eight o'clock.'

'We won't be finished before nine,' she says.

'I know.' I wasn't thinking when I told Will otherwise and now I'm feeling quite sick about it.

I hear the sound of male voices outside the kitchen.

'That's Pete and Dan!' Holly says. 'Go with them!'

'What? Back to the hotel?'

'Yes!' she urges. 'Hitch a ride! I'll see you at that tapas bar later!'

'I can't leave . . .' I look around the kitchen. Everyone is hard at work.

'Go!' she insists. 'Chef!'

'What?' Frederick turns around.

'Holly!' I whisper.

She continues, unperturbed. 'Can Daisy be excused? She has an errand to run for Will.'

'Is Daisy not capable of asking for herself to be excused?' Frederick asks, irritably.

I shift on my feet.

'Go on, then,' Frederick says, turning away.

Holly beams at me so I quickly take off my apron and grab my bag before he changes his mind. The lads are just walking outside to one of our people carriers.

'Pete! Dan!' I call breathlessly. 'Can I get a lift back to the hotel?'

They look surprised, but step back to let me into the car first. 'Sure.'

'Where are we off to tonight?' Pete asks me, when we're all belted up.

'Holly wants to meet at that tapas bar we went to on Friday.'

'What, the one with the bright lighting?' Dan asks me, screwing his nose up.

'Yeah. And all the sexy barmen.' I grin.

'Bollocks to that,' Pete exclaims, nudging Dan. 'We'll go to that other one, won't we, mate? The one on the other side of the road?'

'What, the touristy one?' I frown.

'They're *all* touristy,' Pete rebuffs me.

I sigh. 'Okay, I'll call Holly when I get back to the hotel.'

But when I do, her mobile goes straight through to voicemail. Her battery could be flat, but I'll keep trying.

At ten past eight, I'm still in my hotel room desperately trying to decide what to wear. I did have a change of clothes with me at the track because Holly and I usually get ready there, but now that Will's coming, nothing I have will do. I'm torn between a mini skirt or my black Rock & Republic jeans that I wore on Friday and eventually I decide on the latter, teamed with a gun-metal-grey Diesel T-shirt. The outfit is a bit rock chick, but I decide to run with that look. I have to wear my hair up in a bun for work, but now I take the pins out and it falls dark and wavy, halfway down my back. I go into the bathroom and hurriedly apply some more make-up – black kohl around my green eyes and a smudge of shimmery silver eye-shadow on the lids, followed by black mascara and just a touch of lipgloss. I look at my watch. It's twenty-five past eight. A quick spritz of perfume and I'm ready.

Nerves flutter through me once more. I take a deep breath and try to still them. This is ridiculous. It's not like I'm going on a freaking date, is it? I pull a face and shake my head at my own ridiculousness as I grab my bag and go to the lift. Will's room is on the top floor.

I knock on his door and distractedly survey my fingernails. The beige-pink polish doesn't really go with my rock chick look. I wish I had some rouge noire . . . Oh! I jump as the door swishes open.

'Hello!' I chirp, resisting the urge to take a step backwards. Will is standing in the doorway wearing khaki-coloured G-Star trousers and a black T-shirt. The smell of his aftershave wafts out, but I can see from here that he hasn't shaved. In fact, his jaw has the beginnings of stubble and he looks even hotter than usual. I don't know how I'm going to cope with this.

'All set?' he asks, coming out of the room and pulling the door closed behind him.

'Yes, sorry I'm late.'

'That's alright.' He follows me down the corridor to the lifts and I push the button. 'Is everyone else downstairs?' he asks as the lift doors open and we step inside.

'They should be by now. Holly's meeting us there. She had to stay back at the track a bit longer.'

He nods. A moment later we arrive at the foyer. Pete, Dan and the rest of the lads – about ten in total – whistle at me as we walk towards them.

'Gawd, check you out,' Dan says, wrapping his arm around my neck. 'Are you on the pull tonight, love?'

'Get off.' I push him away, good-naturedly. I'm blushing, but I'm secretly delighted the guys just made a fuss of me in front of Will. I glance at him, but he's chatting to one of his mechanics.

'Shall we go?' I say to Pete.

He turns to Dan. 'Is Luis definitely not coming?'

'No, he said he had a headache.'

Pete scoffs. 'Like that's ever stopped him in the past. Still pissed off at you for that overtaking manoeuvre, I imagine.' He gives Will a mischievous look, but Will just shrugs.

It's only a short walk to Las Ramblas, which are a set of busy shopping streets, crowded with tourists and full of cafés and bars. Because it's race weekend, Barcelona is even more packed with people than usual. I find myself walking between Pete and Dan as we try to avoid street musicians on the bustling pavements. I'm looking at the back of Will's head for most of the way and desperately hoping it's not going to be like this for the rest of the night. If I don't get a chance to speak to him, I think I'll die.

It's standing room only at the bar and when a stool becomes available, the guys insist I take it. I'm the only girl here, and it's quite sweet that they're looking out for me. They get the drinks in, opting for beer while I avoid Sangria and go for a vodka and lemon instead. Then I perch on my stool and make chitchat with one of Luis's mechanics. But twenty minutes in, I'm struggling to focus on what he's saying. Will has just cracked up laughing at something Pete has said. This is driving me nuts. The mechanic I'm talking to excuses himself to go to the gents', and another one of the lads appears in his place. I feel like I'm stranded, but I don't want to seem rude so I smile and try to think of something to say. And then I remember Holly.

'Sorry,' I apologise to the mechanic, Karl, as I pull my phone out of my bag. 'I just have to call Holly,' I explain. 'She's supposed to be meeting us somewhere else.'

I dial her number for the umpteenth time and, once again, it goes straight through to voicemail. I snap the phone shut, impatiently.

'No answer?' Karl asks.

'No.'

'Want another one?' He indicates my almost-empty glass.

'Um, no, I shouldn't.' I stand up. 'I'm going to have to go to the bar to meet her. I'll bring her back,' I promise.

'Cool.' But he's already turned around and is trying to get the bartender's attention.

I squeeze past the other lads in the direction of Pete and Will. Pete steps aside and ushers me into their gang.

'I have to go,' I tell him regretfully.

His face falls. 'Where?'

'Holly's meeting me at that other place. I can't get hold of her.'

'PETE!' Karl shouts.

Pete looks over at the bar.

'ANOTHER ROUND?'

'YEAH, GOOD ONE!' Pete lifts up his beer bottle.

'Where's Holly meeting you?' Will asks me while this is going on.

'Only across the road. But her phone battery must be flat so I'm just going to have to go and wait for her. Hopefully she won't be late.'

'Want me to come and keep you company?'

I stare at him and my spirits lift, but I mindlessly shake my head. 'No, it's okay, you don't have to.' He's only being polite.

'Are you sure?'

No! Please, come with me!

I waver and he notices.

'Come on.' He puts his hand on my back and starts to guide

me towards the door. 'Pete.' He reaches back and taps Pete on his shoulder. 'I'm just going to go with Daisy to get Holly.'

'Sure, mate.' Pete turns back to the lads.

I lead the way out, my heart pounding in my chest as we step onto the crowded pavement.

Chapter 10

'It's just over here,' I say.

We go inside the bar and I scan the room for Holly. 'I can't see her,' I tell Will, 'but she should be here soon.'

'Okay. Let's get a drink.'

At that moment I notice a table come up by the window.

'You grab it,' Will says. 'I'll go to the bar. What are you having?'

I decide to stick to vodka. Will returns shortly afterwards with our drinks and by then I've managed to rack my brain for some things to talk about.

'Thanks for coming with me,' I say, once he's seated.

'Of course, no problem. I didn't want you to have to come on your own.' He's drinking a bottle of beer.

I screw my nose up. 'Do you think Luis has really got a headache or is he just being a sore loser?'

'Probably a bit of both,' Will answers wryly, then adds conspiratorially, 'He thought I was a bit aggressive with my driving today.'

'Did he? Well, he would, wouldn't he? You won and he didn't.'

'Exactly. He'll get over it by the next race.'

'You drivers do seem to forgive and forget pretty quickly. I overheard one of the mechanics yesterday saying something about Emilio Rizzo slating Antonio Aranda to the press for almost taking him off the track at the last race. And then today when Aranda came third, I spotted them slapping each other on the back and acting like best buddies.'

'Yeah.' He nods. 'That's the nature of the business. You can't hold grudges. Saying that, there's a lot of jealousy in this sport, which is probably why Rizzo mouthed off to the press. Aranda's only been in F1 for a year and Rizzo's been around forever. There's talk he's going to retire soon.'

'Oh, right.' I'm not actually that interested in hearing about the slimy old Italian, so I change tack. 'How did *you* get into racing?'

'My grandfather started taking me karting at the age of seven. He was a bit of a race enthusiast.'

'Seven? Wow.'

'Mmm. Anyway, he left me some money when he died—'

'How old were you when that happened?' I interrupt.

'Twelve,' he replies. 'So I was able to fund myself after that. Eventually I secured a drive with a half-decent team, scored a few race wins and that was it, really. Next stop, Formula 1.'

'You make it sound so easy.'

'That's not my intention.'

I lean forward in my seat, interested in his past. Interested in everything about him, actually. 'Your parents didn't help at all?' I ask.

'Nope.' He takes a swig of beer and glances out the window.

'Do they not like racing or something?'

'No, they just don't care what I do.' He stares at me directly for a good few seconds before I tear my eyes away. He's scratching candle wax off the table when I look back.

'Were you close to your granddad?'

'Very.'

'You must've been devastated when he died.'

'Yeah, I was.' He glances up at me, then laughs sharply. 'Can we talk about something else?'

I shift in my seat with embarrassment. I didn't mean to pry, but if he notices my discomfort, he doesn't show it.

'What do you want to talk about?' I try not to sound as brittle as I feel.

'You.' He leans forward and I resist the urge to lean backwards. 'Are you close to your parents? Grandparents?' he asks.

'Grandparents, yes, parents, no.'

'We have that in common, then. Why not?'

'My father is an arsehole.'

'And your mother?'

'She puts up with it. But I adore my grandmother,' I continue. 'She's the only grandparent I have left. She lives in Italy, though, so I hardly ever see her.'

'Where in Italy?'

'Northern Tuscany, in the mountains near Lucca.'

'No shit? You know we're filming an ad for a petrol company around that area next week?'

'No?'

'Yeah. You should come along.'

'Do you think I could?' My voice speeds up in my excitement. 'Won't the hotels already be booked and everything?'

'Ally will be able to squeeze you in.'

'Actually, I could stay with Nonna,' I think out loud.

'Does "nonna" mean "grandmother" in Italian?' he asks.

'Yes. I would *love* to see her again . . .'

'How long has it been?'

'Too long. I was hoping to catch up with her when we go to the Italian Grand Prix later this year, but I didn't think I'd manage to work in a trip beforehand. I wonder if Frederick and Ingrid would release me from a couple of catering jobs?'

'Can't hurt to ask.' He looks out the window while I sit there pondering the possibility. I *mustn't* get my hopes up. He turns back to me.

'So what's the deal with you? Why did you leave the States?'

I'm so caught up in my thoughts about going to Italy that his question catches me off guard and I don't have enough time to come up with a decent lie. I surprise even myself when I answer honestly.

'Oh, I had my heart broken.' My face breaks into a sheepish smile.

'Did you? Who was he?'

'No one you'd kno . . .' My voice trails off. 'Well, saying that . . .' I roll my eyes, jokily, before realising that was a truly stupid thing to do.

'I know him?' Will looks interested.

'No! No, no, no,' I hurriedly try to put a stop to his questioning. 'No, you don't know him.'

'Is he famous?' He sits up in his seat.

'Oh, God, stop talking.' I wave him away and then want to kick myself. As if he's going to drop it now, you idiot!

'Who?' Will demands to know.

'No one! Leave it! How did we get onto this subject, anyway? Let's talk about you, again!'

'Fuck that,' he scoffs. 'Just tell me.'

'No, I can't,' I say.

'Why, did you have to sign a confidentiality clause or something?'

I waver.

'You did, didn't you?' He slaps his hand on the table. 'Oh bollocks, now I'm really curious.'

I stare at him, mortified. I can't believe I've let it get this far. After all this practice at lying!

He looks at me through narrowed eyes. 'Did you work for him?'

'How the hell?' I start. How did he figure that out?

'You did! What did you do?'

I pause, before answering truthfully. That much can't hurt. 'I was his personal assistant. But that's ALL I'm saying.' I determinedly take a gulp of my drink.

'Never mind.' He leans back and swigs from his beer bottle. 'I'll get it out of Holly later.'

I laugh wryly and shake my head. 'She doesn't know.'

'Bullshit.' He plonks his bottle down on the table.

'I'm not joking,' I say. 'And actually, she doesn't even know this much so can you please not say anything?'

He looks at me, trying to suss out whether or not I'm telling him the truth and eventually seems to decide that I am.

'My lips are sealed,' he says.

'Thank you.' I sigh. 'God, that was stressful.'

He laughs. I turn and scan the bar for Holly.

'Still no sign?' Will asks, looking too.

'No. I can't see her.'

'Bet you're wishing you came alone, now, aren't you?'

I look back at him and smile. 'No, I'm still glad you're here.'

He regards me warmly for a moment. He has really nice lips . . .

Suddenly he clears his throat and peers into his beer bottle. 'Want another?' He points to my drink.

'I'll go.' I start to get up.

'Bugger off,' he says, frowning at me as he stands. 'And no crap about you being a feminist, either. Same again?'

I laugh and sit down. 'Yes, please.'

My eyes follow him as he heads off to the bar. A few people turn to stare as they realise who he is. There are a lot of race fans out on the town tonight, and a couple of them approach him asking for autographs. Will signs their caps and T-shirts quite happily, oblivious to me watching.

I smile to myself. *Famous people* . . . But Will is a different kind of famous to . . . you know. I bet he would make a *much* nicer boyfriend. I suddenly recall quite clearly the pain of seeing the love of my life come onto another woman right in front of me. Hot tears prick my eyes, taking me by surprise. To my absolute horror, Will picks this time to return to the table.

'What's wrong?' he asks in alarm.

'Nothing, nothing!' I laugh, embarrassed.

'What is it?' he persists.

'Just having a nasty ex memory.' I quickly swipe my thumbs underneath my eyes to catch the moisture before my rock chick look turns goth.

'Oh. Sorry.'

'It's not your fault,' I say, surreptitiously smearing the mascara from my thumbs onto my jeans.

Will pauses, before saying, 'Well he sounds like a twat, whoever he was.'

I snicker in amusement.

'I'll never go and see any of his films ever again.' He looks at me hopefully.

'Nice try, buster,' I joke.

'Buy one of his albums?' he tries again, raising an eyebrow.

I just shake my head and purse my lips. He chuckles and taps his fingers on the table, eyeing me steadily. 'I'm a bit of a shit for doing that to you,' he says, dryly. 'I get so pissed off when people pry into my love life.'

'Who pries into your love life?'

'The press do all the time. Laura's always getting papped.'

Urgh. Her again. 'Is she? Why?'

He gives me a baffled look.

'Sorry, I don't read the tabloids,' I tell him, apologetically. 'I *genuinely* don't know why they'd bother her.'

'Well, she's kind of . . .' his voice trails off so I prompt him.

'Pretty?' I feel sick as I ask it, and even sicker when he answers.

'Yeah.' He shrugs. 'She's into fashion and all that stuff.'

Great. So she's a stunning socialite. 'Sounds like a Wayne and Coleen situation,' I say, trying to sound light-hearted and unbothered.

'Jesus,' he exclaims. 'I hope you're not trying to say I look like Wayne Rooney.'

I laugh. 'No, I think you look more like Leonardo DiCaprio. Not now,' I quickly add. 'More back in his *Titanic* days when he was really hot.' Dammit, Daisy! Now he thinks I fancy him! I instinctively put my hands to my cheeks to try to stop them from heating up.

He regards me with amusement. I hurriedly turn my attention to my watch. It's ten o'clock. 'Where the hell is Holly?' I ask out loud, thankful for the change of subject. I dig out my mobile phone from my bag. 'Excuse me,' I say. 'I'll just try her again.' This time the phone rings, but she doesn't answer. Eventually it diverts to voicemail so I try again. She picks up on the tenth ring.

'Holly! Where are you?'

'I'm still at the track.' Her voice is muffled.

'*What?*' I screech. 'Why?'

'More to do here than I thought.'

'Oh, no! Is everyone really pissed off with me for ducking out?' I ask worriedly.

'No! Not at all! The others have all left. I'm just helping out with a few little things.'

'Oh, okay. Will you be here soon?'

'Er . . .' She sounds hesitant. 'I'm not sure. Don't wait for me. I'll call you if I can make it. Sorry,' she adds.

'Don't worry, it's okay.'

We hang up and I look at Will. 'I don't think she's coming.'

'She's not?' He looks surprised.

'I'm really sorry.' I feel awful for dragging him here.

'It's alright,' he says.

'Shall we go and rejoin the others?' I ask, making to stand up.

'Sure, let's.' He downs the last of his beer and follows me out.

Back in the other bar I just can't relax. I'm not in the mood for mingling and I can't take up any more of Will's time, so after another hour I tell Pete I'm heading back to the hotel. I refuse his offer to walk me – it's not far and the streets are so full of tourists that I feel safe enough.

When I get there, I find Frederick having a nightcap in the hotel bar with Klaus.

Italy! Ask him about Italy!

'I thought Holly was coming?' Frederick queries, once I've put my 'please-please-please-please-please-let-me-go-to-Italy' face on.

'Holly?' I ask, confused.

'Yes. You know, that girl with the blonde hair. Petite. Goes out and gets pissed a lot with another naughty girl who works for me.'

'Ha ha,' I say sarcastically. 'I know who Holly is, I just didn't know she was going to Italy?'

Frederick looks nonplussed.

'Anyway,' I move on. 'Can I come?'

'What about the catering jobs you had lined up for Ingrid in London?'

I shift from foot to foot. 'Do you think she'd let me out of them?' I ask, pleadingly.

'I suppose Charlotte might be able to step in.'

Charlotte is another girl I work with occasionally. She's doing a fine arts degree, so is only employed part-time.

'So can I?'

'I guess so. You'll have to speak to Ally about booking a hotel . . .'

'That's the best bit.' I grin. 'I'll be able to stay with my grandmother in the mountains. So you'll only have to pay for my plane ticket!'

'Only?' He humphs. 'Well, you'd better speak to Ally about that, then.'

'Yay! Thanks, boss!'

'Be off with you. Let me finish my drink in peace.' He raises it up and knocks it back in one, while I hurry away before he changes his mind.

Holly is in bed when I get up to our room. I shake her roughly.

'What the bleeding hell are you doing?' she snaps, groggily.

'I'm going to Italy! Are you?'

One eye opens. 'What do you mean you're going to Italy?'

'With you! Are you going?' I ask again.

The other eye opens and she props herself up in bed. 'Yes.' She yawns, loudly.

'How did that happen?'

'Simon asked me to come,' she replies.

'When?' I'm a little taken aback. I'm supposed to be his on-hand girl.

'This afternoon. He would have asked you,' she says quickly. 'I'm sure it's just because he knows you have catering jobs in London, that's all.'

'Oh, right.' My voice must be filled with trepidation because she continues to reassure me.

'Don't be offended,' she urges.

'I'm not,' I reply. Holly obviously impressed him much more than I thought when she stood up to him about Catalina. 'Anyway, how cool is that?' I try to inject the enthusiasm back into my voice. 'Only,' I realise suddenly, 'I'm not staying with you lot. I'm staying with my nonna in the mountains. So we probably won't see each other much at all.'

'Oh, that's a shame.' She yawns again.

'Still, it'll be fun, won't it?'

'Yeah. So how are you coming if Simon didn't ask you to?' Holly asks, suddenly curious.

'Will encouraged me to ask Frederick.'

'Will? Hey! How was tonight?'

'It was nice,' I reply offhandedly.

'What did you talk about?' she asks.

'Oh, you know, this and that.'

'Do you still fancy him?' she pries.

I flop down on the mattress and bury my face in the pillow. 'Might do,' I tell her in a muffled voice.

'What did you say? Daisy?' she persists, when I don't immediately answer.

I turn my head on the pillow to face her. 'Might do,' I say, trying to stifle a smile and failing.

'What are you going to do about his girlfriend?' she asks.

Now my smile drops. 'What do you mean, what am I going to do about his girlfriend?' I huff, propping myself up on one elbow. 'I'm not going to do anything. He's got a girlfriend! End of story!'

'Oh, good,' she says.

'I've already told you that,' I continue my rant.

'Yeah, I know,' she says dismissively. 'I just wasn't sure if things had changed.'

'Of course they haven't changed,' I answer, still a touch annoyed. 'I'm not that sort of girl. I just like him as a friend.'

'Sure.' She rolls her tired eyes at me.

'Well, you know, maybe things aren't as rosy with Laura as they seem . . .'

'I knew it!' She slaps the bedcovers.

'What? Oh, *va fanculo*.'

She laughs, then her face becomes serious. 'So you're not sworn off men anymore, then?'

I sigh and, for a brief moment, all the pain and hurt I felt back in America threatens to overcome me. I shake my head and try to black out the memories for the second time that night.

'Daisy? Are you alright?' Holly is suddenly concerned.

'Yes, I'm fine,' I tell her.

'Just be careful,' she says.

'I will be. Careful's my middle name,' I lie. In fact, I've always been a fly-by-the-seat-of-my-pants kinda girl.

'I just don't want you to get hurt,' she adds, sliding back down under the bedsheets.

And that, for now, is the end of our conversation. I take off my make-up in a daze, trying to remember everything Will and I talked about tonight. I climb into bed and picture him staring at me with his beautiful blue eyes. I remember the stubble on his face, and in my mind I reach over and trace my finger along his jaw. His lips, I remember them, too. I wonder if he's a good kisser? I bet he is. I imagine *him* walking me back to the hotel through busy streets full of bars and late-night revelry, and I imagine him pulling me into a dark doorway. My stomach fills with butterflies as I forget all about Laura and Luis and Holly and everyone else I know, and imagine Will kissing me passionately, as though we're both caught up in a moment of time that we can't get out of. But in my mind, when he pulls away, his face is blurry. His eyes are no longer clear. I try to remember his mouth again, and can suddenly see it perfectly, but when I attempt to put it with the rest of his face, it doesn't fit. I've lost him. What the hell is wrong with me? Try as I might, I can't bring the memory of him into focus in my mind. I know it's no good, I've been through this before, so I go back to replaying our conversation instead, and hope that if I don't try too hard, I might be able to see his face again before I reach Italy in a couple of days.

Chapter 11

'Nonna!'

'*La mia stellina! Vieni qui amore, che ti vuole abbracciare la Nonna!*' That means, 'My little star! Come here my love, Grandma wants to give you a hug!' She doesn't speak much English, Nonna, and my Italian is fluent, so we rarely converse in anything else. Don't worry, I'll translate from here on in.

'Look at you! So beautiful, but oh, so thin!' She grabs my cheeks in dismay and attempts to tug some skin between her fingers.

'Ouch, Nonna!' I bat her away and she engulfs me in a big, cuddly hug. I have to stoop down because she's only five foot tall and, of course, I'm five foot nine.

'We'll have to feed you up. The pasta sauce is almost ready!' She ushers me into her small kitchen, where a pot is bubbling on top of her old-fashioned stove.

'Is that what I can smell? What is it?'

'Rabbit.'

Hmm. Thought so. Not really a big fan of rabbit.

'Great!' I fib. Nonna doesn't need to know . . .

'What have you been doing, my darling girl? How is work?'

I fill her in on my time on the racing scene while we sit at the table and drink cups of coffee. It's cool inside these thick stone walls, but the weather outside is mild, even in the mountains.

Nonna lives in an old stone cottage nestled under the rocks, just off the main road. She has a vegetable patch in the garden, and keeps goats and chickens in a small adjoining paddock, but by far the best thing about her place is the view: on a clear day you can see for miles. My favourite thing to do here is sit on the terrace on Nonna's stone bench and look out at the tree-covered mountains while sipping a glass of *acqua alla menta* – mint water.

But it's been a long day, and tomorrow will feel even longer, so after we've eaten, Nonna sees me to my room, a tiny box with a single bed under the window and a small wooden cupboard on the opposite wall. I get ready for bed quickly because the cold has set in, and nestle under the sheets, blankets and Nonna's colourful hand-stitched quilt that I remember from my first ever trip here. I feel more at home in Nonna's place than anywhere else in the world, and while that thought makes me feel momentarily sad, I fall to sleep feeling at peace with the world and everyone in it.

The next day I'm inside the marquee laying out morning tea for the film crew when I feel a gentle nudge on my back. I swivel around to see Will standing there.

'Hi! How are you?' I say. He looks unfamiliar again. Not better, not worse, just unfamiliar.

'Good.' He smiles. He's wearing dark denim jeans and a yellow T-shirt with surfer-style graphics on the front.

'Have you filmed anything, yet?' I ask.

The advert he and Luis are filming today is for a petrol company. They have to pretend-race each other around the bendy mountain roads in fast sports cars.

'Not yet,' he replies. 'We've just been getting our hair and make-up done.' He casts his eyes to the heavens. I peer more closely at him.

'What?' he asks.

'Did they put foundation on you?'

'Yes, unfortunately. Why?'

'I can just see a little spot of it, right there by your eye.' I lean in and smooth it away.

'Thanks.' He awkwardly rubs his finger at the place where mine just was. I glance to my left to see Luis raising his eyebrows at me as he walks in the direction of one of the trailers. I look back at Will to find him staring darkly after Luis.

'Are you okay?' I ask Will, cautiously.

'Yeah, fine,' he assures me.

'Is everything okay with you and Luis?'

'He's being a bit of a dick at the moment.'

'Nothing new there, then.'

He smirks and shakes his head. 'No.'

'Is he still pissed off you won the last race?' I ask. 'I thought you guys got over things like that?'

He shrugs and brushes some fluff off his bare arm and then looks up at me and grins. 'Have you forgiven me for all my prying the other night?'

I smile. 'Yeah. But you know I'm going to have to get you back, right?'

'I look forward to it.' His blue eyes meet my green ones and my heart starts to beat faster in my chest.

'Will, we're ready for you!' A man I don't recognise calls to Will. He's wearing headphones and is carrying a clipboard.

'See ya later . . .'

'For sure.' I hold up my hand in a half wave, but it's ten minutes before my pulse returns to normal.

I barely see Will for the rest of the day – only at lunchtime when Holly and I are busy serving the crew.

'I didn't realise how much work this would be,' Holly says at one point.

'Me neither,' I agree. 'So what are you up to tonight?'

'I don't know. Guess we'll have a few drinks back at the hotel with everyone. What about you? Are you coming along?'

'No, I'd better get back to Nonna. I don't see enough of her as it is.'

We hear an almighty roar and look outside the marquee to see two sports cars – a pale blue one and a lime-green one – zoom past.

'The boys are back,' Holly comments.

'Do you think they'll be finished filming by tomorrow?' I ask. This job was only supposed to take two days.

'I should think so, yes,' Holly says.

'Well, I guess we'd better get this mess tidied up.'

We've been serving snacks throughout the day. Filming is supposed to wrap by six o'clock. It's five forty-five now, but my car isn't coming to collect me to take me back to Nonna's until seven, so we still have over an hour's work to do. By six thirty though, it's all done.

Holly disappeared a few minutes ago and when I come out of the kitchen, she's standing outside talking to Simon.

'All set?' he asks me.

'My car's coming to collect me in half an hour. I'm staying with my grandmother not far from here,' I remind him.

He nods. Behind him, a couple of other crew members approach. The people carriers to take them back to the hotel have been parked up for the past fifteen minutes. Simon hates to be kept waiting so he'd rather pay for someone else to do it.

Holly breaks away from the gathering and comes over to me. 'Will you be okay here on your own?' She looks anxious.

'Yeah, yeah, I'll be fine,' I insist. 'My car will be here shortly.'

I notice Will and Luis come out of one of the trailers. The make-up girl emerges and locks the door behind her.

'Okay, well, I'll see you in the morning,' Holly says, wandering back over to the waiting cars. Luis stops to chat to Simon, but Will continues on towards me.

'What are you up to tonight?' he asks.

'Just going back to see my grandmother,' I say.

'Where does she live?'

'About fifteen minutes' drive away.'

'Want me to give you a ride?'

'No, no,' I brush him off.

'I don't mind. I'm driving the Aston Martin back to the hotel anyway.' That's the blue car he's been racing around the mountains in today.

I hesitate. I would *love* him to drive me! 'I have a taxi coming in half an hour,' I tell him regretfully.

'From Lucca?'

'I presume so.'

'Cancel it,' he suggests.

I guess I could . . .

'Go on,' he urges. 'Here, use my phone.' He hands me a slick iPhone, but I pull out my crappy mobile instead.

'It's okay, I have mine here. Are you sure?'

'Absolutely.'

I dial the number, nervous excitement making me feel a little shaky. I worry Will can hear it in my voice.

'All done?' Will checks when I hang up.

'Yes. Are you sure?' I ask again. 'Will the Aston Martin people mind you going on a detour with their car?'

'Nah. I was thinking about getting one of these babies anyway so they can consider it an extended test drive.'

'Will, are you following us?' Simon calls. Everyone else is piling into the waiting cars, but Holly is still standing outside pulling a sad face, presumably because we're going our separate ways.

'I'm going to drop Daisy back.' Will nods towards me.

Holly purses her lips, mischievously. We hear the sound of a sports car roar into life and, seconds later, Luis pulls around the corner in a lime-green Lamborghini. The window slides down and Simon goes over to talk to him.

'Come on,' Will urges. I follow him over to the pale blue Aston Martin where he unlocks the car and opens the passenger door for me. Just as he closes the door behind me, I notice Luis staring our way with a perplexed expression on his face. He says something to Simon, who glances towards our car before answering Luis. Will climbs into the driver's seat and slams the door, just as Luis screeches out onto the mountain road in front of us, sending a cloud of dust in our direction.

'That was thoughtful of him,' Will comments sarcastically as the dust envelopes the car. 'Someone's going to have to polish that off in the morning.'

He pulls out onto the road slowly, beeping his horn at the others as we go. Holly laughingly shakes her head at this turn of events and I'm relieved when Will doesn't seem to notice. After a minute he kicks up the speed and I have to hold onto the armrest as he manoeuvres the Aston Martin down the windy roads.

'Am I going too fast?' he asks after I do a sharp intake of breath at one particular turn.

'No,' I lie through clenched teeth.

After a while I get used to the speed and start to relax.

'Is it a nice car to drive?' I ask.

'Very,' he replies, glancing across at me with amusement.

'Eyes on the road!' I bark.

He chuckles. 'What car do you drive back in the States?'

'I don't, really,' I admit.

'I thought everyone drove cars in America.'

'I'd drive one of these if I could.' I reach forward and run my fingers across the dashboard.

'You like it?'

'I like the colour.'

'That's such a girl thing to say.'

'No, I like the way it looks, too,' I add quickly. 'And the engine sounds awesome.'

He laughs and looks across at me.

'Road!' I frantically point ahead of us and he returns his attention to his driving.

'I'd let you have a go if I didn't think you might crash it.'

'Oh, thanks very much,' I say sarcastically. 'Take a right, here.'

Eventually we pull into the lane directly outside Nonna's house. Will peers out the windscreen.

'Pretty,' he comments, looking over at the house.

'The view is amazing,' I tell him.

The front door opens and Nonna comes out.

'Do you want to come in for a drink?' I offer.

He unclicks his seatbelt. 'Sure.'

We climb out of the car and I usher Will towards Nonna, who's beaming widely.

'Nonna, this is Will,' I say in English.

I told her about Will yesterday evening, but omitted my feelings for him. Now, she welcomes him like an old friend and leads us into the kitchen. My grandparents lived in this house for decades before Nonno, my grandfather, died of a heart attack five years ago at the age of eighty-seven. It was big enough for the two of them, but right now, with three of us in the kitchen, I feel claustrophobic.

'What would you like to drink?' Nonna asks in Italian.

'Perhaps we could take a glass of mint water out to the terrace?' I suggest. I translate for Will. 'Is that okay?' I ask him. 'You won't be too cold?'

'No, but won't you be?' He casually rubs my arm.

'Maybe,' I tell him, although my sudden goosebumps have nothing to do with the climate. 'I might go and change.'

'Sure.'

I leave him with Nonna, hoping she won't struggle too much with her English, while I head off to my small box room. I pull a dark-green jumper out of the travel bag still squashed into the bottom of my wardrobe – I haven't had the time or inclination to unpack – and swap my black team trousers for jeans. My hair has been tied up into a high bun all day and my scalp is starting to ache, so I unpin it now and it falls down my back in wavy curls.

Back in America I used to straighten it to within an inch of its life, but I rarely bother anymore.

I re-enter the kitchen to find it empty. Nonna and Will have already gone outside.

I find them out in the vegetable garden where Nonna is pointing out her goats in the small paddock.

'She'll have you milking them next.'

Will starts at the sound of my voice.

'I'll just go and get the drinks,' Nonna says in Italian, and bustles away.

'Do you need any help?' I call after her.

'No, no, no!' she assures me.

I turn back to find Will looking at me. He quickly averts his gaze, folding his arms in front of his body.

'Shall we go to the terrace?' I ask.

'Sure.' He motions for me to lead the way, and I do so, intensely aware of him walking behind me. We reach the terrace and I stop, taking a deep breath of crystal-clear air.

'Isn't it beautiful?' I say, staring out at the mountains.

'Mmm,' he says quietly.

'Here you go, children.' I spin around to see Nonna walking towards the terrace. She places a small tray down on the thick stone wall and hands out the glasses of mint water. We sit in a row on the stone bench with me in the middle.

'Have you lived here long?' Will leans forwards to speak to Nonna.

I translate automatically, but she interrupts. 'I understand,' she says slowly in English. 'Fifty-two years.'

'Fifty-two years!' Will exclaims. 'That's exactly twice my age.'

'Mine, too,' I tell him.

'Are you twenty-six?' he asks, interested.

'Yeah.'

'Huh.'

'Did you think I was older?'

'No, I'm just surprised we're the same age,' he says.

'Mmm, I thought it was a coincidence, too, when I found out.'

'That's even more we have in common, then.'

'It is.' We smile at each other. 'Sorry, Nonna.' I lean back on the bench so I'm no longer blocking her view, but she jumps to her feet.

'The lamb!' she exclaims in Italian. 'Will he stay for dinner?' she asks me.

I glance at Will hesitantly. 'I think he'll have to get back.'

'Ask him,' Nonna urges.

'What?' Will interrupts.

'She wants to know if you'll stay for dinner. I said you probably have to get back . . .'

'I don't have to get back.'

'You don't have to get back?'

'No.'

I turn to Nonna. 'He'll stay.' She beams and hurries away to the kitchen.

Will looks at me. 'If you don't mind, that is.'

'Of course I don't mind.'

I stare off into the distance. Dark clouds have begun to invade the mountains.

'That looks ominous,' I comment.

Will nods and we fall silent. A short while later, Nonna calls us to the table.

'This was amazing,' Will says after dinner, indicating his clean plate. 'You're a fantastic cook.'

'Oh, this was nothing,' Nonna replies modestly, but I know she prides herself on her cuisine. She stands up and I quickly join her, helping to clear the table.

'You young things go through to the sitting room. I'll bring coffee through in a minute. Go!' she insists when I hesitate.

Nonna only has two chairs in her small sitting room. One is a sofa and the other is her armchair, so I join Will on the former to leave the latter free for our host.

After a moment he sighs.

'What's wrong?' I ask.

'I wish I could just chill here for a few days.'

'Really?' I look at him in delight.

'Yeah. I'm so sick of staying in hotels. And this is so . . . *homely*.'

'It is homely, isn't it?'

'Very.'

'I know it's small, but it feels—'

'Right,' he finishes my sentence.

'Yes. Exactly.'

'Do you reckon we could persuade your grandma to go and live in my Chelsea pad and we'll camp up here?'

I laugh. 'That'd be nice. But you'd never get her to leave the mountains.'

And I don't suppose your girlfriend would approve, either, I think to myself. But let's not mention her.

'Here we go!' Nonna enters the room with a small tray.

Suddenly a loud crashing sound reverberates through the stone walls.

'Is that thunder?' Will asks, taken aback.

'Yes,' Nonna replies, listening as the heavens open. 'Big storm. Is treacherous, these mountains,' she continues in stilted English as she places the tray on a small side-table and hands us tiny, white espresso cups before sitting down.

'I hope it passes by tomorrow,' Will says.

'*Cazzo*, yes! Sorry Nonna,' I apologise for my language when she looks at me sharply. 'Will was just saying he hopes the storm will have passed by tomorrow otherwise they won't be able to finish filming,' I tell her in Italian.

'Oh, no, no, no!' Nonna cries in dismay, clambering up from her armchair. She rushes away and comes back with a couple of saucepans while we look on, concerned.

'These walls!' she despairs.

Water is leaking through a crack in the far wall.

'Does this happen often?' Will asks, as we both come quickly to Nonna's aid and help patch up the naked stone with old rags.

Nonna replies in Italian so I translate. 'Every time she gets it fixed, the water finds a way back in through somewhere else. She needs to renovate the entire house.'

'Will it cost much?' I ask Nonna.

'Too much,' she replies. 'It's not worth it at my age.'

'Nonna!' I cry. 'Of course it's worth it. You can't live like this.'

'It's fine,' she insists. 'It's not a problem.'

'But it *is* a problem. We can see that ourselves. I could help. I've saved a little money.'

'No, you will not!' she snaps, glaring at me. For an 82-year-old, she's a feisty old bat.

'What are you saying?' Will asks.

'Nothing,' I tell him, when I see my grandmother's face. She wouldn't want Will to feel pity for her.

We mop up the rest of the water and strategically place pots and pans on the floor to catch any drips.

Finally Nonna turns to Will. 'You can't be driving.'

'I'll be okay,' Will says.

'You stay here on sofa.'

'No, no, I'll be fine.' Will laughs.

'Is no laughing matter!' Nonna snaps, wiping the smile off Will's face. 'Carlo, my husband, he died on these roads.'

Hang on, I thought Nonno died of a heart attack?

'Oh, I'm so very sorry.' Will looks mortified.

'So you stay here. Drive in morning when storm gone.'

The sound of thunder comes crashing through the walls again.

'You tell him,' she says to me firmly. 'He not drive in this.'

'You did say you could stay here for a few days . . .' I look at him pleadingly.

'True. I guess it would be okay . . . Are you sure it's alright?' he asks Nonna.

'Of course!'

'I should call Simon and tell him what I'm up to.' He pulls out his mobile.

'There's no reception up here, I'm afraid. Do you want to use the phone? Can Will use the phone, Nonna?'

'Certainly,' she replies.

'Cool. I don't want him to worry.'

I direct him to the phone in the kitchen and return to the sitting room, where Nonna is already making up the sofa with sheets and blankets. Moments later, he joins us.

'All done?' I ask.

'Simon didn't answer so I left a message at reception.'

'It's my bedtime,' Nonna interrupts, collecting our espresso cups. 'I'm going to listen to my radio show. Good night!' she says to Will.

'Good night! Thanks again.'

'You're welcome.' We watch her amble out of the room.

I turn back to Will. 'I could call Holly if you like? Just in case Simon doesn't get your message?'

'I'm sure it will be fine.'

'I don't mind.'

'Okay, then. Just to be on the safe side.'

But there's no answer from Holly's room, either.

'Probably all out on the piss,' Will says.

I take a seat on Nonna's recently vacated armchair because I don't feel right about cosying up next to Will on his makeshift bed, and we fall silent, listening to the rain beating against the windows. Darkness has enveloped the mountains and it's chilly in here. I shiver.

'Are you cold?' Will asks.

'A little.'

'Want one of my blankets?'

'No, it's okay,' I say quickly. 'Actually, I'll go and grab one of my own.' I head to my room to fetch Nonna's hand-stitched quilt and remember the bottle of duty free red wine that I bought at the airport on the way over here. On a whim I get it out of my wardrobe and poke my head around the sitting-room door.

'Do you fancy a drink?' I ask Will, holding out the bottle.

He sits up in his seat. 'Er, sure.'

I put the bottle on the table and my quilt on the chair. 'I'll just go and get some glasses,' I tell him, returning a minute later. Will has already found a bottle opener on top of Nonna's small liquor cabinet, there from the days she used to share an aperitif with Nonno.

I snuggle up on the armchair and tuck my legs underneath myself while Will pours the wine and leans across to hand me a glass.

'Thanks.'

'This is cosy,' he says, climbing under his blankets.

'Isn't it?' I take a sip of my wine and watch him over the rim of my glass as he gets comfortable. 'Did you enjoy driving around the mountains today?' I ask.

He visibly perks up. 'Loved it. At times like this I wish I didn't live in London.'

'You could buy yourself a pad up here.'

He looks thoughtful.

'Have you got a second home?'

'Funny you should ask that,' he says. 'I'm thinking about getting one in Monaco. I know it's a racing driver cliché,' he adds, grinning, 'but it's so bloody beautiful there. Have you ever been?'

'No. I can't wait for that race, actually. Holly's always going on about it.'

'Oh, yeah.' He nods. 'The lads are the same. Non-stop parties, that weekend. You'll have to see if you can go on a yacht.'

'I don't know how I'll manage that unless I'm catering on one.'

'I might be able to get you an invite to something.'

'Really?' My eyes widen in delight. 'That would be amazing!'

He smiles at my excitement.

'Have you ever won at Monaco?'

'No.' He shakes his head. 'Came close a couple of years ago, but some pillock took me out.'

'You crashed?'

'Yep. It wasn't too bad,' he says when he sees my face.

'Have you ever had a bad one?' I ask worriedly.

'Mmm. A few years ago I had a really big accident.'

'What happened?'

He leans back in his seat and pushes his hair off his face. 'I was driving towards a concrete barrier at 190 mph when the steering locked and I hurled straight into it.'

I gasp. 'What did you do?'

'Nothing. There was nothing I could do.'

'What went through your mind?'

'My life didn't flash before my eyes, if that's what you're asking. But I did know, with absolute certainty, that I was going to die.'

I stare at him, troubled.

He continues, 'I landed upside down with zero chance of getting out of the car and then the damn thing caught fire. All I could hear were the track marshals yelling to people to stand back because the car could explode at any second.'

'Jesus . . .'

'I'd only just refuelled so I knew that was a distinct possibility, but luckily the fire truck arrived in time and they managed to get me out of there.'

I shake my head in confusion. 'I don't know how you do it.'

'What? Race?'

'Yes. How did you get behind the wheel again after that?'

'I didn't for a while. Only because I broke my leg,' he explains, grinning.

'How can you smile about it?' Nausea has crept up into my throat. 'Aren't you worried it might happen again?'

'You can't think about that, otherwise it will affect your

driving. But I tell you what, if I ever end up paralysed after a crash, somebody had better shoot me, because I don't want to do anything else. My girlfriend is under strict instructions.'

'To do what?' I don't even baulk at the mention of Laura because I'm too distracted by our morbid discussion. 'Shoot you?'

'Well . . . A lethal injection would be neater.'

'I hope she told you to go fuck yourself,' I say crossly.

He laughs. 'Yeah, she did, actually.'

I take a deep breath. 'I think we'd better talk about something else.'

'Aw, sorry.' He straightens his leg out and kicks my foot. 'I didn't think that sort of thing would bother you.'

'What, the thought of you *dying*?' I ask, outraged.

He laughs, unfazed by my reaction. 'You're just like my girlfriend.'

I'm in two minds about whether or not that's a good thing. I give him a wry look and ask something I've been wondering for some time. 'Do you two live together?'

'No. Well, half and half. She has her own apartment in town.'

'How long have you been a couple?'

'I've known her most of my life, but we got together when we were about fifteen.'

My stomach churns as reality sinks in. I've been living in a fantasy crush world, but he's in love with Laura. He's not going to leave her. He'll never be in love with me. I have to get over him.

'Do you think you'll get married?' I don't want to ask these questions, but I can't stop myself. I hold my breath as he shrugs, oblivious to my pain.

'I don't know. Maybe.'

Only maybe? Is there still some hope? No, no, no!

'Are you getting me back for all my prying in Barcelona?' He raises one eyebrow.

'I told you I would.'

His smile turns into a very loud yawn.

'Tired, are you?' I ask with amusement.

'Shattered.'

'I guess I'd better let you get some sleep, then.' I start to get up. He doesn't try to stop me, sadly.

'Hey, you'd better cancel your taxi for the morning,' he says.

'That's a good point. I'll call them now. Thanks.'

'Night.'

'Sleep well.'

I throw my quilt over my shoulder and head out the door, looking back to see him snuggle down under the covers and lay his head on the armrest. How on earth I'm going to get any sleep knowing he's in the next room, is beyond me.

Chapter 12

Another day, another plane to catch. This time I'm off to Istanbul for the Turkish Grand Prix and I'm flying straight there from Italy. I stayed on for a couple of days to spend some time with Nonna and it was beautifully relaxing, even if I did have a lot on my mind.

Will and I needn't have worried about the weather, because when we woke up, the skies were blue as far as the eye could see and the only reminder of the storm were the puddles on the road.

The last day of filming passed by in such a blur that I barely even spoke to Holly, let alone Will. Holly seemed distracted and not that interested in my evening the night before. I guess it's because she disapproves, and I was reluctant to talk about him for fear of her tainting my memories. Even now we're in Istanbul, she's not saying much.

On the Friday morning before the race, Will comes into the hospitality area where I'm sitting at one of the tables, tidying up the flower arrangement. I start when I see him, because I'd got it into my head that he looked like Leonardo DiCaprio and now I realise that their resemblance is slim.

'Hey,' he says, coming over. 'How was your break?'

'Lovely.' I beam. 'Nonna said to wish you luck, by the way.'

At that moment, Luis walks past. 'No girlfriend this weekend?' he asks Will, slyly.

Will stares at him. 'No. Why?'

'Just wondering.' Luis gives me a look and keeps on going. I feel my face heat up so I quickly go back to my flower arranging.

Will looks after him and frowns. 'Weirdo.'

I giggle and stand up. 'Do you want me to get you some breakfast?'

'No, you carry on. Gertrude can do it.'

I look over to see Gertrude behind the serving table. Will heads off before I have a chance to say anything else.

That evening, he appears in the hotel lobby just as I'm waiting for the lads to come down. We're staying in the old part of town on the Bosphorus Strait – the channel of water that separates the European part of Turkey from the Asian part. The mechanics want to check out some belly dancing in the Beyoğlu district and Holly and I figure it would be a laugh to tag along.

'Coming out for a drink?' I ask Will, hopefully.

'No. I'm going for dinner on the river. Simon and a few of the sponsors are dragging Luis and me to some posh restaurant.'

'Oh, okay.'

'Hey, is your dad's name Stellan?' he asks curiously.

I look at him with shock. 'Yes, why?'

He shrugs as the lads pile out of the lift. 'The car's outside!' Holly calls from the revolving doors. She goes straight back around in a circle again. 'Come on!' she shouts as she goes past. I would laugh, but I'm distracted by Will's question.

'See you later,' he says.

Before I can open my mouth to shout, 'Wait!', Pete and Dan have swamped me.

I can't relax that night. The bar we've ended up in is buzzing and vibrant, but all I want is to talk to Will. Eventually I can stand it no longer.

'I think I'm going to head off,' I tell Holly, who's busy studying her mobile phone.

'Are you?' she asks, distracted. She snaps her phone shut. 'My mum,' she explains. 'Wants to know when I'm going back up to Aberdeen to see her.'

'Oh, right.'

'You off, then?' she asks again.

'If you don't mind.' In fact, I'm astounded she's not giving me any stick.

'Sure, that's fine,' she says. 'I might go and chat to Pete.'

'Good luck getting his attention.' I nod in the direction of Pete and a few of the lads who are ogling a belly dancer undulating across the stage.

Holly just laughs. 'See you later,' she calls, heading in their direction.

I go outside and climb into one of the people carriers waiting for us. It's not recommended for Western girls to venture out alone here, so Simon ensures we always have readily available transport.

I sit and stare out of the car window at the dome-studded skyline as the sun sets luminescent orange over Istanbul's mosques. I'm fully aware that what I'm seeing is beautiful, but I'm too preoccupied to properly appreciate it.

Back at the hotel, I don't know what to do with myself. I wander to the bar, on the off chance Will is there, but he's not.

Frederick is having a quiet drink with Klaus, so I nip back out quickly before they spot me and engage me in a conversation. I call the lift and, once inside, press the button to take me to my floor. Then I stare at the number for Will's floor. On a whim, I press that, too. When we get to my floor, I shift from foot to foot and wait as the doors whoosh closed again and the lift continues to climb. We reach Will's landing and I waver a moment. As the doors start to close, I leap out. Before I can stop myself, I'm walking towards his suite. I stand outside, listening for any sound. Is that the TV? No, it's the room next door. Shall I knock? If he's not there, it won't matter.

Knock, knock, knock.

I wait. And wait. Then knock again.

What the hell am I doing? I'm about to turn and run when the door opens. Will is standing there in a T-shirt and boxer shorts. His hair is all dishevelled and it's obvious I've just woken him up. *Cazzo*, I am so embarrassed.

'Daisy?' he says sleepily.

'Er, hi. Sorry, I don't know what I'm doing. I was just out with Holly and—'

'Come in,' he interrupts.

'I'm sorry, I didn't know you were asleep. What time is it?'

'I have no idea.'

'Sorry,' I say again.

'It's okay,' he replies.

'God, sorry, you've got qualifying tomorrow.'

'Stop apologising!' He laughs. 'Take a seat.' He directs me to one of two opulent-looking sofas in his suite. I perch on it uncomfortably, fully regretting making such a tit out of myself by coming here. I spot the time on the DVD player.

'Oh my God, it's almost midnight. Oh shit, Will, I'm sorry. I'll go.'

'Daisy! Would you shut up? I'll just go and put some jeans on.'

'That's a good idea.' I involuntarily glance at his white Calvin Kleins and quickly look away again.

He wanders off to his bedroom and returns a short while later.

'Do you want a drink?'

'Um, no, it's okay.'

He goes to the minibar and pulls out a Coke, then comes over and collapses on the other sofa. He cracks open the can and takes a swig.

'Are you sure you don't want a drink?' He offers it to me.

'No thanks.'

Silence.

'What are you doing here?' It's he who speaks first.

'What you said . . . About my father . . . Why did you ask that?'

'Oh . . .' Understanding registers.

'How did you find out?'

He takes another swig from his can, then slumps further down into the sofa and eyes me curiously across the coffee table. 'I Googled you,' he says simply.

'Googled me?' I stare at him, confused. 'Why?'

'To try to find out which famous person you worked for.'

'But you didn't find that out?'

He looks perplexed. 'No, I didn't actually. What's with that?'

'Will, I thought you weren't going to pry?'

He shakes his head and leans forward, putting the can back on the coffee table. He doesn't look at me when he answers. 'Curiosity got the better of me.'

So he was thinking about me . . .

'I don't get it,' he says. 'If your dad is Stellan Rogers, what are you doing working here?'

'I *like* working here,' I say firmly. 'And I *don't* like my father.'

He steadily meets my eyes, but this time it's he who looks away first. He rubs his jaw and sighs.

'Sorry, I guess I shouldn't have done that.'

'Don't worry about it. But can you please keep it to yourself?'

'Are you telling me Holly doesn't even know about that one?' He gives me a sardonic look.

'No, she doesn't, actually.'

'Are you serious?' He's incredulous. 'Daisy, what is it with you? Why are you so . . . mysterious?'

I try to keep a straight face at that description, but I can't. After a moment, his face breaks into a grin, too.

I stand up. 'I'm going to bed.'

He sighs and rests his head on the back of the sofa, looking up at me. 'Do you have to wear your hair up for work?'

I'm wearing it down at the moment. 'Yes,' I reply, surprised.

He continues to stare at me.

'Why?' I ask, my stomach fluttering.

'No reason.'

'Why?' I ask again. 'Do you prefer it up?'

He leans forward and grabs his can from the coffee table. 'No.' He slumps back on the sofa. 'I like it better down.'

'Do you?' I'm confused. I wouldn't expect him to have an opinion about my hairdo, but I'm pleased that he does.

'Mmm.'

'Oh, right. Well, I'll be off then.' I make to leave.

'I don't know how I'm going to get back to sleep now,' he says dolefully.

'Serves you right for being such a nosey parker. Goodnight, Will.'

'Goodnight, Daisy Rogers . . .'

I return to my room, my head spinning. I half expected Holly to have arrived back by now, but her bed is empty. I doze in and out of sleep for over three hours before she finally emerges at four o'clock in the morning.

'What time do you call this?' I ask groggily.

'Jesus!' she exclaims. 'You scared the life out of me!'

'I was worried about you.'

'Why? No need for that. Anyway, I thought you'd be asleep.' She looks shifty.

'Nope.'

'Well, I'm really tired.' She changes into her nightclothes quickly, then climbs into bed, not bothering to go into the bathroom to remove her make-up or brush her teeth.

'What did you get up to tonight?' I ask, then snap, 'Holly!' when she doesn't answer.

'Hmm? Tired,' she says sleepily. 'Speak in morning.'

But talking happens to be the last thing on our minds the following day, because after pressing the snooze button on our alarm clock three times in a row, our main priority is just getting to work on time.

Now it's ten o'clock: time to set up morning tea. I'm dozily arranging biscuits on a platter when Frederick speaks up.

'Can you take that lot to the pits?'

'Yes, Chef,' I answer absent-mindedly.

'Come on, chop, chop!' He claps his hands, making me jump out of my skin. 'What is it, Daisy? Another hangover?'

'Hey? Oh, yeah,' I fib.

'You should stop going out with that one.' He indicates Holly.

'Me?' Holly replies, huffily. 'I barely had anything to drink last night!'

'Didn't you?' I ask, surprised. But she stayed out with the lads for hours!

'No.' She looks away.

'Get a bloody move on, would you?' Frederick snaps again.

'I'm on it, Chef.' I quickly place the last few biscuits on the platter and hurry out of the paddock in the direction of the team garages.

I wonder where Will is? He hasn't been into the hospitality area this morning. I'm so on edge that I almost drop the platter when I spot him, dressed in his overalls already, standing by his car in a discussion with one of the team's engineers. He glances my way, but returns his attention to his conversation, not faltering, not acknowledging me. I place the platter on one of the catering tables.

'Got any custard creams?' I turn to see Luis standing there.

'Custard creams? They're not classy enough for this operation, Luis, you should know that. Have a nice piece of shortbread instead.' I offer him some.

'Pah to your shortbread. Get me some goddamn custard creams.'

'*Va se lixar*!'

'Shh!' he urges, looking around in horror. 'My mother's just over there!' He aims his thumb over his shoulder.

'Your mother?' I look past him to see a short, pleasantly plump Brazilian woman standing next to a short, pleasantly plump Brazilian man. There's also a petite brunette who looks to be in her late teens.

'My dad and little sister,' Luis explains before I can ask.

'Aw!' I smile at him in delight. 'Are any of your other brothers and sisters here?' I remember him telling me he has about seven.

'No, just Clara. The others are all either afraid of flying, too busy at work, or have just given birth.'

'Just given birth?'

'Yeah, one of my older sisters had a baby girl last weekend.'

'That's awesome! Have you seen her yet?'

He shakes his head, regretfully. 'I won't get a chance to fly home for a while.'

His mother looks over. 'Mãe, come here,' he calls. All three of them walk towards us. Luis quickly turns to me and says, 'My mum really likes custard creams, too, so you might want to sort that out.' He gives me a mischievous look, but I restrain myself from telling him to piss off in Portuguese again. 'This is Daisy,' Luis says as they arrive. 'My favourite little bun tart,' he adds, wrapping his arm around my neck and giving me a squeeze. I shrug him off and am about to smack him on the arm for calling me a bun tart when his mother speaks.

'Ah, *this* is Daisy.' She beams at me warmly and I look at Luis in confusion. His mother knows who I am?

'I told her you were a troublemaker,' he says as an aside to me. He has a twinkle in his eye. I look back at his mother to see she has the same look in hers.

'Hello, how are you?' I gather myself together and shake hands with all three of them. Clara regards me, shyly. 'Are you enjoying your trip?' I ask.

'Oh, yes, wonderful,' Mrs Castro replies. 'We've been doing all sorts of sightseeing.'

'Have you? Where have you been?' I direct this question at Clara, hoping she'll open up to me.

'Luis!' one of the mechanics calls.

'Gotta go.' He gives his mum a quick peck on the cheek and walks off in the direction of his car. I turn back to Clara.

'We went to the Grand Bazaar yesterday,' she tells me.

'Shopping!' his mother interjects. 'The place to go since the fifteenth century, apparently!'

'And on Monday we're going to the Süleymaniye Mosque, aren't we?' his father butts in. They all speak fluent English.

'Are you staying on in Istanbul for a holiday, then?' I ask them.

'Yes, for another week with Luis,' Mr Castro replies. 'It's our first time in Turkey and we don't see enough of him as it is.'

'Well, I hope you have a lovely time.'

Holly comes into the pits carrying a pot of tea.

'Oh, you've got the tea already. Cool. Thought I was going to have to go back for it,' I say to her.

'No need,' she replies breezily.

'We should let you get on,' Mrs Castro interrupts.

'Okay. Enjoy the qualifying. And help yourself to tea and biscuits!'

As I turn to walk out, I glance back to see Will on the other side of the garage, quietly watching this exchange. We make eye contact for a split-second before he averts his gaze.

Later, I'm in the kitchen washing dishes when Holly appears.

'How's it going?' I ask. She's been working out front of house and watching the qualifying on the big screen.

'Okay. Luis was quickest in Q2.' That's the second qualifying session – there are three in total before the grid positions are determined.

'That's brilliant!' I interrupt.

'But Will was way down in ninth.'

'Oh,' I reply, disappointed.

'Yeah, Simon's not very happy about it.'

'Really?' My stomach tightens.

'Apparently Will didn't sleep well last night.'

'Oh.' I feel quite sick. I'd probably lose my job if Simon knew I'd kept him up.

I leave the kitchen to watch Q3 on the big screen and, even though it's still not great, I'm relieved when Will manages to climb his way up to fifth. Luis will start second tomorrow.

The drivers arrive back soon afterwards, but while Luis sits down at a table with his family, Will goes straight up to his room. I stare after him for a moment, before remembering his spare pair of overalls still needs to have two new sponsorship patches stitched onto them. That's as good an excuse as any . . .

'Come in,' he calls when I knock on the door.

I push it open. 'Hi.'

'Hello.'

'Have you got your overalls handy? The other ones,' I say, when I see him glance down at the pair he's wearing. 'I need to stitch those patches on.'

'Oh, yeah, sure,' he remembers, going to the cupboard and hunting them out. They're still wrapped in dry cleaning plastic from after the last race.

'Are you okay?' I ask tentatively, as I take the package from him.

'Fine,' he brushes me off, indicating a chair. I perch on the edge of it.

'I heard you were tired. I'm sorry.'

He shakes his head dismissively as he pulls off one of his boots. 'That wasn't the problem. There wasn't enough downforce on the car.'

'Oh. Okay. Is there anything I can do?'

'No, no. I'll be down in a minute.' He pulls off the other boot.

'Okay.' I stand up.

The sound of Rihanna's 'Umbrella' starts to pulse out of his mobile phone on the table. Will snatches it up. I've heard his phone ring before, but it just makes a plinkety-plonkety sound, it's not a realtone. And then it dawns on me: this must be the tone he uses for his girlfriend.

'Hey,' he says into the receiver, 'can you hang on a sec?' He covers the mouthpiece as I move to the door and open it. An ache throbs deep inside me. What's that song about? Being there for your beloved, whatever the weather? I haven't got a hope in hell.

'Daisy,' he calls.

I turn back. 'Yes?'

He whispers, 'Better stay away from my room tonight, hey? I could do with a *bit* more sleep if I'm going to beat that dickhead.'

I blush and glance involuntarily at his phone, then force a smile and leave the room, closing the door gently behind me.

I walk back into the kitchen in a daze. I'm so stupid. So very, very stupid. I hate myself. Why can't I stop thinking about him? I have to stop thinking about him. I *have* to!

'What's up with you?' Holly asks, seeing my face.

'Come to the bathroom with me?' I throw a glance at Klaus, Gertrude and the other catering staff working away at nearby counters.

'Oh, God, Holly,' I say as soon as the bathroom door closes

behind her. 'You're going to have to kick me or something. Anything to stop me from falling for him.'

'I take it we're talking about Will?'

I give her a wry look.

'I think you're a bit beyond that, don't you? You've fallen, hook, line and sinker.'

I sigh and lean up against a toilet door. 'Do you know what ringtone he uses for his girlfriend?'

She looks nonplussed.

'"Umbrella", by Rihanna.'

'Oh.' I'm sure she's trying not to smirk.

'It's not funny!'

'Sorry, sorry.' She's contrite.

'Seriously, I've got to stop this. I'm sworn off men for a reason. I don't want any more heartache. And I know you warned me about getting hurt,' I add, when I see the look on her face. 'But what could I do? What *can* I do? I can't stop myself from feeling this way.'

'Why don't you shag Luis instead? That'll take your mind off Will.'

'Holly!' I erupt. 'What sort of a solution is that? No!'

'Why not? I would.'

'Well, why don't you, then?'

She laughs and humorously shakes her head.

'Of all the things to say.' I stare at her in disbelief.

'Don't worry,' she says, patting me on the arm. 'I'm sure things will work out. They always do.'

Great. She's no help at all.

Holly and I are doing the first shift on race day, so when she suggests that we have an early one on Saturday night, I don't disagree. I'm fast asleep when something wakes me up. The door. I look across and see that Holly isn't in her bed. I get up and have a quick check in the bathroom, but she's nowhere to be seen. The glowing red display on the alarm clock tells me it's half twelve. Where the hell has she gone? Is she having it off with Pete? Or maybe she *is* shagging Luis! Something's up, and first thing tomorrow, I'm finding out what.

I wake up the next morning to find her back in bed, sleeping soundly. 'Where did you go last night?' I ask loudly. She moans. 'Holly! Holly!' I reach over and give her body a push.

'What?' she snaps. 'What time is it?'

'Time you told me what's going on.'

'Hey? Daisy, what are you on about?'

'Where did you go last night?'

'Last night?'

'Yes! Holly, for God's sake, just tell me. Are you doing the dirty with Pete?'

'No!' she snaps.

'Luis?'

'*No!*'

'Just tell me!'

'No, Daisy, no! I'm not shagging either of them!'

'Well, where did you go, then?'

'I couldn't sleep, so I went for a wander around the hotel. And then—' She sits up straighter, her eyes lighting up. 'Then I went into the media centre and wrote a few emails. I haven't chatted to any of my pals back home in ages, so I had some catching up to do.'

I can tell she's lying. But I can't accuse her of it, because she's given me a perfectly good explanation. I just know that something's going on, and if she's not going to come clean about it, then maybe I won't be so forthright about my feelings for Will from now on, either.

The sun is shining on the day of the race, but it's chilly when we arrive at the track, ready to set up breakfast at five a.m. I don't say much to Holly in the car on the way over there. I'm still disappointed she's not opening up to me. I don't know if she can sense my mood, but she doesn't say much to me, either.

It's eight o'clock when Luis and his family bustle in.

'Would you like some breakfast?' I ask them.

'Yes, please,' Mrs Castro replies keenly.

'Don't have the muesli,' Luis interjects. 'It's awful. Daisy does the best bacon and eggs.'

'Is that your excuse?' I ask wryly, looking past him to see Will appear. My heart does its usual somersault. I try to focus on serving Luis's family as I see Will stop to talk to Simon at a nearby table. Simon gets up and Will follows him up the stairs. He nods at me as he passes. 'Morning.'

'Hi.' I smile after him and glance back to find Luis giving me a disapproving look. I avert my gaze before he can catch me blushing again.

'Mãe, grab that table, there. I'll be over in a moment,' Luis says. He looks back at me when they've gone.

'Still hanging out for him?'

'No,' I say hotly, plonking a piece of bacon on the plate he's holding out for me. 'Want another?'

'Of course. He's never going to leave her, you know.'

'Shut up, Luis.' I roll my eyes in a huff.

'I saw them together at team HQ the other week. Did I tell you?'

'No?' I look up at him, a familiar sick feeling swirling around inside me.

'She came in for lunch with Will and Simon.'

'What was she like?' I hate myself for being interested, especially in front of Luis.

He shrugs. 'She was alright, actually. Seemed like a nice girl.'

'Have you got enough, there?' I bluntly nod at his plate.

'Yeah, that'll do.'

'Good.' I wipe my hands and stalk off in the direction of the kitchen, leaving him standing alone at the serving table.

Holly and I go to the pits to watch the start of the race, but I'm distracted. I'm standing in Will's garage, but Mrs Castro beckons me into Luis's. Not wanting to seem impolite, I tug on Holly's arm and we go to join the Castros. The cars are already on the grid and we watch as they set off on their warm-up lap. As they pull around the last corner and take their starting positions, my throat starts to feel constricted and my whole body tenses up. The red lights go out to denote the start and, even though Will gets away without any trouble, I can practically hear my heart thumping in my chest.

'Are you okay?' Holly asks me after a few laps. 'You're as white as a sheet.'

I can't look at her. My eyes are glued to the television screen at the front of the garage.

'Daisy?'

I shake my head. I can't speak. Will attempts an overtaking manoeuvre and suddenly I get palpitations and clutch my hands to my chest.

'Bloody hell, Daisy, what's going on?' Holly grabs my arm. Pete sees us and comes over.

'Is she alright?' he asks Holly. Luis's family look on with concern.

'Daisy!' Holly demands.

I feel dizzy. I feel like I'm going to faint. But I can't look away. Will has just taken third place. Suddenly everything goes red in front of my eyes and then black.

When I come to, I'm on the other side of the garage and Holly is fanning my face. The Castros are looking on, worriedly.

I try to sit up.

'Just take it easy,' Mr Castro insists.

'What's happened? Is Will okay?' Panic threatens to engulf me once more.

Holly glances at Luis's family, guardedly.

'*Both* Luis and Will are fine. Will's in third place, Luis is still running second. Come on,' she says, helping me up, 'I think we should go back to the hospitality suite.'

'What's going on?' Frederick demands to know when Holly has sat me down with a glass of cold water.

'She fainted,' Holly explains.

'Hmm. Must be the heat,' he says, even though it's not that hot today. 'Sit there for a while.'

'Are you going to be alright?' Holly asks.

'Yes, I'll be fine,' I reply weakly. 'I'll be back on my feet in a minute.'

'Don't you dare. Just relax. Watch the race.'

But when I look up at the cars on the big screen, the same thing happens. Nausea creeps into my throat. I lean forwards and put my head in my hands.

'Are you okay?' I hear an American man ask.

I look up to see one of the sponsors peering at me.

'Yes, I'm fine,' I quickly tell him, getting to my feet and steadying myself on one of the chairs. 'Thank you.' I hurry back into the kitchen.

'What are you doing?' Holly snaps. 'I thought I told you to chill out.'

'I'd rather keep busy,' I say, steadfastly walking to one of the counters and grabbing a tomato to slice.

She stares at me, hesitantly for a moment, before seeing my determination. After a while, she decides to go back to the pits, but I tell her to take Gertrude. I diligently work away for the next hour, trying not to think about the race. Finally I hear the sound of applause from outside in the hospitality area. I've been using the blender on and off so it's the first commotion I've heard. I hurry out of the kitchen and ask one of the guests what's going on.

'Luis came second!'

Is it over already? 'That's great!' I say. 'What about Will?'

He looks at me like I'm nuts. 'Didn't you see his crash?'

'His crash?' I feel light-headed.

'He's okay,' the man hurriedly assures me. 'It wasn't a bad one.'

'When? What happened?'

'Takahashi span off the track and clipped Will's wing. It happened about half an hour ago,' he explains.

Naoki Takahashi is a Japanese driver for one of the least competitive teams.

'Do you know where Will is now?' I ask, but the man just shrugs. I quickly hurry up the stairs to Will's room. There's no answer when I knock, so I tentatively push the door open. The room is empty. There's no sign of his bags.

I run back down the stairs and crash into Holly. 'Where's Will?'

I demand to know. 'Have you seen him?'

'No.' She gives me a look. 'I thought you were staying away from him from now on?'

I take a deep breath and she obviously feels sorry for me because she says, 'I'll find out, don't worry.'

Ten minutes later she comes to find me. 'He's gone.'

'Gone? Where?'

'Back to the UK. Simon said he could catch an early flight instead of waiting around for the debriefing meeting.'

I'm crushed.

'Don't worry, you'll see him again in a couple of weeks.'

A couple of weeks? I can't bear it! I stare across at my bag, where my mobile phone is buried deep within. I could text him, while I know he's still at the airport or on a plane . . . While I know there's no chance of him being with his girlfriend, yet . . .

I snatch up my bag and hurry to the ladies' room.

'Where are you going? Daisy!' Holly calls after me. I ignore her.

I go inside a cubicle and dig my phone out from inside my bag. What should I say? I think for a moment before typing out:

I HOPE UR OK.

But what if he doesn't know it's from me? I add:

DAISY X

Is the kiss too much? Should I send it? Fuck it. I press send and *instantly* regret it.

I sit on the loo with the seat down scrutinising my phone for a full three minutes before I decide he's not going to reply. Just as

I go to put my phone back in my bag, it beeps. I quickly pull it out again.

I'M OK. THANKS. SORRY I MISSED YOU.

It may only be a short text, but I feel giddy with happiness. Head spinning, I type out another message:

YOU SHOULD HAVE SAID GOODBYE

I press send and he immediately replies:

I COULDN'T SEE YOU ANYWHERE

So he *did* think of me!

I WAS IN THE KITCHEN!

He writes back:

SORRY. WASN'T REALLY WITH IT. SEE YOU IN MONACO X

He signed off with a kiss! I gleefully type out:

I LOOK FORWARD TO IT X

Another kiss. Naughty Daisy! Oh, God, I just can't help myself. I sit there in a daze until I hear an American woman outside the cubicle say, 'I don't know who's in there; she's been ages.'

Mortified, I stuff my phone back into my bag and flush the

toilet, before rushing out with my head down, murmuring, 'Sorry' to the queue of people waiting. It only occurs to me later that I didn't wash my hands. Not a good look for catering staff, but I'm hoping no one saw my uniform.

Chapter 13

Holly and I run towards each other, squealing, before doing a little jig on the spot. We're at Heathrow – again – and are beside ourselves with excitement. This time we're off to Monte Carlo for the most glamorous and historic race of the season. This is the place to see and be seen and Holly and I have spent the last couple of days liaising on the telephone about what going-out outfits we should take with us. As a result, my bag is packed full to breaking point.

'So I reckon we should go to a bar on the harbour tonight,' Holly says, taking my arm as we walk towards the check-in desk.

'Sounds good.' It's Wednesday, and Will isn't due to arrive until four p.m. tomorrow. It'll be about seven o'clock by the time he gets to the hotel. I know this, because I asked Ally for his itinerary. For professional reasons, of course. Anyway, it means there's a whole night and day to kill before I can see him again.

The last week and a half has been torture. I woke up on Monday morning in a cold sweat, severely regretting texting him. I keep telling myself it was completely innocent, but I just hope he sees it like that. I'd be mortified if he suspected I fancied him.

The motorhomes in Monaco are all situated on the port, about five minutes' walk from the pits across the temporary Rascasse bridge. We can see the boats on the glittering ocean from here, and there's a spectacular view looking back up at the hills, which are jagged with apartment blocks and hotels overlooking the harbour.

By Friday morning, I'm so on edge that I can't believe I haven't spontaneously combusted. We went out straight from the track on Thursday night and, as a result, I wasn't at the hotel when Will checked in, which I'm assuming he did.

Frederick pipes up. 'Can you get on with the bacon, Daisy?'

'Yes, Chef!'

Urgh, that's the last thing I feel like doing. I have to grill it out in the hospitality area so it's fresh for our guests, but I always end up smelling like bacon afterwards and with a hangover I feel decidedly queasy. Queasy *and* greasy. A lovely combination.

'Happy there with your nice muesli?' I gripe at Holly.

'Perfectly, thank you.' She smirks. I'm tempted to throw a piece of bacon at her, but Frederick would go mad.

It's only six a.m. but the team members are starting to appear, each looking more worse for wear than the last. Then Simon comes into the hospitality area looking bright-eyed and bushy tailed.

'Can I get you a tea? Coffee?' I offer.

'Coffee, please. White, no sugar.' But, of course, I know this already. He fidgets on the spot impatiently for all of two seconds before snapping, 'Actually, Holly, can you bring that up?'

'Sure,' she replies.

He stalks off.

'That's strange,' she comments.

You're telling me. Why the hell didn't he ask for me to take it to him, considering I'm supposed to be his on-hand girl? But I keep these thoughts to myself.

'Don't you think?' Holly gives me a weird look.

'Yeah, it is a bit,' I agree, uncomfortably. Is he angry with me? Does he know about me keeping Will up before qualifying in Istanbul?

Holly takes the cup from me and heads out and up the stairs, while I get back to flipping bacon.

Then Will walks through the doors, and all my worries about Simon vanish in an instant.

I watch him with anticipation, willing him to look up and see me. Suddenly he does, but there's something not right about his smile.

And then I see her. Tall, slim, blonde, wearing white skinny jeans and a fitted white shirt, looking radiant, glowing with a light tan – the sort of tan only the very rich seem to get right.

Laura. I know it in an instant.

I'm in shock. I realise I'm staring. My eyes flit back to Will as I see him stop to shake hands with some sponsors. He introduces Laura and she shakes their hands, too.

I want to escape. I want to get out of here. But with Holly upstairs, I'm the only person staffing the station. And now they're coming this way.

'Would I be able to have a cup of tea, please?' Laura asks in a posh British accent.

I look around for the teapot and realise Gertrude has just gone into the kitchen to make a fresh pot. I can't wait for her to come back so I pour water into a cup direct from the hot water jug, trying to keep my hands steady. I suddenly realise I haven't put the teabag in, so I quickly rectify my mistake, but it means the tea doesn't brew as well. I stir it with a teaspoon, assuming Laura is currently thinking I'm a total loser.

'Laura, this is Daisy,' Will says.

'Hello!' She leans across and shakes my hand. It's greasy from bacon fat, but she doesn't wipe her hand on her trousers or do anything so common as that afterwards. She probably has a handkerchief in her handbag, for all I know.

'Good morning,' I reply, feeling ever so formal. 'Let me know if you need anything during your stay, won't you? I'm here to help!' I have NO idea where these words are coming from, but I force a bright, albeit shaky, smile.

'Well, thank you very much,' she says warmly, holding her hands out for the tea.

'Milk?' I ask weakly.

'No, thank you. What are you having, darling?' She turns to Will. 'One of those dreadful milkshakes?'

I stare at him as he decides.

'No, maybe later.' He puts his hand on Laura's lower back and steers her away, not meeting my eyes. They take a seat at one of the tables and I do my utmost to focus on the bacon, but my gaze keeps flitting back to them.

She doesn't wear much make-up – only a light slick of the sheerest lipgloss and a touch of blush and mascara. She's too beautiful to need anything else. I can see her fingers, long and slim, wrapped around the handle of her teacup. Her nails are perfectly manicured.

'Alright?' Holly re-emerges, looking comparatively cheerful.

'Laura is here,' I mutter under my breath.

Holly surveys the tables and spots her instantly. She waves. I look at Laura to see her wave back and smile. I remember they've met before.

'Sorry,' Holly whispers to me. 'She saw me; I couldn't ignore her.'

Will suddenly stands up. Laura looks surprised at his sudden movement. He says something to her, then turns and walks towards the stairs leading to his private room. She quickly places her teacup on the saucer and hurries, gazelle-like, after him in her ever-so-high heels.

I turn and look at Holly.

'Oh, dear,' she says.

I don't speak, just stare down at the sizzling bacon. I look back up at her. 'Does my hair look greasy?'

'No, it looks fine,' she lies. 'Gorgeous. You look stunning.'

I smile at her gratefully, even though I know I look like a state. Why oh why did I go out drinking last night? And the bacon! The curse of the bacon! I look like a mess.

'Why did she have to come to this race? Of all the races to come to, this is the one I've been most looking forward to!' I lament.

'Don't let this spoil it for you,' Holly says, but she doesn't understand. My weekend has been ruined already.

Later that afternoon, Holly takes me to one side. 'I know why she's here.'

'Who? Laura?'

Holly nods.

'Why?'

'She's involved in a charity event they're all going to this evening.'

By 'they' I assume she means the drivers and directors.

'I see.' So there's no chance of Will coming out with us tonight.

'We'll have a good time,' she tells me, but she knows I don't believe it.

By ten thirty that night, I've had enough. Everyone else is in high spirits, but I just don't have it in me to enjoy myself. I quietly tell Holly I'm heading back to the hotel. She immediately grabs my arm and pleads with me to stay, before drunkenly insisting she'll come with me. I firmly tell her no. She's been having a laugh with Pete and Dan and I know they'll see she gets back to the hotel safely.

The streets and bars are bustling with people and there's a real party feel about the place. As I set off down the road I'm overcome with sadness that I'm letting Will and Laura ruin my time in Monaco. Holly has raved about this race ever since I got the job with the team last year. I almost stop and go back to the bar, but I feel foolish enough as it is – I don't want to draw more attention to myself.

After a while I spot a couple of front-of-house girls I know from one of the other teams. It's a warm night in May and they're sitting outside at a table on the crowded pavement. One of them, Sarah, beckons me over, so I go to say hello.

'Where are you off to?' Sarah asks me.

'Oh, back to the hotel,' I tell her reluctantly, aware of the response I'm going to get.

'BACK TO THE HOTEL?' she shouts. 'You've got to be kidding me!'

I shrug.

'Sit down here, girl. Get that down ya.' She pours me a glass of champagne from the bottle they've almost polished off.

I dither for a moment. Maybe I could have one drink here and then decide if I should go back and join the others? What would it hurt? I make the decision to do as she says and as soon as the bubbly fizz hits the back of my throat, I feel better. To hell with it, I *am* going to stay out!

We sit there and gossip about the fling Sarah is having with a mechanic from another team, until we eventually drink all the champagne.

'Another one?' I ask, lifting the empty bottle up.

'Yeah!' they chorus.

'I'll go to the bar,' I say, looking around for a waiter and not seeing one. They've been rushed off their feet.

I make my way to the busy bar area and lean in, trying to get the bartender's attention.

'Hello, Daisy Paola Giuseppe Rogers.'

I turn to see Luis standing beside me. I feel bizarrely happy to see him. 'Hello, Luis I Don't Know Your Middle Name Castro.'

'It's just as well. I have about six of them.'

'Six middle names?'

'Yes.'

'Whatever.' I grin. 'How did you remember my full name anyway?' I vaguely remember telling him what it was way back in Bahrain when we had a few drinks that night.

'I have a good memory.'

'Do you?'

'Yep.' He leans up against the bar top, facing me. 'What are you doing here?'

'I should ask you the same question. Aren't you supposed to be at whatshername's do?'

'Yeah. Boring as hell. I left.'

'That's not very charitable of you.'

'I do my bit,' he says, looking around. 'Where are the others?'

'At some other bar.'

'You here alone?' He looks surprised.

'I bumped into a couple of bun tarts' – I say this wryly – 'from another team. They're over there.' I point outside and we both look to see a waiter standing over their table, taking an order.

'Oh,' I say. 'I don't know what I'm doing here.' I indicate the bar.

'Stay and have a drink with me,' he suggests. 'I've been hanging out with Rizzo and Aranda, but now they've buggered off to bed, boring bastards.'

I laugh and pull up a stool that has just been vacated. Sarah glances my way and I point at Luis and pretend to knock back a shot. She gives me the thumbs up, understanding my sign language.

Luis calls over the bartender and orders a beer. I decide to go hardcore and opt for a whisky and Coke.

'Are you Luis Castro?' the bartender asks in a heavy French accent as he whacks our drinks down on the bar top.

'Yes,' Luis answers, pulling out his wallet.

'These are on us,' the bartender replies. 'Good luck for the race.'

'Thanks very much. Cheers.' He holds his bottle up to the bartender and then to me, before gulping some down. 'So you're drowning your sorrows, hey?' He gets straight to the point.

'Mmm.'

'Have you spoken to her?'

'Barely at all. I made her tea. And didn't do a very good job.'

'Did she give you any stick?'

I scoff. 'No, and she'd better not because I won't be standing for it.' I've had too much to drink. This isn't me speaking, at all.

'Will you tell her to go fuck herself like you did me that time?'

I laugh sharply, before saying, 'I don't think I'll be going quite that far.'

'Teach me some other swear words,' he says, grinning.

I swivel on my stool to face him, glad of the distraction he's providing.

'Well, you know, "*cazzo*", right?'

'Dick?'

'Yeah. That's what it literally means, but it pretty much covers everything: fuck, shit, etc. If you want to really express annoyance, you can say, "*Cazzo, cazzo, cazzo!*"'

'Got it.'

'Your turn.'

'*Cazzo, cazzo, cazzo!*' he exclaims, slapping his hand theatrically on the bar top.

'Shh!' I start to giggle. 'I hope none of Emilio Rizzo's fans are in earshot. I want *you* to teach *me* some Portuguese slang! You can never know too many swear words in foreign languages . . .'

He smirks. 'Okay . . .'

'How do you say, "fuck it!"?'

'*Fode-se*. And "fuck off" is *va se foder*.'

'What about, "I couldn't give a shit"?'

'*Estou me cagando*.'

I repeat it: '*Estou me cagando* about William Trust and his goddamn girlfriend!'

Luis chuckles.

'This is great,' I say. 'It's really cheering me up.'

'I bet it is.'

'I wish Will were here.'

Luis looks a little put out, then seems to realise what I mean. 'So you can swear at him?'

'Exactly. Dickhead.'

'*Testa di cazzo*!'

'You got it!'

He raises his beer bottle and loudly chinks the almost empty whisky glass in my hand. 'You want another?'

I glance over at Sarah and her friend. They won't mind if I don't go back and join them.

'Sure.'

The bartender comes over and takes our order, noisily banging down my glass and Luis's beer bottle.

'On the house,' he says.

'Thanks!' Luis and I both enthuse.

'Hey . . .' I lean in and motion to the bartender to do the same.

'Yes?'

'How do you say "fucker" in French?'

He doesn't bat an eyelid. '*Enculé*.'

'Cool. Thanks.'

'What about "fuck off"?' Luis chips in.

'*Va te faire foutre*,' the bartender replies, leaning in further. 'Are you thinking of ways to talk to your team-mate?' His tone is conspiratorial.

I collapse into giggles.

'No!' Luis denies, but the bartender grins knowingly.

'I've read the newspapers,' he says. 'Do you two dislike each other as much as they make out?'

'No,' Luis shakes his head dismissively.

The bartender winks and leaves us to it.

I look at Luis and raise an eyebrow. 'Is that what they're saying in the gossip columns?'

'Surely you've heard about our so-called feud?' He regards me with disbelief.

'I never read the tabloids.' I don't read proper papers much either, but I don't tell him this.

'Don't you?'

'No. Never, ever, EVER.' I tipsily slap my hand down on the bar top to emphasise my point.

'Why not?'

'I have my reasons.'

'When did you stop reading them?'

I pull a face at him. It's not that fascinating a subject, is it? 'A few months after I moved to the UK.'

'Too much about Johnny Jefferson in them, was there?'

I almost fall off my barstool.

'Don't worry, I won't tell anyone,' he says.

'How did you find out?' I raise my hand to my throat. I feel like I'm choking.

'I looked you up on the internet,' he replies. 'Daisy, it's okay.' He touches my arm. 'You can trust me.'

I've heard that before. I can't trust anyone.

'Why did you do that?' I manage to ask. What is it with him and Will? Except Will came back with nothing about Johnny, only my father.

'I'm sorry,' Luis apologises. 'Maybe I shouldn't have. But Will was telling me how you worked for someone famous . . .'

The disappointment that Will gossiped about me when I asked him to keep his mouth shut barely has time to register.

'I remembered about your middle names and searched under

"Paola Giuseppe" instead. Johnny Jefferson's name came up right away.'

I stare at him, still feeling shell-shocked.

'Look, I swear I won't say anything to anyone. Not even Will to annoy him. I *swear*.' He looks at me intently as I consider him warily. 'Is that why you left America?' Luis prompts.

I nod, taking a deep breath. His eyes are full of sympathy. And something happens to me. The weight that I've been feeling on my shoulders for the past two years slowly but surely begins to lift. Once I start talking, I can't stop . . .

I'm a New York City girl, but almost three years ago I went to live in Los Angeles to work as a personal assistant to one of the biggest rock stars in the world. I fell for him instantly. Johnny Jefferson is the ultimate bad boy. The type of guy you should never fall in love with, but the type of guy you inevitably do. The thing that completely caught me off guard was that he fell for me, too. At least, I think he did. It's hard to tell with Johnny. He's complicated, to put it mildly. And that's when it all went wrong. The groupies had always been there, waiting on the sidelines, but Johnny stepped up the drink, drugs and, of course, the sex with countless girls, and he made sure I was a witness to *all* of it. Eventually I couldn't take it anymore. It was devastating to watch the person I loved most in the world self-destruct. And when it was over, when I'd finally walked out his door for the last time, I still couldn't put him behind me. I would see him at parties, at bars and clubs, and even though I soon got a job as a PA to a businessman, the group of friends my new boss mixed with meant that Johnny was never far from my sight. Then Johnny got a new PA, a girl from England, and the rumours circulated that the same thing had happened to her. It was the final straw, to know I wasn't

'The One', to know that I was just another notch on his belt. I was still in love with him, so I quit my job, fled the country and moved to England. I could have gone to Italy. I *should* have gone to Italy. But Johnny is British and the thought of leaving him behind fully was too much. In London there was always the risk of bumping into him again – I've even catered at a party for his own record company – but so far we've managed unwittingly to avoid each other.

'What about your name?' Luis asks finally. 'Why "Paola Giuseppe" and not "Daisy Rogers"?'

'It wasn't intentional,' I say, although quite honestly, at the time I was happy to leave my identity back in New York. 'Johnny discovered my middle names and decided they suited me better. He wouldn't stop calling me Paola Giuseppe and it soon stuck.'

'And when you quit? What did you do, then?'

'I reverted to my real name. I didn't want anything to remind me of him.' I didn't want anything to remind me of my former life in New York either, but even that was preferable to Johnny.

Luis nods and I pause for a moment, thinking.

'I told you I didn't read the tabloids.'

'You did.'

'When I moved to England I read them all the time. I bought every single one and scoured the pages for news of Johnny. It began to eat me up. I realised *I* was addicted, so one day I went cold turkey. I haven't read them since. Of course, I still hear things about him, about all those trips he's had back and forth into rehab, but I do my best to avoid all news of him.'

'You're still not over him?'

I think about this for a moment. 'Do you know what, I actually think that I am. But there's no point testing it. He still hurt me. I don't want those feelings to rise up inside me again. I think that sort of pain takes years to get over.'

'Don't they say it takes twice as much time as the time you went out with someone to get over them?'

I glance at Luis and grin. 'Did you read that in a women's magazine?'

He looks sheepish. 'Might've done.'

'Well, it's taking me a bit longer, to be honest. I only worked with Johnny for eight months, but he made a major impact on me.'

'That's probably why he's famous.'

I cock my head to one side. 'Yeah, you're probably right. He has the X factor . . .' I say this sardonically. 'What about you? Why are you reading women's mags? Were they your girlfriend's?'

Luis almost chokes on his beer. 'Girlfriend, no!'

'Why the strong reaction?'

'I don't have a girlfriend.'

'Why not? You're acting like they're a disease or something.'

He shrugs. 'Not my style.'

'Oh God, another one like Johnny. That's all the world needs.'

He looks thoughtful and stares down at his beer bottle.

'I'm not that bad,' he tells me.

'No?'

'Maybe I was hurt myself once.'

'Oh, Jesus, you really have been reading women's magazines, haven't you!' I start to crack up, but then see his face and realise it's not a laughing matter. 'Sorry. Tell me what happened?'

'Not much to say,' he replies. 'Fell in love with a girl, she ran off with my best mate.'

'Oh, no, that's awful.'

'Yeah, it did suck a bit.'

'When did this happen?'

'When I was about nineteen.'

'Nineteen?' I exclaim. 'Luis! That's ages ago!'

He doesn't say anything.

'But how long did you go out together?'

'Since we were at school.'

'Not another pair of childhood sweethearts . . .' I moan, then apologise for bringing the conversation back to me. 'So does that theory work for you? Has it taken twice as much time as you were together for you to get over her?'

'Hell no, much more. But I'm over her now. I may not have gone to her wedding, but I *am* over her.'

'Wedding? Who did she marry?'

He gives me a wry look.

'Not your best friend?' I pull a face.

He laughs. 'Well, I wouldn't call him that anymore.'

'No, I guess not.' I swallow a mouthful of whisky as the bartender plonks a couple of refills back on the bar top.

'Cheers!' Luis says again. 'I shouldn't really be drinking all this the night before qualifying. Simon and João would go mad.'

I glance at my watch. It's getting close to two a.m. 'Do you think we should call it quits?' I look around. My friends have already left.

'Yeah, you're probably right,' Luis replies, putting his bottle of beer on the bar top.

I slide off my stool and almost topple down a step that I forgot was there.

'Whoa,' Luis says, putting his hands on my arms to steady me. I look up into his dark-brown eyes and a hundred butterflies swarm through my stomach, taking me completely by surprise. I feel my face heat up and quickly look away.

And considering how openly we both spoke earlier on in the night, on the walk back to the hotel we find we have very little to say to each other at all.

Chapter 14

'Have you told him to fuck off in French yet?' Luis asks me the next day during morning tea service.

I laugh. All appears to be normal between us. I don't know what was going on with those butterflies, but my blame falls squarely on the alcohol.

I got back before Holly last night. I tried to ring her because I was worried, then realised she'd already texted me to say everything was fine and they were going to Jimmyz nightclub. Infamous Eurotrash heaven, apparently.

I nod at Luis. 'You look alright considering how much you had to drink.' Klaus and Gertrude did the early shift so this is the first time we've seen each other today.

'Are you saying I normally look like a man who *can't* hold his drink?'

I consider him. 'Well, you are a bit scrawny.'

He laughs and throws a napkin at me.

'Oi!' I'm about to throw it back at him, but spy Frederick by the kitchen door. 'I'll get you back, right when you least expect it,' I warn, evilly.

'Just you try, bun tart.'

We're still chuckling when Will and Laura appear.

'Good morning,' I say, not sounding quite as forced chirpy as I did the day before. 'I'll be with you in a minute.'

'Tucking into the pastries, are you, Luis?' Will says.

'I need something to help me get over my hangover,' Luis casually explains.

'Out drinking the night before qualifying?' Will raises his eyebrows.

'Blame Daisy,' Luis answers, as I hand him tiny pots of butter and jam to go with his croissant.

Will frowns and indicates me with his thumb. 'Daisy? This Daisy?'

Luis nods, picking up a knife and leaning against the serving table. 'Yeah, we had a few, didn't we?'

'That we did,' I agree.

'Were you guys all out together or something?' Will nods towards the kitchen where Holly is working away.

'No, just Daisy and me,' Luis explains, slathering his croissant with butter.

The corners of Will's mouth turn down.

'Aw, did you head off early from the charity event?' Laura pipes up.

'Afraid so.' Luis pulls a face. 'Not really my scene, all that stuff. But don't worry, I left a little something. Anyway, better get this down me before we hit the track. See ya later.' He winks at me and wanders away.

'What can I get for you?' I force a smile at Laura.

'Just a juice, please.'

'Orange? Apple? Grapefruit?' I wave my hand at the glass jugs to my right.

'Ooh, I don't know,' she replies, sweetly. 'Maybe . . . Apple? Are you a little short?' She examines the contents of the jug.

'There's more out the back,' I tell her, trying to keep my tone even. Just hurry up and bugger off.

'Okay, apple then,' she decides.

'Will?' I turn to him.

'Nothing, thanks.'

I serve Laura and then watch as they walk off to an empty table.

'What's up with you?' Holly asks, coming out of the kitchen with a platter of mini lemon tarts. 'You look like you want to murder someone . . . Oh,' she says, spying Will and Laura.

I instantly feel mean. It's not like *she's* done anything wrong. It's not like *he's* done anything wrong, either, for that matter. Am I acting like a crazy person?

'I think we'd better go back to that plan where you kick me,' I say mournfully to Holly.

Later, Frederick asks us both to stock up the snacks in the garages. We traipse across the Rascasse bridge, laden down with cool boxes.

My heart plummets as we walk in to see Will standing next to his car, fully kitted out in racing gear, with Laura at his side. Catalina is talking to Laura, and then Simon joins them, affectionately placing his hand on Laura's back.

I try not to look, but the jealousy is killing me.

Laura's blonde hair is lightly streaked with expensive-looking highlights. She wears it down, around her shoulders. Mine is tied up into a bun as usual. I feel inadequate.

'Stop staring,' Holly whispers.

I quickly turn my attention to the sandwiches we're setting up, but out of the corner of my eye I notice Will climbing into his car. Laura and Catalina move out of the way as mechanics swarm in to push it out of the garage.

I turn to Holly. 'I think I might go back.'

'No, stay,' she pleads. I watch as the mechanics start up Will's car and he zooms away from the pits. There's a white box painted on the floor of Will's garage to show where his car goes and Laura stands right in the centre of it. I study her for a moment as she watches the single television screen above her head following Will's journey as he skilfully manoeuvres the car around the circuit. She looks tense.

No one else stands inside the box with Laura. It's like she owns it. Like she owns Will.

'I'm going,' I say, picking up the empty cool boxes.

'No . . .' Holly blocks me.

'Well, at least let's go through to Luis's garage,' I say.

She perks up. 'Okay!'

Luis is already inside his car, watching Will's lap on the television screen above his head. We stand behind him, watching too, and after a while the mechanics come in to start up his car. He pulls out of the garage.

Towards the end of the qualifying, Catalina comes over to us. 'Don't you have any egg sandwiches?'

I'm about to apologise, but Holly speaks first.

'No,' she snaps.

'The other two. The Germans. They had them yesterday,' Catalina says. That was when Klaus and Gertrude were in charge of the catering in the pits.

'Well, we don't have them today,' Holly answers coolly. I watch in alarm. Isn't she taking this too far?

'Can you make some?' she asks impatiently.

'Too busy for that, I'm afraid.' Holly looks back up at the television screen while I stand there, tensely.

'You don't look very busy to me,' Catalina says, turning her nose up.

'We're on a break,' Holly replies, emphasising the word 'break'. She stares at her directly and after a moment, Catalina crumbles and stalks off to Will's garage. We see her walk outside to the pit wall where Simon is sitting with headphones on. She says something to him and he lifts one of the headphones off his ear to hear her. Holly and I watch this exchange intently, me feeling like we're about to lose our jobs. But Simon shrugs and puts his headphones back on. I glance at Holly to see a satisfied little smirk on her lips. She looks at me smugly, then refocusses her attention on the television screen.

There's a funny feeling in my stomach. An uneasiness. I watch as Catalina makes her way back to the catering table and starts to load up her plate with assorted sandwiches. She glances through to Luis's garage so I quickly avert my gaze. She's a witch, but I feel an odd sense of pity for her, and it's not sitting well with me.

'I feel a bit bad,' I say to Holly.

'Don't,' she bites back, glaring through at Catalina as she perches on a chair in front of the six television screens at the back of the garages.

All of a sudden the mechanics around us cheer. We look back up to see Luis has taken pole position.

'No way!' I exclaim, delighted. 'Where's Will?'

Will is still doing his last lap around the track. As he reaches the start/finish line, we watch in tense silence.

Second!

Everyone claps and I look across at Laura. She's standing in the box, smiling.

Will is going to be disappointed with that time. I know how desperately he wants to win here. Laura knows, too. That's why her smile keeps faltering.

The drivers return and everyone moves out of the way as the mechanics help manoeuvre the cars back onto the white boxes. Luis leaps out to many slaps on the back. In Will's garage, it's more reserved.

'Hey!'

I turn back to see Luis standing in front of me, holding his helmet in his hand. His black hair is damp.

'Well done!' I pat him on the arm and beam, feeling genuinely happy for him.

'Thanks!' He's still grinning. 'You watched it?'

'We did.' I fold my arms across my chest. Luis glances through to Will's garage where Laura is speaking intimately into Will's ear. At that moment, Will looks up and his eyes flit between Luis and I, his brow furrowing. He returns his attention to Laura and shakes his head, seemingly with irritation, as though he couldn't hear what she was saying. She steps backwards in frustration, then leans in again to repeat herself.

Luis and I turn back to each other. 'I'm going to go take a shower,' he says, giving me a knowing look. 'Catch you later, bun tarts!' He smacks Holly on her bum and she squeals as he walks off.

I glance again into Will's garage, but he has his back to me. 'Come on, we should go,' I say to Holly.

'Sure. Let's just grab the cool boxes.'

That evening, we get ready at the track. We're all going to a bar on the harbour, and Holly is expecting big things from me after my drinking session with Luis last night.

Speaking of whom, I spy him jogging down the stairs into the hospitality area. He comes over.

'Are you coming out tonight?' I ask.

'Where are you going?'

'Some bar on the harbour. Bars, Stars . . . something like that.'

'Stars 'N' Bars?'

'That's the one.'

'Yeah, cool. I've got to go to some drinks do on a yacht, but I may catch you there later.'

I feel a tinge of regret as I remember Will saying he'd try to get me an invite to a yacht party. There's no chance of that, now.

Later that night, we're all at Stars 'N' Bars, an American sports bar with a view overlooking the harbour. It's absolutely jam-packed, but we've monopolised a section of the bar. I find myself looking at my watch, wondering if and when Luis will turn up. When he finally does at ten o'clock, flanked by a member of team security, I can't stop smiling.

'You've cheered up,' he comments. 'Had a few?' He indicates the wine glass in my hand.

'Might've done,' I answer. 'You've brought a friend with you tonight?' I nod behind him to the security guard, who's trying to look inconspicuous standing against the wall.

Luis rolls his eyes. 'Simon insisted. You know, pole position, Monaco . . .'

'I didn't think it was likely to be your idea. How was the yacht?'

'Good.' He nods.

'Spot any famous people?'

'No, tomorrow's the best day for that. Make sure you do the grid walk.'

Pete comes over. 'Shouldn't you be in bed, mate?' he shouts.

'Fuck that!' Luis shouts back.

'In that case, cheers!' Pete hands a bottle of beer over and they chink bottles.

'Where are the others?' I ask.

'Will went back to the hotel.' Luis takes a swig of his beer and looks around the bar.

'With Laura?' I find myself asking, but, of course, I know the answer.

'Yep,' he replies.

'*Enculé*!' I shout at the top of my voice.

He's laughing when Holly returns from the ladies' room.

'Luis!' she squeals, enveloping him in a drunken embrace. 'How *are* you?'

'Fine, thanks!' Although he looks decidedly uncomfortable with Holly hanging around his neck.

'How was the yacht?' she shouts, letting go of her grip on him.

'Big!' he replies.

'Was Catalina there with Simon?'

He narrows his eyes as he answers, 'Yes.'

I notice a hardness come over her features as she looks away. Out of the blue, she turns back and plasters a big, false smile on her face.

'I'm going to the bar!' she shouts and pushes past us.

I feel dizzy as realisation comes crashing down on me. I knew something was up. I knew it. And now I know with whom.

Luis is watching me with a strange expression on his face.

'You know, don't you?' I ask him bluntly.

'About what?'

'Simon.'

'What do you mean, Simon?'

'Don't play dumb with me. I saw the look you gave Holly when she asked if Catalina was on the yacht with him.'

'Wait, before we go any further, what do you know?' He pulls me to one side, away from the mechanics, and clocks me straight in the eye. I size him up in return, but even if I wasn't so sure my instincts were correct, something tells me I can trust him.

'Holly is having an affair with Simon.' There. I've said it.

Luis doesn't reply at first, but then he nods and takes a swig of his beer.

'It's true, isn't it?' I speak again as my heart pounds faster. He looks back at me. 'Oh, my God.' I'm dumbfounded.

'I thought she must've told you,' he says, confused.

I stare down at my fingers in a daze. 'I suspected, but I didn't know for sure.' I glance back at him. 'How did *you* know?'

'I saw them together.'

'You saw them together?' I'm still incredulous. 'When?'

'When we were filming that advert in Italy. She came out of his hotel room at five o'clock in the morning. She didn't see me, but later that day I overheard them talking. It was intimate.'

'Catalina wasn't in Italy, was she?'

'No. Nor at the following race in Istanbul.'

'Of course.' I remember Holly disappearing in the middle of the night. 'No wonder she was so rude to Catalina earlier,' I muse.

'Was she?' Luis raises an eyebrow.

'Yeah. A bit too rude, to be honest.'

'Hmm.'

'You don't approve, do you?'

'Do you?' he challenges me.

I think about it for a moment, realising horridly I may not be all that different to Holly if I ever get the chance to be with Will, but I keep my answer true to my heart. 'No. I don't. Catalina may be a bitch, but she doesn't deserve that.'

We both gaze over at Holly, who has collapsed against Pete's shoulder and is laughing hysterically. Pete, also laughing, tries to take her drink away and put it on the bar top, but Holly immediately reaches for it. They have a play fight, which ends with Pete downing Holly's drink and her beating him on the arm. I start to smile, but then remember what Luis and I have been talking about and instantly feel sombre again.

'You haven't told anyone, have you?' I ask, suddenly worried.

'Of course not,' Luis replies irritably.

I can't take my eyes off Holly. And I can't help feeling disappointed. When Luis says after half an hour or so that he should probably head back to the hotel, I decide to walk with him.

I tell Holly I'm off and while she isn't happy, she's too far gone to protest much.

The night is cool and I'm cold. I wrap my arms around myself and walk fast to keep warm.

The security guard follows at a distance. To be honest, there wasn't much need for him. Despite the place being crammed with race fans, I don't think many would expect to see a top driver out on the town. The rest of the grid are probably tucked up in bed or downing protein shakes.

'Do you want my coat?' Luis offers when he overhears my teeth chattering away to themselves. I shake my head. 'Go on, take it.' He shrugs it off and hands it to me, so I put it on.

'I still can't believe it,' I say after a while. We've been walking in silence.

'About Holly and Simon?' Luis checks, glancing at me.

I nod. 'And I know that probably makes me a hypocrite.'

Luis doesn't answer, and his lack of response makes me feel worse.

He follows me through the automatic doors into the bright hotel lobby. I inadvertently glance towards the reception desk and stop in my tracks when I see Will leaning up against it, talking to one of the receptionists.

'Watch it!' Luis puts his hands on my arms to steady himself as he bumps into me. Will turns around to see us and reels backwards ever so slightly.

'Hi!' he says, coming over.

'Hello,' I answer guardedly. 'What are you still doing up?'

'I was checking to see if I had any messages.' He points to the reception desk. 'Have you two been out together again?'

'With the others, yeah,' I tell him, feeling on edge.

Luis walks over to the lift and presses the button. Will follows me in that direction. The lift doors open and Luis steps inside, turning around as I begin to follow him.

'Hey . . .' Will grabs my elbow, pulling me back. Luis puts his finger on the button to hold the doors open. I look at Will, confused. He glances at Luis then at me. 'Can I talk to you for a sec?'

'Er, sure,' I reply, moving away from the lift.

'She'll catch the next one up,' Will tells Luis.

Luis gives him a hard stare and then takes his finger off the button. The lift door closes.

I turn to Will. 'What's up?' I ask, trying to sound indifferent.

'Have a quick drink with me?' He aims his thumb in the direction of the hotel bar.

'Shouldn't you be catching an early one for the race tomorrow?' I ask, warily.

'Can't sleep,' he explains.

'Okay . . .' I give him a baffled look and follow him to the bar. 'I'm not sure I really feel like more alcohol,' I tell him when he asks what I'm having. 'I'll have a cranberry juice.'

'Same,' Will tells the bartender. 'Put it on Room 516. Let's go over here.' He points to a table for two by a window.

I follow him and realise I'm still wearing Luis's jacket. I take it off and hang it over the back of the chair before sitting down.

'Nice time tonight?' Will asks.

'Yes,' I reply. 'How was the yacht?' There's a frostiness to my tone, which I just can't help.

'Okay, yeah.' He looks across at me and frowns. 'Are you alright?'

'Yes, why?' I shift in my seat.

'You seem a bit different with me this weekend.'

'I've barely seen you,' I bite back. 'I don't know how you can say that.'

He leans back in his chair and stretches his legs out underneath the table.

'Where's Laura tonight?' I try to keep my voice sounding casual.

'In bed.'

'Won't she be wondering where you are?'

He shrugs. 'She's probably asleep by now.'

I tuck my hair behind my ears. I wonder if he still prefers it down? I glance up to see him watching me. My insides twinge with jealousy as I remember something he said to me in Italy.

'Have you two been house-hunting together?'

'Here? In Monaco?' he asks.

'Yes. You said you were thinking of buying a place here.'

'Oh, yeah.' He screws his nose up and shakes his head. 'But not this weekend.'

'Why not?'

'There's not enough time.'

'I see.' I reach forward and take my drink from the table, swirling the ice around in the glass before taking a sip. I'm wearing a skirt tonight. A short, black one. I may be imagining it, but did Will's eyes just skim my legs?

'So . . .' He raises one eyebrow. 'What's going on with you and Luis, then?'

I pull a face, about to deny everything, but something makes me hesitate. 'What makes you think something's going on?' I ask, deflecting the question.

'Going out together two nights in a row, you wearing his jacket.' He nods at it hanging over the back of my chair. 'And I saw you chatting to his family in Istanbul.'

'They were nice, actually. Did you speak to them much?'

'No. Not really. But you're not answering my question.'

'Why should you care?'

'I don't,' he replies, before quickly qualifying it. 'Well, I mean, I just don't want you to get hurt, you know?'

I let out a sharp laugh and cross my legs. 'You don't have to worry about me, Will. I have no intention of getting my heart broken again.' Of course, I'm lying. I feel like Will is chipping a little piece of it away, day by day. It's killing me. But I'm not about to tell him that. And if he doesn't like the idea of me having a relationship with Luis, good. Let him suffer for a change.

'What about you?' I change the subject as he pushes his hair back and looks a little frustrated. 'Are you enjoying having your girlfriend at this race?'

'Um, yeah,' he says awkwardly. 'It's alright.'

'Just alright?' I look across at him with interest. 'I would have thought you'd be thrilled?'

He takes a gulp of his cranberry juice and plonks the glass down on the table. 'It's fine,' he says, scratching the back of his head. 'I guess I should be getting to bed.'

'Yes.' I stand up and I lead the way to the lift. We go inside, turning around to face the doors.

Will spies the jacket in my hands. 'Do you want me to drop that off to Luis's room?'

'No, it's fine. I'll do it.'

'Are you sure?' he asks. 'I don't mind.'

'Will . . .' I can't help but laugh. 'I'm not going to go and shag him, if that's what you're worried about.'

He laughs, too, but surprisingly uneasily. 'Okay, then!'

'See you in the morning.' I step out on the landing for my floor. I had no intention of dropping Luis's jacket back tonight, anyway, but Will needn't know that.

'Holy bollocks Old Blighty, what time is it?' Holly moans when I open the curtains in our room the next morning.

'Time we got up,' I reply. I've been lying awake in bed for about an hour, going over in my mind the events of the night before. Now that I know about Holly and Simon, I see the signs everywhere. All those times he asked for her, not me. I wonder if it started before Italy? I wonder if it started before or after she told him to hire someone else to look after Catalina? What was it that Frederick said at the time? '*Simon likes people who stand up for themselves*.'

Well, he obviously liked Holly. A lot. And I can see what she sees in him. He's attractive, if not way too old for her, and he's clearly very powerful. Not to mention rolling in it, although that has never been an appeal for me.

But where is this relationship going to lead? Is he going to divorce Catalina and shack up with Holly instead? Somehow, I doubt it. I toyed with the idea of waking up my friend and questioning her about all of this, but I never actually worked up the nerve. Now that she's awake, I feel even less ready to ask her about it.

And then there was that weird drink with Will last night . . . What was all that about?

At the track a few hours later, Holly urges me to hurry.

'Okay, okay. Just let me go to the bathroom.'

'We'll miss the grid walk at this rate!'

I wipe down my hands and rush into the bathroom to check my reflection. There are so many famous people and VIPs at this race that I want to look my best.

'What are you doing?' Holly screeches as she pokes her head around the door.

'Give me a sec.'

'Lipstick, lipstick . . .' She grabs my make-up bag impatiently, rummaging around for a second before pulling out my burgundy-coloured lipstick and applying some to her lips. It suits my olive skin tone, but on Holly's pale complexion it looks too harsh. I tell her.

'Bollocks!' she exclaims, wiping it off on the back of her hand and then immediately attempting to scrub the consequent mark off with soap.

'Here, use this.' I hand her some sheer lipgloss and she tries that instead, pursing her lips at me afterwards. 'Much better,' I decide. She shoves everything back into my bag and drags me out of the bathroom.

The bridge is crowded with pedestrians and we hurry past them towards the pits. Balconies overlooking the track are packed with well-dressed 'suits' and socialites wearing large sunglasses as they bask in the sunshine. Monte Carlo is a beautiful city and today is a glorious day, barely a cloud in the sky. I can well understand why Will would like a place here. For a split-second I see myself sitting up on one of those balconies with him and have to inwardly berate myself.

The garages are practically empty when we arrive. The cars are already on the grid and most of the mechanics are out there with them. Holly and I go to the pit wall.

'Let's walk down to the start/finish line,' she suggests. 'See who we can see.'

I follow her as we climb over the wall into the throng.

'Look, it's Prince Albert!' she says, pointing out a handsome man surrounded by important-looking people. 'And I heard Brad Pitt was here!' Holly nudges me.

'Really?' I look at her with interest. I met him once at a film premiere I went to with—

'Johnny Jefferson!' Holly squeals.

I feel like the world is closing in on me. I see him instantly, regardless of the fact that Holly is pointing right at him. He's being mobbed by camera crews and is wearing dark shades so I can't see his piercing green eyes, but I'd recognise his dirty blond hair a mile away.

Holly is practically jumping on the spot. 'Let's follow him!' She tugs on my shirt.

'No, no.' I pull back and she looks at me in surprise.

'What's up with you? You're not having another funny turn, are you?'

'Yes, I think I am.'

'Daisy!' Her disappointment is fierce.

'I'll see you back in the garages,' I say weakly. I don't wait for her to answer, just walk away. Seconds later I feel a hand on my arm and spin around to see Luis standing there. His eyes convey his concern and I know he's seen Johnny, too.

'Luis, can we have a few words?' a man with a film crew interrupts.

'In a minute.' Luis puts his hand up to ward off the journalist.

'No, you go on,' I urge, embarrassed.

He watches me as I rush away to the relative safety of the garages. I busy myself tidying up the small catering table at the back, while trying to keep my tears at bay.

I saw Johnny's last PA once. She was in Soho, London, walking down Old Compton Street with a dark-haired man and a baby in a pushchair. I recognised the man as being Johnny's best friend Christian – he was always nice to me – but I couldn't place the girl at first. I was in two minds about whether or not to say hello to Christian, but then it dawned on me who he was with and I was too shocked to do anything except hide back in a dark doorway and let them pass. They seemed happy together, like a couple, and as my eyes flicked down to their little boy, he glanced up and saw me. His hair was blond, like his mother's, but his eyes, they were green, like Johnny's.

I wonder if he knows he's a father.

I scoured the papers compulsively after that, every single one of them. But there was nothing in them about Johnny fathering a son. That was when I told myself I had to end my tabloid obsession. I haven't read them since.

Now I have an unbearable urge to surf the internet for everything and anything there is to read about Johnny Jefferson. But I compress this desire right down into a tiny ball and hide it away, deep inside. I'm not going down that path again.

The grid begins to clear because the race is about to start. I take a few deep breaths to steady myself and then go to watch the action on the television screens. The camera zooms in on the two black, white and gold cars at the front and I push thoughts of my ex to the back of my mind as I focus my attention on Will and Luis.

'You're still here!' Holly exclaims in surprise.

I nod and manage a tight smile. The drivers set off on their warm-up lap, around Casino Square and through the tunnel, then the shimmering harbour, crowded with white yachts, is laid out before them. The cars come around the last turn and take their places on the grid, then the five lights go red, and they're off!

Will has a good start and almost beats Luis to the first corner, but Luis keeps his nerve. The television screens cut to Will's on-car camera and suddenly I get a sense of what it would be like to be in the car with him. He's flying around the corners, missing the steel and concrete barriers at the edge of the track by a matter of millimetres. This circuit is so much more dangerous than the modern equivalents.

At that thought, my heart starts racing and I begin to feel dizzy, but this time, Holly cottons on quickly that something isn't right.

'Are you pregnant?' she hisses, once she's sat me down in a chair at the back of the garages.

'Jesus! No! How the hell could I be pregnant? I haven't had sex for almost two years!'

'Blimey. No wonder you fancy Will so much – you're desperate for a good seeing to.'

'Pass me that water. Please,' I add weakly. I glance over to see Laura standing alone within the lines of the white box in Will's garage. She's staring up at the single television screen above her head.

'WHOA!'

The sound of several team members shouting makes me spin around and stare back up at the television. Will is hot on Luis's tail and now he's attempting to overtake. I see Laura cover her mouth with her hands and it distracts me for a second, and in that moment another collective gasp erupts from the two garages as Will and Luis zoom out of the tunnel and Will outbreaks Luis into the chicane. But no, it's too tight, there's not enough room. Suddenly both cars are spinning and then one after the other slams into a wall, shattering car parts across the track.

I watch, white knuckled with fear, as the camera zooms in on the wreckage. And then both Luis and Will are climbing out of their cockpits and over the wall to safety. They're still wearing their helmets – you can't see their faces – but it doesn't take a genius to work out that they'll both be fuming.

Simon gets down from the control desk on the pit wall and stalks into the garage, his jaw clenched as he opens the door to the meeting room. Luis arrives back at the pits first, with Will only metres behind him. Neither of them has spoken to the press – or each other – along the way. They both tug off their helmets angrily and head towards Simon. The team's technical director follows the boys into the meeting room and Simon firmly shuts the door behind him. Laura put her hand out to Will as he passed, but he didn't meet her eyes.

Holly and I throw each other a glance. We look up to see the television screens broadcasting a crane hauling the wrecked cars off the track.

'Two new cars . . . Jesus,' Holly murmurs. 'That's going to cost the team, big time. Simon will be really pissed off.'

I'm sure you'll cheer him up, I think to myself. 'At least no one was hurt,' is what I actually say.

'They'll probably still have to go to the Medical Centre for a check-up,' Holly replies.

There are no celebrations that evening and the atmosphere is decidedly subdued. I see Will come back into the hospitality area after the doctors give him and Luis the okay, but Laura is by his side so I can't – and don't want to – get near him. Finally Frederick sends me back to the pits on clean-up duty and by the time I return to the already partially disassembled motorhomes, both Luis and Will have gone.

Chapter 15

I'm getting a bit bored with this flying business, now. I'm back at Heathrow again, and this time we're off to Shanghai for the Chinese Grand Prix. This race used to come towards the end of the season, but races can be moved around on the calendar – or even removed completely. The French and Canadian Grands Prix recently succumbed to this fate.

I've had a lot to think about since Monaco, but right now I feel like I have very little to say to Holly. I'm still upset she hasn't confided in me about Simon, and I certainly don't feel like talking about Will. It was all very well daydreaming about him when 'Laura' was just a name, but now that I've met her, it's a whole different ballgame. I know I have to try even harder to put my feelings for him to the back of my mind. Luckily we're flying at night, so I can pretend to sleep, even if I can't.

When Will turns up at the track in Shanghai on the Friday morning before the race, he looks unfamiliar again, but my heart still jolts at the sight of him. No, Daisy, I tell myself. Enough of this.

'Hey,' he says warmly, coming over to the serving table. 'How are you?'

'Okay, thanks,' I reply coolly. 'What can I get you?'

'Er . . .' He looks taken aback by my reaction.

'Actually,' I interrupt, then call over my shoulder. 'Gertrude, can you see to Will?'

'Of course,' she says pleasantly, joining us at the table.

Will gives me a strange look before I walk away in the direction of the kitchen.

'So have you heard the latest about their feud?' Holly asks, appearing by my side.

'Whose feud? Will and Luis's?'

Holly rolls her eyes impatiently. She's been in a foul mood the last couple of days, I'm guessing because Catalina is at this race. 'Yes, Daisy. Who else's? Are you still not reading the papers?'

I shake my head. I wanted to after Monaco to see if I could spot any pictures of Johnny in them, but for that reason alone I stopped myself.

'I thought drivers were supposed to get over incidents quickly?'

'Not our two,' she says ominously. 'Team-mates. Too close for comfort, I guess.'

'Fill me in,' I say to Holly.

'Apparently,' she whispers, checking to make sure no one is in earshot. 'Luis blames Will for the accident in Monaco, saying that Will was showing off in front of his girlfriend because it's the only race she's gone to this year.'

I shake my head dismissively. 'I don't believe Luis said that.'

'That's what they wrote in the papers.'

'And you wonder why I don't read them?'

'Well, they also reckoned that Will's jealousy must've got the better of him because he feels like he's over-the-hill compared to Luis, who hasn't even reached his peak, yet.'

I scoff. 'Yeah, right.'

'I'm just telling you what I read.'

'Okay, thanks,' I say wryly, grabbing a bowl of hard-boiled eggs and tapping one against the counter to break the shell.

Holly joins me. 'What's up with you? Why don't you believe it?'

'Because Luis isn't a gossip, for one thing,' I say, peeling the shell off that egg before reaching for another one. 'He's not going to go running to the papers and spouting his mouth off.'

'You've changed your tune,' she says.

'And as for Will being over-the-hill,' I continue. 'That's just ridiculous.'

'You would say that.' She gives me a look.

'They're both only twenty-six, for crying out loud. If Will were forty, I'd agree.'

Holly falls silent and I realise what I've said. Simon is in his forties.

'Do you think we should offer Catalina an egg sandwich?' I don't know why I just said that, but I have a mean desire to wind her up.

'Fuck that,' she snaps.

I put down the third hard-boiled egg that I've peeled and turn to face her, suddenly desperate to know the truth about her relationship with Simon.

'What?' she asks, glancing at me. She's clearly still riled about Catalina.

'Nothing.' I lose my nerve and get back to work.

The modern track facilities in Shanghai are stunning – we've left our portable 'motorhomes' back in Europe. The circuit here is designed in the shape of the Chinese character 'shang', which stands for 'high' or 'above', and the hospitality buildings are arranged like pavilions on a lake to resemble the ancient Yuyuan Garden in the Old City.

The weather today is mild, with the humidity only moderate, and some of our guests are sitting outside at tables overlooking the water. I put together a tray of drinks and take it out to them. Luis is sharing a table with a couple of mechanics. They get up and go inside while he turns his attention to a newspaper.

'Not catching up on all that ridiculous gossip about you and Will, are you?' I ask him, placing the tray on his table to rest my arms for a moment.

He puts the paper down and looks up at me. 'Have you been reading about it?'

'No, Holly told me.'

'Oh, I see. So how are you? I didn't see you after the race in Monaco.'

'Nor I you,' I say. 'And I should be asking how *you* are.'

'Fine.' His response is blunt. He pulls out a chair. 'Take a break for a minute?'

I pause, then sit down. 'So you weren't hurt, then?'

'What? In the crash?'

I nod.

'No.' He shakes his head. 'No thanks to you know who.'

'Will?'

'Yes, Daisy,' he replies pedantically, before changing the subject. 'Did Johnny see you?'

I flinch a little at the sound of his name, then pull myself together. 'I doubt it. He would have been far too caught up in himself to notice me.'

'Does he know you're working for a Formula 1 team?' he asks.

'No, I'm sure he doesn't.'

'He's quite into racing, isn't he? Doesn't he have loads of sports cars?'

'Yeah. How do you know all this?'

'It's just common knowledge. I'm not a massive fan or anything.'

'Good.' I flash him a wry smile. 'Because I can't get you an autograph anymore.'

He rolls his eyes.

'Anyway,' I add, 'from the sounds of it, you and Will are more famous than he is at the moment, with this alleged spat going on.'

Luis's face hardens as he looks past me towards the lake.

'I don't believe you gossiped about it, but do you blame him for the accident?' I ask, tentatively.

'Yeah. It was his fault.' He glares at me and defiantly folds his arms.

'Was it?' I don't honestly know.

'Yes! He's far too aggressive at overtaking, he didn't leave enough room and clipped my wing. What does he expect at a track like Monaco? It's not like he hasn't driven there before – he should know better! Now I've lost ten points in the championship and I'm going to have to race twice as hard to get them back again!'

'Alright, alright!' I interrupt his rant, looking left and right. 'I hope there aren't any journalists listening in.'

He picks up the newspaper again. Now I'm not so sure he *didn't* gossip.

'Did you say that about his girlfriend?' I can't help asking. 'About him showing off in front of her?'

'Of course I bloody didn't.' He slaps the newspaper back down on the table, crossly.

'No, I didn't think so,' I hurriedly tell him. 'Did you get your jacket back, by the way?'

'Yep.'

I left it for him at reception.

'Right, well, I'd better get on.'

He nods and starts to read.

Moody bastard.

Later that afternoon I'm in the kitchen washing dishes when Will pokes his head around the door, making me jump with surprise. He's never done that before.

'Can I borrow you a sec?' he asks me, before glancing at Frederick. 'Is that alright?'

'Sure.' Frederick waves me out of the kitchen.

I join Will in the hospitality area. 'Everything okay?' I ask.

'Yeah.' He glances behind him and spies one of the front-of-house girls wiping down a nearby table. He looks back at me. 'Can we go upstairs?'

'Er, okay . . .' I follow him, hesitantly, as he leads the way to the drivers' suite situated directly above the hospitality area. He has to share a room here with Luis, so he checks it's empty before ushering me inside.

'What's up?' I prompt, standing just inside the door as he closes it behind him.

'Um . . . Are you going out tonight?'

'Yes, to a club in the Pudong district. You're welcome to come, if you like.'

'Er, no, thanks.'

I look at him, perplexed.

'I was just wondering if . . . I'm sure you won't, but . . .'

'What?' Now I'm dying of curiosity.

'I think I'm just going to watch a movie in my room.' He crosses his arms and then uncrosses them again. 'If you fancy it . . .' he adds.

'Oh.' I'm gobsmacked. To be honest, I wasn't really up for another night on the town. I'm getting a bit bored with the late nights and drinking. I must be getting old.

'But no chick flicks,' he adds, forcing a grin. He looks uncomfortable, which is odd because he's usually so composed.

'Okay,' I say. 'What time?'

He looks relieved. 'What time do you finish here?'

I glance at my watch. 'Probably not for another couple of hours. Are you going to the hotel, now?'

'Yeah.'

'Shall I come up to your suite later, then?'

'Sure.' He uncrosses his arms.

I reach for the door handle, but he gets there before me, holding the door open.

'See you later, then?' I say, awkwardly stepping under his arm.

'Cool. Okay.'

He shuts the door behind me, staying inside the room. I walk back down the stairs into the hospitality area, my mind racing.

Holly is not very impressed when I tell her I'm blowing her out, but when I come clean and explain what happened, she's all ears.

'Do you think he fancies you?' she asks, her eyes wide.

I shake my head. 'I doubt it.' Although a tiny little voice inside my head isn't so sure.

'Then what's going on?'

'I don't know. But I'll fill you in later.' I refrain from adding, *I won't keep secrets from you . . .*

Does he like me? His behaviour in Monaco when he asked me for a drink was strange, and he clearly didn't like me spending time with Luis. Maybe he's just bored and wants some company?

But what if it's not just that? What if it's something more? If he made a move on me, would I have the willpower to say no? Nerves bombard me at the thought.

I don't want to look like I've made too much of an effort, so when I get back to the hotel, I just change into some jeans and throw on my green jumper. I *do* take my hair down, though. What the hell, right?

'Hey,' Will says, stepping aside to let me pass when I turn up at his door. 'I was just looking at the room service menu.' I spy the card in his hand. 'Are you hungry?' he asks.

'Depends what they've got,' I reply.

'Go through, go through,' he says, using the menu card to wave me in the direction of the living area as he shuts the door behind me.

'Wow!' Floor to ceiling windows look out over the city of Shanghai, its vibrant lights shining like multicoloured stars in the darkness. My room is only on the third floor, so I don't have much of a view, whereas Will is up on the forty-third.

The living room is softly lit by myriad table lamps. There's a two-seater, soft cream leather sofa and a yellow fibreglass Eames chair in front of a large television. I opt for the sofa, thinking he can have the hard chair if he wants it. But he slumps down on the sofa to my right, making me move involuntarily a little to my left.

'Can I have a look, then?' I nod at the menu.

'Sure.' He puts it in front of me, but doesn't let go, shifting in closer so he can continue to study his options. I feel distinctly on edge and struggle to stop myself from moving away again.

'What are you having?' I glance at him, sideways. He looks back at me with those beautiful blue eyes and my stomach flips.

'Um . . .' He studies the menu again. 'I'll have a burger,' he decides, letting go of the card so that I'm left holding it. He shifts back to his side of the sofa and I stifle a sigh of relief.

'I'll have the same.' I put the menu down on the dark-wooden coffee table.

'Cool.' He grabs the phone from the side-table next to him and calls room service, placing the order.

I squash myself further into my corner and tuck my feet up underneath myself. Feeling much safer, I turn to face him. He puts his foot up on his opposite knee and looks across at me.

'I missed you after Monaco,' he says.

'I know. You'd already gone when I came back from cleaning up the pits.'

'I was half-expecting you to text me again.'

I shake my head, resolutely. 'Not with your girlfriend around. She might've found that a bit weird.'

'Mmm,' he says dryly, raising his eyebrows.

'What?' I ask, confused by his expression.

'Oh, you don't want to know,' he brushes me off.

'Tell me,' I insist.

'Ah, things are a bit strange between Laura and me at the moment.'

'What do you mean?' I ask cautiously.

'Do you want a drink?' He stands up and goes to the minibar, opening up the fridge and peering inside. He pulls out a bottle of water.

'What is there?' I ask.

'Vodka, whisky, wine . . .'

'I'll just have a Diet Coke.'

He pulls out a can and cracks it open, pouring it into a glass. He brings the glass over and hands it to me, then slumps down again and swigs water straight from the bottle.

'You were saying about your girlfriend?' I prompt, grabbing one of the pale-yellow cushions adorning the sofa and hugging it to my chest.

He puts the bottle on the table.

'Things are a bit weird?'

'Yeah. You know, she doesn't come to many races.' He reaches down and scratches his knee. 'So I'm not used to having her there.'

Oh. Is that all?

But then he sighs and leans back against the sofa, running his hands through his hair and peering up at the ceiling. 'God, Daisy, this is really doing my head in.' He stares at me and we hold eye contact until I break away.

'What's doing your head in?' I ask warily, looking back to find he's still watching me.

He doesn't answer immediately and I hold my nerve. 'You.' That's all he says: 'You.'

'*I'm* doing your head in?' Oh, God. Is this really happening?

He rests his head back on the sofa and continues to stare at me sideways as my heart begins to beat faster.

'I don't understand,' I say to him, desperately needing him to spell it out and avoid any confusion.

But he's silent. And then he reaches over and touches the tips of my fingers with his, sending an electric shock shooting all the way up my arm and into my head. Then he pulls his hand away and stands up, pacing the room.

'Shit, this is a really bad idea. I don't know what I'm doing.' His expression is anguished.

'Do you want me to go?' I ask hesitantly, my heart pounding so loud I can't believe he can't hear it.

'Yes, I think you should go.' He sounds determined.

Shakily I get to my feet and step away from the sofa.

'No, don't.' He comes over to me, but almost immediately walks away again. He looks so confused.

My autopilot kicks in. 'I'll go.'

'Yes, yes, that's a good idea.'

I walk to the door, my head spinning as I reach for the handle. Is he going to stop me? I pause, wavering, then pull on the door so that it opens a crack, letting the harsh fluorescent lighting from the corridor spill into the room. No. He doesn't stop me.

I walk out into the corridor to see one of the hotel's catering staff wheeling a room service trolley in our direction. Never mind. I wouldn't have been able to eat anyway.

Needless to say I barely sleep that night. I cannot for the life of me believe what just happened. How the hell is he going to act now? My head hurts just thinking about it. I can't let my heart hope. I just can't. I keep unwittingly picturing him kissing me and I have to shake my head so it doesn't run away with my thoughts.

I hear Holly come in later, but pretend to be out cold, and that's exactly what she is when I wake up the next morning. I get up quietly and go into the bathroom, feeling overwhelmingly surreal about the night before. She comes in while I'm brushing my teeth.

'You alright?' she murmurs sleepily.

'Um, not really.' If I felt sick with nerves yesterday, that's nothing compared to how I feel now.

'Why?' She yawns. 'What happened last night?'

'Will told me he likes me.' I spit toothpaste out into the basin and rinse my mouth out.

'*What?!*' That wakes her up.

'Well, more or less.'

'Shit! What did you do?'

'Nothing.' I lean back on the basin and cross my arms. 'After that, he asked me to leave.'

'*Really?*'

'Yes. I think he's confused.'

'God.' She stares at me, open-mouthed. 'I wonder how this is going to pan out.'

'You're not the only one.'

She perches on the side of the bath and looks up at me. 'Do you think he'll leave Laura?'

'I don't know.'

'Bloody hell. Childhood sweethearts . . . Over. Kaput!'

I glance down at her, unhappily.

'Will you be able to cope with all the press?' she asks.

'What do you mean?' I sit down on the toilet seat. I don't like being on a different level to her while we're having this conversation.

'Well, you know, Will and Laura are in the papers all the time. They're one of Britain's hottest young celebrity couples. The tabloids are going to go bonkers if they break up.'

I look away from Holly and stare at the door. I'm starting to feel quite nauseous.

'Still . . .' She nudges me, trying to perk me up. 'You'll be William Trust's hot new American girlfriend. Ooh, it'll be like a Jennifer Aniston, Brad Pitt, Angelina Jolie scenario!'

'What? And I'm supposed to be Angelina Jolie? Are you kidding me? Everyone hated her when all that came out! Jennifer Aniston was like a freakin' saint!'

'Everyone likes Angelina Jolie now, though,' Holly says, defensively.

'Yeah, but that took ages! I can't believe we're actually talking about this, anyway. Fancy comparing me to Angelina Jolie.'

'Well, you do have long, dark hair. And Will looks a little bit like Brad Pitt.'

'He does not! I think he looks more like Leonardo DiCaprio.'

Holly considers this thoughtfully. 'Yeah, I know what you mean.'

'Anyway!' I snap. 'I don't know how we got onto that, but you're basically telling me that if I break up Will and Laura's happy relationship, then the whole of Britain will hate me forever.'

'Not forever, maybe just a couple of years.'

'Great.'

I go to the track that morning feeling tense and anxious. I don't know what he'll be like when I see him again, but thankfully I don't have to wait too long. Will walks through the doors and momentarily falters when we make eye contact. Then he continues to walk towards me, raising his hand in a half wave at some of the sponsors to his right.

'Hi,' he says, meeting my eyes for a moment before looking away. He hasn't shaved this morning and stubble graces his jaw.

'You look tired,' I say, wanting to reach over and stroke his face.

'Mmm. Didn't get much sleep.' He stares down at the table.

'At least it's not my fault this time.' I'm trying to make light of the situation.

'Yeah, it is.' He looks up at me and his expression is so troubled that my heart goes out to him.

'What can I get you?' I change the subject in the hope that it'll put him out of his misery.

'Daisy—' he starts, but at that moment Gertrude comes out of the kitchen with more breakfast supplies. 'Just the usual, please,' he says, folding his arms and glancing around behind him while I put his breakfast together.

'Here you go.'

'Thanks.'

He takes his plate and goes to a table, but five minutes later gets up again and heads upstairs to his room. I look over to see he's barely touched his muesli. I toy with the idea of going to see him, but I honestly don't know what to say. After weeks of dreaming about him, this has come to a head in a way that I never expected. I don't want to be the person who breaks Laura's heart. I don't want the whole of Britain to hate me. I don't want to be the other woman. There is no clean way out of this. All I know is that I like him. *Really* like him. And somehow, somewhere, there's got to be a resolution.

I want to stay away from the pits during qualifying to allow Will to concentrate, but Holly has other ideas.

'Come on,' she says, after the first two qualifying sessions have taken place. 'Will is quickest, but Luis is ridiculously close. Q3 is going to be really exciting.'

'I don't want to distract him,' I say.

She grins at me. 'Daisy, are we talking about the same guy? He's far too focussed to let you put him off! He's the quickest out there, for goodness' sake.'

Now I feel a bit silly.

'Okay, let's go,' I tell her.

Will is sitting in his car, watching the television screen above his head, when we arrive. I look through to the other garage to see Luis is doing the same. I stare at the back of Will's navy blue and silver helmet, willing him to do well. Luis goes out first and, shortly afterwards, the mechanics send Will out. I'm tense as the television cameras follow Will's lap. It doesn't matter that he was quickest in the last qualifying session. Any one of the nine remaining drivers could easily swipe pole position in the last lap. And then my head starts to spin and I feel dizzy again. Think of something else, think of something else, think of something else . . .

'YAY!' Applause breaks out in the garages.

'Who? What?' I ask, glancing up at the television screens.

'Luis!' Holly shrieks with delight. 'He's on pole!'

My face breaks into a grin. 'Where's Will?'

'Hang on,' she says, eyes glued to the screen. I look up just in time to see Will beat Luis's lap time.

'Pole!' Holly and I shout at the same time. So that relegates Luis down to second. Another stellar one/two start tomorrow.

The cars roar down the pit lane and turn into the garages. Happiness bubbles over inside me as I watch Will leap out of his car to back slaps from his team-mates. He rips off his helmet and is grinning as he pushes his damp hair back, then he glances my way, before turning his attention to Simon.

'Simon is going to be *so* pleased,' Holly says, watching as the team boss pats Will on his arm. 'As long as Will and Luis don't take each other out again tomorrow,' she adds darkly.

I glance through to Luis's garage to see him having an intense discussion with his engineer, then I hear Simon's voice behind me. 'Maybe you should go the whole hog and grow a beard, if that's the result you're going to get.'

Simon and Will are at the nearby catering table. Will shakes his head good-naturedly as he helps himself to a glass of orange squash.

'Ah, Holly, there you are,' Simon says. 'Did you manage to sort out that thing for me?'

'Er, yeah.' She looks uncomfortable as she follows him out of the garages.

I turn to Will. He scratches his stubble and raises his eyebrows. 'Guess I'd better shave before the race tomorrow.'

'Don't,' I whisper, checking no one is in earshot. 'I think you look really sexy like that.'

He chuckles and looks down at a platter of biscuits.

'Still no goddamn custard creams, bun tart!'

I spin around to see Luis.

'My mother would be so disappointed in you.' He squeezes himself between Will and I. 'What were you two gossiping about?'

'Nothing,' we both say in unison.

'Doesn't look like nothing to me,' he says.

'Well, if you must know,' I reply, 'we were talking about Will not having a shave this morning.'

'Yeah, what's with that?' Luis studies him.

Will shrugs. 'Just didn't get around to it.'

'No girlfriend here to keep you in check, hey?'

Will glares at him and stalks out of the garage.

I give Luis a look.

'What's up with him?' he asks innocently.

'You don't want to know.' I make to leave, but Luis pulls me back.

'Hey, where are you going?'

'Back to work.'

'Stay and chat to me a minute.'

I pause. 'Okay, what do you want to chat about?'

'What's going on with you two?' He nods towards the door that Will has just walked out of.

'Nothing,' I snap, then change the subject. 'I just saw Simon grab Holly.'

'What, literally?'

'No, no, he just wanted to talk to her in private.'

'Bet she's pissed off Catalina's here.'

'She is.' I glance at the door. I wonder if I can catch up with Will before he retires to his room again? 'I'd better get on,' I tell Luis. But when I walk out into the bright sunlight, Will is nowhere to be seen.

Chapter 16

Holly and I are in the lobby, waiting for the lads to come down. I don't want to go out tonight, but I heard Will is attending some charity event anyway, so I need something to take my mind off him.

The lift beeps to announce its arrival. 'Here they are,' Holly says. 'Hurry up! You take longer than us to get ready!' she shouts as they pile out of the ornately carved golden lift doors. I start when I see Will with them, wearing a slim-fitting, expensive-looking black suit with a white shirt.

'What are you doing?' I ask in surprise. 'Aren't you going to some event tonight?'

'Yeah, I am. I'm just waiting for Simon.'

'Oh.' The disappointment is even more immense after that little spark of hope.

'Nice dress,' he comments.

'Thanks,' I answer absent-mindedly. I'm wearing a red dress with a hemline that falls just above my knee. Everyone starts to move outside to the waiting cars. I stay where I am, reluctant to leave Will.

'Hey,' he says quietly, 'we still need to talk.'

'Mmm.' I look at him, then glance awkwardly after the others. 'Are you sure you can't come with us?' I ask quickly.

'No.' He shakes his head. 'I don't think I'll be out late, though. What about you?'

'Um, I don't know.' I see Holly looking back at me through the enormous lobby windows as the lads pile into the waiting cars. I feel horribly on edge.

'I could text you when I get back? See where you are?' Will suggests.

The weight lifts off my shoulders. 'That's a good idea,' I say, breathing a sigh of relief. 'I'd better go.'

'Okay.' And then he ever-so-lightly traces his thumb down my bare arm, making the hairs stand up on the back of my neck. I look around nervously to make sure no one saw and then hurry outside to join the others.

The wait for that text is torturous.

'Why don't you just go back to the hotel?' Holly snaps eventually. She's not very impressed with me. She knows my mind is on other things.

'Maybe I should.'

'Go on, then.' She waves me away as I slide out of the booth we're sitting in.

'Sorry,' I apologise, but she doesn't answer.

I've been checking my phone constantly for the last two hours, but haven't heard anything from Will. There's every chance he's changed his mind and doesn't want to see me after all, but I'm trying not to think about that. I just want to see him, to find out where his head is at. There's so much we need to talk about.

I get back to my hotel room and pace the floor, then lie down on the bed and turn on the television. I can't be bothered to change out of my dress. I flick through the channels until I come across *The Beach.* Leonardo DiCaprio with his top off, that should take my mind off things, right? But no, it doesn't.

When I hear a key turn in the lock after forty-five minutes, I sit up, startled. But it's just Holly arriving back.

'You're early?' I say.

'Yeah.' She doesn't look that happy. 'He hasn't texted you, then?' she asks wryly.

'No, not yet.' What if he's not going to?

She comes in and kicks off her shoes. Suddenly there's a knock at the door. She turns back to answer it.

'Oh, hello!' She sounds surprised.

'Is Daisy there?' I hear Will ask, and I sit upright in bed.

He's here!

'I was wondering if she knows where my team shirts are.'

'Sure you were,' Holly says wryly, stepping aside to let him pass.

I stand up and give her an annoyed little look for making Will feel uncomfortable. 'Do you want me to come and have a look for them?' I ask.

'Sure, if that's okay.'

'She knows,' I say to Will once we're in the lift.

'She knows?' he looks at me in horror. 'You told her?'

'Yeah,' I say nonchalantly. 'She won't tell anyone.'

'You told her about me, yet you won't even tell her who you used to work for?'

I shift on my feet. I actually feel quite guilty that Luis knows about Johnny when Will doesn't.

He doesn't say anything else, though, and soon we arrive at his room.

'Have you really lost your team shirts or was that just an excuse?' I ask.

'The latter,' he says bluntly, unlocking the door.

'I thought you were going to text me?'

'I forgot to charge my phone.'

His suite is messier than it was yesterday evening. Clothes are trailed across the bed and sofa.

'Couldn't you decide what to wear tonight?' I ask him as I survey the scene.

'Er, no, I just couldn't find my shirt.'

'You shaved, then.' I glance at his face.

'Thought I'd better.'

Shame. I twirl my hair around my fingers and stand there, waiting for him to say something.

'Sit down, sit down,' he says eventually, bundling up the clothes from the sofa and chucking them through onto his bed. 'Actually, I'm just going to put on something a little less poncey.' He goes into the bedroom and returns a short while later wearing jeans and a black T-shirt. He sits down at the other end of the sofa.

'Here we are again,' I say.

He raises his eyebrows and smiles. 'Fancy a burger?'

I laugh. 'No thanks.'

He leans back against the armrest and puts his feet up on the sofa so they're nearly touching my bum. I'm sitting with my legs crossed. I glance across at him.

'Comfy, there?'

'Yeah, not bad.'

I take my shoes off and do the same so I'm facing him, my knees in between his. We're not touching, but are not far off.

'How was the do tonight?' I feel more comfortable sticking to small talk for the moment. I'm sure Will's the same.

'It was alright.'

'You have to go to a lot of those things during race weekends, don't you?'

'A fair few. And a fair few when I'm not racing, too.'

'Is that because your girlfriend organises a lot of them?' My stomach tenses up.

'One of the reasons.'

'Have you spoken to her about any of this?' So much for small talk.

'No.' He frowns. 'Not yet.'

'Not yet?'

'I'm not going to cheat on her, if that's what you're asking. Not that I expect anything to happen between us,' he hurriedly adds. 'I just mean . . .'

'I know what you mean.'

He sighs.

'Was she your first girlfriend?'

He nods. 'Yeah.'

'You've never been with anyone else?'

'Well . . . You're going to think I'm a bastard, but I was unfaithful to her, once. I told her about it,' he hastens to add. 'And she forgave me. Well,' he humphs, 'only after she'd got me back by sleeping with someone else.'

That's a bit feisty of her. I wouldn't have expected her to have it in her.

'Who did you cheat on her with?' I ask.

'She was just a girl,' he replies. That's not very specific, is it? 'I haven't done it since.'

I stare across at him and then ask a pertinent question, 'Are you going to end it with Laura?'

He meets my eyes before replying, 'I guess that depends on you.'

'Me?'

He shakes his head. 'I don't even know how you feel about me.'

I lean my head against the sofa, coyly. 'I can't believe you can't tell.'

My knees fall to one side so they're resting against his. He closes his other knee in on me so we're lying there, intertwined. I'm all jittery inside. He reaches over and takes my hand, pushing his fingers through mine. It's blissful, like I'm experiencing my first high school crush all over again.

We lie there in silence for a moment, just staring at each other. An image of Laura's face flicks through my mind and I feel a twinge of guilt before pushing it out again.

Eventually I sit up and he does, too. I tuck my legs back underneath myself and move closer to him on the sofa, so my knees are touching his left thigh. He casually rests his right ankle on his opposite knee and takes my hand again, looking at me sideways. I sit there and let him trace his forefinger in circles on my palm.

'Do you remember when I fell off my scooter?' I ask, smiling.

'Mmm.' His tone is wry.

'You held my hand, like you're doing now.'

'Did I?'

'Yes. That was the moment I fell for you.'

'Seriously?' He raises his eyebrows in surprise.

'Yep. Instantly.'

'Huh.'

'What about you?' I ask.

He thinks for a moment. 'I think it was at your nonna's place. When you came out of the house wearing that green jumper. It matched the colour of your eyes, and you had your hair down . . .'

I gaze across at him, but his expression changes and he looks away. His grip on my hand goes limp.

I take my hand away and move back a little on the sofa so I'm no longer touching him. 'Do you want me to go?' It's like déjà vu, this.

'No,' he replies, looking across at me with regret in his eyes. 'But I think you should. You know, until I sort it out with . . .' His voice trails off and I'm glad he doesn't say her name.

'Of course. I understand.' I get to my feet and walk to the door. 'Good luck for the race tomorrow,' I say as he stands up and comes to the door.

'You'll see me in the morning.' He smiles ruefully.

'Okay, well, night.' I reach for the door handle, but he leans against the door, folding his arms and staring at me.

'What?' I ask.

'Maybe we should have a goodnight kiss . . .'

I don't speak, just stare at him, and my silence appears to be all the encouragement he needs to move forward and take my face in his hands.

He kisses me, slowly, languidly, his tongue touching mine so lightly that it sends electric sparks tingling throughout my entire body. He runs his fingers through my hair and down my back, and then he pulls me back to the sofa and I'm on top of him. He pushes the hemline of my red dress up and over my bare legs as his kiss deepens and becomes more intense. I reach down to his jeans and unbutton them, unable to wait any longer. I want his T-shirt off. Right now. He tugs it over his head and is kissing me again as I run my hands over his smooth, toned chest.

'Take your knickers off,' he whispers into my ear. I stand up and do as he says, while he shrugs off his jeans. I straddle him again and can feel him pressing against me, with only the flimsy fabric of his Calvin Kleins keeping us apart.

I want him so much . . .

'Let's go to the bedroom,' he says, but as I jump up to follow him, smoothing down my dress as he leads the way, niggly doubts start to race through my mind. I try to ignore them, but I can't, and they're bothering me. Maybe we should wait. Maybe we should wait until it's all over between him and Laura.

We reach the bedroom and he turns back to see me hesitating.

'What's wrong?' he asks.

'I don't know.'

His face falls and I suddenly feel very much like I'd like my underwear back on. I turn and hurry back out of the bedroom and over to the sofa to retrieve it. I can't meet Will's eyes as I hand him his clothes. I wait anxiously while he turns his black T-shirt the right way out before pulling it over his head. He steps into his jeans and buttons them up.

I walk to the door, my heart throbbing with disappointment, even though it's all my own doing. My hand takes the handle and pushes down, then I look back to find him right behind me. He leans against the door and gently runs his fingers down my spine as he looks into my eyes.

'I can't believe I'm letting you go,' he says.

'I can't believe it either,' I reply. 'But it's the right thing to do.' He pushes himself off the door and steps back, while I walk out onto the landing feeling regret course through my blood like a drug.

Chapter 17

Will won the race the next day, but Luis didn't give it up without a fight. Holly told me afterwards that Simon had to order Luis to back off at one point, not wanting a repeat of Monaco. She also said that after the race, Luis went ballistic with anger and he and Simon had a massive barney. Luis flew back to Brazil instead of returning to the UK for testing. The team had hired a racetrack to test some new car components they'd fitted – it's something each team does at some stage, to make sure everything is reliable and effective. Luis was supposed to do some laps in the car himself, but in the end, the team's test driver, a Frenchman called Pierre, had to do it all.

I don't even bother to ask Holly how she knows all of this anymore. Anyway, maybe it will do Luis good to have a break and see his baby niece for the first time, although the last thing any driver should do is fall out with the team boss, especially when your contract expires at the end of the season.

As for me, I'm back in the UK myself and it's a relief because I don't have to get on another flight until we go to the German Grand Prix in July – a whole month away. The next race on the calendar is the British Grand Prix and Frederick and Ingrid have been keeping me busy with lots of catering jobs in the interim. It's a far cry from the work I do on the Formula 1 circuit and can vary from ten ladies who lunch to dinnertime ballroom glitz for a thousand people. It's solely waitressing though – no actual food prep involved – so I don't really enjoy it.

I haven't heard from Will and it's been seriously doing my head in. The second week after China was the hardest. After the race he pulled me aside to tell me he needed some space to talk to Laura, but would give me a call when he could. I thought a week would be more than enough time, but two weeks later, I'm starting to seriously ask if he's changed his mind about me completely.

My other horrible news is that my landlord is throwing me out. He's putting my flat on the market, and as I can't afford to buy it, I have to start searching for a new place immediately. I'm devastated. It may only be a tiny studio flat, but it's warm and it's sunny and I like it. I have been to look at a few places, but they were all either damp and dingy or way out of my price range so I've had to keep looking. Luckily, Holly has told me I can always stay with her if I'm stuck. I may have to take her up on it at this rate.

On Sunday, the week before the British Grand Prix, I'm on my way into Camden to pick up some supplies for a rare night in when I walk past a newsagent's. My feet come to an automatic stop when I see Will's face staring out from one of the newspapers. Someone has put one of the papers back on the shelf the wrong way, and a story about him is gracing the front of the sports pages. I know I shouldn't, but I can't help myself. I pull it off the shelf and study the picture of Will. He looks different again. It's so strange, but pictures just don't capture what he looks like in person.

'Are you going to buy that?' the man behind the counter calls.

I huffily go to the cash desk, getting the correct change out of my purse, then I leave the shop with my head engrossed in the story.

It's perfectly harmless, all about Will and how the nation is backing him to win. The Brits don't like Luis too much, from what I can gather, and want Will to knock him off the top of the championship at the next couple of races. This is the last year that the British Grand Prix will be held at Silverstone before it moves to another venue and the organisers are desperate for a Brit to win. Blah, blah, blah, and then I see the italic smallprint at the end of the story:

Go to page 23 for Will's stunning girlfriend Laura's hot summer style tips . . .

Crap. I flick to page 23 and there she is: beautiful, blonde and slim, wearing six different outfits of varying colours and styles. I pass a bin and impulsively stuff the paper in it, feeling disgusted with myself. My phone rings. I pause on the street and rummage around in my handbag to get it out. It's Holly.

'Have you found a place yet?' she asks. 'No,' I answer woefully. A bus whizzes past and I don't hold my breath fast enough to avoid breathing in the fumes.

'And how long is it before your landlord kicks you out?'

'Ten days.'

'Shit. You haven't got long.'

'Tell me about it.'

'At least there's a few weeks' break before we head to Hockenheim.'

'True,' I concede. 'Is it still okay for me to crash at yours if I'm stuck?'

'Er, yeah, that should be okay,' she answers.

Oh, no. She doesn't sound too keen.

'Are you sure?' I check again.

'Yes, it's fine.' Again, not very convincing. I'll be seriously screwed if I can't stay with her. I wonder if it's because she and Simon have been shagging round at hers? *Cazzo*! I wish she'd just be honest with me!

'Are you still there?' Holly interrupts my train of thought.

'Yes, I'm here. Don't worry, I'm going to see another estate agent this afternoon.'

'Cool,' she replies.

'I've gotta go. I'm outside the supermarket and I need to pick up some ravioli for dinner.'

'Okay. Chat soon.'

'Bye.'

I hang up unhappily and stuff my phone back into my bag as I walk through the supermarket doors. My phone rings again. I distractedly snap it open without even looking at the caller ID.

'Hello?'

'Daisy?'

I halt in my tracks. 'Will?'

'Hi,' he says. 'Is this an okay time to talk?'

'Um . . .' I look around at my surroundings and then quickly walk back outside. 'Yes, sure.'

'Where are you?'

'Just at the supermarket, getting some pasta for my tea.'

'Sounds nice. Wish I could join you.'

'Do you?' My heart flutters. I lean up against the wall. It's dirty with pollution, but like I care about that right now.

'I'm sorry I haven't called before. I've had a lot going on.'

'I understand.' Well, I'm trying to. 'Have you spoken to . . .?' I ask hopefully.

'Yeah.' My heart lifts. 'Well, kind of.' And falls flat again.

'Kind of?'

'It's been . . . Difficult.'

What does that mean? I don't speak.

'Daisy? Are you there?'

'Yes. I'm here.'

'Where are you exactly? There's a lot of background noise.'

'I'm on a street in Camden. There are a bunch of cars going past.'

'Will you be home soon?'

A Number 29 bus pulls up a few feet away. To hell with the ravioli. 'I'll be home in ten.'

'I'll call you back.'

'Okay.' I hang up and make a run for the bus.

He doesn't call me in ten. He doesn't call me in fifteen, either. By twenty I'm practically climbing the walls. Finally, he calls.

'Hello?'

'Hi. Are you home?'

I've been home forever, you idiot! 'Just,' I fib.

'Cool.'

'So what's going on?' I sit down on the sofa and wrap my left arm around my knees.

I hear him sigh. 'It feels like ages since I've seen you.'

My heart swells with happiness. I've been so worried he'd gone off me.

'Won't be long, now,' I say. 'What day are you coming to Silverstone?'

'I'll be there Thursday morning.'

'Really? Brilliant!'

'Yeah, I've got some interviews and stuff to do. And it'll be nice to see you again.'

I beam and tap my fingers impatiently on my leg. So much small talk, so many big things to say.

'What else is up?' I pause. 'Are you going to tell me what happened?'

'With Laura?'

I still flinch when he says her name. 'Yes.'

'Well, you know things were a bit strained at Monaco?'

'I didn't, but go on.'

'She wanted to talk to me after that, but it was so hectic between then and Shanghai. We finally got a chance to catch up when I got back from China, and after everything that had happened with you, she could tell we had a problem.'

We had a problem . . .

'Okay,' I say, willing him to continue.

'I told her I thought it was over.'

I hold my breath.

'She was pretty upset.'

From the sound of his voice, I can tell that's an understatement.

'It was a bit traumatic.'

Now I feel awful. I don't want to cause her pain. But holy shit! Has he *split up* with her?

He continues. 'She wanted another chance. I said I didn't think so, that we'd been growing apart for some time, and she begged me to consider taking a break.'

My stomach freefalls. 'A break? As in to get back together again afterwards?'

'That's what she's hoping, but it won't happen.'

Take a deep breath, Daisy. Calm down. 'Did you tell her that?'

'Well,' he sighs, 'there are other complications.'

I can't bear this!

'Yes?'

'She's organising a charity event at Silverstone.'

'Right . . .' Oh, here we go.

'A lot of people are going because . . . of me. I know that sounds conceited, but . . .'

'No, I know,' I say reluctantly. 'It's true.'

'So if we're not together anymore . . .' His voice trails off again. I can see where he's going with this.

'I understand.' My voice is monotone as the light at the end of the tunnel dims, flickers and then goes out completely. 'You have to keep up pretences.'

'Daisy, I'm sorry.'

'It's okay.'

'No, I know it's going to be difficult. Especially after China and everything that happened there.'

'Or didn't happen,' I interject wryly.

There's silence on the other end of the line, and then he speaks. 'It will be different after the British Grand Prix. I promise.'

'Okay.' That's all I say.

'See you on Thursday?' he asks hopefully.

'Of course.' I try not to let him hear the disappointment in my voice.

So it's with a certain amount of trepidation that I arrive at the track on Wednesday afternoon. I tell Holly about our exchange because there's no point in keeping it from her.

'That's not going to be pleasant,' she says. 'Seeing Laura get all the attention this weekend.'

'Hopefully it won't be too bad.'

'Daisy, you're living in a dream world. I don't think you know fully what you're dealing with when it comes to Will and Laura and the British press.'

'Yes, yes, I know, they're like royalty and all that.'

'Well, if you want a reality check to see what you're getting yourself into, I guess this is the way to do it,' Holly comments.

'I *don't* want a reality check, thanks very much. I just want Will. After that I'll bury my head in the sand and won't have to deal with it.'

'Whatever you say, pal, whatever you say. I just hope he's worth it.'

A shiver goes through me as I remember our kiss and the feeling of him pressed up against me.

'He is,' I tell her firmly.

On Thursday morning I'm upstairs in the director's suite, tidying away some coffee cups, when someone grabs my waist from behind.

'Argh! Will!' I leap away in shock. 'You scared the life out of me!'

He just regards me with amusement. 'Sorry, I heard you were up here.' He sits on the table that I've been precariously piling crockery upon. 'How are you?'

'Okay, thanks.' I look away, suddenly feeling shy. 'You?' I glance up at him.

'Alright, yeah. Do you need help carrying those down?' He nods at the cups.

'No, I'll be fine. When did you get here?'

'A little while ago. I've got to head over to the BRDC' – that's the British Racing Drivers' Club – 'in a minute for an interview.'

'Is . . . Laura here, yet?'

'No. She arrives tomorrow.'

I look down.

'What are you up to tonight?' he asks.

'I don't know, why?'

'Do you want to have dinner with me?'

'Won't that be a bit dodgy if we get spotted?'

'I know a little pub about forty minutes from here. It's very small and full of locals. I doubt anyone will pay attention to us.'

'In that case, I'd love to.' I can't keep the smile from my face.

'You're staying at the hotel, right?' he asks, hopping down from the table.

'Yes, aren't you?'

'I have a room there, yeah. Shall I come and get you at around eight?'

'Sure. I should be finished by then. Room twenty-three.'

'Cool.'

I don't know what the pub is like, but I'm guessing it's a no-frills affair so I opt for my black Rock & Republic jeans and an emerald green top from Reiss. I remember what Will said about green and the colour of my eyes and as it's a warm night in early July, I don't need long sleeves.

I'm staying on the ground floor of the hotel and the car park is just behind my room. Will leads me towards a black Porsche, pointing his key at it and unlocking the doors with a bleep.

'Nice car,' I say, climbing inside.

He starts it up, glancing across at me with a cheeky grin. 'Do you like the colour?'

'Oh, bugger off.'

He chuckles and pulls out of the car park. It's still light and I watch as the countryside whizzes past outside my window. We drive through villages and past farms and fields until we finally pull up outside a little stone pub. There's smoke coming out of the chimney, despite the fact that it's the middle of summer. I follow Will inside and he leads me to a table, tucked away in a corner with a view of the rolling hills spread out before us.

A waitress comes over to take our order.

'Sorry, we haven't had a chance to look at the menu yet,' Will says.

'I'll come back in a minute,' she replies. She walks away and glances back over her shoulder at us. Will gives me an uneasy look.

'Do you think she recognised you?' I ask.

'I don't know. Maybe I should put my cap on.'

'No, too obvious.'

We study the menu, but I can tell he's on edge. There won't be any hand-holding across the table tonight, that's for sure.

We place our order and then I stare out of the window. The sun is just starting to dip below the far-off horizon.

'What have you been up to since China?' Will asks.

'Flat-hunting.' I tell him my whole sorry saga.

'Why wouldn't Holly want you to stay with her?' He looks confused.

Oh, *cazzo*. He doesn't know about Holly and Simon's affair.

'I think she just likes her space.' I don't like lying to him, but I can't betray my friend.

'Why don't you stay in a hotel for a bit?'

'I can't really afford that,' I tell him.

He gives me an odd look. 'Well, I'll help out if that makes things any easier.'

'No!' My reply is instinctive, although I'm touched.

'Why not? It's not like I don't have enough to go round. Come and stay nearby so we can see each other.'

Well now, that would be *lovely* . . .

'I would say you could stay at my place, but it's probably a little soon.'

'Oh, yeah,' I brush him off, 'definitely too soon for that.'

He laughs and glances over to the bar area. I follow his gaze to see our waitress and the bartender talking and looking our way.

'Bollocks,' he mutters. 'I thought we'd be okay here.'

'It doesn't look good, does it? I know.' I pull a notepad out of my handbag.

'What are you doing?' he asks.

'Let's make it look like we're having a business meeting.'

'Good plan.'

But we can't relax after that, and we leave soon after we've eaten.

'I could do with an early night, anyway,' he tells me as we pull into the hotel car park.

'It's going to be very early at this rate.'

'I think I might drive back to London,' he says.

'Really?' I'm surprised.

'Yeah, I don't have to be at the track until ten o'clock tomorrow, and it'd be nice to be home for a change.'

'Are you going right now?' He hasn't turned the ignition off.

'May as well. I don't need anything from my room.'

'Okay, then.' I open the door and hesitate for a second, wondering if he might kiss me. But he doesn't, so I climb out. 'See you tomorrow.'

'Night.'

I close the door and I hear the low growl of the Porsche pulling away behind me as I walk back into the hotel. That wasn't exactly a night to remember after all that waiting . . .

The next morning, Luis arrives before Will.

'Have you seen my spare helmet anywhere?' he asks me.

'No. Isn't it upstairs?'

'No. I don't *think* I left it behind in China . . .'

'I doubt you would have done that,' I reply. 'Anyway, what's wrong with your other one?'

'Some of the stickers are coming unstuck. And it's a bit grubby.'

'Want me to have a look at it for you?'

He shrugs. 'If you wouldn't mind.'

I turn to Holly. She nods, having overheard. I follow Luis up the stairs to his room. 'Where is it?'

'Here.' He hands it to me.

'It looks alright,' I say.

'No, look.' He snatches the helmet back and smoothes down the corner of one sponsorship sticker which is very, very slightly raised up.

'Give it here.' I hold my hand out for the helmet and he complies, then I perch on a chair and give it a good polish.

'So how are you after China?' I ask. 'I heard you had a bit of a run-in with Simon?'

'Where did you hear that?' He looks annoyed.

'Holly,' I reply, and he rolls his eyes.

'Yeah, well, he's screwing up my championship chances.'

'That's not *strictly* true, is it?'

'That's what it felt like at the time.'

'Anyway, you got back to Brazil? Was it nice? Did you see your niece?'

'Yeah. Cute little thing. So light!'

'Light?'

'As in, not heavy. Tiny! Yeah, it was good to get home for a bit.'

'How are your parents?'

'Fine. Mãe told me off for giving you stick about the biscuits.'

'Did she?' I laugh. 'So how do you feel about being on Will's home turf? Worried?'

'Ha! He's the one who should be worried.'

I smirk and turn my attention back to the job at hand. 'I think you're going to have to replace it with a new one.' I'm referring to the sticker, not the helmet.

'I could have told you that ages ago.'

I stand up. 'I'll sort it for you.' He also gets to his feet. '*Thank* you,' I prompt, giving him a meaningful look.

'Thanks,' he replies indifferently. He follows me out of the room and down the stairs, back into the hospitality area, where I'm greeted with the sight of Laura happily chatting away to a group of sponsors.

'Watch it!' Luis exclaims, bumping into me.

'Sorry,' I mutter, averting my gaze. The sponsors all seem to know her – *and* adore her from the looks on their simpering faces.

'Oh,' Luis says, spying the reason for our two-person pile-up.

'I'll get this sorted for you,' I tell him, holding up his helmet and hurrying away. I don't expect him to follow, so I'm surprised when he does. He drags me into the corridor leading to the toilets and spins me around to face him. 'He's never going to leave her, you know.'

I look at him defiantly. 'He already has.'

'What?' he barks.

'He already has left her.'

'Then what the *cazzo* is she doing here?'

I grin involuntarily at the sound of his Italian. 'They're keeping it quiet until after Silverstone. She's got some charity event going on.'

Luis scoffs.

'It's true,' I continue. 'Ask him yourself if you don't believe me. But don't tell anyone else. She doesn't know about me yet,' I add, to which Luis gives me a wry look. 'What?' I ask defensively. 'It's too soon for him to tell her.'

He nods. 'So you just have to be bun tart this weekend while she sits back and acts like a princess? That'll be fun,' he adds, sarcasm dripping from his voice.

'Well, I didn't say it would be *fun*, Luis, but what choice do I have?'

A woman comes out of the ladies' room and Luis pulls me to one side so she can get past.

'Is she staying at the hotel with him?' he asks suddenly.

'No!' I'm outraged. 'Of course, she isn't!' At least, I don't *think* she is . . .

Luis raises his eyebrows.

'What are you looking like that for?' I demand to know. 'Do *you* know if she's staying at the hotel?' Bile seeps into my throat.

He shakes his head and his lips turn down. 'No . . .'

'Then what's with the questions?' Now I'm angry. When he

doesn't reply I spin around to leave, and at that exact moment, Laura walks around the corner and almost crashes into me.

'Sorry!' she exclaims, putting her hands on my arms to steady us both.

'Excuse me,' I murmur, squeezing past her and scampering back into the safety of the kitchen.

I keep poking my head out of the door to see if I can spy Will, and when I finally do, I make to leave the kitchen.

'Where are you going, now?' Frederick demands to know.

'I, er, just have to go and see Will for a minute,' I stutter.

'Those dishes aren't going to wash themselves,' he snaps.

'No, I'm sorry, I won't be long.' I look at him anxiously, but he turns away. He's obviously been noticing my recent disappearing acts.

I walk out just in time to see Will going up the stairs. I hurry after him, glancing around me to see Laura sitting at a table with Catalina. I hope she doesn't follow him up. I knock on his door and don't wait for him to tell me to enter before pushing it open.

'Is she staying with you? At the hotel?' I barely have time to close the door before I start my interrogation.

'Hi!' He looks startled.

'Just tell me, Will. Is she staying with you?'

He looks uncomfortable. 'She *is* staying at the hotel, yes.'

'In your room?'

He hesitates before answering. 'Yes. But we're not sleeping together.'

'Oh, God.' I feel overwrought. I want to cry. I turn to walk out.

'Daisy, wait!' He gets up and puts his hand on the door, blocking my exit. 'It's not like that.'

'Yes, I know, Will, you're just keeping up appearances. Well, to hell with that! Sorry, but this is too hard!' I try to turn the handle, but he blocks me again.

'Please. It's only for this race. She won't come to any more.'

'I have to go,' I say dully. 'I have to get back to work.'

'Stay for a minute,' he begs, putting his hand on my arm. I can't look at him.

'No. Frederick's getting annoyed with me.'

'Is he?'

'Yes.'

'Okay.' He lets go of my arm and I walk out, feeling even worse than I did when I walked in.

I refuse to go out that night, preferring to stay in my hotel room and torture myself with my thoughts instead. It's the night of Laura's charity do, and everyone who's anyone is going. Holly is furious because Simon is attending it with Catalina. Not that she's telling me that, mind. She's out drowning her sorrows with Pete and the lads. The next morning, both of us are in horrible moods when we arrive at the track. It's Saturday, the day for qualifying, and a huge turnout is expected in Will's honour.

I'm outside at the serving table when Will and Laura appear together. I'm guessing he gave her a lift into the track from the hotel. He flashes me an awkward glance, then stops to talk to Simon at a nearby table. A moment later he turns around to speak to a man and a woman who walked in the door behind him. He says something to them and points in my direction, then pulls up a chair at Simon's table. Laura leads them my way and they're almost upon me before I realise they could be Will's parents.

They appear to be in their late fifties and are both wearing smart tweed suits with pristine white shirts. The woman has a matching tweed hat.

'Good morning,' I say brightly, hoping to make a good impression.

Neither of them answer, but the woman looks me up and down, disdainfully.

'Hello,' Laura says to me. 'Daisy, isn't it?'

'Yes,' I reply, taken aback. I don't want her to be nice enough to remember my name.

She turns to the woman. 'What would you like?'

'I'll take a tea,' she replies, in an upper-crust British accent.

'Mr Trust?' Laura asks. Doesn't she even call them by their first names?

'Yes, that'll do.' His tone is curt.

'Three teas, please,' Laura says to me, forcing a smile. She looks as uncomfortable as I feel. Considering she's known Will's parents most of her life, I don't fancy *my* chances much.

I pick up the teapot and begin pouring the tea, before remembering to ask if they take milk.

'Start again,' Will's mother insists, glaring at the half-full teacups in front of her.

'Sorry,' I mutter, feeling my face heat up as Laura fidgets with her gold bracelet in front of me. I wonder if Will bought it for her? Trying not to be distracted by that thought, I put the spoiled cups to one side and pour in a little milk before adding the tea this time. I pass them over, aware that my hands are shaking.

Will's mother glances at Laura and a small smile forms on her lips. I'm about to breathe a sigh of relief when she says, 'One couldn't expect an American to make a decent cup of tea, could one?'

Laura smiles awkwardly and leads them away, giving me a sympathetic look over her shoulder.

'They look like they've got – what do you say? – pokers shoved up their arses.' Luis appears out of nowhere.

I meet his eyes and my nose starts to prickle. Oh God, please don't cry. He looks shocked as he realises I'm about to do just that, but I quickly rush off to the bathroom.

No, no, no, I tell myself after I've locked the door and sat down on the seat. I will not cry. This is ridiculous. I haven't cried over him yet, and I can handle this situation. The end is nigh, Daisy, the end is nigh! I wave my hands in front of my face and try not to be melodramatic. Happy things. Think happy things. Puppies, kittens . . . I've always wanted a pet, but my father wouldn't let me. No! That's not a happy thought! Nonna . . . Nice Nonna. I miss her. I hardly ever see her. No! Another horrid thought! Holly . . . Laughing, smiling Holly . . . Who's lying to me about her relationship with a married man. Argh! Luis and I in Monaco pestering the French bartender for new swear words. I start to smirk and moments later feel better about returning outside. Luis has gone, but Holly looks at me with concern.

'Don't give me any sympathy,' I warn. She understands it will only set me off again, so we work away in silence.

Mr and Mrs Trust are sitting with Laura at a table. Will isn't with them, but after a while he comes downstairs kitted out in his racing gear. He goes straight over to them.

'I have to get to the pits for qualifying,' I overhear him say. 'Would you like to come?'

'Fine, yes,' his mother replies, sipping the last of her tea. She turns to Laura. 'Will you join us?'

'Yes. Thank you.' Laura smiles and all three stand up. Will doesn't look my way as they follow him out of the hospitality area.

'Are you coming to watch qualifying?' Holly asks as soon as they're out of eyesight.

'No.' My reply is blunt. I damn well won't.

It was an exciting session, I discover later, when team members start to spill back into the hospitality area. Will sneaked pole position with Luis less than one tenth of a second behind him, so he'll start in second place on the grid tomorrow. I don't feel as happy as I know I should. My run-in with Will's parents has left a seriously nasty taste in my mouth, and the other thing that's bothering me is how I feel about Laura. She seems like a nice person and if *I* feel bad about breaking her heart, how is everyone else going to feel about me?

Will is completely oblivious to my dilemma when he returns from the pits with a spring in his step. He comes over to me, grinning.

'Did you see it?'

'No, I was here. Well done,' I add unsmiling.

He gives me a querying look, but doesn't say anything because people are in earshot. 'Can you sort me out with a team shirt?' he prompts eventually.

'Now?'

'Yes, please.'

I come out from behind the serving table and stalk off towards the stairs.

'What's up with you?' he asks as soon as we're inside his private room.

'I met your parents,' I reply sombrely.

'Were they okay with you?'

'Not really, Will. I get the feeling they don't like Americans very much.'

'Well . . .' He looks away from me. 'I told you what they were like.'

'I didn't think they'd be *that* bad. And they're going to hate me even more when they discover . . .' I can feel myself getting slightly hysterical now.

'It will be alright,' he lies. 'Anyway, I don't care what my parents think. If my dad writes me out of his will, fuck it!'

'Writes you out of his will?' I ask, horrified. 'Would it really come to that? Over your relationship with me?'

'Calm down,' he insists, putting his hands on my arms. I shrug him off. 'I can't handle this.' I turn to leave. 'It's all too much, Will.'

'Daisy, please . . .' He tries to grab my hand, but I won't let him. I start to open the door, but he slams it shut again.

'You almost got my fingers!' I squawk.

'Sorry,' he says. 'Just wait a minute, would you?' He's frustrated now. I glare at him. 'Why don't we go for a drive tonight? Just the two of us?'

'Oh, that sounds like such a fun night out,' I reply sarcastically.

He frowns at me.

'Did you sleep well last night?' I snap.

'No. I slept on the sofa,' he replies pedantically.

'Did you?' My heart lifts a little.

'Yes, of course.' He takes my hand and pulls me to him, staring into my eyes. I instinctively want to look away, but I steady myself. 'Daisy . . .' He cups my jaw with his hand and strokes the side of my face with his thumb, sending butterflies spiralling through my stomach. 'I'm sorry this is hurting you.'

'It's okay,' I murmur, looking at his lips.

'I just want to be with you,' he says in a low voice, and I stare back at him, feeling like I'm drowning. 'I'll come and get you later.'

He doesn't come and get me, instead I get a text, asking me to meet him in the car park.

'This is very cloak and dagger,' I comment, when we've pulled onto the road and are speeding back down the country lanes. He doesn't reply. 'Where are we going?' I ask.

'Just for a drive,' he says.

'Where does Laura think you've gone?'

'That's what I've told her, too.'

We fall silent for a while. Will reaches across and turns the radio on. The sound of The Verve fills the car.

'Um . . .' he says after a while. I look across at him. 'I've just had a thought.' I wait for him to continue. He glances at me. 'We could go back to mine?'

'What, in Chelsea?'

'Yeah.'

'That's a bit of a trek, isn't it?'

'It'll only take an hour or so.'

'Okay, then.' I sit up straighter in my seat, feeling much happier with this plan. I'm dying to see his house.

But by the time we get there, it's nine thirty and I'm starting to wonder if this was the best idea. Will needs to get his sleep for the race tomorrow and, at this rate, we should probably be turning around and going straight back again.

'What's wrong?' he asks as we step over the threshold into his hall. I tell him my concerns and he shrugs as he kicks off his shoes. 'I'll be okay. Luis manages on barely any sleep, doesn't he?'

I take off my shoes, too, and leave them by the door. 'Yeah, but Luis is Luis.'

'What's that supposed to mean?' He looks irritated.

'Nothing. You two are just a bit different, that's all. Wow, I like your place.' He lives in a white stucco four-storey Victorian townhouse and we've entered on the first – or upper-ground – floor. He takes me straight through to the living room and it's very much a lad's pad, lots of black, white and silver with a humungous flatscreen TV up against the far wall. I go and peer out of one of three, very tall windows, but it's dark outside.

'Do you have a garden?' I ask.

'A small one, yes. It's nice in this weather.'

'I bet.'

'Do you want a drink? Actually, are you hungry? We haven't really eaten anything,' he comments.

'I could cook us something . . .'

'There's not a lot in the fridge.'

'Where's your kitchen?' I ask. 'Let's go and see what you've got.' Spaghetti, onions, garlic, tinned tomatoes, dried herbs and extra virgin olive oil. That'll do. I get on with our meal while he sits at the stainless steel table and watches me. The underfloor heating is keeping my bare feet warm.

'Do you do much cooking for Frederick?' he asks as I plate up our food.

'Not a lot,' I tell him. 'I wish I could do more.'

'Why don't you?'

'Frederick always wants me out front of house.'

'That's because you're so gorgeous.'

I laugh. 'Flattery will get you everywhere.'

'Will it?' he asks flirtatiously.

'Eat your dinner.'

'Mmm. It's really good,' he comments between mouthfuls.

As I look across the table at him, I'm suddenly hit with realisation. He's almost mine. And I didn't even go out of my way to get him. I can barely believe it.

'What time do we need to set off?' I ask after a while.

He pushes spaghetti around on his plate with his fork. 'We could always stay here . . .'

'Here? What? And drive back in the morning?'

'Set off early, yeah. Don't worry, you can sleep in one of the guest rooms,' he says when he sees me wavering.

'No, it's not that,' I reply.

'Isn't it?' He raises one eyebrow at me.

'Stop it, you.' I roll my eyes. 'I want to start with a clean slate.'

'Yeah, me too.' He looks away. 'I'll keep my hands to myself.'

After we've eaten, I text Holly to let her know my plans and then start to wash the dishes while Will goes off to text Laura.

'Did she text you back?' I ask, when he re-enters the kitchen.

'Not yet, no. I doubt she will at this hour. She'll be too pissed off with me.'

I don't say anything, just continue to scrub at the plates.

'Hey, what are you doing?' he says suddenly. 'I've got a dishwasher.'

'Yes, I know, but I didn't think we should leave any evidence of us being here together. You know, in case anyone comes over after the race . . .'

He joins me at the sink and picks up a tea towel, drying the plates as I hand them to him.

When the surfaces have been wiped down and everything put away, I follow him out of the kitchen. He reaches back to switch off the lights and then leads the way up the stairs.

'First floor you've seen . . .' Massive living room area. 'Second floor is all guest bedrooms.' He gives me a quick tour around the three of them. Two have en-suites and there's a third large bathroom.

'Which one should I sleep in?' I ask.

'Take your pick.' He continues up the stairs.

'And this is where I am.' He pushes open the door to the master suite. It's enormous, running from the front to the back of the house with a huge bathroom set off to the right. His giant bed is covered with a bronze bedspread and the furniture is dark mahogany. Very masculine.

'Nice. I like it.'

'Laura thinks it's too boysey.'

I don't say anything.

'Sorry,' he apologises when he sees my face. 'I shouldn't keep bringing her up.'

I sit down on his bed. 'It must be hard. You've known her so many years.'

He sits down beside me and looks ahead solemnly. 'It is a bit sad,' he concedes. 'But these things happen. We've been together so long and, I don't know, we've both changed.'

I turn to look at him. 'Would you have broken up with her if you hadn't met me?'

He glances at me and looks away again. 'I don't know.'

'I feel terrible,' I say suddenly. 'She seems like a really nice girl.'

'She is.' He turns to face me and puts his hand on my knee. 'But you are, too.'

'I don't think anyone else is going to see it like that. Holly thinks the British press are going to hate me.'

Will frowns. 'That's not a very nice thing to say.'

'It's true, though.'

He grins. 'Let's move to Monaco, then.'

I laugh. 'Okay!'

He collapses back on the bed and shuffles up so his head is resting on a pillow. He pats the space next to him so I join him. We stare up at the ceiling as he takes my hand in his.

'Do you ever think you'll go back to America?' he asks.

'I will someday. But not for a while.'

'Do you miss it?'

'No.' My reply is blunt.

A memory flickers back to me of walking through Central Park on a frosty morning in January a few years ago. I was on the phone to my mother and she was telling me that my father wanted me to come home for dinner that night. I told her I was busy, like I usually do, and I now recall the disappointment in her voice.

I know I should call her.

And I also know that I won't.

I shake my head to rid myself of my thoughts.

'What are you thinking about?' Will asks.

'My parents.'

'How long has it been since you've seen them?'

'About three years.'

'Wow.'

'Have you thought any more about coming to stay in a hotel near here?'

'Yes, and I couldn't do that,' I reply.

'Why not?' He shifts to face me.

'I just couldn't, Will.'

'You know what I'm going to do?' He raises one eyebrow, teasingly.

'What are you going to do?'

'I'm going to book you into The Knightsbridge for a month and pay up front. Then you'll have no choice but to stay there.'

'You'd better not,' I say.

'I'm going to.'

'I won't use the room.'

'Yes, you will.' He wraps his arm around me and pulls me to him. I rest my head on his chest and listen to his heartbeat, smiling. It feels so right in his arms. 'Or you could just stay here, with me.'

'I wish I could,' I tell him. 'But that wouldn't be fair on Laura.'

He doesn't say anything for a while, then he speaks.

'I'll have to tell her about you sooner rather than later.'

I prop myself up and look at him. 'Why?'

'She won't accept that our relationship is over unless I do.' He pulls me back down.

'Oh God, everyone's going to think I'm the wicked witch of the west.'

'North-east,' he corrects me.

'Oi!' I slap his stomach and it automatically tenses beneath me. 'It's not funny.'

'Monaco,' he jokes, as he pulls me in tighter.

I smile and relax.

We lie there in silence for a long time until his breathing slows and I glance up to see that his eyes have closed. I start to detach myself.

'Where are you going?' he asks groggily.

'To bed,' I reply. 'You need to sleep.'

'No, stay here.' He pulls me back down and, a moment later, tugs on the bedcovers underneath us, wriggling around until I get up and help him pull them back. We climb under the sheets and snuggle up together again, still fully dressed. Soon the sound of his breathing slows again, but I lie there for a long time afterwards before I finally fall asleep.

In the early hours of the morning, just as the birds are beginning to sing in the trees outside the window, I wake up. Will is sleeping on his side, facing me. I resist the urge to reach over and stroke his face, but then he stirs and his eyes open. We lie there, staring at each other in the darkness for a minute. And then he pulls me to him and we kiss, unspeaking. My whole body tingles as our kiss deepens to become more passionate. And then he's unbuttoning my jeans and I'm doing the same to his, before we both tear off our T-shirts and he lowers himself onto me.

It's intense, so intense, and it's over too quickly. He stays inside me for a while afterwards as our breathing steadies, and then he rolls off and pulls me back into his warm arms.

He soon falls into a deep sleep again, but I doze in and out of slumber until the dawn begins to brighten and light spills underneath the blinds. Will's watch starts to beep and he comes to, stretching his arms over his head so they press up against the headboard. He looks across at me and smiles sleepily.

'We'd better get going.'

I nod and reach for my clothes down the side of the bed. If it weren't for the fact that I'm naked, I would think that what happened between us was just a dream.

'Shall I drop you back to the hotel?' Will asks an hour and a half later. It's six thirty.

'Yeah, that'd be great. We're doing the late shift today.' By late, it means eight o'clock, so it's still disastrous if you've got a hangover.

He drives into the car park.

'You'd better go first,' he says.

I put my hand on the door handle, but he pulls me back.

'If I don't get a chance to speak to you much today, I'll call you tomorrow.'

'Okay.' I turn back to leave.

'Daisy . . .'

'Yes?'

He puts his hand around the back of my neck and pulls me to him, touching his lips to mine. 'See ya later.'

'Bye.'

Chapter 18

'Go on, you can spare another muffin. I'm wasting away here!' The fat American man in front of me cracks up laughing as I stifle a yawn and add a chocolate muffin to the collection of pastries on his plate. Will's parents walk into the hospitality area behind him, making me automatically stiffen as I hand his plate over.

'Thanks, bun tart!' Fatty dissolves into giggles again, before walking away. I'm distracted watching Will's parents stop to talk to Laura.

Will and Laura arrived at the track together again this morning and he didn't meet my eyes. Laura was immaculate, wearing a blue sundress with white trim and white heels, and I'm certain everyone here was thinking that she and Will looked like the perfect couple. I felt a rush of jealousy when I saw her, followed by several sharp pangs of guilt at the thought of what happened last night.

But the jealousy soon prevailed. Laura doesn't seem like someone who's worried they're about to lose the love of their life, and her confidence concerns me. If she's not worried, should I be?

I'm debating whether I can bear to watch the race from the

garages with Laura and Will's parents there when Frederick takes the decision away from me.

'I need you girls doing the catering in the pits. Come and get the supplies from the kitchen, would you?'

By the time we get there, Laura and the Trusts have already settled themselves in Will's half of the garage. I'm bristling with annoyance and jealousy as I set up the catering while the three of them chatter away, ignoring me.

'Come on, let's go and do some celeb spotting,' Holly suggests, aware of my pain. I follow her gladly.

As we climb over the wall that separates the pits from the starting grid, the thought occurs to me that Johnny Jefferson might be milling around the track, seeing as this is his home Grand Prix, but I can't see him, thankfully. That would have been the last straw, I think, although if I had a choice between Johnny or Laura being here, I'd choose the former every time. I'm taking this as proof that I am definitely over him.

Holly and I wander to the front of the grid where we spot Will being interviewed by a television crew. He glances my way but carries on, unfaltering. I dither for a moment before deciding that yes, I do want to wait until he's finished so I can wish him good luck for the race. Holly complies and we lean up against a nearby wall. Luis is being chatted up by some of the brolly dollies. Stunning girls in hotpants and advertisements splayed across their straining T-shirts . . . He's in his element.

'Where's the lovely Laura today?' I hear the interviewer ask Will and my attention is immediately diverted.

'She's in the garage, I think.' Will looks uncomfortable to me, but I'm not sure the interviewer would pick up on it.

'And will we be hearing wedding bells anytime soon?'

What?

'Er, I'd better just concentrate on the racing for now.' Will flashes the interviewer a grin.

Holly and I wait for the interviewer to finish up his piece to camera. Will glances at us and raises his eyebrows. Finally the television crew moves away and we start towards him. But then out of the corner of my eye I see her – the blonde in the blue sundress. I hold Holly back as a smiling Laura reaches Will's side and affectionately rubs his arm. Holly pulls on my hand. 'You're staring,' she says quietly.

I quickly avert my gaze and it falls instead on Luis. He meets my eyes, ignoring the pretty grid girl fawning all over him.

'Let's go,' I mutter to Holly, giving Will one last glance before turning to climb the wall. As we get to the other side, I look back to see Laura departing and Will staring regretfully after me. Then Luis stalks over to Will, his expression furious. I only catch the look of surprise on Will's face before I have to concentrate on getting across the pit lane without bumping into the hordes vacating the grid. What on earth is Luis saying to him?

Will's parents are standing within the lines of the white box painted on the floor of Will's garage. Moments later, Laura joins them. I suddenly feel angry. This isn't right. This isn't right at all.

'Let's go through here,' Holly urges, but I'm rooted to the spot. 'Daisy,' she prompts. I reluctantly follow her. By the time we reach Luis's garage, the cars have set off on their warm-up lap. The camera shows hundreds of race fans in the grandstands blowing whistles and holding up banners in support of Will. My heart starts to beat faster as the camera zooms in on his car.

I don't want to be here.

But I'm not leaving if she's not leaving.

The cars come around the last corner and take their places on the grid, then the lights go out and they're off.

I feel sick. Dizzy. Will makes it around the first corner and keeps his position, but Luis is hot on his tail.

Focus, Daisy! If you leave, they'll win! They'll all win! His parents detest you, Laura barely knows you exist, but you have a right to be here. You should be standing in that box, not them!

I look away from the cars on the television screen and stare at the back of Pete's helmet-encased head, trying to distract myself from the dizziness I'm feeling.

A collective gasp of shock brings me back to my senses. I glance up at the television screen again to see a car turning in the air like a spinning top, car parts shattering and splintering across the track as it smashes into a tyre wall and lands the wrong side up on a gravel pit. The blood drains from my face as I realise it's Will. Flames flicker underneath his car as track marshals clamber across the race wall to get to him.

I'm vaguely aware of Holly's hand on my arm and the sound of Will's mother shrieking in the garage next door.

Everyone else is eerily silent, just staring at the footage on the television screens. The track marshals have put out the fire and an ambulance crew has arrived. Moments later they're pulling out a white sheet to shield Will from the spectators.

'What's going on? Why have they covered him up?' Laura sounds slightly hysterical.

Whereas I feel frighteningly calm.

'He'll be okay,' Holly says. 'Don't worry.' It sounds like she's very, very small and is speaking in a tiny, tinny voice. I barely register her words. A chill goes through me as I remember what Will said about topping himself if he ever got paralysed.

Suddenly Will's parents and Laura are being bustled out of the garages and I watch after them, panicked.

'Where are they going?' I hear myself ask Holly.

'With the ambulance.'

'I should go.' I start to move, but she puts her hand on my arm to hold me back.

'Daisy, you can't,' she says firmly. 'Family only.'

My heart races. Will I even be able to visit him at the hospital?

'Let's go back to the kitchen,' Holly says. I hesitate, suddenly tearful. 'Come on. We can't let anyone see you like this.' She helps me to my feet and ushers me across the asphalt outside the garages to the hospitality area.

'I want to go to Will's room,' I murmur as we walk through the doors to the hospitality suite. 'Tell Frederick I'm not feeling well.'

She nods and lets go of my arm as I rush towards the stairs. Once inside Will's private room, I close the door and lean up against it, breathing deeply with my eyes closed. When I open them again, I notice the contents of Will's bag are spilling out on the floor. I need something to do so I kneel on the floor and start to fold up his clothes, placing them in a little pile on the coffee table. I come across the black T-shirt that he was wearing on Thursday night and press it to my nose, breathing it in. It still smells of him.

In a daze, I fold up the T-shirt and put it, along with everything else, into his bag before zipping the bag up and taking a seat on the sofa. I don't know how much time passes, but Holly comes in eventually. I stare up at her, my eyes hopeful, but she won't look at me. Why won't she look at me?

'Have you heard anything?' I come to life and ask this question as she kneels in front of the sofa and puts her hands on my knees. 'Holly?' My voice sounds squeaky, different.

And then she meets my eyes. Hers are filled with tears.

'No . . .' I start to say. She tries to pull me in for a hug, but I push her away. 'No, no, no . . .'

'Daisy, I'm sorry.'

'No, no, no . . .'

'Daisy, please . . .'

'No, no, no, no, no, no, no, NO! NO! NO!' I start to scream.

'Daisy! Daisy!' She pulls on me frantically as I stand up.

'NO! NO!' My hands claw my face, but I can't feel the pain. All the pain I have is caught up inside me. It's in my heart. My heart is dying.

'NO!'

He can't be . . . He can't be . . .

'I'm sorry!' Holly cries, once again trying to comfort me. She grabs my hands, pulling them away from my scratched-raw face, but I fight back, unable to calm down, unable to accept what I know she's trying to tell me.

He's not . . . He's not . . . He's not . . .

My whole world is crashing down around my ears and all I can think about is his face in the darkness this morning. His body pressed up against mine. I want him back. He can't be!

I turn to Holly. 'He's not, is he? Tell me he's going to be okay!'

She shakes her head at me.

'TELL ME HE'S GOING TO BE OKAY!' I scream.

'Daisy! People will hear!'

Her words are like a slap in the face. I stare at her in shock. She comes over to me and takes my hands. I let her sit me down on the sofa. Neither of us speaks as I look off into space.

Finally I break the silence. 'Where is he?'

'His body is at the hospital.'

'His body? Oh God, oh God, oh God . . .'

She places her hand on my arm to still me.

'Where's Luis?'

She looks surprised at my question. 'I think he's with Simon. He won the race,' she adds and immediately looks mortified as I stare at her with bewilderment. And then I start to cry. I curl up into a ball on the sofa and press my face into a cushion to muffle the sound of my sobs. Thoughts and memories spin fast around my head, so fast that they make me dizzy. Will helping me pick up my scooter in Melbourne after I crashed it . . . Will standing on the landing outside the lift in Bahrain where I handed him his cap . . . Will staring across the table at me as we waited for Holly in Barcelona . . . Will on the stone terrace looking out over the mountains at my nonna's house . . . Will last night . . . Will last night . . . Will last night . . .

I vaguely register a knock at the door, but I'm too caught up in my thoughts to care who it is. I stay curled up on the sofa with my face pressed into a cushion as I hear Holly talking to a man – it sounds like one of the mechanics – followed by a shuffling sound. The man leaves and, after a while, Holly puts her hand on my arm.

'Why don't you come back downstairs to the kitchen?'

'No.' I shake my head and look up at her. 'Where's his bag?' Panic throbs through me as I see the empty room. 'Where's his bag?' I ask again when she doesn't immediately answer.

'Karl took it for his family.'

'But his T-shirt! I want his T-shirt!' I need his T-shirt. I have to have his T-shirt. It's MY T-shirt! It's all I have of him!

'I'm sorry!' she cries.

'Stop saying you're sorry!' I scream at her, and she backs off. 'I NEED HIS FUCKING T-SHIRT!' I scream again.

'Daisy, please! It's gone! His bag's gone!'

'BUT I NEED IT!'

'What's going on here?' Frederick suddenly storms in. 'Enough! We're ALL upset! Go home, Daisy.' He turns to Holly. 'Take her home.'

'But—'

'Get her out of here!' he shouts.

I don't remember what happens next. It's all a muddle. I vaguely remember Holly speaking to a doctor. I vaguely remember taking the pills she told me to take. I vaguely remember sitting in a car as we crawled bumper-to-bumper out of the car park, and then staring out of the window at greenery flashing past. I vaguely remember being in my own bed in my flat on Camden Road, surrounded by bags ready for my forthcoming move. I vaguely remember Holly checking on me during the night and giving me another pill to take in the morning.

When I finally come out of my drug-fuelled daze, it's Tuesday, and she's asleep on the sofa.

The flat is bright and warm, light spilling in from the south-facing windows. Holly didn't pull the curtains last night, and for a moment I bask in the heat of the sun, completely unaware of what happened just two days previously. Then reality sinks in and I feel my throat close up with the pain.

'Holly!' I try to rouse her as tears fill my eyes. 'Holly!'

'Yes?' she mumbles, before reality sinks in for her, too, because she shoots upright in bed.

'When's his funeral?' I demand to know. 'When's his funeral?'

'Today. This afternoon,' she replies, rubbing her eyes.

'Where? In Cambridge?' That's his home town.

She nods groggily. I climb out of bed.

'What are you doing?' she asks, alarmed.

'Getting ready for his funeral! Jesus, how the hell are we going to get there? Can you ring the train station to find out about tickets? Or would a bus be better?'

'No, Daisy, wait.'

'Come on!' I shout. 'We've got to hurry!'

'Daisy, *wait!*' She climbs out of bed.

'*What?*' I'm annoyed now.

Her expression is pained. 'You can't go to the funeral.'

I stare at her, dumbfounded.

'It's for family and close friends only.'

'What do you mean?' I cry. 'I'm a close friend! I was almost his girlfriend!'

'I know, but . . .' She puts her hands on my arms. 'No one knows about you. As far as the rest of the world is concerned, Laura is the one he left behind.'

Laura is the one he left behind . . .

I collapse down on the sofa, too shocked even to cry. I can't go to Will's funeral? I can't say goodbye to him?

'Who else is going?' I ask. 'Is Simon going?'

She looks shifty. 'Yes, I think so.'

That means she knows so. 'What about Luis?' My tone is hard.

'I think he's going with Simon.'

I stare at her angrily. I don't know why. It's not her fault. But I *so* want to shoot the messenger right now. She doesn't meet my eyes, looking balefully down at the bags on the floor.

Oh, God. I was going to go and stay near Will.

I fall to my knees and burst into tears, sobs coursing through my body as I place my hands on one of my bags.

'Daisy, it's okay,' Holly says. 'You can move in with me.'

And then my tear-blurred vision makes out the tiny corner of a newspaper poking out of Holly's bag.

I rush over, tugging it out amid her protests.

A LOVE LOST

The headline screams out from the front page, and underneath it is a picture of Laura, tear-stricken and anguished.

I scan the story. It's all about Will and Laura, how they grew up together, how they fell in love, how they were destined to be wed. The journalist recalls Will's answer on the grid to the marriage question, and how he flashed a mischievous grin at the interviewer, implying that a wedding wouldn't be far off. Only I know that he was avoiding the question because of me.

I suddenly see his face – quite clearly – staring after me regretfully as I climbed the pit wall before the race. I didn't even wish him good luck! And then his face goes blurry.

No! Not this! Not this, now! Where is he? I hastily turn the pages of the paper until I come to the continuation of the story. There are pictures of the crash – the remains of Will's destroyed car – and there! There is a picture of him and Laura dressed up to the nines on their way to some do or another. I bring the page in close and study it, trying my hardest to ignore the image of Laura at Will's side. He looks kind of familiar, but no! It doesn't capture what he's really like.

'Daisy?' Holly interrupts my thoughts. I look up at her, tears streaming down my face. And then another memory comes back to me. Luis. Luis angrily stalking over to Will before the race started.

What did he say to him? I have to know. And then another thought strikes me.

'Luis will take me.' I leap up and grab my mobile phone from my bag.

'Daisy, what do you mean, Luis will take you?'

'Luis will take me. He can pretend I'm his girlfriend, I don't give a shit! But I am going to that funeral!'

The phone rings and rings, and eventually he picks up.

'Luis, it's Daisy.'

'Hello!' He sounds surprised to hear from me.

'What time are you going to Will's funeral?'

'Er, it starts at two o'clock, so we'll be leaving in an hour, I think. Why?'

'I need you to take me with you.'

'But I, we, there won't be enough room in Simon's car.'

'You've got a car, haven't you?'

'Yes . . .'

'So drive that.'

'Daisy,' he says reasonably, 'have you thought this through?' Holly is tense beside me. 'Laura . . . Will's parents . . . Do you think it's that appropriate—'

'Luis,' I interrupt, steel in my voice, 'if you don't take me to his funeral, I never, *ever* want to see you again.'

He's silent for a moment and then he speaks. 'Give me your address.'

Even up until the point he rings on the doorbell, Holly tries to talk me out of it. I ignore her, putting on a black dress and brushing my hair before leaving it down, the way Will liked it. I don't bother with make-up.

I manage to mumble a brief thank you to Luis when I answer the door, but I can't meet his eyes and hope that will be enough to convey my gratitude for the time being. We barely speak during the car journey on the way up to Cambridge. I know we have a lot to say – there are still unanswered questions in my mind – but that can wait. Right now, I just need to focus on the job in hand.

The funeral is being held in one of the grand university churches and from what I can see, Will had *a lot* of so-called close friends and family.

I spy Simon, Catalina, the team's technical and financial directors and their wives, plus a couple of important sponsors. They're standing together in a group on a pathway near the church entrance, but Luis keeps our distance, waiting for the church to fill before leading me in to a pew at the back. I don't argue with him. I'm not going to make a scene.

It's the most surreal feeling. I feel like I'm in another person's body, experiencing another person's emotions. I'm not tuned in to what's happening at all. There's a coffin up at the front of the church, and it's covered with white flowers. Will's body is inside.

Will's body is inside! Oh, my God, Will is dead! My throat closes up and I put my hand on my chest to steady myself. Luis looks across at me in alarm, just as the priest begins to take the service. I try to listen to what he's saying, but I can hear stifled sobs reverberating through the church. The sound of other people's pain calms me, bizarrely, and if I don't think about what is making them cry, I might just be able to get through this.

A blond man in his early thirties gets up to do a reading. He looks sort of familiar.

'Is that Will's brother?' I ask Luis. He glances at me and nods. I know the priest must've introduced him, but I can't concentrate. I don't take in his words, but instead crane my neck towards the front of the church. There's a little girl sitting on the second row. Is that Will's niece? The one who likes *In the Night Garden*?

'Why didn't Will's brother or sister come to any of the races?' I ask Luis.

He shrugs.

'But your family came. Why didn't Will's?' I ignore the looks I'm getting from other mourners listening intently to the reading. 'I don't understand,' I continue.

'Maybe it's because of his job,' Luis whispers. 'Isn't his brother an important banker or something?' A woman in front of us shuffles in her seat and tuts.

'What about his sister?'

'High-flying lawyer?'

'*Would you be quiet?*' the woman in front of us turns around and hisses before facing forward again. I stare at the back of her head, nonplussed. I'm back in someone else's body again. She can't hurt me. No one can.

More prayers, another reading . . . What should I have for dinner tonight? I feel like I haven't eaten in days. I *haven't* eaten in days! A woman takes to the stand at the front of the church. Who's this, now? I wonder indifferently. And then she turns around, and even though her face is half-covered with black netting, I know instantly that it's Laura.

'I've known – sorry, I *knew* William most of his life . . .'

She called him William?

'. . . and he was the kindest, sweetest, most loyal guy you could ever meet . . .'

My fingernails are digging into my palms. I wonder if I can draw blood?

'I hated the racing. I always hated it. And William knew that. It's why he forgave me for my absence at so many Grands Prix. But he loved it. With all his heart and soul he loved racing so much, and I loved him. I still love him. I'll always love him.'

Her voice breaks and she puts her head down as her body starts to shake with silent sobs.

'I'm sorry,' she apologises, her voice unsteady. 'He died doing what he loved best . . .' She can't finish her sentence. She collapses into sobs again as Will's brother steps up to the altar to lead her away. The church echoes with the sound of people weeping.

What am I doing here? I shouldn't be here. I can't be here. Suddenly I'm on my feet and rushing out of the church, not caring that the doors will bang behind me. I run, run, run down the gravel path to the gate.

'Daisy!'

Luis grabs my arm to stop me, spinning me around.

'No, no, no!' I shout. 'NO!' My knees buckle beneath me and I crumble as Luis tries to hold me up.

'What did you say to him?' I cry. 'What did you say to him before the race?'

'Daisy, now is not—'

'Tell me!' I claw at his arms as I try to tear him away from me. 'Tell me, right now!'

He looks overwrought. 'It wasn't my fault! I didn't mean to upset him!'

I stare at him and take deep breaths, one after the other. When

I finally speak, my voice sounds deadly calm. 'What. Did. You. Say.'

'I was angry with him. Over his treatment of you.'

'Go on.'

'I was angry because he hadn't told Laura about you.'

'Why?' I snap. 'I was okay with that!'

'Were you?' He gives me a hard stare.

'What else did you say? What exactly did you say?'

'I told him . . . I thought he was . . . a prick.'

'*How could you?*' I feel like something has just rushed through my head. Suddenly white rage fills every pore in my body. 'YOU KILLED HIM!' I find myself screaming. 'YOU! IT WAS YOUR FAULT!' I feel like I'm having an out-of-body experience as I start to slap at him, pummelling his chest and his arms.

'Stop!' he shouts, trying to calm me down.

'GET AWAY FROM ME!' I scream, backing away. 'I NEVER WANT TO SEE YOU AGAIN!'

And then I turn and run. I don't know where I run, but I can't stop. Tiny shop windows blur past me as I run down narrow streets lined with cream stone buildings. I run across a bridge and I am vaguely aware of punters on the river below as I leave the city centre and enter a green field opposite one of the picture-postcard college buildings. Exhausted, I come to a stop in front of an enormous oak tree and collapse down on the dirt between its roots. And then I cry. I cry until I feel like I have no more tears left in me.

'Are you okay, miss?'

I look up to see a man in his forties walking by with a brown and white springer spaniel.

'I've lost my boyfriend,' I find myself telling him.

'Don't worry,' he says. 'He'll come back.'

I nod and smile and let him go on his way, then stare ahead in shock.

I don't know what time it is. The funeral will be over by now. I guess I'd better find the bus station. But I don't want to go back to my flat. I don't want to go to Holly's. I don't want to be here. I don't want to be anywhere.

I have no one. No one. No one.

My phone rings. It sounds distant, far off. In a trance I get it out of my bag, pressing the green button to answer the call. I don't speak, just put the phone to my ear and listen, breathing heavily.

'*La mia stellina*!'

My little star. Nonna.

And then the tears return.

'Oh my darling girl, I know, I know . . . I've been waiting for you to call.' I sob down the line, unable to catch my breath as my grandmother makes soothing sounds.

'How did you get my number?' I ask eventually. I haven't given it to anyone except the people at work.

'I tracked you down through your boss at the team's headquarters,' she explains. 'Are you still in England?'

'Yes,' I reply, trying to catch my breath.

'Have you spoken to your parents?'

'No.' I rest my head on one hand in despair and cradle the phone to my ear as the roots at the base of the tree dig into my backside.

'Your mother called me,' Nonna says.

'Did she?'

'She hasn't been able to get hold of you.'

That was my intention when I didn't give out my number.

'Have you called her recently?' Nonna pries.

I don't answer.

'I think you should,' she continues. 'She wants to hear from you.'

My tears slowly come to a stop.

'What will you do, now?' Nonna asks.

I look around at the green field and nearby river and it suddenly becomes very, very clear.

'I think it's time to go home,' I reply.

Chapter 19

The yellow taxi cab pulls up outside the tall building on Fifth Avenue. I hand the driver some money and tell him I don't need help with my bags. I have just one suitcase – the rest I left with Holly, who promised to send them on later. I only need to reach into the trunk before the doorman waiting under the gilded canopy comes running to my aid. He pulls out the suitcase and then turns to me, before leaping back in shock.

'Miss Rogers! I wasn't expecting you!'

'Don't worry, Barney, no one was,' I reassure him as I lead the way into the marbled lobby. He hurries after me. 'Just leave it there, Barney. Thanks,' I tell him as I reach the elevator. He starts to protest about accompanying me, but I firmly assure him there's no need. I step inside and put my key in the slot on the elevator panel – the only slot there is – and the elevator doors whoosh closed. Floor after floor I shoot past until I finally reach the very top. The penthouse. I hear the buzz of the intercom as the doors begin to open, and know that Barney has hurried to inform my parents about my arrival, but I get there first, and the look on my mother's face as I step out onto the landing inside my parents' apartment – once my home – is a sight to behold.

'Hello, Mother,' I say as I put my bags down on the plush, cream-carpeted floor.

She drops the intercom receiver so it swings on its flimsy cord and bashes against the wall. 'Daisy!' she cries in shock.

My mother is a well-dressed woman in her late forties. Her clothes are tailor-made, created for her personally by the world's best designers, and her dark hair has been highlighted blonde and is neatly coiffed. I take after my mother and her side of the family – although you'd hardly know she's Italian when looking at her. Her once-olive skin tones appear lightened from avoiding the sun and wearing too much face powder. She doesn't look any older than when I left her three years ago. I'll put that down to the Botox.

'You'd better pick that up.' I nod to the receiver. 'Barney is probably still on the other end of the line.'

She hastily does as I say, before turning back to me, not knowing if she should hug me, kiss me, or even, God forbid, shake my hand. I save her the trouble of deciding, calmly walking to her and planting a quick peck on her cheek.

'You're back,' she says to me. 'Are you back?' she asks again, not sure what's going on.

'For now,' I reply.

'Come in, come in.' I leave my suitcase where it is as she ushers me through to the sitting room. Floor-to-ceiling windows look out over Central Park, green with summer's leaf-laden trees. I take a deep breath. I'd forgotten how beautiful this view was. In fact, I don't think I ever properly appreciated it before.

'We didn't know. Did you call? Martina will have to make up your room. Martina!' my mother shouts.

'Don't worry, it's fine,' I quickly tell her. 'Don't make a fuss. I can sleep in one of the guest rooms for now.'

'No, you cannot!' she snaps. 'Your room is *your* room. MARTINA!'

'Yes, ma'am?' A maid I haven't seen before hurries into the room wearing a light-grey dress and a white pinny.

'Daisy is back. Daisy is back!' My mother sounds slightly unhinged, but that's always been her way. 'Make up her room immediately!'

I look apologetic as Martina nods her assent and scuttles away again.

My mother turns back to me. 'Tea? Would you like some tea?'

'Sure,' I reply, beginning to walk towards the kitchen. She looks startled.

'Where are you going?'

'To the kitchen. To make a cup of tea.'

She looks at me as though I'm mad. 'Candida will do it,' she says, confused.

'Is that the cook?' I ask. The last cook I knew was called Gita.

'Yes. She's excellent,' my mother replies. Her Italian accent is only slight these days. I don't know how she rid herself of it or if it was even intentional, but many people would assume she's American.

I slump down on one of the armchairs and immediately sink into its depths as my mother hurries out of the room. I take another deep breath and stare out at the view as I hear the high-pitched tones of my mother's voice directing the cook.

My memory takes me away from the present for a short while as I remember working with Rosa, Johnny Jefferson's cuddly Mexican cook. How I adored her. She taught me how to cook. In fact, it was she who inspired me to go into catering in the first place. I still dream of running my own company one day. I've dreamed of lots of things recently, and most will never come true . . .

I shake my head quickly to free my mind of my memories. I can't think of Will now.

'She'll be through with the tea in a minute.' My mother stands in front of me.

'Why don't you sit down?' I suggest, and she perches on the edge of one sofa while anxiously fidgeting with her hands.

Neither of us says anything for a while and I enjoy the silence. I'm surprised when she speaks first. 'It's been a long time, Daisy.'

'I know.'

'I spoke to your grandmother. She told me what happened with the racing driver.'

The racing driver . . .

'Why didn't you call?' Her expression is pained.

'I'm sorry,' I say, but my apology sounds cold and unsatisfactory. 'I just didn't think you'd miss me.'

'Of course I missed you!'

'You would have been the only one.'

She says nothing. She has nothing else *to* say about that.

Candida brings through the tea and leaves again.

'Where is my father?' I ask suddenly. I want to call him Stellan, because that's his name. 'Father' sounds wrong, and 'Dad' is almost laughable.

'At work,' my mother replies.

I nod. Of course he is. It's Sunday. Where else would he be? At home with his family?

My father is a billionaire. He made his money by being a ruthless bastard, buying up failing companies and selling them off piece by piece. You know that job that Richard Gere did in *Pretty Woman*? That's my dad. Except, unlike Julia Roberts, my mother wasn't the making of him.

I don't know if they've ever been happy, but she's stood by his side, for richer or poorer.

What the hell am I saying? For richer, richer, richer . . .

I grew up with what most people would assume was everything I ever wanted. Except all I ever wanted was a warm and happy family, and that was so far from being in my life that I went to bed each night feeling cold, despite the expensive goose-down duvets and underfloor heating. For all my father's money, he rarely took us on family holidays and we never travelled to Italy to see my grandparents. I saw them every few years when they came to England or the States, but the most contact I had was through letters and the occasional phone call. Then, when I was eleven, I went to stay with them in the mountains and for the first time I knew what it was like to live in a happy household.

I hated my parents even more after that trip. But try as I might, I couldn't escape them. I always felt my father despised me, so I couldn't understand why he wouldn't let me attend college as far away as possible – on the other side of the country or even abroad. I was forced to study law in New York and, with no money of my own, I felt I had no choice but to comply. Of course, I did have a choice, but deep down I think I just wanted to please him, just wanted him to love me.

I graduated with honours, and as a reward of sorts, my father opened a bank account in my name and transferred 10 million dollars into it. I don't know why, but that was the catalyst to me leaving. I packed my bags and went to Los Angeles, and perhaps it was my father's name that did it, or even my lawyer credentials, but I scored a job through an agency and ended up working for Johnny Jefferson. You know the rest.

As for my father's money, I've never spent a cent of it.

I tell my mother I need to rest and walk via the elevator entrance on the off chance my suitcase will still be there. Of course, it's not. In fact, when I reach my bedroom, my drawers are already full of my bag's contents, neatly folded, with the items of my cosmetics case precisely placed on the shelves in the bathroom.

I used to love it when our servants unpacked my bags, but now I can't stand it. I'm too used to a life without 'help', and I don't like the idea of anyone – paid or unpaid – going through my things. But there's nothing I can do about it. This is the way it is. This is my life for the moment. I came back, so I'm just going to have to get used to it.

I go to the bed, a giant super-kingsize one with an enormous cushioned bedhead pressed up against the far wall. I lie down on it and curl up on my side, staring out of the opposite window with its view of New York City's skyscrapers.

I must have dozed off, because when I awake the city is glittering with lights. I groan and put my hand to my head. I have a storming headache. I stagger into the bathroom, in search of ibuprofen. I down a couple of tablets and drink straight from the faucet, before remembering the crystal glasses resting on the sink on a solid silver tray. Oh, well. I stare at my reflection in the mirror. I look a state: haggard, tired, bags under my eyes the size of suitcases. I turn and switch the bathroom light off, then head out of the bedroom.

The lights on in the rest of the apartment are overpowering. Halogens spike down at me with every step. In a far-off corner, I can hear the sound of knives and forks scraping on plates. I look at my watch. It's nine o'clock. My father is probably only now eating dinner.

I reach the dining room and push open the door. My mother and father are eating in silence, as is their way, with each of them at either end of a fourteen-seater dining table. You've seen this scene in movies countless times, but who would have ever believed it actually happens?

My father's eyes flicker as he glances up and sees me at the door. But they fall hard again as my mother looks on nervously.

'Daisy. Come in. Have a seat,' my father says.

My mother stands up.

'Sit down, Christine.' My mother's name is actually Cristina I found out when I was eleven, but my father always calls her the British equivalent.

'I was just going to ask Candida to prepare something for Daisy's dinner.'

'I'm not hungr—' I start, but my father interrupts.

'CANDIDA!' he barks. The cook comes running. 'Get something for Daisy.'

'Yes, sir.' She hurries off again. I pull up a chair. There is no halfway point between my mother and father, so I choose a chair three away from him and four away from her. I don't know why I'd opt to be closer to my father, but I guess I'm still drawn to him in that way.

'You need a hair cut,' my father says.

I'm not wearing it up – it's falling halfway down my back. I don't reply.

My father is in his late fifties with silver grey hair and grey eyes. You rarely see him out of a suit.

'And you need to go shopping,' my father adds, glancing at my favourite green jumper – the one that Will first fell for me in. No, no, no, don't think about that . . .

I gather myself together. 'I have enough clothes, thank you,' I reply tautly.

'Except that you don't,' he says, slicing through a piece of carrot and balancing it on his fork.

'How would you know how many clothes I have?' That's the rebellious teenager in me, rearing its head.

'The servants informed me.' He puts the piece of carrot in his mouth and chews it, while calmly and coldly meeting my eyes.

I avert my gaze. Of course they did.

Candida comes through with my meal. 'Thank you very much,' I tell her warmly, as she places it on the table in front of me. She hurries away again, not acknowledging my gratitude. I bravely look back at my father. 'I still have a wardrobe full of clothes that I left here.' My tone is petulant.

'You can't wear those.'

'Why not? They're only three years old.'

'Exactly. What would people think?'

I stifle a sigh. There's no point. He always gets his own way and it's just a waste of energy to argue with him. In fact, the only time he hasn't got his own way was probably when I moved to LA. That must've been quite a shock . . .

'Do you have any funds left in your bank account?'

I assume he's referring to the 10 million. He probably thinks I've come home to top it up. I don't say this, just nod.

'Leave it there. Speak to Martin. He'll sort you out.'

Martin is my father's lawyer and on-hand man. He's practically a member of the family. Except that I can't stand him since he started making eyes at me at the age of thirteen. Fat, bald, disgusting. I shudder as I recall how he was the first person to comment on the fact that I had breasts.

'I might have to ask daddy to give you money for a bra and some little panties . . .'

The sound of my father putting his knife and fork down on his plate brings me back to the present. He stands up.

'Will you not have dessert?' my mother asks anxiously.

'No,' is my father's blunt reply. He looks down at me. I pause chewing my fillet steak. 'I have an early start.'

'Okay,' I say with my mouth full.

'Good night.' He stalks out of the room.

No questions about what I've been doing, what I've been up to, how I am . . . But he probably knows all this already. Knowing my father, he could have had his lackeys checking up on me ever since I left New York.

My mother and I finish the rest of our meal in silence and afterwards I tell her I'm going outside for some fresh air. She wants one of the family's minders to accompany me, but I leave before she has time to do anything about it. I know she's most concerned about what my father would say if he knew she'd let me out alone.

I grab my lightweight cream-coloured jacket from French Connection and non-designer handbag and walk into the elevator, pushing my penthouse apartment key into the slot so the elevator goes straight down to the lobby without stopping at other floors, even if other people are waiting. Barney hurries to open the door for me, wildly looking around for my minder, but not seeing one.

'I'm going out alone, thanks Barney,' I tell him, not waiting for his reply before walking quickly out onto Fifth Avenue and setting off in the direction of the city.

It's Sunday night, but New York never sleeps and the sound of cars honking their horns from far away resounds through the air. I don't know where I'm going, but I head towards Times Square, craving the need for lights and sounds and anything that will take me away from where I've been. The shops here are still open and the pavements are crowded with pedestrians. I clutch my handbag tightly to my side and push my way through the throng, enjoying the feeling of anonymity amongst the tourists. It's eleven o'clock, but I don't feel the least bit tired after my nap earlier, and now I don't know what to do with myself. I wander aimlessly through a couple of shops, before finally heading away from the noise and the giant neon displays towards a quieter back street. I come across one of my favourite nightclub haunts of years gone past and feel surprisingly nostalgic as I spy the queue of people waiting. Back in the day I would have gone straight to the front, doormen falling over themselves to let me pass through with my well-dressed friends. I wonder what those friends are doing now? I haven't kept in touch with any of them. I finally came to the conclusion that they were shallow princesses, but at the time it didn't occur to me to mind.

Eventually exhausted, I head back to the apartment. It's one o'clock and I'm surprised to see the lights still blaring in the living room. I pop my head around the door to find my mother waiting alone on one of the sofas. She leaps up when she sees me.

'You still up?' I say stupidly. Clearly, she is.

'Yes. I wanted to . . . Wanted to . . .'

I nod my head in frustration, willing her to go on.

'You got back safely,' she says eventually.

'Yes. I'm off to bed,' I tell her, barely waiting for her to reply before I head off back down the corridor to the other side of the apartment where my bedroom is.

I did love my mother, once. I'm sure I did. When I was little – very little – before I lost all respect for her for staying with my father. Now she's just this meek little mouse who stutters and worries. I don't know why *he* hasn't left *her*, come to think about it.

My father has already gone to work by the time I wake up at seven o'clock the next morning. I barely slept, despite not going to bed until after two a.m. I read a book for a while and then tossed and turned, trying to clear my mind of things.

Martin, my father's lawyer, comes to find me later that morning. I'm sitting on one of the windowsills in the sitting room, looking down at the park. I've been watching the joggers go round and around, round and around . . .

'Well, look who it is . . .'

The sound of his voice sends a chill spiralling down my spine. I turn to look at him. 'Hello,' I say coldly. I make no attempt to get up.

'Ooh, haven't you grown up.' He looks me up and down, smarmily. When I don't reply, he continues. 'Your father said you needed some funds to go shopping. Anywhere nice?'

'The usual.'

'Right, yes, okay.'

He takes a few steps towards me and hands over an expensive red leather Hermes purse – whatever happened to a simple envelope? A quick look inside tells me I have a wad of 100 dollar notes and a single credit card.

'Do you have anything smaller?' I ask, pulling out one of the hundred dollar bills.

Martin looks at me warily, before his face breaks into a slimy smile. 'Oh, you're joking.'

'I'm not actually.'

He laughs again and turns away. 'Well, you have fun. Perhaps you could give me a little fashion show later.'

I hold my tongue and quash the urge to kick him where it hurts as he walks out of the room, snickering to himself.

I look down at the purse and feel empty. But there's nothing much else I can get my head into. I may as well go shopping.

Prada, Chanel, Dolce and Gabbana, Donna Karen . . . I used to love going to these shops with my friends and spending vast amounts of my father's money.

Arnold, one of my family's minders, keeps guard outside on the pavement as I rifle through the racks, horribly aware of the eagle-eyed sales assistants watching my every move. I pick some clothes out and don't even bother to try them on – one of the servants will return them for me if they don't look right.

I pause at the racks for a moment as I think this, and just feel sad. I can't believe how quickly I'm slipping back into this life; this life I despise. But it takes me away from my memories. The thought of Holly, fun, bubbly, lovely Holly, is enough to make my eyes well up. I tell myself that she lied to me about Simon and my heart hardens. I go back to rifling through the racks.

News travels quickly here and soon my old friends and acquaintances begin to call. I receive invite-after-invite to attend various glittering parties and bar openings and I decide on the spot to accept them all. I don't want to go out – it's the last thing I want to do – but I figure if I sink back into this lifestyle it might make the pain go away. I'm not thinking of Will. Hardly ever. And it's just as well because I can't remember what he looks like.

So I accept these invitations and ten days after arriving don my new designer gear and go downstairs where one of our drivers is waiting diligently with the limo. It's shiny and new inside and the leather still smells like leather. I see that someone has put a bottle of champagne on ice for me, and I hesitate for a moment before opening it. I'll only have one glass – the rest will go to waste – but there's plenty more where that came from.

'DAISY!' As soon as my high-heeled Jimmy Choo is on the pavement, I hear my name being screamed. I turn to see Donna, one of my old friends, standing on the sidewalk having only just exited her own limo. More screams follow as two other friends spy us both.

I've known Donna, Lisa and Cindy most of my life. Their fathers work in banking, law and banking respectively and have known my own father for years. Their mothers do nothing except shop, eat and exercise, much like my own. The girls and I went to school together, holidayed in the Hamptons together, and as we got older, partied together. Cindy's dad spent 1½ million dollars on her eighteenth birthday party. Which was pretty amazing until Donna's daddy trumped it with a cool 2 million on hers. My father spent even more on mine. He's a competitive son of a bitch.

I suddenly see Nonna with her pots and pans, trying to catch the water coming through the walls. Why haven't my parents seen her right? How much money would it take? It's less than a drop in the ocean to them.

'Daisy! It's so good to see you!'

I turn my attention to my friends. 'Hello!'

'Wow, what are you wearing? And is that the latest Dolce bag?' They don't wait for me to answer before moving onto their next question. 'Where have you been? Come on, come on, let's go in!'

The queue to the club is already snaking around the building, but I follow the girls to the front. The doormen unclip the red rope and stand back to let us pass. Cindy, Donna and Lisa barely acknowledge them, but I smile and say thank you, and immediately wish I hadn't because I don't get anything other than a scowl in return.

Buff men in black-tie suits offer us cocktails on silver trays as we reach the bottom of the plush red-carpeted stairs. The latest new bar to see and be seen in stretches out in front of us. Everything is silver and white. The tables are mirrored cubes, the chairs are glossy white, the floor is polished chrome, and white velvet drapes hang from the walls. I feel like I'm standing inside an icicle and I shiver even though it's the middle of summer.

Donna manages to sweet-talk two men in their fifties into giving up their seats in a silver leatherette booth and the four of us slide in and make ourselves comfortable. Only I don't feel comfortable. Not like I used to. Everything is different, now. The deep ache inside that has been bothering me recently is throbbing away now. I reach for my cocktail and take a large gulp, before motioning for one of the suited waiters to bring me another. The girls collapse into giggles.

'That's the Daisy we know!' Lisa squeals.

I ignore her and take another large mouthful and as alcohol infuses my body, I start to relax.

'So tell us what you've been up to?' Cindy says.

'I want to hear about Johnny Jefferson!' Lisa interrupts.

'Is he really as hot as he looks?' Donna chips in.

I don't want to talk about Johnny, but it's preferable to talking about . . . you know. So I divulge trivial details that the girls could just read about in magazines without going into any depth. It seems to satisfy them.

'What's been going on here?' I ask eventually.

'Oh my God, did you hear about Portia Levistone?' Donna's eyes are wide with the anticipation of telling me a story about one of our old school friends.

'No,' I reply.

'Oh. My. God,' she says again, glancing at Lisa and Cindy.

I go along with it. 'Tell me,' I urge, although I couldn't really care less what Portia has been getting up to.

'You know how she married that banker?'

'I didn't, but . . .'

'Ew! He's, like, totally disgusting. Fat and old, but really, really rich. And you know how Portia's daddy lost all his money on the stock market?'

'Did he?'

'Yes! Daisy, you've been living in a bubble for three years!'

Er, no, I just haven't given a damn about any of this stuff . . .

'Never mind,' Donna continues. 'Portia's daddy introduced her to this *old* guy, like really old – forty or something like that – and they got married!'

'Oh, right.'

'Yes! But that's not it. She's PREGNANT! They've only been married, like, a couple of months or something.'

Lisa turns her nose up. 'I can't believe she had sex with him!'

Loud chorus of 'EWs' all around.

Jesus, they still sound like they're sixteen.

'Maybe it's not his?' Cindy looks at the others, wide-eyed.

'Oh my God, maybe it's not!' Donna screeches. 'She was *totally* into that bartender at her hen party!'

This is how rumours start, I think to myself indifferently. And then a thought slams into me.

What if I'm *pregnant?*

'So tell me about Fifi,' Cindy turns to Lisa. 'Did you manage to get that diamond-encrusted coat in her size?'

I stare ahead in shock. Will and I didn't use contraception . . .

'Oh, no, I couldn't,' Lisa replies sadly. 'They're going to order it in for me.'

My hand instinctively goes to my stomach.

'Fifi is Lisa's new chihuahua,' Donna explains to me, but I'm already on my feet. 'Where are you going?' she asks, taken aback by my sudden movement.

'I'm not feeling well. I'm going to head home.'

'Oh.' One, two, three put-out faces around the table. I don't wait for them to say anything else before hurrying out of the venue.

I set off down the street, deciding to walk rather than call the driver.

Pregnant? *Pregnant?* What would I do? Of course, I would keep it. What if it was a boy? What if he looked like Will?

A lump forms in my throat and tears prick at my eyes as I run across the street in my three-inch heels. I'm not used to wearing them and my feet are already starting to ache, but that's good. Physical pain helps deflect from the emotional kind.

Would I tell Laura? Would Laura want to know that Will had a son? What about his parents? Would they accept me? They would have to. I would be the mother of their only grandson . . .

Or perhaps it's a girl. A little girl who takes after me. But she could have her daddy's eyes . . .

Tears start to stream down my face and I brush them away,

quickly. My soles are burning. I should have called the limo. It was probably only waiting around the corner.

I want to speak to Holly, but no, I'm not ready.

Oh God, I want to be pregnant. Please let me be pregnant. When did I last have my period? It was ages ago. I start to cry properly as I stumble down the sidewalk. Passers-by glance at me warily, but no one asks me if I'm okay and I don't want them to. And then up ahead, I see a limo parked on the side of the street. Is it mine? I reach it and realise with a wave of relief that it is, banging on the window at the driver who leaps out of the car in shock.

'Take me home!' I wail.

'Miss Rogers! Did you call me? I'm so sorry.'

I shake my head at him wildly and climb into the car. He knows better than to ask any more questions.

There's a fresh bottle of champagne chilling on ice. I can't believe I drank so much tonight! What if I've harmed the baby?

Oh, please God, let me be pregnant!

No one knows about you . . . Laura is the one he left behind . . .

I thought Holly's words would haunt me forever, but they'd all know about me if I were the mother of Will's only child. I wouldn't have to hide. I wouldn't have to grieve in silence . . .

I want his baby, so much!

I could go to a pharmacy . . . Get a pregnancy test . . .

No. No. I don't want to do that.

What if I'm not?

Don't think it, don't think it, don't think it.

I wipe away my tears as we pull up in front of my apartment block. Barney comes to hold open the door and I step out, calmly thanking him. He looks concerned when he sees my red and no-doubt puffy eyes, but I walk past him with my head held high.

Most of the lights are off in the apartment and I go straight to my bedroom. In the bathroom I lift up my top and stare at my stomach. Flat as a pancake. But I wouldn't be showing, yet. I must eat healthily tomorrow. Make up for all the booze I've had tonight.

Would I have the baby here? Or would I go back to England? I could go to Italy! Nonna would look after us both!

Italy . . . That was where he said he first fell for me . . .

Sobs ricochet through me as I stare at my reflection in the mirror. I miss him so much. It's been over two weeks, but I want him back. He can't be gone forever!

He was trying to block Luis from overtaking him, and ran wide, crashing into a wall and spinning through the air before landing the wrong side up on a gravel pit. He broke his neck, they said. It was quick, painless. But he must've known he was about to have an accident.

I wonder if he knew he was going to die . . .

No, no, NO! He was mine! But his life was snatched away on the very day he became so. We could have spent our lives together. I was on the verge of being happy – the happiest I have ever been. How can I cope with the pain of his loss, now?

I love him!

How dare she love him, too! How dare she!

I run and throw myself on the bed and cry, hard, into my pillows. It should have been me. It should have been me at the front of the church. It should have been me on the front of the papers staring out at me at Heathrow. I should have been reading about *me* as I knelt on the floor of the newsagent's at the airport, my fingers turning black from the newspaper print.

But it was her. It's all about her.

Italy. Italy. That's where I'll go. Nonna, me and the baby. He'll like living in the mountains. I'll bring him up bilingually . . .

Two days later, I get my period. I sit on the toilet in shock, unable to cry, unable to do anything except sit there and stare into space. My hopes, my dreams have vanished. I feel lost and alone. I have nothing.

Chapter 20

What am I doing, here?

Forgetting . . . Forgetting . . . Forgetting . . .

I've been back in New York for two weeks and I'm sitting on the windowsill again, watching the joggers. I have a sudden urge to go down to Central Park and join them, but no, I can't be bothered.

I had an 'interesting' conversation with my father last night at dinner. We were halfway through our main course when he came out with a question that has clearly been on his mind for some time.

'What are you going to do with yourself, now?'

'Are you actually asking me?'

He gave me a hard stare but didn't answer, so I looked away before replying.

'I was thinking about going to catering school.'

He actually laughed. A cold, brittle laugh. 'All that money I spent on law school and you want to become a meagre cook?'

'It's a difficult job! There's nothing meagre about it.'

'You will do no such thing. I've spoken to Martin. There's a job in his law firm. I expect you to take it.'

He continued to chew on his beef while I sat there in silence, my blood beginning to boil.

'No.' My tone was firm, resolute.

His knife and fork froze in mid-air as he turned his grey eyes to look at me. 'What did you say?'

'I said, no.' But my voice was wavering.

'You have the summer,' he coolly replied, ignoring my refusal. 'Have your fun, go to parties, see your friends, but after that I expect you to settle down and start this job.'

I bit my tongue. It's now the middle of July. By September, who knows where I'll be? I can't even think further than the weekend at the moment.

'And get your hair cut,' he continued. 'Stacey will make you an appointment for the morning.' Stacey is one of my father's assistants.

I closed my eyes in defeat. Years ago I would have argued. Weeks ago I would have laughed. Now I let his comments slide over me. I just want to be numb for a while.

A few seconds later I opened my eyes again and continued to eat.

I still haven't listened to my mobile phone messages. I know I have some because I saw the reminder on the screen before my phone ran out of battery. Since then, it's been sitting on my bedside table, staring at me every time I go to sleep or wake up. And that's not just in the morning and at night; I've been napping in the daytime, too. Anything to pass the time.

Maybe my father's right. Maybe I should get a job. Not with Martin, I'm not that desperate, but somewhere. Maybe even at a coffee shop?

I actually smile to myself and shake my head at this thought. As if he'd allow me to do that.

'Ahem.'

I turn to see my mother standing in the doorway of the sitting room.

'Oh, that looks nice,' she says, nodding in my direction.

'What looks nice?' I ask.

'Your hair,' she replies.

This morning I went to the hairdresser, as agreed. I had the tiniest trim and am now wearing my hair up where it will probably stay for the rest of the summer. My father will never know the difference.

'Oh, right. Thanks,' I add generously.

'Did you have a nice time last night?' she asks.

'Yeah, it was fine.'

After dinner, I went to see a movie with Lisa. I may not particularly like those girls, but my need for distraction outweighs my moral responsibility to tell them to piss off.

How I miss Holly . . .

Right, that's it. I'm calling her. I've been thinking about her on and off for the last couple of weeks, but I haven't felt like speaking to her until now.

I get up so suddenly from the windowsill that my mother looks startled.

'Where are you going?'

'To my bedroom.'

'Not for another sleep?'

'Why?' I snap. 'What's your problem with that?'

She doesn't answer, so I storm out of the room in a huff and even go as far as slamming my bedroom door like a petulant child. I may be twenty-six, but I sure as hell don't feel like it, right now.

I snatch up my phone from the bedside table and commence

my search for the lead to charge it up. Where the hell have the servants put it? I find it eventually, in the top drawer inside my wardrobe, neatly folded and secured with a piece of string. I tug it off and find an American adaptor, then plug it in, turn the phone on, and wait for the LCD display to light up. There we go. Voicemail . . .

'*You have nine new messages* . . .'

Play.

'Hi, Daisy, it's me, Holly. I just want to know if you got home safely. Give me a call . . .'

'Hi, Daisy, it's me, Holly. I'm just wondering how you are? Give me a call . . .'

'Hi, Daisy, it's me, Holly. I know you're probably really busy settling back into New York City life, but I'd really love to just have a chat and see how you are. I miss you. Call me back . . .'

'Hi again Daisy, it's me, Holly. Are you there? I hope I've got the right number for you. No, I definitely do because I called you on this when you were still here. Oh, I'm rambling. Just give me a call when you can.'

'Daisy? It's Holly. Are you checking your phone? Please call me.'

'Hi, it's just me again, wondering where you are and what you're up to . . .'

And so on. Guilt prickles inside me as I listen to her voice. I should have called sooner. I'll make up for it now. *Cazzo*, what time is it in the UK? Ten o'clock. Too late? No . . .

Ring, ring, ring . . .

Damn, it probably *is* too late.

Ring, ring, ring . . .

Should I hang up?

Ring, ring, ring . . .

I've probably woken her up now, anyway. If I hang up now she'll be really annoyed.

Ring . . .

Does this phone have voicemail, or what?'

'Hello?' Bummer. She sounds sleepy.

'Holly? Sorry, have I woken you up?'

'Daisy? Daisy!' She instantly perks up. 'You called! At last! Did you get my messages?'

'Only just now, I'm afraid.'

'I've called you about twenty times!'

'Nine, actually.'

'Not counting the times I hung up . . .'

'Oh. I'm sorry.'

'What have you been doing? How's it all going?'

'You know . . . It's alright.'

'No, I don't know. Tell me everything. What have you been up to? How are you feeling?'

'Um, just keeping myself busy, catching up with old friends, that sort of thing. And shopping. Lots of shopping.'

'Wicked! Ooh, you've got Banana Republic on practically every corner there, haven't you? I'm so jealous.'

'Mmm, yeah.' Although I haven't been in. It's all designer, designer, designer, but I keep that to myself. 'What about you? How's it going?'

'Good, good . . .'

Still shagging Simon? No, I don't ask that question.

'Hey, what do you want me to do with your bags?' she asks. 'You never left me your address, but should I send them on now?'

'Actually, Holly, have you got enough room for them in your loft for the moment?'

'Sure, yes, of course.'

'In fact, you could even just give everything away to charity.'

'Don't be ridiculous!' she scoffs. 'I can't give all your things away!'

I don't tell her that I have more than enough 'things' here.

'So what's been happening?' I ask.

'Well, we're off to Germany this weekend and Pierre, the test driver, has taken over Will's drive—'

'I don't want to hear about that,' I bluntly interject, feeling light-headed.

'Oh.'

'Sorry. I just . . . can't.'

'Alright,' she says sympathetically.

'How are Pete and Dan?' I ask.

'They're, you know, okay,' she replies. 'And Luis is—'

'I don't want to hear about Luis, either.' My tone is hard.

'Oh, right. Sure.'

Silence.

'Did I wake you up?' I change the subject.

'Um . . . No, I was just dozing, you know.'

'Is there anyone else with you?'

'Hey?' She sounds startled. 'No, no, I'm here on my own, just little old me.'

Right. So Simon *is* there, then.

'Well, I guess I'd better let you get back to it.'

'Okay. Well, it was lovely to hear your voice. I've missed you so much.'

I feel warm inside. 'I miss you, too.' But once I've hung up, I just feel cold again.

July turns into August and New York becomes stifling hot. I

stay inside the air-conditioned apartment as much as boredom allows, and the rest of the time I go shopping or out to the movies. Yesterday I spent all afternoon at the Guggenheim Museum, just sitting in front of the paintings and trying to lose myself in the abstract colours.

Holly calls me a few more times – I usually miss her phone calls and rarely call her back, but I will speak to her soon. I'm still upset she won't confide in me the way I confided in her.

Well, I didn't tell her everything. And she still knows nothing about my life in America or Johnny, but that's not the point. Is it? No, it's definitely not the same thing. Anyway . . .

One day in early August, I'm flicking through the channels on the television and almost fall off the sofa when I come across Luis being interviewed. It's a foreign channel, so I can't understand much of what's being said, but he looks distraught. I immediately try to dismiss it as him losing his latest race, but I know in my heart that's not it. It bothers me for hours until eventually I call Holly.

'Hello!' She sounds delighted to hear from me. 'How are you?'

'I'm okay,' I reply. 'I just saw Luis on the television.'

'Did you?'

'Yeah. He looked a bit worse for wear. Is everything alright?'

'I thought you didn't want to hear about Luis?' I don't answer so she continues. 'He hasn't been that great, to be honest.'

'What, isn't he winning or something?' Sarcasm kicks in.

'It's not that.' Holly hastily corrects me. 'Daisy, he pulled out of the last race.'

'He pulled out? What do you mean?' I'm confused. 'Was this in Hungary?' The Hungarian Grand Prix follows the German one.

'Yes,' she replies.

'What happened?'

'Well, he did this whole speech about how he was going to win it for Will.'

'I bet he did,' I interrupt nastily.

Holly continues. 'But he just couldn't get it together. He's lost it, Daisy. He's devastated about Will's death. He blames himself.'

'So he damn well should!' I erupt. 'It was his fault!'

'Daisy, it wasn't,' Holly says reasonably. 'The FIA' – that's the Formula 1 governing body – 'looked into it and everything.'

'Do they know that Luis called him a prick before the race? No!' I don't even give Holly a chance to answer. 'They bloody well don't! What happened in Germany?'

'It was almost as bad,' Holly explains. 'He qualified sixth—'

'I wouldn't call that bad,' I interject.

'But he started poorly and just kept getting overtaken by backmarkers. He ended up finishing thirteenth.'

'Boo bloody hoo. I bet Simon wasn't too happy about that.'

'Simon understands,' Holly replies.

'And is he still leading the championship?'

'No. He's slipped down to third.'

'Tough luck.'

'Daisy, don't be too hard on him . . .'

'Why not? He killed Will! He killed him!' My head feels like it's swelling from all the pressure inside of me and then I'm sobbing uncontrollably.

'Daisy, Daisy, I'm sorry . . .' Holly tries to comfort me in the background, but I'm beyond help. I just need to cry.

Oh God, I want him back. I'd give anything to have him back.

'Why did he have to die?' I wail. 'I miss him, Holly, I miss him so much.'

'Oh, Daisy . . .'

I eventually calm down and take a few deep breaths while neither of us speaks.

'Are you alright?' Holly asks.

I take another raggedy breath and reply that I am. And then I remember the TV interview. 'What was Luis doing on telly, anyway? You said something about a big speech he did?'

'That's right. Are you sure you want to hear this now?' Holly sounds wary.

'Yes. Go on, I won't break down again, I promise.'

'Well, after, you know, the funeral, the press turned on Luis. He got a terribly hard time about going on to win the race when his team-mate had had such a horrific crash. Simon fears someone from the team leaked the fact that Luis blames himself for Will's death, because suddenly the tabloids cottoned onto the story and wouldn't let it drop. Instead of feeling sorry for Luis, they became even more bloodthirsty. They managed to get an interview with Will's father and he slated Luis for winning at Silverstone.'

'Has Laura spoken to the press?' I interrupt.

'No.'

'Oh. Go on.' I can't even feel angry with her.

'Anyway, Luis did terribly in Germany, refused to do any interviews himself, and the furore finally seemed to be dying down. Then, just before the race in Hungary, an interviewer must've caught Luis at a weak moment because he broke down on the grid.'

I butt in. 'What do you mean he broke down?'

'In tears,' Holly explains. 'He started to cry as he was getting into his car.'

I'm dumbstruck. I can't imagine Luis doing that.

Holly continues. 'He told the interviewer he was going to win the race for Will.'

'But he didn't.'

'No, he pulled out after ten laps.'

'Was there something wrong with the car? Was he doing really badly?' I'm confused.

'No. On the contrary, he started off really well. He started way down in eleventh place on the grid, but he overtook four people at the start, and was climbing up through the pack when suddenly he just seemed to slow right down. Seven people went past him before he pulled into the garages and climbed out of the car. Simon went bonkers.'

I listen intently as she continues.

'Anyway, that interview you saw was probably the only one he gave after the race because he just couldn't keep it together. He hasn't been into team HQ since and I think he's properly screwed up. I don't know what Simon's going to do.'

'What do you mean, you don't know what Simon's going to do?'

'About Luis. He can't keep him in the car when he's so obviously affected by Will's death.'

'He can't keep him in the car? What, he's going to fire him?'

'He might not have a choice.'

'Of course he has a choice! He was leading the championship. Why would Simon get rid of him, just because he's had a couple of dodgy races? His team-mate is dead!' I can feel the sobs building up inside me again.

'Hey, hey,' Holly soothes. 'I thought you'd be pleased to hear it.'

'No. I'm not pleased,' I tell her. In fact, I'm worried about Luis.

He doesn't deserve this. Do I really blame him for Will's death? Do I? 'When's the next race?' I ask.

'In a couple of weeks. European Grand Prix.'

'Well, wish him good luck from me.'

'Really?'

'Yes.'

'Daisy . . .' Holly's voice is tentative. 'Are you really going to stay in America?'

'I don't know,' I reply.

'Why don't you come back? There's still a job waiting for you. We all miss you.'

I pause. 'I miss you all, too.'

'You could come back in time for the next race. Stay with me. You wouldn't even need to find another flat.'

For a moment I picture myself back at work, behind the serving table, dishing up greasy bacon, and then I see Will, asking for a quick word, and my throat closes up so quickly I have to gasp for air. I start to wail. Holly's shock is immense.

'Daisy, please stop crying!'

'I can't . . . I can't . . . I can't . . .' I manage to say.

'I know, I know,' she hushes me. 'It's too soon.'

'I can't bear it!' I promised her I wouldn't break down again, but the floodgates have well and truly opened. 'I can't believe he's dead!' And that's it, all Holly can hear for ages afterwards is the sound of me sobbing.

Finally I calm down. 'I have to go,' I say morosely.

'I'm so sorry, Daisy.' Her voice sounds husky, like she's been crying, too.

'It's okay,' I whisper. And then I hang up.

Moments later I hear a knock on my bedroom door. I don't

answer, so the door opens slowly and I look up to see my mother standing there.

'Daisy? Are you okay?'

'No, no, no, I'm not.' I shake my head and stare down at the carpet in despair.

'What's wrong?' she asks quietly.

'Just let me be,' I tell her and collapse face down on the bed. 'Go!' I shout crossly when she doesn't make any attempt to move. Seconds later I hear the door shut behind her and I'm alone once more.

Chapter 21

'He's seriously considering it.'

I'm on the phone to Holly. It's a week after the European Grand Prix and she has just told me that Simon is thinking about replacing Luis with another driver. He qualified badly and then crashed the car into Naoki Takahashi after making a stupid mistake at the start.

'I can't believe he'd do that to Luis.' I'm mortified.

'He's a businessman, Daisy, he has to do what's right for the team,' Holly says reasonably.

'Yes, but *is* that right for the team? *Do* the team want Luis to be replaced?'

'Well . . .' She hesitates. 'I guess not.'

'Exactly! They all love Luis! They couldn't bear to lose another driver!' My eyes well up with tears. I quickly brush them away.

After my last conversation with Holly, I had a brief look on the internet to see if anyone else from the industry had been speculating about Simon's intentions for Luis. I came across a photo of all the drivers before the race in Germany. They were standing with their arms around each other's shoulders, taking part in a minute's silence for Will. Several drivers – Kit Bryson, Nils Broden, Antonio Aranda – looked tearful, but Luis was the only one with his head down, unable to face the camera.

I don't know how he's able to race at all . . . That's the hardest thing about this – or any – sport: carrying on when one of your own has died.

'Did you tell him what I said?' I ask Holly.

'Who? Luis?' Holly checks.

'Yes.'

'What did you say again?' Holly sounds guilty.

'So you didn't, then.'

'I'm sorry, I forgot.'

'Don't worry about it. But please will you send him my best?'

'Of course I will,' she replies warmly.

A few days later I call her again. 'Did you speak to Luis?' I ask.

'About you sending him your best?' she checks.

'Yes.' I smile.

'No, I haven't had a chance, yet.'

Oh.

'I haven't seen him at team HQ,' she explains. 'Why don't you give him a call?'

'Oh no, I couldn't do that.' I brush her off.

'Why not?'

'No. I just couldn't.'

'Well, I'll tell him you're thinking of him.'

'He's still got a drive, then?' I ask.

'Yes. For now,' she replies ominously.

'It's Belgium next, isn't it?'

'Yes. Next week.' Pause. 'Have you thought any more about coming back?'

'No,' I reply.

'I really miss you,' she tells me once more.

'I miss you, too.'

'Frederick was only asking after you the other day. He said you could have your job back anytime you wanted it. Simon said the same thing.'

'Really? They haven't replaced me?'

'Other staff from Frederick and Ingrid's business in London have been filling in, but no one permanent. I've been helping out Simon and the drivers since you've been gone, but I'll happily step down.'

'There wouldn't be any need.'

'No?'

'No. I wouldn't want to work closely with the drivers if . . .' My voice trails off. I don't want to say, 'If Will's not there'.

'I understand,' she says, before desperately adding, 'Oh, *please* come back, Daisy.'

I close my eyes for a moment and cradle the phone to my ear, listening to her voice. I miss her so much. It's just not the same being here. I was never happy in New York before, and now I know what it's like to *be* happy, I feel like I'll never be happy again. I don't know if that makes any sense whatsoever, but it's the closest way I can think of to describe how I feel.

'I think it's too soon,' I tell her, my head ruling my heart this time.

'Really?' she checks.

'Yes.'

That evening my father joins us for dinner – a rare occasion since I've been here. In fact, most of the time I eat out or don't eat at all because I can't bear to sit at the dining table in silence with my mother. He broaches the subject of the position with Martin's firm.

'He suggested the ninth of September as a starting date,' my father tells me. That's just over a week from now.

'I told you before, I'm not interested,' I say sulkily.

He raises one eyebrow and stares at me. I look away. I can never hold his gaze for long. 'Just for the sake of argument, what is it you intend to do? Because you can't sit around in your bedroom forever.'

'If you don't want me here, I'll go.'

He doesn't answer for a moment, but then he speaks, his voice laced with sarcasm. 'And where will you go, exactly?'

'I don't know! England! Italy!'

'Italy?' my father barks. 'Italy?'

'Yes! To stay with Nonna!' I latch onto this idea, fervently.

'Ha!' He lets out a sharp laugh. 'In that hovel? You couldn't stand it.'

'How would you know what I can or cannot stand?' I demand to know. 'I haven't been living it up for the last few years, I can tell you.'

'Sure you haven't,' he says wryly.

'I haven't! And I would love to stay with Nonna! Have you ever even been to her house? It's magical!'

'Magical? Don't be ridiculous. It's a crumbling mess. God knows why she's still there. God knows why she's still on this earth, for that matter.'

'Stellan!'

I turn sharply to see my mother's shocked face. She hardly ever speaks up. The sound of a chair scraping across the wooden floor brings my attention back to my father.

'I've had enough.' He throws his napkin down on his food and I watch as the gravy seeps up into the white linen fabric. 'YOU!' He points at me. 'You will take the job with Martin on the ninth of September. Otherwise you will not get another cent from me! EVER!' And with that he stalks out of the room.

I sit there, white-knuckled, my heart beating fast. Only my father can make me feel this way. I hate him. I hate him.

I stand up, scraping my own chair across the floor.

'Daisy, sit down,' my mother says. Her tone is harder than I've ever heard it and it makes me freeze on the spot.

'I'm going to my room,' I tell her, but without much conviction.

'Finish your dinner.' She picks up her knife and fork.

But I suddenly feel angry and hot-headed and nothing she can say or do will keep me there. 'No,' I reply, and with that, I storm out of the room.

I will NOT go and work for Martin! I could go back to England and stay with Holly . . . That idea is becoming more and more attractive. Or I could stay with Nonna. Keep her company. How *dare* he say she lives in a hovel? And why *does* she live in a house that's crumbling down around her ears when he has all the money in the world?

I halt in my tracks and spin around on the spot, storming back into the dining room. My mother is just standing up.

'Why the hell does Nonna live like that in the mountains?' I demand to know. 'Water leaks through the walls when it rains, but she can't afford to fix it! It's disgusting! You're her daughter! How COULD you?'

My mother stares at me calmly, then sits back down in her chair.

'Answer me!' I screech.

She answers in Italian. I'm surprised – my mother never speaks to me in Italian – but this time she does, and I have to concentrate hard so it doesn't throw me off guard.

'She wouldn't take any money,' my mother tells me.

I falter before speaking, also in Italian. 'She wouldn't take money from me, either, but you're her daughter! She must know you're rolling in it!'

'It's not my money, though, Daisy.'

'It bloody well is. I mean, I know he might be the one who goes out to work, but you've stayed by his side. You earned it, too!'

'Yes, but my mother doesn't see it like that.'

'Even so, who cares? Why won't she let you help her? Or is it my father? Will he not let you help her?' I'm starting to see red. 'Is that it?' Fury bubbles up inside me, but my mother puts a stop to it.

'That's not it,' she says calmly, holding her hand up. 'She doesn't want anything to do with your father – my husband. She'd rather live in squalor than accept his help.'

'But that's crazy. It may be only a matter of time before the walls collapse on her!'

My mother looks startled. 'I didn't know it was as bad as that.'

'Well, you *should* know! Why don't you know? Why the hell don't you ever go and see her?' I don't know why I've never thought to ask any of these questions before. 'Did you even go to Nonno's funeral?'

'Of course I went to his funeral!' she snaps.

'Did you? When? I don't remember that.'

'You were on holiday in the Hamptons with your friends.'

'But I didn't know you'd gone! Why didn't you ask me to come with you? You must have known I would!'

'Yes, I . . .'

'What? *Why?*'

She looks shifty. The words come out with difficulty. 'I . . . needed to go . . . alone . . .'

'But why? I don't understand!'

She sighs. 'Oh, Daisy . . .'

I look at her in confusion. I've never seen her like this before, so composed and reasonable.

'Tell me!' I raise my voice.

She looks at me and her eyes are filled with pain. Then she looks away again and her answer is firm. 'I just wanted to spend some time with my mother and be there for her without worrying about you. Okay?'

I shake my head. 'No. That's not it. There's something else. What is it you're not telling me?'

'That's enough, now.' She stands up and walks out of the dining room.

'No, it's not!' I follow her into the kitchen. 'Tell me what's going on?' Candida is at the sink. She gives us a wary glance before quickly exiting the room. She's probably startled to hear us speaking in another language. In fact, she probably had no idea about our Italian heritage at all.

My mother turns her back on me and faces the far wall.

'Hey!' I shout. I go to her and spin her around. There are tears in her eyes and . . . something else . . . Fear?

'What is it? You have to tell me. You can't *not*.'

'Okay,' she says.

'Okay?' I step back in surprise.

'Okay. Let's go for a walk.'

'A walk? Alone?'

'Yes, alone.'

'At this time?' It's after nine o'clock at night. 'Without a minder?'

'Yes.'

I'm taken aback – this is very out of character for my mother – but I go along with it.

We're silent on the elevator ride down to the lobby, and silent on the walk along the street. It's only when we've turned the corner and are out of sight of our apartment block towering up above that my mother begins to speak.

'I left your father once.'

I turn to her in surprise. She's staring off into the distance, as though lost in her thoughts.

'When?' I ask.

'It was before you were born.'

'When you were living in England?'

'Yes. Although I went back to Italy.'

'To stay with Nonna?'

'And your grandfather, yes. They welcomed me back. They didn't want me to marry him in the first place. They said he had bad blood.'

I know what they mean.

'Why *did* you marry him?'

She sighs. 'I thought I loved him. I think I just loved the idea of him. I was at university in England on a scholarship.'

'I didn't know you went to university?' It strikes me that I don't actually know an awful lot about my mother. 'What were you studying?'

'English.' She waves me away, a touch impatiently. I'm sidetracking. She continues. 'I had this one friend, a well-meaning girl from a wealthy family who took pity on this poor soul from the mountains. She dragged me out one night to her father's private members' club and we got dressed up to the nines – me in a borrowed outfit. We sat on high stools at the bar while drinking martinis in cocktail glasses.' I glance at my mother to see her smiling wistfully as she remembers. 'Your father walked in. He was so handsome and well dressed. He took . . . an interest in me, I think you could say. He wanted to take me out on a date. I was flattered. I agreed.'

'Then what happened?' I prompt. I'm utterly intrigued by this story.

'We got . . . carried away,' she says, with difficulty.

'What do you mean?'

She takes a deep breath.

'You had sex with him?' I ask. She looks at me sharply. We never speak about intimate things. I've never had that sort of relationship with her. 'On the first date?' She doesn't answer, but suddenly I see it clearly. 'And you fell pregnant with me,' I say dully. So I'm the reason she ended up in an unhappy marriage. But her next words shock me.

'Not with you,' she says.

I stop on the sidewalk and stare at her, unable to walk any further.

'Then with whom?' I ask, the words threatening to choke me.

'Perhaps this isn't the place.' She indicates the street around her, the sidewalk, the nearby canopy from a cheap Italian restaurant.

'You can't stop now,' I warn, feeling sick to the pit of my stomach. 'Tell me.'

'I miscarried at twenty-two weeks. Five and a half months,' she explains, when she sees me trying to calculate it in my head. 'It was a boy,' she says sadly.

'I almost had a brother?' I ask.

She nods.

'Were you married to my father by then?'

'Yes. Only a month before. I wasn't even showing yet. Your father was devastated. He always wanted a son.' She glances at me apologetically, and in that instant I remember something my father said to me when I was only about five or six.

'*At the very least you could have been a boy . . .*'

'Didn't you try to have any more children after me?'

She looks off down the street. 'Yes. I miscarried them all.'

'All?' I look at her in horror.

'Six in total, but all in the first trimester. I never knew the sex of the others.'

'What about me? Why didn't you miscarry me?' It's a crazy question, and I don't really expect her to know the answer, so I'm startled when she suddenly looks on edge. 'Mother?'

'Let's keep walking.' I hurry after her down the sidewalk, waiting for her to continue. Eventually she does. 'I felt like your father hated me.'

I glance at her in confusion as she continues.

'I lost him his son.'

'It wasn't your fault!'

'But he didn't see it that way. He wanted to try again. Straight away. But I had another miscarriage. I didn't fall pregnant again for some time after that, and he just became bitter and resentful.'

'But how did you cope with that? You must've been devastated yourself.'

'I was,' she says simply. 'More devastated than I could ever describe. And to live with his hatred . . . It was too much.'

'So you left him?'

'Yes.'

'And you say this was before I was born?' I'm breathless from walking so fast.

'About ten months before, yes.'

'Wow. So you didn't leave him for long, then?'

She shakes her head. Her expression is pained.

'What is it?'

In the light of the streetlamps I see her eyes have filled with tears. I stop suddenly, struck down with realisation. She stops, too, and turns around to face me.

'He's not my father, is he?'

She doesn't speak, she doesn't nod or shake her head. Her eyes steadily meet mine as time seems to stand still.

'I don't know,' is her reply.

'You don't know?' My voice is wavering.

'I don't know,' she confirms.

'How can you not know?' I'm starting to feel hysterical. 'Who was he? Who did you screw?' My last words sound bitter.

'He was my childhood sweetheart.'

'Argh!' I shout, all too familiar with that term.

She regards me warily, but my anger is not as strong as my need to know the truth. I breathe heavily as I wait for her to continue.

'He was my boyfriend. We broke up before I went to England.

He was angry I was leaving him and said he wouldn't wait for me. We left a lot of things unfinished.'

'So you went back home and slept with him, while you were still married to my father?'

She doesn't reply. 'Go on,' I prompt. 'What happened next? Did you go running back to England?'

She shakes his head. 'He came looking for me.'

'Who? My father?'

'Yes. He wanted to make amends. He wanted me back.'

'And what about poor old whatshisname?'

She actually shrugs. 'I was married. I felt it was my duty to go back to England with my husband.'

'Fuck your duty!' I shout. 'Why didn't you do what was in your heart?' I'm so confused. I feel all over the place, sometimes *with* her, sometimes *against* her. I don't know what to think.

'My heart was torn, Daisy. And then when I realised I was pregnant again, I almost expected to miscarry. But I didn't.'

'No, you had me. And I bet 'daddy' was absolutely delighted with his little girl,' I say sarcastically.

'He *was* happy,' she tells me.

'But he still wanted a son.'

'Yes.'

'And you never gave him one.'

'No.'

'Does he know about the other guy?' I ask unhappily.

'His name was Andrea.'

I suck in a sharp breath as I hear the name of the man who *could* be my father.

'No,' my mother replies. 'I never told your father what happened.'

'Does . . . Andrea know about me?'

My mother shakes her head. 'I don't think so. But I can't be sure.'

'Maybe I could have a paternity test? Find out if he's my real father? Perhaps I could get to know him?'

'He's dead.'

Her words resonate through me.

'He's dead?'

'Yes. I found out when I went back for your grandfather's funeral.'

I feel crushed. Suddenly I can't walk anymore. 'Do I look like him?' I ask quietly.

My mother studies my face and, finally, shakes her head. 'No. You look like me,' she says. We stare at each other as tears begin to streak down both our cheeks.

'I don't understand why you never left my father when he's always been so hateful towards you.'

'I thought I was doing the right thing. Doing the best thing for you.'

I shake my head. 'You weren't doing the best thing for me.'

'But we would have had nothing!' Her face is anguished.

'I have nothing, now,' I say, angry all of a sudden. 'I don't want the money. It's never been what I wanted. I just wanted to grow up in a happy household with a family who loved me.'

'We do love you.'

'Don't make me laugh. You don't have to lie to protect me. I'm sure you've done more than enough of that over the years and I haven't appreciated it or respected you for it.'

She says nothing.

'Why don't you leave him now?' I ask eventually. 'You could find love again, be happy . . .'

She steadfastly shakes her head. 'No. This is my life now. And I'm fine. I have everything I could ever want.'

'What? The latest Gucci bag and Prada shoes?' My tone is sarcastic.

'It makes me happy, Daisy.'

As I continue to stare at her, disappointment seeps up through my pores and suddenly I understand. She likes the money. She likes the wealth. She's used to this life now.

'I'm used to this life now.' She uses the same words that have just passed through my mind. 'I couldn't go back. Not to Italy, not to the mountains. I like it here in New York.'

She's trapped by her wealth, I can see that so clearly. But I won't let that happen to me. I won't.

That night when we return to the apartment, I go straight to my bedroom and call Holly.

'Can I stay with you?'

'Yes!' she shrieks. 'A million times, yes! When are you coming back?'

'Give me a few days to get it sorted.'

'You know we're in Belgium this weekend?'

'That's right, yes. Do you get back on Sunday?'

'Yes.'

'I could come then . . .' I think aloud.

'If you fly into Heathrow around the same time, we could share a cab back to my place. I'll get my itinerary and text you the details.'

'Cool.' Pause. 'Do you still have my things?'

'Of course. They're in the loft. I'll put them in your bedroom.'

'So you didn't give them away to charity?' I check, smiling.

'Hell, no. Who do you think I am, Laura? Sorry, bad joke.'

I don't speak.

'Daisy?' she says tentatively. 'Are you going to be okay?'

'I don't know, Holly. But I'm sure as hell going to try.'

Chapter 22

My plane ticket is booked, my bags are packed and, yes, I even packed them myself. I'm taking with me only what I brought here – the designer outfits I've boxed up and sent to Cindy, Lisa and Donna. They may be rich, but they still like a freebie, and they'll have more use for them than I will. The only thing left to do is tell my parents, and my father is typically late home from work again. My flight leaves in a few hours, so I don't have long. Part of me hopes he doesn't return in time, but three years ago I left without saying goodbye and now I'm determined to be stronger.

I find my mother in the living room. She's doing what I usually do, sitting on the windowsill, staring down at the joggers in Central Park. I stand there and watch her quietly for a moment, feeling a rush of love for her. It surprises me. Maybe one day I'll understand what she's been through and the choices that she's made, but right now I'm still finding it difficult. If anything, perhaps being away from her again will give me the space to forgive her for being the person that she is.

'You're leaving, aren't you?' she asks quietly, slowly turning her head to look at me.

'Yes,' I reply.

She nods. 'When?'

'Tonight.'

'And what will you do?'

'I'm going back to work with the Formula 1 team.' I turn around and look towards the door as I fidget with my hands.

'He's not going to be happy about it,' my mother says.

'I know.'

'Daisy . . .' she starts.

'Yes?'

She begins to speak in Italian again. 'I'm sorry.'

'For what?' I answer back, also in Italian.

'For everything. I'm sorry you didn't have a happy childhood. Or adulthood,' she adds. 'I wish you would stay.'

'I'm sorry, too,' I reply, 'because I can't.'

'I know. And I will miss you. Please don't leave for as long this time.'

'I won't.' I hesitate while standing there, and then walk to the sofa and sit down. She joins me. 'What was he like?' I ask. 'Andrea.'

She's not surprised by my question. 'He was fiery, passionate, but we were only young. I don't know what sort of a man he turned into.'

'Did he get married? Have children?'

'Married, yes, children, no.'

'So I don't have any half brothers or sisters.' It's not really a question, more a statement.

'I don't know if he was your father,' my mother says. 'I don't know how important it is for you to find out. But I know that it would kill Stellan.'

'Kill his reputation, you mean.'

'It's the same thing.'

I stare at her and wonder to myself if I need to know. What would I do? How would I handle it? Is there any point, now Andrea is dead? Perhaps not. I don't know how I'll feel in the years to come, but I guess I don't have to decide anything right now.

'I think I'll leave it alone for the moment,' I say.

She smiles tearfully and reaches over to hold my hand. 'I'll miss you, my little star.'

I'm taken aback. 'That's what Nonna calls me!'

'It's what she called me, too, when I was growing up.'

The sound of my father's voice makes both of us jump. 'What are you saying to each other? Why are you speaking in that language?' He's standing at the doorway, staring at us angrily. I notice a figure creeping around in the corridor behind him and realise it's Martin.

My mother immediately looks fearful at his words, but I feel brave. 'We're speaking in *Italian*. It's *our* language.' I motion to my mother and me.

'It's not your language,' he spits. 'That's not how I raised you.'

I try to stay calm. I know he just feels threatened because he doesn't understand.

'Hello, Martin.' I change the subject.

'Hello!' He scoots past my father and comes into the living room. 'Two more days to go before the big day. I don't have an office for you, but I thought you could perch in the corner of mine for the time being. Keep me company.'

'Thank you for the offer.' I try to keep my sarcasm at bay, but I'm speaking through clenched teeth. 'But as I've already told my father, I'll have to politely decline.'

'Daisy,' my father interrupts. 'Do not disobey me.'

'She's a feisty one!' Martin rubs his hands together with glee. 'But I like a challenge.'

'That's enough!' I raise my voice and leap to my feet. 'I am NOT coming to work with you, I'm going back to England.'

'You are doing no such thing,' my father says angrily.

'Just try and stop her.' That was my mother speaking and the sound of her deadly calm voice makes us all spin around. 'Martin, can you wait in the office, please,' she says.

'Why?' my father demands to know.

'Thank you.' My mother gives Martin a pointed look as he scuttles away.

'How dare you embarrass me like that!' my father erupts.

My mother ignores him. She turns to me and speaks in Italian. 'What time is your car coming?'

'I just planned on hailing a taxi downstairs.'

'But you should have taken the car!' she exclaims.

'What are you saying? What are you saying?' My father is glaring at each of us in turn. He looks almost comical.

'A taxi is fine,' I tell my mother. 'I'm going now,' I say in English to my father. 'I have a plane to catch tonight.'

'Don't you dare,' he warns. 'You will never get another cent from me. Don't you dare!'

'I don't want your money,' I say, and for once my voice doesn't shake. 'I want to make it on my own.'

'What?' he barks. 'By washing dishes? Peeling potatoes?'

'If that's what it takes.'

'You're a disgrace!'

'Goodbye, mother.' I turn to look at her.

'I'll see you out,' she says.

'Get back here!' my father shouts as we both exit the room. 'Get back here!'

'He doesn't mean it,' my mother says as the elevator whooshes downwards.

'He does. And it doesn't matter, because I meant what I said.'

She nods. 'I know. You're just like your grandmother in that respect.'

At least I know *she's* my blood, I think sadly.

'What will you do? He's going to be very angry when you go back up.'

'He will be. But he'll calm down. And Candida has cooked a lovely leg of lamb so that will cheer him up.'

What an odd thought.

It's raining when I board the plane, and as it zooms off down the runway and soars up into the sky, I only catch a glimpse of New York before we fly through the clouds. I lied to my mother. It will be a long, long time before I come back again.

Chapter 23

'Will you have a glass?' Holly is holding up a bottle of red wine.

'Sure.'

Her face breaks into a grin.

'But you won't need that.' I point at the bottle opener she's just grabbed from the kitchen drawer. She looks at me in confusion. 'It's a screw top,' I tell her.

'Aah . . . And you could see that from there?'

I'm sitting at the kitchen table and she's at the counter top a few paces away.

'Of course. When it comes to opening bottles of booze, I'm a pro.'

'God, I've missed you.' She cracks the bottle open, pouring out two very large glasses and bringing them over.

'Thanks for letting me stay,' I say.

'No problem. Stay as long as you like. Oh, I know you'll want to find a place of your own again, but there's no rush and no pressure from me. It's not like there's anyone else here. Just me, myself and I!'

Right, enough of this.

'Holly, I know about Simon.' I look her straight in the eyes.

'You what?' she asks weakly.

'I know you're having an affair with him.'

The blood drains out of her face. 'How did you find out?' she whispers, sinking into a chair. 'Does everyone know?'

I immediately feel sorry for her. 'No, no, no. Just me. And Luis,' I add.

'Luis?' She looks shocked.

'He won't tell anyone.'

'How do you know? Why? How did he find out? How did you two end up talking about it?' Her voice is rising more with each question.

'Listen, it's okay,' I say sympathetically. 'I just guessed after seeing the way you were with Catalina. And all those times you weren't around when we were staying in the same room.'

'Was I really that obvious?' she asks worriedly.

'Only to me,' I reply.

'What about Luis?'

'He saw you coming out of Simon's room in the early hours of the morning when we were in Italy filming that advert.'

I go on to explain how Luis and I both ended up figuring out how the other person knew. 'He won't tell another soul, I know he won't.'

'You sound very sure,' she says, half warily, half hopefully.

'I am sure,' I tell her. 'I trust him.'

'Okay.'

'So are you still seeing him?' I ask.

She nods guiltily. 'And I know what you must think, especially considering I gave you such a hard time over Laura at the beginning.'

I don't answer.

'But I really like him,' she continues. 'I know he's a lot older than me, but he's just so much more worldly than the boys I've been out with in the past, and, underneath that serious exterior, he's a really kind and gentle man.'

So kind that he's cheating on his wife . . .

'I do feel bad about Catalina,' she adds.

I take a sip of my wine.

'I do!' she insists. 'But she's such a bitch and they don't get on.'

'So why doesn't he divorce her?' I ask.

She looks down at the table. 'He said it would cost him too much money. They don't have a pre-nup,' she explains.

I nod. I don't really understand, but what can you do?

'I know you must think it sounds dodge, dodge, dodge, but . . . Oh, I don't know.'

'Where do you see it going?' It's a question I've been wondering for some time.

'I don't know.' Her shoulders slump dejectedly. 'I'm trying not to get too . . . attached to him. Just in case.'

'And what about your job? You love working for the team.'

'He's not going to fire me!' She frowns.

'I'm not saying he'd do that, but if it all ended, could you keep working for him?'

'Maybe not,' she admits. 'But I guess I'll deal with that if I have to.'

'Aren't you worried about Catalina finding out?' I ask.

'Every day. She almost did in Hockenheim.'

'Really?'

'She wasn't going to come to that race at first, so Simon booked my room next to his, and then she did come and it was a total surprise to me.'

'Were you in his bedroom?'

'Oh no, he told me she was coming the day before, but I was a bit peeved, to be honest. He had to make it up to me in the directors' suite . . .'

She smirks and I feel a bit queasy.

'Anyway,' she continues, 'Catalina came in when we were finishing up . . .' Sorry, but *ew*! '. . . and luckily just thought I was there to iron . . . What? What are you looking like that for?'

I must be pulling quite a face because Holly has stopped mid-sentence. 'It just seems a bit weird to me,' I say.

'What? What seems weird?' She's confused.

'You and Simon.' I'm still screwing my nose up, I can't help it.

'Why?'

'Well, he's just so . . . middle-aged.'

'He's not middle-aged!' she says hotly. 'Well, okay,' she concedes, 'he is, but he doesn't seem it.'

'I just . . . Sorry.' I flap my hand and look away.

'No, tell me,' she urges. 'What?'

I lean in and look at her. 'Do you actually *fancy* him?'

'Of course I do!'

'So it's not just the money?'

'No!' She looks horrified – and a little annoyed. Am I taking this too far? 'It's him. There's something about him. Sorry if you can't see it,' she says petulantly.

'Catalina obviously sees it, too,' I say.

'Now she *is* in it for the money,' Holly snaps.

'And she's going to end up with quite a bucketload if he ever divorces her.'

'If he ever does,' she says sadly.

I'm vaguely curious as to how Holly and Simon got together in the first place, but the thought of him coming on to her, of him sticking his tongue down her throat . . . God knows how I'll feel if I spot him here, going into the bathroom with his boxer shorts on. I shudder and change the subject.

'So what time do we fly out to Italy on Wednesday?'

The next Grand Prix is at Monza, Italy, and it's Sunday night now so I only have a couple of days to settle in and get over my jetlag before we head off again. Holly is working at the team's headquarters in the canteen and she's not at home on Monday or Tuesday, so I spend my time sitting on the sofa in my pyjamas watching rubbish daytime television while eating bowls of nachos. I'm bored out of my brains – I don't know how I ever lasted two months in New York doing little more than this – and by the time Wednesday morning comes around, I'm dying to get back to work.

We're catching the first flight of the day and, as usual, the hospitality staff are setting off to the track the day before anyone else arrives, so I have time to prepare before facing the lads. But I hadn't factored in seeing Frederick again, and as I stand in the terminal, waiting to check in for our flight, I remember what he said the last time he saw me.

'We're ALL upset, Daisy!'

He didn't know about Will and me. And I didn't even tell him I was quitting. I just left. I'm lucky he's taking me back. Nerves flutter through me as I wonder how he'll be with me again. I don't have to wait long. He arrives with Klaus and Gertrude, the latter of whom embraces me warmly.

'Daisy, you're back!'

Gertrude's hug is hefty and I gasp for air as I pull away before

Klaus happily clumps me on my back. I start to cough, while Holly tries not to laugh, but comical as we must look, I am absolutely delighted to see them again. I turn to Frederick. He nods down at me. 'Welcome back.'

'Thank you. Thank you for having me back.' I can't help sounding formal.

'Are you well?' he asks.

'Much better.'

'Good. Because no one fries the bacon as well as you. Let's go.' He motions to the check-in queue in front of us, and that for the moment, is that.

I'm nervous in the car on the way to the track. I'm worried about being in the motorhome again. When we pile out of our standard black people carriers the others file off inside, but I look up for a moment at the team's shiny, portable hospitality building. Holly glances back and sees me.

'Are you okay?' she asks, concerned.

I nod and hesitantly follow her in.

The hospitality area is always empty two days before the first practice session, although this afternoon it feels eerily so. Holly walks off towards the kitchen with the others, while I take in my surroundings slowly. I try not to look to my left where the stairs are, the stairs that used to lead me to Will's private room, but I can't help myself. A lump forms in my throat, but I swallow in quick succession, forcing it back down again. I need to keep busy.

By Friday, I feel like I've settled in somewhat. It was weird seeing Pete, Dan and the lads yesterday. They arrived at the track to start getting the cars ready and I don't think they knew I was going to be back at work. They were definitely pleased to see me, but the atmosphere here seems changed. It's more strained, somehow. Maybe it will be different when race day comes around, I don't know.

On Friday morning I'm serving breakfast when I see a dark-haired guy walk through the hospitality doors. I don't recognise him at first – he has a beard for starters – but suddenly he takes off his dark glasses and I'm floored. It's Luis. He's halfway across the room before he notices me and falters. He's a shadow of his former self, and right now he looks like he's seen a ghost.

He reaches the table. 'Daisy?' he asks quietly, as though not believing it's me standing there.

'Hey,' I reply, my face softening.

'I didn't know you were back.' He looks unsure of himself, so different to the Luis from a couple of months ago. His usually olive-skin tone seems paler and even his beard can't disguise the fact that he's lost a lot of weight.

I nod. 'I thought it was time.'

He doesn't say anything, just meets my eyes for what seems like a long while.

'How are you?' I ask.

He shrugs and looks down.

'Can I get you some bacon?' I smile, trying to cheer him up, but he barely looks at me as he shakes his head.

'No, thanks. I'm not really hungry.'

My blood runs cold.

'I'm just going to head upstairs.' He backs away from the serving table and then turns and walks off with his head down. I look after him worriedly.

'Was that Luis?' Holly asks, coming out of the kitchen.

I glance at her. 'I didn't know he was that bad.'

She nods. 'I told you he wasn't good.'

'But Holly, he looks awful,' I murmur. 'Isn't he eating?'

'He eats,' she says. 'Just not a lot. He doesn't stray from the diet designed for him and you won't catch him out on the town with the lads for beer nor money.'

'Maybe I should go and check on him.' I look towards the stairs. The thought terrifies me. I haven't been near Will's old room since I've been here and have been wondering how I can get through the rest of the season by avoiding it completely.

'I wouldn't,' Holly says.

I look at her in surprise. I didn't expect her to disagree.

'Maybe just leave him be for a little while,' she explains. 'He'll need to get his head together before practice.'

I avert my gaze, feeling a little put-out. The last thing I want to do is upset Luis even more, and I'm sad she thinks I'm capable of it.

By Saturday, it's become quite clear that Luis is avoiding me. He now seems to prefer eating in the privacy of his upstairs room, and as Holly is the drivers' new on-hand front-of-house girl – and I certainly don't want the position back – she's the person who deals with him.

I haven't been into the garages yet, but on the morning of qualifying, Frederick sends Holly and me there to handle the catering. I try to keep my breathing steady as I head across the asphalt to the pits, but my heart jolts when we walk through the door to see Pierre, the test driver who took over Will's drive, standing in Will's garage.

'Daisy, can you sort out the coffee cups?' Holly asks firmly. I know she's trying to distract me and I'm grateful. I get on with my work.

Luis comes in just before qualifying is due to start.

'Come on, man,' Dan urges and even from the other side of the garage I can see frustration etched across his face at Luis's late arrival.

Luis glances my way and quickly averts his gaze before walking unhurriedly towards his car. He climbs in and Dan helps him get settled. The atmosphere in here is tense, but it's a different kind of tension to the one I'm used to. There's no anticipation or excitement, just stress and strain. For the first time I wonder if it was a mistake coming back.

Q1 goes badly. Luis just scrapes into the top fifteen, meaning he'll get another chance to qualify better in the second session. He climbs out of the car.

'It's not handling well,' he exclaims hotly, ripping off his helmet.

'What's wrong with it?' Dan asks.

'It's just not right!' Luis tugs off his gloves.

'Mate, we can't help you if you don't tell us what's wrong.'

'I don't know what's wrong!' Luis shouts, before Dan leads him away towards the private meeting room.

'Is this what it's been like?' I ask Holly.

She nods. I don't think I can watch any more.

Luis qualifies twelfth in the end and doesn't even make it through to the third qualifying session. Pierre does better and will start sixth tomorrow, but that's hardly anything to get excited about.

That night, Saturday night, Holly tentatively broaches the subject of the evening's plans. We're staying at a hotel in the middle of Milan and it's only a short walk to the Piazza del Duomo in the centre of town and a whole host of super-cool bars and clubs.

'I'm not going out,' I tell her flatly.

'I understand,' she says, perching on the end of my bed. I'm lying down, my head propped up on three pillows as I reach for the television remote.

'You go out, though,' I insist. 'I don't need you to keep me company again.' We stayed in the room last night, watching a chick flick and eating room service.

'Well . . .' She looks on edge. 'I might pop up and see Simon later. Only if you don't mind,' she quickly adds. Catalina isn't at this race, and last night Simon had to attend dinner with the sponsors.

'Oh, sure,' I say. After all this time wishing she'd open up to me, now I find it very strange hearing her talk about him.

Holly goes to get changed in the bathroom and I flick through the channels trying not to think about the fact that she's probably putting on lacy underwear in Simon's honour. When she eventually heads out looking sheepish, I sigh and turn the television off. Perhaps I'll read a book? But no, three pages in and half an hour later, I realise I haven't taken in a single word.

Something makes me think back to Bahrain and the sight of Luis speeding around the desert track. The commentators were comparing him to Ayrton Senna, one of the greatest drivers of our time. There's no word of such comparisons now. I wonder if the British press still have their knives out?

I could go and see him . . . If Holly is right, Luis won't be out on the town with the lads. I wonder if he'd let me in? He may just slam the door in my face. Only one way to find out. I leap off the bed full of determination and grab my door key. I don't bother to change out of my work clothes or check my reflection.

Luis is staying in a room three floors above me. I run up the stairs instead of taking the lift and I'm slightly out of breath by the time I get there.

He answers after twenty seconds, opening the door and staring at me with a confused frown.

'Hello,' he says.

'Luis, hi.' I try to catch my breath and give him a hopeful look. 'Can I come in?'

He stands back to let me pass, not speaking.

His room is a tip. Clothes are strewn across the floor and living area. A quick glance through to the bathroom and I can see dirty towels discarded on the floor. The television is blaring out at high volume.

Luis doesn't apologise for the mess as he leads me to the sofa. I pick up his helmet and team overalls and place them on the coffee table, then perch on the edge of an armchair and wait while he digs around down the side of the sofa. Eventually his hand emerges with the remote control. He points it and turns the volume down on the TV before leaning back on the sofa and putting his feet up on the coffee table. He doesn't look at me.

'How are you?' I ask.

'What are you doing here?' he hits back.

'I wanted to see how you are,' I reply, flummoxed.

'Why should you care?' His dark eyes meet mine and I'm taken aback by the intensity of them.

I glance away at the flickering, soundless television for a moment before looking back at him. 'I *do* care.'

He scratches his beard. 'I thought you'd left for good.'

'Sorry to disappoint you.'

He rests his head down on the back of the sofa and takes a deep breath.

'You don't look well, Luis,' I say eventually.

He shrugs.

'What are you going to do about it?' I press.

He shrugs again. 'Nothing.'

'You can't keep hurting yourself like this,' I say. 'You have to forgive yourself.'

'Have *you* forgiven me?' he bites back.

'Yes!' I exclaim. 'There wasn't really anything to forgive! It wasn't your fault!'

His face crumbles and I stare on in shock as I realise he's about to cry.

'Oh, God, Luis, I'm sorry.' I get up from my chair and go to sit next to him on the sofa.

'No, no.' He puts his hand out to wave me away, but I grab it and hold it tightly. 'Please,' he begs, turning his face away.

'It wasn't your fault,' I say again, quietly and sympathetically.

'Don't!' He chokes and I pull him to me, wrapping my arms around his neck as he buries his face into me and starts to sob. My throat swells and tears well up in my eyes because his pain is hurting me, too. I can't let myself think of Will, otherwise I'll be in an even worse state than he is, and I need to be strong for him right now.

Eventually he pulls away.

'Do you want a tissue?' I ask belatedly, digging around in my pocket for one. I never go anywhere without them these days.

'Thanks,' he answers groggily, taking it from me and loudly blowing his nose. I edge away to give us both some space.

'*Nossa Senhora*,' he sighs, leaning back on the sofa and staring up at the ceiling. 'You didn't go out tonight?' He turns to look at me, his eyes red and still a little teary.

I shake my head. 'No.'

'Holly?'

'She's with Simon.'

He nods and looks up at the ceiling again.

'It's strange being back,' I comment.

It's a while before he answers. 'Where did you go?'

'New York. To see my parents.'

'How was it?' He glances at me.

'Awful.' Pause. 'How are your family?'

'Good. Well, yeah . . .' He hesitates.

'What?'

'No, nothing.' He brushes me off.

'Tell me. How's your mother?'

'Um . . . All this . . .' He waves his hand around the room. 'You know, it's bothering her,' he says with difficulty.

'What do you mean? The *racing* is bothering her?'

'Everything. It's all bothering her.'

I'm confused. 'Has she been reading about you in the papers?'

'Mmm, yeah.' He sits up straighter and looks jittery.

'Luis, she can't believe everything she reads. Maybe she should just avoid the tabloids like I do.'

He nods, clearly on edge.

I sigh. I hate seeing him like this. I want to try to make it better. 'I'm sorry I ran away from you after the funeral.'

'It's okay.'

'I wasn't myself, you know?'

'I know.'

'Luis, please!' I just want him to return to normal. I can't handle this!

'What? What? It's okay,' he adds absent-mindedly. Even his voice sounds strange.

'You have to let it go,' I plead. 'You have to let him go.' My eyes well up again as he turns to look at me.

'Have you let him go?'

We stare at each other for a long while before I shake my head. He looks away again. 'No. I didn't think so.'

'Are the press still giving you a hard time?' I ask after a moment.

'It's not so bad.'

'Good. They'll lay off soon.'

'I didn't mean to win the race,' he says suddenly in a detached voice.

'What race? The one that . . . Silverstone?'

He nods. 'I didn't know the accident was as bad as that.'

'I know. I'm sure everyone understands.'

'No, they don't.' He slowly shakes his head. 'I don't know if I can do this anymore.'

I grab his hand again and clutch it tightly. 'Yes, you can,' I tell him fervently. 'Yes, you can. You're a brilliant racing driver. They were comparing you to Ayrton Senna, for Christ's sake!'

'They're not anymore.'

'Well, they will be again. You just have to get back on your feet, get back behind the wheel. You said you wanted to win a race for Will, well do it!'

He looks at me in surprise. 'You heard about that?'

I nod. 'I saw you on the telly in America.'

'Huh.' He looks away again. 'I didn't do a very good job of it.'

'No, well, don't worry,' I say lamely, before clutching his hand fiercely once more. 'You can do it now. Tomorrow!'

'From twelfth?' He gives me a wry look, and for the first time I get a glimpse of the Luis I used to know.

'Well, maybe not win it, but you know, finish it. Or something. I don't know! Just stop being such a lame-arse and get out there. *I'll* be proud of you.'

He grins at me and squeezes my hand, then almost instantly snatches his away and covers his face as his body starts to shake with sobs.

'Oh, Luis . . .' I rub his back, feeling utterly mortified. 'I'm sorry. I'm sorry.' I rest my head on his shoulder and just stay there for a while, waiting for him to calm down. Eventually he sits up and composes himself, brushing his tears away.

'You'd better go,' he says morosely. 'I need to get to bed.'

I stand up unsteadily. I don't know if I've made it worse by coming here. He follows me to the door and pulls it open. I step out onto the landing and turn around.

'I'm sorry,' I say. 'I'm sorry for all of this. I don't know . . .' I hesitate. 'Maybe I shouldn't have come back.'

'No,' he says fervently, meeting my eyes. 'That's not true. I'm glad you're back.' And then his face crumbles again and he quickly closes the door in my face.

Chapter 24

I don't tell Holly about my visit to see Luis. She stayed in Simon's room anyway, so the first I see of her is in the morning when I'm putting on my team uniform. I had terrible nightmares last night, about a man or a monster hunting me down. I kept waking up in cold sweats, trying to tell myself it was just a dream, but then I'd fall straight back into it again. Needless to say, I'm in a vile mood today.

Luis turns up at ten o'clock and goes straight up to his room. I'm in the kitchen looking out, but he doesn't see me, just keeps his head down and walks quickly. I suppose he's feeling embarrassed about losing it in front of me . . .

To hell with this! I go to the serving table and grab a plate, loading it up with bacon and eggs.

'What are you doing?' Holly asks, frowning.

'Don't try to stop me,' I reply, coming out from behind the table and walking towards the stairs.

'Daisy!' she calls in dismay, but I ignore her.

At the top of the stairs I inadvertently glance to my right and see that the door to Will's one-time driver's room has been left open. I halt in my tracks and stare inside. There's a black team carry case, identical to Will's – identical to all of ours – resting on the table. I feel like the blood is literally draining from my face. The door to Luis's room opens and he comes out with his head down. And then he looks up and sees me.

'Daisy? Are you alright?'

I shake my head quickly as my nose starts to prickle. He ushers me into his room. My hand is shaking so I put his plate of food down onto the table with a clatter.

'Is that for me?' he asks.

I nod, silently, unable to meet his eyes.

'I'm not hungry.'

'You have to eat!' I exclaim, suddenly cross.

'I don't want to eat,' he replies nonchalantly.

'Well, tough! Because you're going to!'

He raises one eyebrow at me with amusement. 'And how are you going to manage that, exactly?'

'I'll shove it down your throat if you're not careful,' I warn.

He sighs and collapses onto the sofa. 'Give me one piece of bacon,' he demands. I grab the plate and sit down next to him, picking out the crispiest piece I can see. He takes it from me, reluctantly, and chews along the edge of it before finally popping it into his mouth.

'If João could see me now . . .' he comments.

'João would just be damned relieved you're eating at all,' I say hotly.

He holds out his hand for another piece.

'Are you coming to watch the race today?' he asks after a moment.

'I don't know,' I reply. 'I don't think so.'

'Why not?'

'Luis, you know why not. I'm just trying to, you know, break myself in gently.'

He chucks the piece of bacon back onto the plate and slumps into the sofa. '*Fode-se*,' he mutters.

'What does that mean?' I ask, but he ignores me. 'Fuck it? Luis, did you just say, "fuck it"?'

He doesn't answer.

'Well, fuck you,' I tell him.

'*Fottiti*?' He glances at me hopefully and my face breaks into a grin.

'You're such a *testa di cazzo*. When are you going to have a shave?'

He shrugs. 'Who gives a shit?'

'I do. You look weird with a beard.'

'Weirdy beardy?'

'Yes!' I laugh.

'I'll have a shave if you come and watch the race.'

My face falls and I stare at him. 'I don't know if I can.'

'Sure you can.' He pats me casually on the knee before standing up and stretching his arms over his head. His T-shirt rides up and I can see his far-too-skinny torso underneath.

'Eat another piece – no, two more pieces – of bacon and you've got yourself a deal,' I say, joining him on his feet and offering up the plate. He gives me a wry look, but reaches down and grabs two pieces, shovelling them both into his mouth at the same time.

'That's disgusting,' I say, grimacing at the sight. He grins at me, making it even worse. 'Oh, stop!' I insist, but he swallows and puts me out of my misery.

'Where's my coffee?' he asks suddenly, looking on the table.

'I didn't bring one,' I reply.

'Jesus. And you're supposed to be a bun tart.'

'Oi!' I go to slap him on his arm, but he blocks me. 'I don't know why I've been worrying about you, Luis Castro.' I shake my head and start to head out of the room. He follows me.

'See you in the pits in a couple of hours.'

'I'll be there,' I promise, as a chill goes through me.

Red, red, red, red, red, GO! I can barely make out Luis's car so far back, but it looks like he's overtaking several cars at the start. After a while the race positions flash up on the television screens above our heads and my thoughts are confirmed: Luis has made up four places on the grid and is now running eighth. That's not bad. At least it's in the points. Pierre, in the other car, is still sixth.

Luis is now hot on the tail of Germany's Benni Fischer in seventh place.

'WHOA!' a few people in the garages shout as he nips out from behind him and outbreaks him into a corner. Seventh!

'Bloody hell!' Holly exclaims from my side. 'What's gotten into him?'

I don't answer, just stare up at the screens in anticipation. We're standing in Luis's garage. I've made a concerted effort not to look through to Pierre's.

It was raining this morning, but when the race started it was dry. Suddenly the heavens open again and the mechanics go into overdrive as Luis pulls into the pits for a tyre change. Cars still wearing their 'dry' tyres are spinning off the track and fear begins to creep back into my heart.

A few laps later and on his 'wet' tyres, Luis has climbed another two places on the grid. He's now running sixth and Pierre has climbed a place into fifth. Suddenly the camera cuts to Nils Broden's car, wrecked and smoking in a gravel pit. The television screens show a replay of the accident which put it there, and I watch, white-knuckled and sick to my bones, as Broden's car smashes into a concrete wall and shatters across the track.

And then I see Will, clear as day, in my mind. His car is upside down on the gravel pit as an ambulance crew brings out a white sheet. I start to feel dizzy. I hear Holly's voice beside me asking if I'm okay. She puts her hands on my arms to steady me and tries to tell me that Broden is fine, that he's climbed out of his car and is already over the wall and on his way back to the pits, but I'm in another place, another time. All I can see is Will's car, the front end completely gone. And then I see Will, staring at me in the darkness as we lay side-by-side in bed.

I break down in uncontrollable sobs.

'Daisy . . . Daisy . . .' Holly's voice tries to soothe me, but I'm beyond help. I fall to my knees and am vaguely aware of people in the garage turning to stare at me.

'Daisy, please,' Holly begs. 'Come back to the hospitality area.'

'I can't . . . I can't . . .'

'It's okay.' She crouches beside me and puts her arm around my shoulder while several mechanics worriedly look our way. I know it will be a struggle for them to concentrate with this going on.

Klaus comes into the garage with Frederick. He must've gone to fetch him.

'Come with me,' Frederick says firmly. He pulls me to my feet and I stumble out of the garage with him. Holly follows.

'I'm sorry!' I cry. 'I can't be here!'

'No, Daisy, please don't leave again!' Holly begs, her hand on my arm. 'Chef, don't let her quit!'

'Enough!' Frederick snaps at her. 'Take a couple of days,' he tells me as my sobs quieten. 'Go and stay with your grandmother. Call Ally to arrange a car.'

I nod dumbly as Holly relaxes her grip on my arm.

'But I want you back at work next week,' Frederick adds. 'And after that we're off to Singapore, so don't let me down.'

We return to the kitchen in the hospitality area where Holly helps me gather my things before walking me outside to one of the team's people carriers.

'Can you take me back to the hotel?' I ask the driver, who's leaning up against the front of the car, listening to a hand-held radio.

'Sure,' he replies.

'I'll call Ally from there,' I tell Holly. 'And I'll see you back in the UK.'

'You will come back, won't you?' Her face is etched with worry.

'Yes,' I tell her, although at this stage I'm really not sure.

Chapter 25

The track in Monza is on the outskirts, north-east of the city, but I have to collect my bag from the hotel and arrange a car before I can set off. Nonna lives about three hours' drive south-west from Milan, so I have a lot of time to think as I stare out of the window. To the far right I catch occasional glimpses of the sea, while to my left there are hills and forests, but the route is mostly dull – long stretches of motorway until we finally reach the bendy mountain roads north of Lucca.

I remember Will driving me around here in the Aston Martin that he was thinking of buying. There are so many things he wanted to do. Sometimes it hits me how his life was cut short and I have to gasp for air before I can push yet another memory to the back of my mind.

Nonna comes out of her front door as the taxi pulls into the lane outside her house. I called her from the hotel so she's been expecting me.

As soon as she engulfs me in a warm hug, I start to feel better.

'*La mia stellina* . . .' she murmurs into my hair, before pulling away and studying my face. 'You have lost even more weight.' She shakes her head in dismay.

I glance around at the mountains, which are shrouded in dark clouds. A storm is imminent.

Nonna leads me inside to her warm kitchen and immediately starts to serve up some *ribollita* soup. It's made from the leftovers of minestrone and it's delicious, but I'm not hungry, so I swirl my spoon around and take the odd mouthful while Nonna looks on sympathetically.

'Are you okay, my love?' she asks eventually.

I shake my head. 'Not really, no.'

'Would you like to talk about it?'

'Maybe tomorrow,' I reply softly. 'I'm very tired.'

The sky outside the window begins to flash with lightning. Nonna gets to her feet and pulls pots and pans out of a cupboard before exiting the kitchen. I get up wearily and put my bowl in the sink before following her through to the sitting room. Old bits of rag are still stuffed in the walls from the last time I was here. I sigh, too drawn to comment.

'Come,' she says to me, indicating the sofa. I falter for a moment, remembering the sight of Will falling asleep there, but she takes my hand and pulls me down to sit beside her. I curl up and lay my head on her lap as she quietly and soothingly strokes my hair.

The sound of a car screeching to a stop outside the house wakes me up. I look, bleary-eyed, up at Nonna.

We both react at the same time, leaping to our feet and staring out of the window in alarm. A man climbs out of the car and holds his jacket above his head to shield himself from the pelting rain as he runs towards the door.

'Who is it?' I ask.

'I don't know,' Nonna replies.

We hurry through to the kitchen as the man starts pounding on the door.

'Shall I open it?' Nonna asks me, clearly not used to expecting visitors, especially this late on a Sunday night.

'I'll do it,' I insist, going to the door.

'Daisy, it's me!' I hear the man shout.

Luis? I open the door in surprise and he stares out at me from underneath his drenched coat.

'Can I come in?' he asks quickly.

I step back in shock. 'What are you doing here?'

'Good evening.' He nods at Nonna, who's watching this interaction with some interest. She takes his coat, going to the old-fashioned stove and hanging it out to dry. 'Thank you,' he calls. He sounds oddly formal.

'Who is this?' Nonna asks me in Italian.

'Luis Castro,' I reply. 'He's the other driver for the team.'

'He doesn't look much like a driver,' she mutters.

'He doesn't usually have a beard. He was just, you know, he hasn't been himself since . . . the accident.'

Luis glances with confusion at each of us, but Nonna's face softens after my last comment. 'Come in, come in,' she urges in English. 'Sit down.'

'Er, thank you,' Luis replies awkwardly. He pulls out a chair at the kitchen table.

'Have you had dinner?' Nonna asks in Italian. I translate.

'No, but I'm fine, thank you,' Luis replies.

'You can't say no to my nonna's cooking,' I tell him.

He gives me a look, not sure if I'm tricking him into eating or not.

'In that case, yes please.' He sounds so polite for a change. I would giggle if I weren't so confused.

'How did you find me?' I ask while Nonna ladles some soup out of the saucepan still sitting on the stove.

'I asked Holly where you'd gone, then called Ally to find out the address.'

'But I don't understand? Why did you come at all?'

Nonna places a bowl in front of him. He looks up and says thank you, then picks up his spoon.

'Don't worry,' I say, glancing at Nonna. 'You can fill me in, later.'

He starts to eat while Nonna and I sit there and watch him for a moment. I realise we're staring.

'How did the race go?' I ask, coming to my senses.

'I came third,' he replies, taking another mouthful.

'Luis, that's brilliant!' I exclaim.

'What?' Nonna interrupts. I quickly fill her in about Luis qualifying twelfth, but finishing on the podium. I turn back to him, feeling absolutely delighted.

'Simon must've been thrilled!'

He shrugs. 'I wouldn't know.'

'What do you mean?'

'I came straight here.'

'What, after the press conference?'

'Nope. Didn't do it.'

'But that's immediately after the awards' ceremony. How did you even know I'd left?'

'You weren't in the crowd. I shouted down to Holly and she told me you'd gone.'

I'm too taken aback to comment.

Luis puts his spoon down. 'I'm sorry,' he says. 'My appetite isn't what it was.'

Nonna waves away his apology and clears the bowl. 'Why don't you go to the sitting room and I'll bring through coffee,' she suggests. I lead the way.

'I guess I wasn't really thinking, turning up like this.' Luis glances around the room. 'It's not very good manners to land on someone's doorstep, uninvited. I hope your grandmother doesn't hold it against me.'

'Don't worry, she won't.' We sit next to each other on the sofa. 'You still haven't told me why you're here?' I prompt.

He looks uncomfortable. 'Spur of the moment. I didn't want you to leave again.'

'I was only taking a break for a few days.'

'I couldn't be sure of that. I couldn't take the risk.'

'I'm surprised you'd care that much.'

He looks up suddenly and stares straight into my eyes. 'I need you more than you think.'

My heart does something funny and it dawns on me at that moment that maybe I need him, too. I know I need him to be right again, and if he thinks I can help, then I'll consider that my job for the time being.

Nonna comes into the room. 'Here you go,' she says, handing coffee cups to each of us.

'So when are you going to have that shave?' I give Luis an amused look.

He shrugs. 'Sometime before the next race. I was quite liking my beardy look.'

'I bet Simon hates it.'

'Simon's not my biggest fan at the moment, anyway.'

'So I've heard.'

He takes a sip of his coffee.

'What's this?' Nonna asks. I fill her in about Luis's promise to shave off his beard and she stands up and hurries out of the room with determination. Luis and I look after her, curiously. She returns a minute later with a small bag and hands it to Luis. He opens it and pulls out an old-fashioned razor and shaving brush.

'Carlo's,' Nonna tells me. 'They were my husband's,' she says to Luis.

'Er, thanks,' he replies, lifting up the blade and inspecting it. 'I'm, um, not sure I'll know how to use this. I usually use an electric one,' he explains to Nonna. I translate.

'Give them to me,' she urges, and Luis hands them over. 'I'll do it for you.'

'What, *now*?' he asks, disconcerted.

'Yes, now,' Nonna replies, standing up and pointing in the direction of the bathroom. 'Time for a fresh start. You wait here,' Nonna tells me. 'Not enough room. Come.' She holds her hand down to Luis, who reluctantly takes it and follows her, shooting a worried look at me over his shoulder. I stifle a giggle. Ten minutes later, Nonna produces a clean-shaven Luis.

'Wow,' I say, as he jokingly rubs his face. 'No cuts?'

'Not a single one.' He grins and sits back down on the sofa. 'Thank you,' he says to Nonna.

'You're welcome,' she replies in English, with wry amusement.

Luis sighs. 'I guess I should be getting off.'

'Off? Where is he going?' Nonna asks me in Italian.

'I have to get back to Milan,' Luis explains, and I translate.

'You can't drive in this weather. No. You stay on sofa,' Nonna says, as I experience a feeling of déjà vu.

'No, honestly, I'll be fine,' Luis assures her, making to stand up.

'Absolutely not!' she insists. 'This storm is too fierce!' A loud crack of thunder helpfully illustrates her point.

'I'm a racing driver.' Luis grins. 'I'm used to driving in tough conditions.'

'Tell him to wipe that smile off his face.' Nonna's tone is ferocious. She glares at Luis. 'My husband, he died on these roads!'

I stare at my grandmother through narrowed eyes as Luis looks shamefaced. 'I'm so sorry.'

'I'll be back with the bedding.' She bustles off.

'Sorry about that,' I say to Luis. 'But you may as well sleep here and set off in the morning.'

'Will you come back to Milan with me?' he asks hopefully.

'No,' I reply. 'I'd like to spend some time with Nonna. But I *will* come back. I promise.'

He relaxes back into the sofa as she re-enters the room with sheets and blankets.

'Just leave them there, Nonna, I'll do it,' I say.

'Fine. I'm off to listen to my radio show,' Nonna replies. 'Good night!' she calls as she hurries off.

'I'm going to head off to bed, too,' I say, sadly recalling my evening here with Will.

'Okay,' Luis answers. He helps me make up the sofa and then climbs under the covers.

'Well done on your podium result,' I say, standing by the door.

'Thanks, bun tart.'

He leaves early the next morning, but not before Nonna has persuaded him to eat some breakfast. The storm has passed, although it's still overcast. We wave him off from the door as he pulls his rental car out of the lane onto the main mountain road, tooting the horn as he goes.

I follow Nonna back inside, still dumbfounded that he came all this way for me. We sit at the kitchen table and I sip at my coffee.

'I like that one,' she says after a moment.

'Luis?'

'Yes.'

'More than Will?' I can't help but ask.

'Not more. They're very different. He likes you.'

'Will liked me?'

'No, this one. Luis. He likes you.'

I scoff. 'No, he doesn't.'

She eyes me shrewdly over the rim of her coffee cup. 'Yes, he does.'

I don't say anything for a moment, then a thought comes to me.

'Nonna . . .'

'Yes?'

'I thought Nonno died of a heart attack?'

She shrugs. 'He did.'

'But you told both Will and Luis that he died on the mountain roads.'

'They wouldn't have stayed otherwise.'

'But Nonna, that's so sneaky!' I exclaim.

'A girl's gotta do what a girl's gotta do,' she casually replies. I can't believe she's speaking like this. At her age! She's eighty-two!

'Anyway, why would you want them to stay?' I ask.

'To give them more time with you, of course.'

'But *why*?'

'You need a man!' she erupts.

'*What?* Nonna, what are you going on about? We don't live in the dark ages!'

'Don't patronise me, young lady. I know what's good for you.'

'Well, Will had a *girlfriend*,' I pedantically point out.

'Oh, I know that,' she waves me away.

'How did you know that?' I ask, confused. I never told her.

'It was obvious,' she replies. 'But you can't let things like that stand in your way.'

'Nonna!' I'm outraged. 'I would have never allowed myself to be the other woman.' But even as I say it, a little shred of doubt niggles away at me. I glance down at my fingernails.

'Did you know Nonno was set to be engaged to another girl when I met him?'

'No?' I sit up in my seat.

'Yes,' she replies. 'But they weren't in love. I could see it. It was to be a marriage of convenience. To please their parents. When Carlo and I set eyes on each other . . .' Her voice trails off as she becomes lost in her thoughts. She turns back to me. 'It was meant to be, your grandfather and me. You can't always wait for fate, you have to step in.'

'Is that what you did?' I ask.

'Yes,' she says firmly.

I don't really like the idea of my grandmother stealing another woman's man, but she doesn't seem at all repentant. And I guess I wouldn't be here if she hadn't.

'Well, it's all in the past now,' I say sadly, thinking of Will.

'No,' she says bluntly. 'There's still Luis.'

'Nonna, I couldn't be interested in Luis!'

'Why not? He's better suited to you than the other one.'

'No, he's not! Anyway, I'm still in love with Will, so I can't think about anyone else.'

'Give it time,' she says wisely. 'Give it time.'

I roll my eyes, but let it be.

She stands up and leaves the kitchen, bringing back a couple of pots and pans from last night. Water swishes around inside them as she takes them to the sink and pours out the contents.

'Nonna, why won't you let my mother help you fix the walls?' I follow her back through to the sitting room and help retrieve the remaining pots.

'No,' she says bluntly, returning to the kitchen sink and tipping the water down the plughole.

'Why do you have to be so stubborn?' I complain and she shoots me a ferocious look over her shoulder before sitting down again.

I join her back at the table. 'My mother told me something in New York,' I start. 'About my father.' I'll leave the subject of house maintenance alone for the time being.

'Yes?'

'About Andrea . . .'

'Andrea?' she barks.

'Well, I don't know if he's my real father or not . . .'

Nonna's eyes widen.

'And neither does my mother.'

Cue a knowing look. 'I see.'

'Did she not tell you? Did you ever suspect it?'

She pauses before answering. 'She didn't tell me, but I did suspect it, yes. She spent a lot of time with Andrea when she left your father and returned home. And she fell pregnant very soon after she went back to him. I thought it was *too* soon.'

'Did you ever say anything?'

'What *could* I say? I told her not to go back to your father, to stay with me and your grandfather, but she chose not to.'

'And what about Andrea? Did he know that my mother was pregnant?'

Nonna looks down at the table. 'Yes.'

'And he didn't think to chase after her? To find out if the baby – if *I* – was his?'

My grandmother doesn't answer.

'I guess not.' I'm disappointed in my father, whoever he is, then.

'He would have been too proud to run after her,' Nonna says finally. 'And Stellan was a very daunting man.'

'What happened to Andrea?'

'He got married to a local girl and lived a simple life here in the mountains.'

'How did he die?'

'Cancer. He was ill for a long time before he finally passed away.'

'And they had no children?' I know my mother said they didn't, but I want to be sure.

'No. No children.' Pause. 'Your mother couldn't have handled it, you know.'

'What?'

'Caring for him. She wasn't the type. She was always looking for something better, a better life for herself. It drove her mad that your grandfather and I were so settled here for all those years. When Carlo died, she wanted me to move to New York.'

'Did she really?' I can't imagine my grandmother in New York.

'Yes. Of course, I refused. Although I was tempted just to annoy your father.'

I look away.

'Sorry,' she apologises. 'I shouldn't speak badly of him. He's still your father.'

'Is he, though?'

She studies me for a moment. 'I think so. You look nothing like Andrea. I think you have your father's nose.'

I can't help but snort at the triviality of that resemblance.

I return to England four days later.

'Have you seen the papers?' Holly asks me the moment we settle ourselves down on the sofa with a nice glass of wine.

'No? Why?'

'God, it's all about Luis, Luis, Luis.'

I sigh with frustration. 'Why won't they just leave him alone?'

'No, it's not that,' she says excitedly. 'They're all interested in him now. After that last race result, and then running off after the awards ceremony like that and turning up at the airport the next day with his beard shaven off. It's like he's a new man! They can't stop talking about him!'

'Seriously?'

'Yep, ooh, the other drivers are all going to be jealous again.'

'Jealous? Why would they be jealous?'

'Daisy, you are so out of touch! He was like the hot new thing when he started out in F1. The other drivers all felt massively threatened!'

'Oh, right. So . . . Does anyone know where he went when he ran off like that?' I ask hesitantly.

She grins at me. 'He went to see you, didn't he?'

I nod awkwardly.

'Ally told Simon about Luis ringing up to find out your address, so he wasn't worried.'

'Does anyone else know?' I ask.

'No. Just Simon, Ally and me. Bloody hell, though, Daisy. What did you say to him to get him to clean up his act like that? Simon's over the moon! He'd decided Monza was Luis's last chance!'

'Seriously?'

'Yes! So whatever it was, you saved Luis's butt. I hope he knows it.'

'I think he does,' I say quietly. 'But hey, tell me what else has been going on?' I don't really want to discuss Luis anymore.

The following week, one of Holly's colleagues at the canteen calls in sick. Holly asks me if I can cover for her. I've never been to team HQ before and I'm keen to see it, so I agree.

It's like something out of a James Bond film, all shiny black, white and gold with a series of high-security gates to get through before I'm finally allowed inside the hallowed doors. The team's headquarters are enormous, and racing cars from past seasons line up along the polished concrete floor. I walk quickly past them, not wanting to know if one of Will's old cars is there.

The so-called canteen is like a Michelin-starred restaurant, so there are no cheese and pickle sandwiches packaged up in cardboard. I'm lucky I'm trained in silver service from my time working functions for Frederick and Ingrid, because some of the most important sponsors are coming in for a lunch meeting today and Holly has wangled it for me to help her wait on them. We're in the boardroom where they're dining, dishing out freshly baked bread rolls, when the door opens with a whoosh and Luis comes in.

I look up with surprise. There was an empty seat, but I had no idea it was for him.

'Sorry I'm late,' he apologises to the sponsors. 'Terrible traffic.'

'No problem,' Simon replies, indicating Luis's chair. He sits down in it before he sees me, and then jolts a little in shock.

'Oh, hello! I didn't know you worked here?'

'Just helping out,' I reply, embarrassed, because now everyone is looking at me and before that I was just an anonymous waitress. 'Brown, white or granary?' I ask, holding up the bread basket.

'No thanks.'

I give Luis a look.

'Oh, alright, then. That one, there.' He points to a granary roll. Out of the corner of my eye I see Simon looking amused.

'How was Italy?' Luis asks me. Everyone is listening.

'Fine, fine,' I reply quickly, following Holly out of the room. We return a few minutes later with the smoked salmon starters.

'Thanks.' Luis looks up at me and grins, a familiar twinkle back in his dark-brown eyes. I try to keep a straight face as I serve the sponsor next to him. Norm Gelltron is the managing director and main money man behind our team.

'I'm liking your new fresh-faced look, Luis,' Norm says in a loud, booming American accent.

'Blame this one.' Luis aims his thumb at me.

'Is that right?' Norm asks with interest.

'Yep. Well, actually, blame her grandmother. She shaved it off for me.'

Cue a loud chorus of impressed and surprised 'oohs' around the table.

'Your grandmother, hey? You two know each other well, then?'

Twelve sets of eyes are now focused on me. Before I was invisible, now I'm the centre of attention.

'Um . . .' I start.

'We're friends,' Luis interrupts. 'Aren't we, Daisy?' He raises one eyebrow at me and tucks into his salmon.

'Mmm, yes,' I murmur, blushing but secretly pleased.

Holly smirks at me as I hurry out of the room.

'Friends?' she says, once outside. 'And to think you used to hate him.'

'I didn't hate him,' I reply, brushing her off.

'Sure you didn't,' she says sardonically.

Ten minutes later, we go back in to clear the plates. Luis produces a clean one. 'Look!' he says, delighted with himself, a bit like an 8-year-old.

'Well done,' I mutter, amused.

'Daisy's trying to get me to eat properly,' he tells everyone.

'Oh, *really*?' Norm says. 'Gosh, Daisy, you seem to be one hell of a woman,' he booms.

My face immediately heats up again.

'You are one hell of a woman, aren't you, bun tart?' Luis pats my bum.

'Oi!' I whack him on the arm.

'Feisty, too.' Luis laughs.

By the time dessert comes around, I've blushed so many times I'm surprised my face hasn't turned red permanently. Holly is finding the whole thing highly amusing.

'It's mortifying!' I exclaim.

'No, it's not,' she scoffs. 'Simon will be loving it.'

'Will he?' I ask hopefully.

'Absolutely. He hates it when the sponsors act like we don't exist.'

'Huh. I didn't think he cared about things like that.'

'Yeah, well, there's a lot you don't know about Simon. I wish you could see him like I do.'

'Ew!' Whoops. Didn't mean to say that out loud. 'Sorry, I was just imagining him with his pants down!' I dissolve into giggles and after her initial perturbed reaction, Holly soon joins in.

'Why are you always rushing away?' Luis complains as I clear up his dessert plate.

'I'm *working*,' I say quietly. Once again, the others are all ears.

'Stay and talk to me,' he says, as I move on to clear the next plate.

'I can't.' I give him a look to warn him off.

'What are you doing after this?' Luis asks. I'm halfway around the table by now.

'*Still* working.'

'Want to take the afternoon off and come for a drive with me?'

'I can't.' This is *so* embarrassing!

'Aw, come on, how can you say no to an offer like that?' Norm booms. 'One of the world's top racing talent offering to take you for a drive? You'll let her off an afternoon's work, won't you?' Norm turns to Simon.

'Of course,' Simon casually replies.

'There you go!' Luis chirps. I stand at the end of the table, my hands piled with plates, and stare at him with pursed lips. 'Ready in five?' he asks.

'I've got to get your coffees, first.'

'Don't really fancy a coffee. You don't mind if I shoot off, do you?' Luis asks the faces around the table.

I frown. 'I can't just leave.'

Holly grins at me. 'I can manage the coffees.'

'Off you go, then!' Norm booms.

I glance at Luis and he winks at me, then I leave the room to the sound of him shouting that he'll meet me back here. Holly cracks up laughing the second the door shuts behind us.

'That was hilarious!' she squawks between guffaws.

'I can't believe he just did that to me,' I reply, walking quickly down the corridor in the direction of the kitchen.

'*So* funny . . .'

I decide to help out Holly with the coffees, but when we get back to the boardroom, Luis is leaning up against a wall outside the door.

'Come on, then,' he says, jokily glancing at his watch. 'I haven't got all day.'

'Let me just put this down,' I say, nodding at the filtered coffee jug I'm holding.

'I'll do it.' He takes it from me and follows Holly into the room. A moment later, the door opens again and the sound of cheering applause rings out as Luis emerges. 'If the racing doesn't pick up, I could always get a job as a bun tart,' he says.

I roll my eyes at him. 'No chance.'

In the car park, he points his key at a grey and white Bugatti Veyron. I know what the car is, because Johnny had one, and I also know that they're one of the fastest – and most expensive – cars in the world. I try not to look too impressed, but fail.

'It's not mine,' Luis comments, seeing my face. 'The CEO of some company is lending it to me. They're trying to persuade me to take part in an advertising campaign.'

'What do they want you to endorse?'

'Watches. Posh ones,' he adds, climbing in the car.

'Have you been asked to do a lot of that sort of thing?' I ask, once we're buckled in.

'A fair bit. I'll get more offers next year if I win the championship.'

'Do you think you're still in with a chance?'

He flashes me a cheeky grin. 'Honey, I'm always in with a chance.'

'You dick.' I shake my head and chuckle to myself as he drives slowly back out towards the first security gate. 'Where are we going?' I ask.

'Just for a drive,' he says. 'And then maybe we'll go to Marlow and feed the swans.'

I crack up laughing.

'What?' he asks.

'I didn't take you to be a "feeding swans" type,' I reply.

He glances at me sideways and teasingly says, 'There's a lot you don't know about me, Daisy Rogers.'

'Is that right, Luis Castro?'

We exit the last set of security gates and Luis cranks up his speed.

A thought pops into my head. 'Does it bother you when people pronounce your name "Lewis" instead of "Lew-eesh"?'

'It's a bit annoying,' he says. 'But the main thing is that they're talking about me at all.'

'Even when they're saying horrible things?'

He pulls a face. 'Hmm. Maybe not.'

'Holly told me the papers are being much nicer now.'

'We'll see how long that lasts. I was thinking I was going to have to move back to Brazil if that kept up.'

'Where *do* you live?' I ask suddenly. I don't even know if he has a house in the UK.

'Hampstead,' he replies. 'North London.'

'I know Hampstead.' Now I'm properly impressed. 'It's beautiful there. What's your house like?'

'Come over sometime and you can see it for yourself.'

'Well, I don't know about that . . .'

'Why not? We're friends, aren't we?'

'*Are* we?'

'Sure we are. You know things about me and I know things about you that no one else knows. And I trust you. I hope you trust me.'

I think about his words for a moment before answering. 'Yeah, I do. I have done for a long time.'

Is Nonna right? Does Luis have feelings for me? Or am I just someone he can talk to? When I think about all those Screwdrivers he hooks up with, I can't believe he'd want me to be anything more than just a friend. Which is good, because I wouldn't touch him with a bargepole.

I suddenly remember the night in Monaco when butterflies fluttered through me as I looked at him. It makes me feel uneasy. And then I'm thinking of Will. I see him quite clearly, his blue eyes staring into mine, before he goes blurry again.

'What are you thinking about?' Luis asks.

'Hmm?'

'I asked what you were thinking about?'

'I was just thinking about Will, actually.'

He falls silent as he pulls off a roundabout and the road starts to climb uphill. We've been travelling on main roads, but now we've reached the country lanes and Luis picks up his speed. I cling on to the armrest as my stomach tenses.

'Did you ever go to Will's house?' Luis asks suddenly.

I hesitate before answering truthfully. 'Yes. The night

before . . . Silverstone.' I wanted to say, 'The night before he died', but those words still come with difficulty.

'Really?' He glances across at me.

I don't reply and I swear he puts his foot down.

'Luis! Slow down!'

'Why?'

'Because you're going too fast!'

'Am I scaring you?' he asks dryly.

'Yes, actually.'

Bizarrely, that does the trick. He slows right down. In fact, he's suddenly going *so* slow that I can't believe he's not going to stop. Oh. He *has* stopped.

'What the hell did you think was going to happen?' He looks across at me angrily.

I give him a wary look. 'I don't know what you're talking about.'

'With Will. Do you really think he was going to leave Laura?'

'Luis, seriously, shut the fuck up.' Fury bubbles up inside me. 'Anyway! Why does it even *matter* anymore?'

'It DOES matter!'

'WHY?'

'It just does!'

We glare at each other for a moment before I finally calm down enough to speak. 'Are we going to drive anywhere or am I going to get out and walk?'

'We're going to feed the fucking swans!' he snaps.

'Well, let's go and feed the fucking swans, then!'

'Okay! We fucking well will!'

I start to laugh. Seconds later, he does, too.

'You drive me nuts,' he says, pulling away from the kerb. 'Jesus, I think Will had a lucky escape.'

My face instantly falls and my heart feels like someone is crushing it. 'That's not even funny,' I manage to say.

'I didn't mean it like that,' he quickly tells me, looking worried.

But suddenly Will is everywhere. My head is filled with him and I can't push him out. He's leading me up the stairs to his bedroom, he's kissing me up against the hotel room door in China, he's pushing his hair off his face in Bahrain, he's rubbing my arm and giving me goosebumps on my nonna's terrace . . . A lump forms in my throat and I can feel sobs building up in the centre of my chest. I don't want to cry again. I feel like I've done enough crying. I try to swallow the lump, but it won't go away.

'Are you okay?' Luis asks, concerned.

I shake my head quickly.

'I was only joking,' he says.

But I can't speak. He falls silent for a moment, then glances across at me before saying tentatively, 'Do you remember back in Bahrain when I told you it was *me* who asked for you to be our on-hand girl?'

My brow furrows. I nod, confused as to why he's bringing this up now.

'I lied.'

My head shoots across to look at him. 'You lied?'

'I was just winding you up. It *was* Will,' he explains.

'And you're telling me this *now*?' I ask bitterly, as tears fill my eyes.

'I thought it would make you feel better,' he says, confused.

'Well, it doesn't,' I bite back, as a wave of anger pulses through me.

'We'll be there soon,' he comments, oblivious to my encroaching rage.

'I don't want to go,' I reply through clenched teeth. 'I want you to take me back to Holly's.'

'Daisy—'

'NOW!' I interrupt.

'Come on, we'll have a nice ti—'

'Take me back to my fucking friend's house, right now,' I warn menacingly.

And so he does, and I swivel in my seat and face away from him for the rest of the journey, feeling like I'm drowning in a haze of loss and regret.

Chapter 26

'It was damn out of order! He shouldn't have said it!'

'He obviously didn't mean it. Honestly, Daisy, you need to give that guy a break.'

For the last week, Holly has been giving me stick about my behaviour with Luis. We're on our way to Singapore for the only night race on the calendar. I went to the first-ever Singapore Grand Prix last year. On the Thursday night before everything kicked off, we went out in the city and got wasted on Singapore Slings, ate a plate full of chicken and beef satays at a hawker centre and then got a lift back to the hotel on a rickshaw. We almost fell off, we were laughing so hard. I have a feeling this time around the atmosphere won't be quite so joyous.

Because Singapore is a night race, the first practice session on Friday doesn't kick off until the evening, and the second doesn't even finish until after eleven o'clock, so Holly and I aren't needed at the track until late afternoon. I'm at the serving table preparing the evening's meal when Main Money Man Norm Gelltron shouts out to me.

'Hey! Daisy!'

He remembers me?

'Hello, sir!' I chirp. 'Can I get you anything?'

'No, I just want to know how your drive went the other week?'

'Er, it was fast. Very fast.'

'I bet it was. And have you managed to keep his beard at bay?'

I'm about to answer that I don't know, but a clean-shaven Luis walks in through the door behind him.

'See for yourself.' Phew. Lucky escape.

'Luis!' he shouts. 'I see Daisy's done another great job of keeping up your appearances!'

Everyone in the hospitality area is staring at us. I will my face not to go red, but there's no stopping it.

Luis glances from Norm to me and back again before twigging. He rubs his jaw.

'Oh, yeah. She's good at cracking a whip, this one.'

Norm guffaws and wanders off, leaving us alone. I look at Luis awkwardly. I don't know what to say so I settle on my usual.

'Can I get you anything?'

'Is that all you're going to say? "Can I get you anything?"'

'Sorry, I'm a bit lost for words after our last encounter.' I give him a challenging look, but he's unperturbed.

'How about, "How are you, Luis? What have you been up to? Sorry for depriving the swans of their dinner last week."'

'Oi, that was *your* fault,' I say warningly. 'If you hadn't said something so stupid . . .'

He stares at me directly and I struggle to keep eye contact, but I'm too stubborn to look away. I start to feel jittery and it strikes me as odd before suddenly he comes around the side of the serving table and grabs my hand. 'Come with me.'

'Hey, what are you doing?'

'I want to talk to you.'

I glance back to see a few people watching. 'Everyone's looking!' I hiss as he drags me out of eyesight and up the stairs.

'Who cares?'

'*I* care! They'll all think something's going on! Or something.'

'Or something?' He grins at me over his shoulder and leads me into his room. I shake my hand free.

'What was all that about?' I demand to know.

'Look, Daisy, I'm sorry I said what I said. I didn't mean it. You know I didn't mean it. So can we just drop it?'

I'm kind of pleased he wants things to go back to normal, but no, I can't drop it.

'I'd love to, but it still bugs me that you think Will wouldn't have left Laura. How the hell would you know?'

'I *don't* know.'

'Exactly!' I can't help but feel a little angry. 'You have no idea how close we were.'

He puts his hand up and looks pained. 'Just . . . Can we just . . .'

'What?' I ask crossly.

'Can we just leave it?' he asks again.

'Just promise me to stop going on about it.'

'I promise. What are you up to tomorrow?'

'Oh. I don't know.' I'm flummoxed by his sudden change of subject. 'Why?'

'Want to come out to lunch with me?'

'Um, I, yes, I guess I could . . .'

'Good. I'll come and get you at eleven thirty.' He balances on one foot and tugs off a shoe. I stand there, still feeling confused, as he hops around and takes off the other shoe, before reaching for his flies. 'Are you going, or what?'

'Hmm?'

'I need to get changed. So unless you want to see me with my kit off, you'd better leave.'

'Of course, yes.' I hurry out of the room.

Catalina is here this weekend and she wasn't originally going to come. Simon told Holly about this on Thursday night, which was their only night together before his wife arrived, so she and I haven't been out on the town at all. Last year's rickshaw fun seems like a distant memory, so to be honest, I'll be glad to escape the hotel for a couple of hours, even if it is just with Luis.

'Where are we going?' I ask, when he comes to pick me up twenty minutes late on Saturday morning. Holly went out earlier to sneak some time with Simon while Catalina went shopping and she's still not back.

'Raffles,' Luis replies.

'Ooh, fancy,' I tease.

'Simon and some of the sponsors are meeting us there.'

'Oh.' I feel a bit put-out. 'Don't you think you should have warned me about that?'

'I didn't think you'd mind.'

'Well, I might've worn something different.' I indicate the khaki green sundress I'm wearing.

'You look fine.'

'I might not have.'

'In which case, I could have told you when I came to collect you.'

He's already doing my head in. Why did I agree to this?

The humidity hits you like a brick wall, here. Sometimes it feels difficult to breathe. We're staying at a five-star hotel on Orchard Road, which is Singapore's equivalent to Fifth Avenue.

The concierge hails us a taxi and we climb in. Raffles Hotel is only about a ten-minute drive away.

I've never been to the famous colonial-style hotel, but I've heard about it. We're dining in the Long Bar Steakhouse and quite a few people are already seated at the table when we arrive. I count five men and one woman.

Oh, *cazzo*, it's Catalina.

'Luis, hi,' Simon says, standing up to shake Luis's hand. I notice Pierre, the ex-test driver who replaced you know who, seated next to Catalina. He's French, has floppy light-brown hair and is shorter than me by a couple of inches.

'Daisy, hi!' Simon jolts slightly as he reaches across to shake my hand. He's clearly surprised to see me here, which makes me feel even more out of my comfort zone. I glance down at Catalina to see her mouth drop open as she places me as a front-of-house girl. Her eyes flit from Luis to me and back again and a nasty expression falls over her features. I realise that she probably thinks I'm one of his Screwdrivers and, needless to say, that does *not* sit well with me.

'Take a seat, take a seat,' Simon insists, indicating the last two chairs at the table. Luis pulls out one for me and I sit down next to Norm Gelltron.

'And so here you are again!' Norm booms, as a waitress comes over to take our drinks order.

'Shall we order food, too?' Simon suggests to a buzz of agreement.

'Sorry,' I apologise to Norm as Luis and I quickly scan the menu. Clearly we've arrived late and everyone is hungry. I'm not going to be able to relax for the life of me. I order a grilled seafood dish and decide to stick to still water, a bottle of which is already on the table.

'I'm surprised to see *you* here,' Catalina comments, turning her nose up at me. 'Yes, I'll have some of that.' She nods at the water bottle I've just reached for, but I have to stand up and lean across the table to fill her glass. 'That's better,' she says, giving me an evil smile. I look confused. 'I recognise you now you're being the waitress.'

I don't really know how to respond to that, but several people around the table shift uncomfortably in their seats. I'm angry, but I try to keep my emotions in check. I can't make a scene here.

'Have you spoken to my cousin recently?' Catalina turns her attention to Luis.

'No,' he replies bluntly.

'Luis got up close and personal with my *beautiful* cousin, Alberta, earlier in the season,' she tells the sponsors around the table.

'Cat . . .' Simon warns, clearly embarrassed.

'What, darling?' she asks, playing innocent.

'Aah, here come the starters,' he says, breathing a sigh of relief.

I am absolutely fuming. That bitch! How dare she try to humiliate me in front of everyone! At this moment, I strongly believe she deserves everything she gets. I can't wait to get back to the hotel to tell Holly.

The conversation carries on around me for a while as everyone tucks into their starters.

'Can you spare a prawn?' Catalina asks Simon, eyeing his plate.

'Sure,' he replies, pushing it towards her.

'Oh, no, actually, I can't,' she says suddenly, glancing around the table as she pushes his plate back. A few raised eyebrows, but no one says anything, much to her dismay as I imagine she was just seeking attention.

'All set for the race tomorrow, Luis?' one of the sponsors asks him.

'Sure am.'

He was quickest in practice last night.

'Must have something to do with the beard, eh, Daisy?' Norm booms as a waiter appears to clear the table.

'Beard? What's this about?' Catalina enquires.

'Daisy's grandmother shaved off his beard. Ever since then he's had fire behind his wheels.'

'How strange.' Catalina sniffs, turning to Simon. 'Didn't you say Will drove better when he *hadn't* shaved?'

I tense up as Simon nods.

'For Luis it seems to be the other way around,' she comments, amused. 'Oh, isn't it a tragedy about Will . . .'

Lots of 'yes, yes, oh, yeses' around the table. Pierre has the good grace to look awkward.

'His poor girlfriend . . . Oh, what a lovely girl. He had *such* good taste in women.' Catalina gives me a look that says, 'unlike Luis', and I'm about to stand up and throw a glass of water in her face when I feel Luis's hand on my thigh, trying to calm me down. The waiters bring out our main course and everyone digs in, but I can barely swallow, I'm so angry.

'So what about you, then?' Norm turns to Luis and me. 'Are you two an item?'

'Hell, no,' I snap.

'That's some reaction.' He frowns and points his steak knife in Luis's direction. 'I would have thought this guy here would be a damn good catch for a girl like you.'

'What do you mean, a girl like me?' Right, I've had enough. If I lose my job, so be it.

'Hey, hey, don't get your panties in a wad.' He holds up his hands, patronisingly, then gets stuck into his steak again.

Luis speaks and his tone is hard. 'You might know Daisy's father, actually.'

'Oh?' Norm looks mildly interested.

'Stellan Rogers. I believe he's the main shareholder in your company?'

I've never seen anyone backtrack quite so quickly.

'Mr Rogers! Stellan Rogers! He's your father?'

'*Is* he?' an astounded Simon interrupts. Catalina looks on, confused.

'Mmm, yes,' I reply. I didn't really want the world and his wife knowing about my family, but quite frankly, fuck it.

'Well, I never . . . I never . . .' Norm stutters. 'Goodness me, you pass on my respects next time you see him, won't you? Goodness me.'

Out of the corner of my eye, I see Luis smirk. It's everything I can do to keep a straight face myself.

'Who's Stellan Rogers?' Catalina interrupts.

'Daisy's father, from the sounds of it,' Simon replies, looking uncomfortable. My phone starts to ring inside my bag.

'I'm sorry,' I murmur, rummaging around in my bag to dismiss the call. Moments later it rings again.

'Don't mind us,' Norm urges. 'You take it. It might be urgent. In fact, it could be your daddy!'

'Excuse me.' I stand up and answer the call. 'Can you hang on for a moment, please?' Then I walk quickly out of the restaurant before putting my phone back to my ear. 'Hello?'

'Daisy, it's me!'

Holly.

'Hi. What's up?'

'Where are you?'

'I'm at Raffles Hotel having the time of my life,' I answer sarcastically.

'Will you be long?'

'I don't know, why?'

She sniffs.

'Are you okay?' I ask, concerned.

'No.' She bursts into tears. 'Can you come back?'

'Um, yes, I won't be long.' It won't look good for me to walk out like this, but I've just about reached the end of my tether.

'Thanks.' A muffled sob and the line goes dead.

I stare down at the phone with concern. 'What's up?' I turn to see Luis standing there.

'That was Holly. I have to go back to the hotel.'

'Why?'

'She's in floods of tears, I don't know why. Probably something to do with Simon.'

'Hmm.'

'I guess I'd better come and make my excuses.' I motion in the direction of the dining room.

'No, it's okay. I don't want to put you through any more. I'll tell them you had a family drama or something, that'll shut them up.'

I breathe a sigh of relief. 'Thanks.'

'Let me walk you out.'

I don't argue with him. 'How did you know about my father being his main shareholder?' I ask as we head down the stairs. 'Have you been researching me again?' I give him a wary glance, but he dismissively shakes his head.

'No. I saw that the first – and *only* – time I looked you up.

Gelltron's our top sponsor so, of course, I noticed his company name when I saw it.'

'I had no idea.' I don't know anything about my father's businesses. It strikes me that perhaps I should.

'The look on Norm's face . . .' Luis grins at me.

'It was pretty funny, wasn't it?' I grin back.

'Well, seriously. He deserved it. What was he thinking, saying something like that?'

'Mmm.'

'He'll be fawning all over you tomorrow, you mark my words.'

'I'd rather he just kept his distance, to be honest. *Cazzo*!' I halt in my tracks for a split-second before continuing.

'What?'

'Do you think Simon and the others will talk about it to anyone else? I don't want it getting around, about me. Even Holly doesn't know.'

'Really? Why not?' We reach the doors and Luis pushes through.

'I just don't want to go on about it.'

'Holly doesn't know about your family, yet you were upset she didn't confide in you about Simon?' His lips turn down at the corners as he nods for the hotel concierge to hail a taxi.

'It's not the same thing,' I reply defensively.

He doesn't answer and I feel irritable. 'Do you think I'm out of order?' I ask suddenly. 'Not telling Holly about my family? Where I came from?'

'Yeah, I do a bit,' he answers honestly. 'What would it hurt?'

'I don't know. I guess I'm always just a bit worried that people will treat me differently, or think differently about me.'

'Not Holly. Holly wouldn't.'

I don't say anything. I know he's right.

'And I don't either, for that matter,' he adds as a taxi pulls up.

'No, I know you don't.' I look at him and smile. 'You'd give me just as much grief if I was a goddamn princess.'

'Probably more,' he replies and I laugh as he opens the door for me. I climb in as he tells the driver where to take me and hands him some money.

'You don't have to do that,' I call through to the front window at Luis.

'*Va se lixar*,' he shouts back with a grin. The driver puts up the window and pulls away.

Holly's face is red and puffy when I get back to the hotel. She looks like she's been sobbing her heart out into her pillow and there's a pile of snotty tissues next to her to prove it.

'What's wrong?' I ask with alarm, rushing to her side. She sits up on the bed and draws me in for a hug as she cries into my hair. I let her carry on for a while before I gently pull away. 'Tell me what's wrong?'

'He said they didn't sleep together anymore.'

'Who? Simon?'

'And . . . that witchy bitch!'

I take it she's talking about Catalina.

'And do they?' I ask, tentatively.

'SHE'S PREGNANT!' Holly starts to wail.

'Oh, Jesus,' I murmur, although I'm not surprised something like this has happened. I put my arms around her and hug her tightly, half as a comforting gesture, half-hoping to muffle the sound of her sobs. It may be a pricey hotel, but the walls are so thin I heard our neighbours sneeze earlier.

'I swear she did it on purpose. She must've suspected something was up,' she says fervently. 'She's trying to trick him into staying with her, I'm sure of it.'

'Does he even want children?' I ask.

'I don't know! We've never talked about it. I kind of got the impression he was past all that, although I'm sure I could have persuaded him if I'd wanted to.'

A wave of compassion passes through me. The fact that she was even thinking that she might one day be in a position to have children with Simon . . . Well, she's more deluded than I thought, and I don't mean that in a nasty way.

'What are you going to do?' I ask. 'Has he called it off with you?'

'No.' She shakes her head.

'Have you called it off with him?'

'No.'

'But you will, right?' I frown at her.

'I don't know! Daisy, don't look at me like that! I don't know what I'm doing yet!'

I back right off. It was bad enough when he was married, but now his wife is *pregnant* . . .

His witchy, bitchy wife for that matter. But no, I still don't approve. Yet Holly is my friend, and I need to be there for her.

'So *that's* why Catalina wouldn't eat any of Simon's prawn starter. You're not allowed to eat shellfish when you're pregnant, are you?'

'What are you going on about?' Holly looks confused.

'Oh . . .' I forgot she didn't know I'd been out with them. I explain. 'Luis took me for lunch with the sponsors and Catalina was there. Ooh, she was such a bitch!'

'Was she?' Holly perks up.

'Yes.' I tell her what she said to me and then hesitate before remembering Luis's words about my lack of honesty. 'Actually, Holly, there's something else I haven't told you.'

'Oh, really?' She looks intrigued.

'It's about my family.'

'Right . . .'

I sigh and spill the beans. Several 'Oh my Gods' and 'Holy shits' later, I finally get to the story about my dad being a shareholder in Norm's company. Holly claps her hand over her mouth at the start, but is squealing with hilarity by the end. Surely it's only a matter of time before the people in the next room complain.

'How did Luis know about your family?' she asks when she's finally calmed down.

Do I really have the energy for all of this today? No, but what the hell . . . I take a deep breath and tell her about Johnny. Nothing that would break the terms of my confidentially agreement, just the bare basics, that I worked for him and, yes, that I fell in love with him. I know my secret is safe with her.

She's dumbfounded by the end of my story. She shakes her head at me with awe. 'God, you really are full of surprises. How did you keep all that to yourself?'

'With difficulty.'

She pulls a face. 'And Luis knows everything?'

I nod.

'And he didn't say anything to anyone?'

'No. I'm telling you, he's not a gossip. I trust him.'

'You've said that to me before. And why is it you don't want to get into his pants, exactly?'

'Holly!' Her comment takes me by surprise. 'I just don't!'

She gives me a wry look.

'Jesus, will everyone please stop going on about how much I should be with Luis!'

'Who else is going on about it?'

'My nonna. She's thinks he's better suited to me than Will was.'

My heart clenches. It's funny how sometimes I can say Will's name so easily without thinking about him, but other times reality will hit me, and the pain does, too. It's been almost three months and while the grief is definitely lessening, it often still hurts like he died only yesterday.

'Are you okay?' Holly sees my face.

'I'm just tired. I don't know how I'm going to work tonight.'

'Shit! What's the time?'

I glance at my watch. 'Car will be here in twenty.'

'Bollocks.' She leaps off the bed and rushes through to the bathroom. I hear the tap turn on and assume she's splashing her face with cold water to tone down the redness.

I change into my team uniform and she emerges a short while later.

'Ready?'

'As I'll ever be.'

It feels surreal going to work late in the afternoon like this. I barely see anyone from lunchtime during qualifying – I don't know if they're avoiding me or if it's just a coincidence, but I'm relieved nonetheless. Holly and I watch from the pits as Luis swipes pole position before Kit Bryson, who's now leading the championship, takes it back from him. The team is in high spirits regardless, because Luis is still on the front row of the grid.

Now it's race day – or should that be, race night – and I'm back in the pits again for the start. The track is floodlit so it almost replicates daylight conditions to make it less dangerous for the drivers. With the city's stunning skyline and a view of the Singapore Flyer Ferris wheel glowing blue, purple and yellow in the background, the atmosphere here is electric.

Luis was sitting on a table at the back of the garage when Holly and I arrived. His car was already on the grid, but he seemed in no rush to get out there. I was about to go and talk to him, but his expression was so serious and determined, I was worried I might distract him. Then he got up, pulled white earphones from his ears and stalked out of the garage to the pit wall. I had no idea he was listening to music. Now I'm wondering if he does so before every race, to psyche himself up. I was always so sidetracked with Will in the past, I never paid Luis that much attention.

He has a fantastic start, overtaking Kit Bryson before the first corner and immediately putting some distance between him and the rest of the pack. But when, a third of the race later, he has to come in for a pit stop, something goes wrong with the fuel rig. It doesn't detach from the car properly and Luis pulls away, dragging poor Dan with him. Luis stops a split-second later when he realises something's wrong, and luckily Dan is unharmed, because mechanics in the past have broken their arms in similar situations. It soon transpires that the accident has relegated Luis down to fourth. What follows is one of the most tense and exciting races I've ever witnessed. In fact, if I weren't so rooted to the spot, I'd be quite happy to watch on the big screen in the hospitality area so I could hear what the commentators are saying. One by one, Luis outbreaks Antonio Aranda and Nils Broden in front of him. The next pit stop goes perfectly and soon he's right behind Kit Bryson again.

'Frederick is going to kill us,' Holly shouts over the noise of the engines. We should have been back half an hour ago.

'I don't care!' I shout back and she giggles.

'Neither do I!'

It all comes down to the last lap. There's less than half a second between Kit and Luis. Will Kit make a mistake? Will Simon warn Luis to keep his distance rather than risk another crash? If he does, Luis ignores him because, suddenly, he pulls out from behind Kit and everyone in the garage holds their breath as he takes the corner. They're so close, surely they're going to touch, but no! Oh my God, Luis has done it! The chequered flag is waving up ahead as Kit pulls out and tries to overtake Luis again, but he fails. Luis is too quick. I'm screaming with elation as he crosses the start/finish line and everyone around me is cheering. Holly turns and hugs me. Will flicks through my mind, but I push him away. I can't think of him now. I don't want to.

We run outside to wait for Luis, Kit and Nils to pull up and watch as Luis leaps out of his car and punches the air. He runs straight over to the mechanics and I want him to see me there, cheering and laughing with the rest of them, but he doesn't look my way and my stomach momentarily falls flat as he jogs inside to be weighed before the podium celebrations. A couple of minutes later he appears up above us, waving and clapping the crowd. All around there is the sound of whistles and horns going off. There's such a buzz about the place, and it feels like all the spectators are behind Luis and his incredible race win.

The national anthems start up and everyone falls silent, then the trophies are handed out. Luis kisses his and raises it up high as we all cheer again, and then it's champagne time . . . Luis, Kit and Nils drench each other first before spraying the crowd below.

I haven't seen Luis this happy, I don't think ever, and as he reaches down to drop the champagne bottle to Pete, he catches my eye. I beam up at him and he winks at me with those twinkly brown eyes. Seconds later, the drivers file off for the press conference.

Did he really run out from the race in Monza to come and find me? I'm floored as the reality of this sinks in. Is my nonna right? *Does* he have feelings for me? Butterflies flit through my stomach and for the first time I wonder if I could have feelings for him, too.

Chapter 27

Frederick and Ingrid have got me working at a daytime function in Hampstead and I've been toying with the idea of texting Luis to see if I can drop over to his place for a drink afterwards.

He's probably not in. But it *is* a Wednesday afternoon . . . Perhaps he's at team HQ? Shall I? What the hell.

HI, DAISY HERE. R U IN? WORKING IN HAMPSTEAD – CLD POP ROUND?

Send.

I feel nervous. *Why*? It's only Luis, for Christ's sake.

But I've been thinking about him *a lot* since last weekend. He's starting to get under my skin, and I don't know how I feel about it.

Ooh, a reply:

SURE. I'M AT . . .

He adds the address.

Short and sweet. Too short and sweet? Does he even want to see me? Stop overthinking it, Daisy. But, of course, that's easier said than done . . .

I finish the rest of my shift, then change out of my uniform into jeans and a jumper. I double check with one of my colleagues that he lives on the road that I'm thinking of, then set off down the High Street, trying not to be lured into French Connection and Reiss along the way.

I turn left on Downshire Hill and walk in the direction of the heath. On my left, the tall, white Regency houses are beautiful, nestled away from the footpath under leafy trees the shade of burnt amber. Does he seriously live along here? I count the numbers on the houses I can see, until finally I come to Luis's. I swing open the black wrought-iron gate and walk up the stone footpath. It's early evening and the house lights are already glowing in the encroaching darkness. I feel like I'm inside a fairytale and suddenly feel nervous again.

Will puts his hand around the back of my neck and pulls me to him, touching his lips to mine. 'See ya later.'

No. Why am I thinking about Will now? Guilt passes through me like a wave on an ocean and I try to still it. I have nothing to feel guilty about. I'm just going for a drink with a friend.

Yes. A friend.

I knock and wait. Moments later I hear shuffling behind the heavy, aubergine-painted wooden door and then Luis opens it, his hands full of post.

'Come in,' he says, plonking the post down on an antique wooden side-table. There's already a pile of letters there.

'Don't you ever sort your post?' I ask, my brow furrowing.

'When I can be bothered. Have you come round to nag me?'

'No.'

He grins at me. 'Come on through.'

'I like your house,' I say as I follow him along the wide corridor. The oak floors knock underneath my boots.

He leads me through to a bright, open kitchen. Large double doors lead out to a green garden beyond. I go straight over to look out. Growing up, I never had a garden. My garden was Central Park and, as a result, I'm always drawn to other people's.

It's actually quite large. A dusky-green painted gazebo is down the far end, and there's a magnolia tree in the centre which I bet is stunning in the spring.

'Thanks,' he replies. 'Do you want a coffee? Glass of wine?'

'What's the time?' I glance at my watch. Five o'clock. 'A wine would be nice. I'm exhausted after working.'

'Red or white?'

'I don't mind. What are you having?'

'Let's go for white.' He goes to the fridge and pulls out a bottle, then digs around in a drawer for a bottle opener.

'How was work?' he asks.

'It was okay.' I pull up a stool at the bar and watch him pour the wine into outsize glasses. 'Society wife hosting a posh lunch for thirty of her closest friends. Amazing how those sorts of dos require so much more energy than catering for 300 people.'

'I don't know how you do it.'

I don't reply.

'Do you like it?' He sits down at the bar opposite me.

'I'd prefer to be out the back, cooking.'

'Really?'

'Yeah.'

'I didn't know that.'

'I didn't always want to be a bun tart, you know.' I narrow my eyes at him and he smiles at me.

'So why don't you work in the kitchen for the team?'

'Frederick won't let me. He wants me out front of house.' I sigh. 'I guess I haven't had any real training, so it's understandable.'

'Why don't you get some training, then?' He gives me an inquisitive look.

'Um . . . I don't know. I haven't really considered it.'

He takes a sip of his wine while I stare off into the distance, thoughtfully. Why haven't I applied to catering college? I know I threatened my father I'd do it in New York, but I've never actually looked into the possibility . . .

'Anyway, what have you been up to?' I change the subject.

'Not much. Just hanging out here.'

'When did you buy this place? It's absolutely stunning.'

'At the beginning of the year after I got the drive for the team.'

'It must've cost a fortune,' I muse.

'I still have a hefty mortgage. I would have had to be in F1 for a couple of years before I could afford to buy a house like this outright.'

'Sorry, that was a bit of a rude of me.'

'Don't worry,' he brushes me off. 'Anyway, it's not like *you're* obsessed with money, is it?'

'Do you get a lot of that? Women going after you because you're a rich bastard?'

He cracks up laughing. 'I think they're into me because I'm devastatingly good-looking.'

'Modest, too.'

'Have you had that problem?' he asks.

'What, men going after me because I'm devastatingly good-looking?'

'Well, that as well.' He winks at me. 'But no, because of your dad's wealth?'

'Oh, the boys I hung out with when I was growing up all had bucketloads of money, too. And then there was Johnny Jefferson. Hardly lacking in cash.'

'Yet you live in that studio flat on Camden Road . . .'

'*Lived*,' I correct him, fleetingly recalling how he picked me up to take me to the funeral. 'I still miss it.'

'Why?'

'Because it was mine. Okay, so I didn't actually own it, but it was still the first and only place I actually had all to myself.'

He nods. 'Well, I grew up in a tiny house, shared a room with my four brothers, and couldn't wait to get the hell out of there.'

'I thought you were close to your family?'

'Oh, we're *close*. But that was too close for comfort.'

I laugh. 'And now you live here in this big house all on your own.'

'Rub it in, why don't you?'

'I'm joking! Don't you love it? You must, surely.'

'Well, it is pretty big. But no, I don't really like being on my own.'

'I'm sure you could find some willing women to bring back here.' I give him a wry look and he rolls his eyes at me.

'I've never brought *anyone* back here if you must know.'

'Seriously?' I regard him with surprise.

'Seriously.' He shrugs and looks away.

There's something overwhelmingly nice about that. The

thought that no other woman has tainted this house . . . Unlike Laura with Will's house.

Oh, there I go again. I really must stop comparing them.

Would he have left Laura?

Would he have had a fling with me before going back to her?

Stop it! Stop torturing yourself!

Luis reaches over and tops up my wine glass, then gets to his feet and goes to the cupboard. I watch as he pulls out a packet of honey-roasted cashew nuts and decants them into a bowl. He looks – dare I say it? – sexy tonight. He's wearing a grey sweatshirt with the sleeves pushed up to just below his elbows so I can see his olive-toned forearms. His black hair is longer than it was when I first met him and now falls just below his eye-line. I stare at him as he pushes the bowl of nuts in my direction.

'How are you feeling about the next race?' I ask.

'Good. The car handled like a dream in Singapore, so . . .'

'Fingers crossed for Japan. And after that, it's Brazil.'

'Mmm.'

'Your home race. Are your family going to come?'

He chuckles. 'If there's enough room for them.'

'Hey,' I remember suddenly. 'Do you listen to music before the races to psyche yourself up?'

'Yeah,' he replies hesitantly.

'I saw you with your earphones in,' I explain. 'What were you listening to?'

'I think it was The Chemical Brothers.'

'The music worked, then. You won.'

'It wasn't just the music, Daisy.' He stares straight at me for five, very long seconds before breaking away to have a drink. 'How's Holly?' he asks. 'You never told me why she was upset in Singapore.'

'No,' I reply hesitantly. 'I probably shouldn't now, either.'

'Top secret, is it?'

I consider him, undecided. I know he'd keep it to himself, but would Holly mind? I don't *think* so . . . 'It's okay. I trust you.'

He folds his arms in front of him on the bar top.

'Catalina is pregnant.'

'Really?' His eyes widen and I fill him in on the whole shebang.

'I have something top secret to tell you, too,' he says eventually, after we've exhausted that topic.

I look at him with interest. 'What's that?'

'I've been offered a drive with another team.'

'No way?' My heart sinks. 'Which one?'

Luis tells me it's for the team Kit Bryson drives for. His teammate Emilio Rizzo's contract has expired and as Rizzo has underperformed all season, he's been given the boot. The press will be told he made his own decision to retire from F1. He is thirty-five, after all.

'But that's like, the best team, isn't it?'

He nods seriously. They've won the championship for the past three years. Our team usually ranks fourth or fifth.

'Are you going to accept it?'

'It's for a lot more money,' he says casually, and he doesn't sound boastful. 'But I don't know. Part of me feels loyal to Simon, but he was going to fire me if I didn't perform in Italy so I don't know . . .'

'I don't think I'd enjoy working there as much if you left,' I say in a small voice, screwing my nose up.

He chuckles and reaches across to pat my hand. 'Well *you*, bun tart, should get yourself into catering college and then you wouldn't have to miss me at all.'

I laugh. 'But then I *would* miss you, because I'd *never* see you!'

I'm feeling a little tipsy after all this wine. It's making me feel quite affectionate.

'Aw,' he says, grinning at me. 'And to think you almost scratched my Ferrari . . .'

'You almost ran me over, you moron!' I jokily exclaim. 'And you called me a crazy bitch.'

'I didn't!' He looks horrified.

'Yes, you did.'

'I didn't, did I?'

'Yep.'

'That's horrendous. I'm sorry,' he adds.

'Hmm. I might forgive you one of these days.'

We sit there and chat for another half an hour before he asks if I'm hungry.

'I am a bit,' I reply.

'We could nip down the road for a Chinese if you like?'

'That'd be nice.'

'Okay, I'll just grab my coat.'

I go and stand in his hall while he rummages around in the cupboard under the stairs and pulls out a black biker-style jacket. I poke my head around the door and take a quick peek at his living room. There's a large bay window overlooking the front garden. It's dark outside now, but for a split-second I picture myself sitting in the white designer armchair, drinking a cup of espresso coffee while the sunlight spills in. I shake my head. I must be drunk.

'Ready?' he asks. 'I'm just going to set the alarm.'

I walk to the front door and moments later he opens it and ushers me out to the sound of beeping. We walk down the footpath to the road.

'I can't believe Hampstead is only a short tube ride away from the city,' I muse. 'It's like you're in the middle of nowhere, here.'

'That's what I like about it,' he says. 'Best of both worlds. Hampstead Heath is just there.' He points over his shoulder. 'Lots of swans and ducks to feed.'

I crack up laughing as he wraps his arm around my neck and gives me a squeeze. I feel my face heat up in the darkness as he pulls away again, but I don't think he notices.

Dinner is a delight. We talk about anything and everything and I realise I haven't felt so relaxed in a long time. By the time dessert comes around and Luis insists on ordering toffee apples and bananas with ice-cream, I really don't want the evening to end.

We walk out into the crisp night air and I look at my watch. It's ten o'clock.

'I should be getting home.'

'Don't want to come back for a coffee?'

'No.' I shake my head. 'I've got a bit of a trek back to Holly's. I don't think I could stand it if it were much later.'

'You could always stay over, if you like.'

'No, no, I couldn't.' Could I?

'Why not? I've got plenty of room.'

'No, I'd better get back.'

'Yet you persuaded me to crash at your nonna's . . .' He tuts and I continue to waver before he brushes me off. 'Suit yourself. Shall I call you a cab?'

'It's alright, I'll go by tube.' I pause before adding, 'Thanks for a lovely night.'

'You're welcome. Thanks for dropping round.'

We stand and smile at each other for a moment. I want to give him a kiss on the cheek – at the *very* least – but we haven't had that sort of touchy feely relationship in the past. I take a step backwards.

'Well, bye, then.'

'Bye.' He turns to walk away. 'See you next week,' he calls over his shoulder.

'For sure,' I call back, feeling bizarrely deflated as I start to climb the steep hill back towards the tube.

I think about him the whole way home. Holly's bedroom light is on when I arrive and I knock on her door, desperately wanting to tell her about my evening.

'Come in,' she calls.

'Hi!' I excitedly push the door open. And then I see her face. She's been crying again. 'What's wrong?' I ask with concern.

Her face crumbles. 'He's not going to leave her.' And then she starts to sob.

'What are you going to do?' I ask, after rubbing her back for a few minutes.

'I don't know. I don't think I could stand to see her get bigger and bigger and know that he's going to be the father to that . . . that . . . *little demon*!'

I make a face at the description, but obviously don't pull her up on it. 'So will you quit?'

'No. Oh, I don't know! It's a bloody nightmare! Maybe she'll lose it?' Her eyes brighten up.

'*Holly*,' I warn, and she starts to cry again.

Needless to say, I think any discussions about Luis are going to have to be put on hold for the time being.

Chapter 28

'Will you come with me?'

'Are any of the sponsors going to be there?'

'Probably all of them. And Simon and Catalina. But seriously, who gives a shit?'

'I do!'

'We don't have to talk to them. It'll be fun. Go on.'

It's Saturday and Luis has asked me to go to a charity ball with him tonight. We're in Japan for the penultimate race of the season. Holly has been miserable. She toyed with the idea of not coming to this race at all, but then managed to pull some strength from somewhere.

'Do you think I should go?' I ask her later.

'Absolutely,' she replies without a moment's hesitation. 'It'll make a nice change from the usual bars and clubs we hang out in.'

'What will you do?'

'I might go out with the lads, get rat-arsed and shag Pete to take my mind off things.'

'Holly!' I crack up laughing.

'I'm not joking,' she says. 'That'll piss Simon off.'

'Hey,' I berate her. 'Don't mess Pete around. He's a good guy and you'll probably get him fired if you do something like that.'

She takes a deep breath and chews on one of her thumbnails. 'Alright, Mum. What are you going to wear?' she asks after a moment.

'I have no idea. It's black tie, apparently.'

'You should check out that shop in the hotel lobby. I saw some beautiful dresses in there while I was waiting for you to come down yesterday.'

I'm strangely nervous by the time I get back to the hotel at six thirty. I pop into the shop Holly mentioned before going upstairs. There are indeed some beautiful gowns here, but a quick glance at one price tag tells me I'd have to break into my father's 10 million before I could afford even a single sequin. I go up to my room, racking my brains to try to think of an outfit that would suffice as I get on with my hair and make-up. I'm just starting to wonder if I should back out when there's a knock at the door. I open it to find the hotel concierge standing outside on the landing.

'Good evening, madam. I have a delivery for you.'

He hands over a box and I take it, confused. I thank him and shut the door before putting the box on the bed and opening it up.

I do a sharp intake of breath as I lift out the contents of the box and a floor-length gown spills out, shimmering with gold beads. There's a note:

Just in case you're stuck for something to wear – Luis

Luis bought me a dress? That's like something out of a film. I would laugh, but I'm too astounded.

I can't possibly accept it. It looks like it cost an absolute fortune. No. It's not appropriate. What was he thinking?

But oh . . . It's so beautiful. Perhaps I'll just try it on?

It fits like a glove, skimming my curves, and is low-cut enough to accentuate my breasts. I go and stand in front of the mirror by the door and stare at my reflection. Oh my God, it's stunning. I don't think I've ever owned anything this beautiful, even when I lived in my billionaire father's penthouse apartment.

There's another knock at the door. I answer it absent-mindedly.

'Wow,' Luis says, his eyes wide. He's wearing a black-tie suit, except said black tie is hanging loose around his neck. Dammit, he looks hot. 'I never in a million years thought you'd wear it,' he comments.

'I, er, wasn't going to,' I stutter, stepping backwards to let him come in. 'I was just trying it on.'

'You look . . .' He shakes his head, lost for words.

'Thanks.' I blush and put my hands to my face. 'I'm not ready yet.'

'You seem ready to me.'

'I haven't done my hair or anything.' It's still hanging loose down my back.

'Leave it.'

I come to my senses. 'Sorry, Luis, but I can't accept this.'

'Don't be ridiculous,' he brushes me off.

'No, I can't. I'm sorry. You'd better wait outside while I take it off.'

'I'm not going anywhere unless you're coming with me. Now.'

'Stop being a bully,' I snap. 'I have to get changed.'

'You're not getting changed. I can't return that dress, you

know. They said no refunds. So you are coming to the charity event with me. And you're wearing that dress.'

'No.'

'Yes.'

'No.'

'YES!' He grabs my hand and pulls me towards the door. I let myself be dragged reluctantly. Well, if they said no refunds . . .

'Wait! I need my bag.'

He sighs while I break away and run back to grab it.

'Okay. I'm ready.'

'Thank Christ for that,' he murmurs, guiding me out onto the landing.

'Anyway, what did you mean, you never in a million years thought I'd wear it?' I ask as he pushes the button for the lift. 'What about the no refunds policy? Wasn't that a bit of a risk?'

He waits until the doors open and we step inside before he answers. 'I like taking risks.'

The charity event is being held in a nearby five-star hotel. Hundreds of candles glimmer in the darkness, uplighting the banzai trees and ornate Japanese gardens as our car pulls up. Men in dinner jackets and women in evening gowns climb up the steps ahead of us into the glowing hotel lobby. I've been to plenty of functions like this in my time, but not for a few years now, and certainly not since I've worked as a front-of-house girl.

Luis guides me through to the ballroom. Chandeliers sparkle overhead and candelabras adorn every table. I feel dozens of sets of eyes upon us as the crowd parts to let us through.

'You've got a lot of fans here,' I murmur.

'They're not looking at me.'

I smile at him, but he's staring straight ahead.

He leads me in the direction of the bar where tall flutes of fizzing champagne are laid out on silver trays. He takes one and passes it to me, then takes another for himself.

We stand and scan the room for a moment.

'There's Simon and Catalina,' Luis says, nodding in their direction.

'I've barely seen the boss this weekend,' I muse.

Simon looks over and catches my eye. He says something to Catalina, whose face instantly sours, then walks in our direction. She follows him, reluctantly.

'Daisy, hi!' Simon bends down to give me a kiss on the cheek. I try not to look as astonished as I feel. 'Luis.' They shake hands. 'Daisy, you remember my wife, Catalina.'

'Hello.' I nod at her and force a smile, aware she's forcing one back.

'Out together again?' Catalina comments, pulling a face. 'And you say you're not an item?' She looks from Luis to me.

'Lovely to see you here, Daisy,' Simon interrupts. 'How are you finding everything with the team at the moment?'

'It's great, thanks,' I reply warily.

'Good. Good,' he says determinedly. 'You know, sorry to interrupt, Luis.' He puts his hand on my arm and takes me to one side, leaving Luis to speak to Catalina. 'Are you happy doing what you're doing? Would you like to swap back with Holly to be the drivers' on-hand girl?'

'No, no!' I answer vehemently. 'I'm fine where I am, thanks.'

'Well, if you ever change your mind, you come and speak to me. Okay?'

'Okay . . .'

'Right.' He turns back to his wife. 'We should probably mingle, darling.'

'Absolutely.' She turns away, not giving me another glance.

'That was weird,' I comment.

'What did he say?'

I fill him in. 'Do you think it's because of my dad?' I ask worriedly.

'I don't know . . .'

I sigh. 'That's the last thing I wanted, people to treat me differently.'

He casually squeezes my arm and looks away. 'I'm sorry about that.'

'Don't worry. It's not your fault.'

'I think you'll find that it is.'

'No, honestly, I'd rather you said what you said than let that prick get away with his comment.'

'Speaking of whom . . .'

I follow Luis's gaze to see Norm jiggling our way.

'Daisy! Luis! Great to see you both!' He bends down to kiss my hand, then turns to Luis and shakes his. I resist the urge to wipe his slobber away on my dress. 'WOW! You look stunning!' he booms at me, and I can actually feel his hot breath on my face from a foot away.

'Thank you,' I reply, trying not to flinch.

'*Now*, you don't look like a bun tart.' He shakes with laughter, before adding, 'I spoke to your daddy a few days ago.'

My blood runs cold. 'Did you?'

'Yes. He said to pass on his regards.'

'That's nice,' I lie, knowing that my father will have meant nothing of the sort.

'Would you excuse us?' Luis chips in. 'I've just seen my team-mate and have to talk tactics.'

'Of course!' Norm waves us through.

'Oh, God,' I say under my breath.

'That's not good, is it?' Luis checks.

'No. I don't think my father knows I work here.'

'Is it likely to be a problem?'

'Oh, yeah,' I say with absolutely certainty. 'It's likely to be a *big* problem.'

'What do you think he'll do?'

'I'll find out soon enough.'

Quite a few racing drivers are here tonight. Pierre is chatting to Antonio Aranda and Kit Bryson, so we stop to say hello. Antonio seems happy enough to see Luis, but Kit makes his excuses and wanders off. I wonder if Holly was right when she said some of the other drivers were jealous of him.

It takes two hours and several glasses of champagne before I can relax again. The auction is now over. People have been bidding for items that previously belonged to celebrities, all in aid of charity. Luis didn't bid for anything, but Naoki Takahashi won a rug that Madonna used to have in her living room.

'Shall we go and join the others?' Luis asks me. 'Dan texted me a little while ago. They're all at some karaoke bar.'

'Let's do it!' I squeal a little too loudly.

'We'll do it later, if you're lucky, but let's go and sing some karaoke in the meantime.'

I whack him on his arm as he stands up and offers his hand down to me. I take it, my head fizzing with all the champagne.

Holly detains me the second we walk through the doors of the low-lit venue.

'Come with me.' She drags me in the direction of the ladies' room.

'Was he there?' No prizes for guessing that she's talking about Simon.

'Yes.'

'Was she?'

'Yes.'

'Did you speak to her?'

'Hardly. He was a bit weird, though.' I relate Simon's behaviour.

'Strange.' Her brow furrows. 'Do you think he's trying to get rid of me?' she asks suddenly.

'No! Of course not!' I reply, although I hadn't actually considered that possibility.

'What else happened?' she asks morosely, then suddenly seems to notice my appearance and perks right up. 'Oh my God! That is the most amazing dress!'

I smile and give her a twirl.

'Did you get it from that shop in the lobby?'

'Er, no.' I screw my nose up in embarrassment. 'Luis bought it for me.'

'No way!'

'Yeah, he did.'

'Holy fuck! That's like, so *Indecent Proposal*!'

'I'm hardly Demi Moore and he's hardly Robert Redford. And anyway! I'm not shagging him!'

'You added that almost as an afterthought.' She gives me an amused look.

'Stop teasing me.'

'I'm just going to the loo. Wait for me.'

She goes inside a cubicle and I turn to stare at my reflection. I'd almost forgotten I was wearing this dress, this beautiful dress. Nerves flicker through me at the thought of Luis.

'Look at you, checking yourself out,' Holly jokes as she re-emerges.

I turn to her and lean up against a basin. 'Do you think it's strange that he bought me a dress?'

'No,' she replies. 'He obviously wants to get you into bed.'

'Holly!'

'It's true! Any idiot can see it.'

I don't say anything.

'You fancy him, don't you?' She nudges me. 'I knew you did!'

'Holly, no, stop it, don't say that,' I plead.

'Why not? It's true. Just shag him and get it over with. Move on.'

'What do you mean, move on?'

'Well, he's hardly marriage material, is he?' She rolls her eyes and giggles.

I try to laugh. 'No, I guess not.'

'But he's supposedly brilliant in bed, so I'd get your kicks and be done with it, if I were you.'

I have a sinking feeling she's right. In fact, it wouldn't surprise me if Luis were outside in the bar, trying to pull a woman at this very minute. Saying that, I haven't seen that side of him since Silverstone. He seems different these days. More responsible. Maybe he's changed . . .

'What's up?' Holly asks, frowning.

'Nothing.'

'Oh my God,' she says worriedly. 'You don't really like him, do you?'

'No!'

'Seriously, Daisy, that's a bad idea.'

'I know!' I snap. 'You don't have to tell me that, I know it already!'

'Good.' She gives me a wary look. 'Because I don't want to see you get hurt.'

I stop short of telling her *she* can talk.

I follow her back outside to the bar. Luis is squashed into a curved booth with Dan, Pete and a few of the lads. He pats the space beside him. After what Holly said, I'm reluctant to sit next to him, but my friend goes to the other side of the booth and there's no room anywhere else for me, so I don't have a choice. He immediately wraps his arm around my waist and pulls me affectionately back into him. I tense up, but don't think he notices.

'Hey! It's Dan's song!' Pete shouts, as the big screen opposite starts to show the words to Bon Jovi's 'Livin' On A Prayer'.

'WOOHOO!' Dan shouts, before throwing himself into the song with great gusto. As the chorus kicks in, he climbs up onto the table and starts playing air guitar. Holly and I scream with laughter as the boys cheer and Luis takes his arm from around my waist to clap. Seconds later, a petite Japanese woman with her hair tied up in a bun pads over to ask Dan, very politely, to sit back down.

My waist feels cold . . .

He's just like Johnny! Stay away from him!

But then he puts his arm back around me and a feeling of warmth floods my entire body. I tell the annoying little voice inside my head to go away.

'Daisy, this one's ours!' Holly screams.

'What?' I ask in alarm as she passes me a microphone. 'I can't sing!'

'That's the point,' Luis says, grinning.

'Right, well you'd better do the next one.' I smack him on his chest and take the mic as Holly and I launch into 'Heaven On Earth' by Belinda Carlisle.

An hour and a couple of glasses of whisky and Coke later, we've all made complete tits of ourselves, including Luis who pulled off a ridiculous rendition of Vanilla Ice's 'Ice, Ice Baby'.

I've never laughed so much in my life. We're all in high spirits and even Holly is having a blast, which is a relief after all her moping about.

Pete launches into Wham's 'Wake Me Up Before You Go Go', but my mind is elsewhere because Luis's thumb has just started to stroke the curve of my waist. I'm quite drunk now, and this is beginning to feel dangerous. I lean into him as Holly, across from me, grins. Her eyes flit towards Luis and back again. I know she's encouraging me to do the dirty deed, and right now, I don't think I'd be able to resist.

'I'm going to have to go back to the hotel and get some sleep before the race tomorrow,' Luis says to me. My stomach crashes downwards until he says in my ear, 'Want to come with me?'

I glance at him, his dark eyes confirming he means what I think he means, and nod.

We stand up and he makes his excuses about leaving early. I don't know if the lads suspect anything is going on between us, but right now I don't care.

We don't speak in the short taxi ride back to the hotel. That annoying little voice pops back to ask me if this is such a good idea. YES! It's a brilliant idea, I scream back at it. I fancy him like mad tonight!

But how will he feel about you tomorrow?

Shut up, shut up, shut up!

We walk into the lift together and I look at the buttons. He presses the number for his floor, then leans back against the gold-gilded railing and stares at me.

He's just like Johnny . . .

As a reaction to that thought I reach over and punch the number for my floor, then defiantly look at Luis. A split-second later I'm in his arms and he's kissing me passionately as my head tingles with anticipation. The lift comes to my floor and stops, and we break away from each other to stare out onto the empty landing. Then he's kissing me again and the doors close before we shoot upwards once more.

Inside his suite, he can't keep his hands to himself. I can see his bedroom up ahead, but I don't even know if we'll make it that far, because we've kicked off our shoes, he's taken off his jacket, I'm unbuttoning his shirt and now he's unzipping my dress. He grabs my hand as I step out of the beaded gold garment discarded on the floor, and leads me through to the bedroom. I don't feel as naked as I am, because his eyes stare straight into mine as we climb onto the bed and kneel, facing each other. I push his shirt off his shoulders and run my hands over his hard chest and then he's pressing his lips to my neck.

He takes his time with me and it's slow, sensuous, erotic. I can hardly bear it because I want him *so badly*, but when he finally does take me, it's worth waiting for.

I can't catch my breath for a long time afterwards as we lie, tangled in the bedsheets, hot and sweaty in each other's arms. He turns to face me, running his forefinger along my jawline. I don't know what to say, so I don't say anything, just lie there staring into his dark eyes.

'I should probably get some sleep,' he says finally.

'What is the time?' I turn and look at the red digital display on the alarm clock next to his bed. 'It's almost two o'clock in the morning!'

He grins. 'I know.'

'Will you be alright racing tomorrow on this little sleep?' I ask in alarm.

'I'll be fine, don't worry.'

'Are you sure?'

'Yes. I drive better after sex.' He winks at me and I remember how he's made that joke before. I pull my pillow out from behind my head and wallop him with it.

'Oi,' he warns, trying to keep a straight face. 'You don't want to have a pillow fight with me.'

I do, actually, but perhaps now is not the best time. 'I'll leave you to it, then,' I say, climbing out of bed.

'You don't have to go,' he calls as I walk to the door.

'No, you won't sleep properly if I stay.' I go out into the living space and pick up my dress, climbing back into it and zipping it up.

'Come here,' he calls from the bedroom.

I walk back through to him and stand beside the bed as he props himself up on one elbow and looks at me. I try to show him the same respect as he did to me and stare at his face rather than his chest, but it's harder than you'd think.

He takes my hand and pulls me down, then kisses me languidly.

'Sleep well,' I say, breaking away from him. 'Thanks for the dress.'

'You look better out of it than in, and I didn't think that was possible.'

He flashes me a cheeky grin and I smile back, before turning and walking out of the room.

Chapter 29

I'm a Screwdriver.

That's my first thought when I wake up the following morning with a stonking hangover.

What was I thinking, going to bed with Luis? Of all people! I remember that time he turned up in Melbourne with Alberta on his arm and feel sick to the pit of my stomach. Thank God he used a condom. At least I won't be going through another pregnancy scare . . .

Oh, Will. Will! How could I have done it? I see his face quite clearly for a fleeting moment and then he turns into Leonardo DiCaprio. I would bang my hand on my head to try to bring the memory back into focus, but it hurts enough as it is.

'Good time last night?' Holly asks, grinning.

'No,' I moan.

'*Really?*' she sits up in bed, surprised.

'I shouldn't have done it, Holly.'

'Why not?' she asks, pulling a face.

'He's not good for me.'

'We know *that*,' she brushes me off. 'But was he a good shag?'

I don't answer.

'He was, wasn't he?' She gives me an amused look.

Some of the details come back to me and a shiver goes through my entire body.

'You're blushing!' she squeals. 'Tell me everything!'

'No way,' I say firmly. 'I never kiss and tell.' I climb out of bed and go into the bathroom, ignoring her protests. I grab my toothbrush and squeeze out some toothpaste then commence brushing my teeth.

God, he *was* a good kisser . . .

Another shiver.

Oh, and that body . . .

I pause in my brushing and just remember for a moment. Then I spit out the toothpaste and rinse out my mouth before impulsively splashing my face with cold water. I need something to cool me down.

I've never felt so nervous as I wait for him to appear at the track that morning. I can't believe he has to race today, because my head is pounding with a terrible headache.

When he walks through the doors to the hospitality area at Japan's Suzuka circuit, my heart starts to pound like a jackhammer. I busy myself with the bacon while it occurs to me he might go straight to his room, but he doesn't. The next time I glance up, he's standing at the serving table looking straight at me.

'Morning,' he says, raising one eyebrow.

'Good morning.' I look down, then up again, before looking back down at the bacon. I want to ask if I can get him anything, but don't think that will go down too well.

'How are you feeling?' He has an amused expression on his face.

'Okay. Apart from my hangover. I was *really* drunk.'

'Were you?' He frowns. 'You didn't seem that bad to me.'

'Oh, I was,' I assure him. 'Weren't you?'

'No.'

'Really? I thought you were wasted! Weren't you drinking whisky and Cokes like they were going out of fashion?'

'No whisky, just Cokes.'

'Oh.'

We both fall silent.

'Can I get you anything?' I ask reluctantly. Well, sorry, but I don't know what else to say.

'Sure. The usual.'

'Is that the usual you *used* to have, or the usual your new, improved, healthy self would opt for?'

'Just get me some bacon and eggs, bun tart.'

We grin at each other and I breathe a very large sigh of relief as I load up his plate and hand it over. He winks and a thrill passes through me as I watch him walk away.

Okay, so I still fancy him. What's the big deal?

'I am totally going to go on that rollercoaster later. Are you coming or what?' Holly interrupts my thoughts. Suzuka circuit has an amazing theme park on site and its Ferris wheel dominates the skyline.

'You've got to be joking. I'd probably throw up.'

'Hey, was that Luis?' she asks suddenly. 'What did he say to you?'

'Nothing,' I reply casually.

'Nothing? What, he ignored you?'

'No!' I exclaim. 'I mean, nothing of interest.'

'Oh. I can't believe you're not kissing and telling,' she says disappointedly.

'Well, I'm not, so get over it.'

I don't speak to Luis again before the race starts, and when I do see him, he doesn't meet my eyes. I tell myself he's just trying to get his head together and stay focussed, but the insecure part of me thinks it's something more sinister. I'm not sure I want to go to the pits to watch the action, and when Holly persuades me, I don't feel comfortable when we stand in Luis's garage. I can't help but think all the mechanics are judging me. Do they all think I'm a Screwdriver? God, I hate that term now . . .

Luis wins the race, but I'm not full of elation along with the rest of the team. Those niggly doubts that have been bothering me are right in the forefront of my mind. I go outside to watch the podium celebrations because it would look odd if I didn't, but afterwards, I hurry back to the kitchen to commence the clean-up mission.

A couple of hours later, Luis comes to find me.

'Where have you been?' he asks, standing by the door.

'Just in here, tidying up.'

He gives me a weird look. 'Well, I'm off now.'

'Okay. I guess I'll see you in Brazil.' I don't go over to him.

'Are you alright?' he asks quietly, glancing around to make sure no one is in earshot.

'I'm fine,' I reply, nodding behind him to warn him of Frederick's encroaching presence.

'Well, okay, then.' He backs away from the door, looking put-out as Frederick budges past him into the kitchen.

'Bye.' I put my head down, moments later realising I didn't even congratulate him on his win. Should I go after him? No. I can't.

*

Back in England I throw myself into my work and try to forget all about my night with Luis. One of Holly's colleagues at the canteen is on maternity leave, so I fill in whenever I'm not working in London for Ingrid and Frederick. I'm too busy to even hunt for a new flat, but Holly assures me there's no rush.

'It's not like anyone else is staying here,' she moans one night when we're sitting on the sofa watching television. 'Catalina was at team HQ again today,' she says. 'That's three times in a week. I swear she's keeping her eye on me.'

'Do you honestly think she suspects anything?' I ask.

'I don't know. Simon and I haven't shagged since we were in Singapore, so there's nothing to suspect.'

'Has he spoken to you about it again?'

'What do you mean, called it off?'

'Yes.'

'No. I reckon he's just keeping me on the backburner in case it turns out to be a big scam.'

'A scam? What, you think she's not pregnant?'

'Well, she's not showing, is she?'

'No, but how far gone is she?'

'Only a couple of months.'

'She wouldn't be showing yet, then.'

Holly takes a gulp of her wine and plonks it down on the coffee table. 'I've had enough now, anyway.'

'Really?'

'Yep. I'm telling him it's over. No more booty call.'

I give her a sympathetic look, but don't patronise her by saying it's the right thing to do. 'When?'

'When I can next get a minute alone with him without that devil bitch poking her nose in.'

I laugh. 'Good luck with that.'

'What about you, have you heard from Luis?'

It's been over a week since Japan.

'No.' My reply is blunt.

'Why don't you text him? You left things a little *too* abruptly at Suzuka.'

'*Now* you're telling me this? Look, if he wanted to hear from me, he would have contacted me himself.'

'Maybe he's too scared to after you told him how drunk you were on the night you shagged and then ignored him after his race win.'

'Holly!' I exclaim. 'I didn't tell you all that so you could use it against me.'

'I'm not using it against you. Oh, whatever. Suit yourself.'

She grabs the television remote control and starts channel surfing, but irritation is eating me up. 'What do you want to watch?' she murmurs.

'I don't care,' I reply hotly.

'Have I pissed you off?' she asks, surprised.

'Yeah, you have a bit.'

'Why?'

'I can't believe you encouraged me to shag him and move on afterwards and when I actually did that – and no, I didn't particularly want to – you tell me to chase after him again.'

'What do you mean, you didn't particularly want to? Shag him or move on?'

'Move on!' I snap.

She smirks at me. 'I knew you had feelings for him . . .'

'I bloody don't, anymore.'

'Yes, you do,' she says, grinning.

'Well, it's a bit of a shame, then, isn't it, because he clearly thinks I'm just another tart he's managed to get into bed.'

Her face turns serious. 'That's not what I heard.'

'What are you going on about?'

'Something Pete said.'

'What?'

'Luis came into headquarters yesterday and was asking if you were around. Apparently his face fell when Pete told him you were working in London.'

'Really?' My heart lifts.

'Just text him,' Holly pleads.

'No.'

'You're both so stubborn!' she exclaims.

'I thought you said he was going to hurt me?'

'Now I'm not so sure,' she admits.

'Well, I'm going to see him in a few days, so I'm not doing anything until then.'

Our next race is in Brazil and I have to say I'm relieved it's the last one of the season. This whistlestop tour of the world has been fun, but the countries have all started to blur into one. All those airports, planes, setting up and cleaning up, non-stop partying, cars going round and around on a track . . . I don't think I could do much more of it. Which is just as well, because when we reach São Paulo, Simon calls me into the directors' suite.

'Hi,' I say, sitting down on an armchair, as instructed.

'I'm afraid we have a bit of a problem,' he says, looking concerned.

'Oh?'

He gets straight to the point. 'Your father has threatened to withdraw sponsorship if I continue to let you work for me.'

'*What?*' I'm shocked. 'But isn't he just a shareholder? Can he do that?'

'Apparently, he can. He's a major shareholder, and he has a *big* say in the company's expenditure.'

'But what does he expect me to do? I'm not going to go running back to New York if that's what he thinks.'

'I guess that's something you'll have to discuss with him.'

'Fuck that!' I snap, before apologising. Simon is still my boss, even if it's only for a short while longer. 'Is that it, then? Am I fired?'

'I'll write you an excellent reference,' he replies.

'Should I pack my bags now?'

'Please stay until the end of the weekend.'

I don't suppose they have anyone to cover for me, my cynical side says.

'There's a big bonus waiting for you if you do,' Simon continues.

I'll need it, at this rate.

He shakes his head, sadly. 'It just won't be the same without you girls next year.'

'Us girls? What, you're firing Holly, too?'

He looks taken aback. 'She handed in her resignation this morning. Didn't she tell you?'

'No.'

I back out of the room and run straight into Luis.

'Hi!' His face lights up, but falls instantly when he sees mine. 'What's up?'

'Why should you care?' I bite back angrily.

'Hey, come on.' He frowns. 'Can I talk to you for a sec?' He points to his room.

'That's what Will used to say to me. And no, you can't.'

I may as well have slapped him across the face. His features harden and he turns away. 'Suit yourself, Daisy.'

I storm into the kitchen and spin Holly around. 'You quit?'

She looks shamefaced.

'When were you going to tell me?'

She glances around the kitchen. 'Let's go to the bathroom.'

I follow her in there and she explains. 'It was a spur-of-the-moment decision.'

'Why? How?'

'Please keep your voice down. I don't want anyone else to hear.'

'Go on,' I tell her bluntly, trying to oblige.

'He just tried it on with me. I told him I wasn't interested in shagging him again until he got a divorce. He actually laughed in my face.'

'Really?'

'Yes. Loudly. He said that was just ridiculous, he was never going to divorce the bitch, baby or no baby. But he didn't see why we couldn't carry on as we were because she was going to be – get this – even less interested in sex once she had a kid. Can you believe he said that to me?'

I sigh in empathy.

'So I told him I was quitting. I said I'd see the weekend out, but after that I'd find another position.'

'What will you do?'

'I don't know. Maybe Frederick and Ingrid could hire me?'

'Perhaps.' I pause. 'Do you know that I've been fired?'

'*WHAT?*'

I fill her in.

'Oh my God, Daisy, I'm so sorry.'

'It's okay, I'm not surprised.'

'I didn't realise your father was as cruel as that.'

'Oh, he's worse, but that's something I've had to learn the hard way.'

'What will *you* do?'

'I'm still thinking about it.'

Norm can barely look at me. The other sponsors seem uncomfortable around me, too. A couple of them have managed a small smile and a slight nod, but my shifts have never been so quiet because so many people seem to be avoiding the serving table when I'm behind it.

'Do you think I can work in the kitchen?' I ask Frederick eventually, when I can stand it no more.

He gives me a sympathetic look, which is so out-of-the-ordinary from him that I feel my eyes prick with tears.

'Fillet the fish,' he replies, pointing with his knife to the other side of the kitchen.

I go to the counter and get on with the job at hand, quietly and diligently working away as I skin and debone a sea bass.

My head is spinning with all that's happened. It doesn't feel real. None of it feels real. I don't feel like myself, I feel like I'm in someone else's body. Is all this really coming to an end?

I work away in the kitchen for the rest of the afternoon, not taking a break to watch practice. Early that evening, I hear a couple of the front-of-house girls gossiping as they collect their things from the kitchen.

'He was, like, properly shouting.'

My ears prick up.

'What was he saying?'

'He said he had no balls!' one of them whispers loudly.

'What's this?' I can't help but ask.

They both look sheepish. 'Oh, it's nothing. Sorry, I didn't know anyone was there.' They both grab their bags and hurry out of the kitchen.

'Do you know anything about a shouting match earlier?' I ask Holly.

'Simon and Luis,' she replies without a moment's hesitation. 'Luis has taken a drive for another team.'

I slam my knife down on the counter. 'Seriously?'

'Oh for God's sake, go and talk to him,' she snaps. 'What have you got to lose?'

I scrub my hands and wipe them on a tea-towel before stalking determinedly out of the kitchen, ignoring her satisfied smile. I jog up the stairs and pound on his door, then push it open before he even has a chance to answer. He's sitting on a chair with his head in his hands and looks up at the loud interruption.

'You took it, then?' I ask.

'What?'

'The drive for the other team.'

'Oh, yeah,' he replies dully.

'Heard about your shouting match,' I explain.

He raises his eyebrows and looks away. 'We weren't arguing about that.'

I regard him with interest. 'What, then?'

'I can't believe he fired you,' he replies.

'Oh, that,' I dismiss him. 'I'm not surprised. I told you what my father was like.'

'Simon's a bastard for not standing up to him.'

'Forget about it. I've had enough of all this anyway.' I wave my hands around the room.

'Have you?' He frowns. 'I was thinking you could come with me?'

'No. I don't want to be a bun tart anymore.' I take a seat on a chair next to him.

'You seem surprisingly okay about it.'

'I am. I just wish I'd sorted myself out and resigned before my father had a chance to stick his nose in. At least I'm not going back to New York, which is what I'm sure he's expecting.'

'What will you do?'

'I'm going to look into catering colleges.'

He stands up, going to his team carry case. I watch, intrigued, as he pulls out a green folder and hands it to me.

'What's this?'

'I tried to drop it to you at HQ last week, but you weren't there.'

I open it up and pull out application forms for London catering schools. I stare at them, feeling utterly astounded. I can't believe he went to that effort for me.

'Thank you.' I look up at him as my eyes fill with tears.

'Hey, don't get upset.' He sits down next to me and puts his hand on my back. I stare down at the forms as my stomach is overrun with butterflies.

'What are you doing tonight?' Luis asks casually.

'I don't know.'

'Will you come for dinner at my house?'

'Your family's house?' I double check.

'No, *my* house, but my family is going to be there. My mum is cooking dinner for us all,' he explains. 'I know she'd like to see you again.'

'Does she even remember me?' I'm pleasantly surprised.

'Oh, yeah. She warned me not to mess you around.'

My face breaks into a grin. 'She didn't?'

'She did.'

'How did she even know . . .'

'That I had the hots for you? Come on, that must've been obvious.'

These are not the words of someone who thinks I'm just a Screwdriver, even I can see that.

'I'd love to come,' I tell him.

'Cool.' He smiles at me as the butterflies go into overdrive, but he doesn't attempt anything. It's funny how sometimes the second kiss comes so much harder than the first.

He picks me up in his yellow Ferrari.

'No way,' I exclaim. 'You're really letting me near it?'

'You can drive it, if you like.'

I burst out laughing. 'You'd let me behind the wheel of this thing? Are you mad?'

'Why not? Don't you have a driving licence?'

'Barely. I got driven round in limos when I lived in New York.'

He rolls his eyes at me and grins. 'Get in, then.'

'I knew that'd change your mind.'

'No, you can drive it later if you want to.'

'What if I scratch it?'

'Just get in and shut the door,' he jokily snaps.

He drives me north out of the city until we reach a small airfield.

'What are we doing here?' I ask, perplexed.

'You're not afraid of flying, are you?'

'Luckily, no, otherwise I wouldn't enjoy my job very much.'

'Good.'

Twenty minutes later I'm wearing earphones and I'm strapped into the front seat of Luis's private helicopter. He's next to me in the pilot's seat.

'I cannot believe I'm letting you fly me around in this thing,' I say into my earpiece.

'Just relax and enjoy the ride.'

He starts up the rotors and moments later we've left the ground and are soon swooping over towns and houses far below. I wanted to scream at first, but now I'm just taking in the sights. I'm still stunned that he can fly as well as drive so fast. I wonder what else I don't know about him.

His home is a sprawling mansion surrounded by acres of private land. It's dark now, but the lights around the house are welcoming. Luis sets down the helicopter, switches off the engine and comes around to help me out.

'That was crazy,' I exclaim.

'Crazy good or crazy bad?' he checks.

'Crazy amazing. What other surprises have you got lined up for me?'

'No surprises, just family.'

'Come on, then.'

When he said his family was big, I didn't know he meant this big. There must be thirty-odd people here, including siblings, cousins and aunts and uncles, not forgetting his parents, of course. It turns out they live in the house along with his teenage sister, Clara, because he's so rarely here to look after the place. His other brothers and sisters live in the surrounding area and it doesn't take a genius to work out that Luis is looking after his family very well.

His mother embraces me in a big hug the second we walk through the door.

'What about me?' Luis berates her.

'Daisy, first,' she jokes, before turning to engulf her son in a suffocating squeeze.

Clara is standing just behind Luis's father and she smiles shyly at me. 'Hello,' I call, after getting a hug from Mr Castro. Clara comes through to kiss my cheeks, but I impulsively give her a hug, too. And that's the way it goes from then on. I've never been hugged so many times by so many people. There is so much warmth in this one enormous room, and I can't help compare Luis's family to my own. How I wish I had been raised in surroundings like this. Not in a mansion, you understand, just with people who loved me. And they're all so proud of Luis. I've been swept away by Mrs Castro to meet various members of his family, but I keep looking back and catching glimpses of him laughing and chatting away.

I wonder how he copes in England when his family are all here. He must miss them. Suddenly I feel bad about saying he lives in that big house in Hampstead, all on his own. He *must* be lonely.

'And this is my granddaughter, Rosa,' Mrs Castro says, after introducing me first to Fatima, another one of Luis's sisters, and then to Fatima's little baby girl.

'She's beautiful,' I say, as Rosa coos and gurgles in Fatima's arms.

'Would you like to hold her?'

'Um, will she cry?' I ask hesitantly.

'No, no, she's as good as gold.'

Fatima hands her over and, after a moment, I realise the baby isn't going to scream so I relax. 'How old is she?' I ask her mother.

'Just under six months.'

'I think she has Luis's eyes,' I comment, looking into the baby's brown ones.

'Daisy thinks Rosa has your eyes!' Fatima calls to her brother. Luis glances at me, amused.

'I used to know a Rosa,' I say to Fatima, handing the baby back. 'She was an excellent cook.' I think of Johnny Jefferson's cook and how she inspired me. I wish I could tell her I'm going to apply to catering college – I know she'd be proud.

'Speaking of cooking, it's time to serve up!' Mrs Castro exclaims.

'Can I help with anything?' I ask her.

'Absolutely not! You're our star guest. Please go through to the dining room.' She points to large double doors on the far wall, then turns and shouts in Portuguese to her vast family. Everyone starts to file through to the other room.

Luis appears by my side. 'Are you okay?'

'I'm good.' I smile at him. 'Your family are so lovely.'

'You're going down pretty well with them, too.'

As he leads me through to the other room, I suddenly feel very strange. What am I doing here? He's brought me to meet all his loved ones. That's so personal and . . . I don't know, odd? Why would he open himself up to me like that? I'm seeing Luis in a whole new light, here, and it scares me how much I like it.

Two hours later, he tells his family we have to leave. His mother protests, suggesting we stay the night, but Luis is quite firm in his negative response, which is something I have mixed feelings about. Doesn't he want to spend the night with me? Then again, the thought of having breakfast with his parents in the morning . . . Well, that's too much, too soon.

And so we say our many goodbyes and set off on the short walk to the helicopter. The flight back to the airfield seems to pass more quickly this time around and, before I know it, he's parking his Ferrari in the hotel car park.

I'm on edge. What happens now? I've been too busy talking to drink much alcohol, and he's stone-cold sober, so there will be no drunken antics.

He glances at me as we walk up the steps into the lobby. 'Want to come up to my room?'

I raise one eyebrow at him. 'For a coffee?'

'I was thinking more along the lines of a shag.'

I crack up laughing.

'But we can start with a coffee, if you like,' he adds, his eyes twinkling.

Inside his suite, he directs me to the sofa area while he gets on with the drinks.

'That was such a nice night, thank you,' I tell him as he brings two steaming cups over. 'I can't believe you can fly a helicopter.'

'I can fly a plane, too. I'll take you on one of those next,' he says, sitting down next to me.

I shake my head in wonder. 'There's so much I don't know about you. And to think you once said *I* was the mysterious one.'

'When did I say that?' he asks, gently placing the cups on the coffee table.

'Oh, sorry,' I quickly reply as my memory starts serving me properly. I feel my face heat up.

'You were thinking about Will, weren't you?' he asks quietly, turning to look at me.

'Sorry,' I say again, but he averts his gaze.

I feel tense and a little bit nauseous. He meets my eyes again.

'Are you over him?'

I don't answer for a moment, then reply honestly, 'I don't know.'

'That's not good, Daisy.'

'No, I know it's not good, Luis,' I snap. 'But what do you expect me to do about it?'

He looks away and shakes his head. 'Were you in love with him?' He asks the question so softly I can barely hear him.

Was I in love with him? I don't want to remember, but now I can't help it. Images flood my mind of my time with Will. How he sat on a sofa not dissimilar to this one and told me he preferred my hair down to up. How he said I was doing his head in before he came clean about his feelings for me. How his eyes were full of regret when Laura got to him on the grid before me and I never wished him good luck.

And then I see that crash, that terrible crash . . . The white sheet coming out by the ambulance crew, Laura and his family being rushed out of the pits, me packing his bag in his room and then losing his black T-shirt that still smelled of him . . . A lump forms in my throat and my eyes fill with tears, and then I desperately want to sob my heart out, but I can't, not here with Luis.

'I think you should go,' he says morosely. 'I have to get some sleep before qualifying tomorrow.'

I nod and stand up. 'I'm sorry,' I tell him again.

He doesn't answer so I walk to the door and leave him alone on the sofa.

Luis qualifies third the following day, and I can't help but feel somewhat to blame because yesterday he was quickest in practice. I want to talk to him about it, but his parents are here now, and I don't feel comfortable seeing them after what happened – or didn't happen – between Luis and I last night. So I hide away in the kitchen because Frederick is still letting me help with the catering.

'Very good,' he comments, when I show him a platter of fresh seafood that I've prepared. My heart swells with pride because compliments don't come easy to him. 'I should have had you helping out with the cooking more often.'

'I would have loved to have done that,' I tell him.

'Well, it's too late now,' he says, before erupting. 'It's a bloody disgrace!'

I crack a smile. 'Don't worry about it.'

He shakes his head angrily, and I'm touched that he cares about losing me.

'I'm applying to catering college, you know,' I tell him.

He regards me with interest. 'Are you? If you want me to write you a reference, let me know.'

'Would you really?'

'Absolutely. Just don't go into competition with me on the Formula 1 scene.'

I laugh. 'I hardly think that's likely. I'd be happy working in a restaurant in London.'

'For some celebrity chef, no doubt,' he scoffs.

I smile and hand the platter to Gertrude to take outside to the serving table.

Later, Pete, Dan and the lads drag Holly and me out on the town for our last night out together.

'I can't believe you two are leaving,' Pete says sadly. We're seated by the window at a piano bar called Terraço Itália and the view of São Paulo city laid out below is incredible. I've seen the twinkling lights of so many cities around the world and it still takes my breath away. I've been ridiculously lucky to have had this experience. I hope I didn't take it too much for granted.

'Me neither,' I reply. I don't feel like drinking, but the lads have insisted on caipirinhas all round. Brazil's notorious cachaca-based cocktail is very alcoholic, so I'm making mine last.

Pete turns to me. 'I had no idea you were a rich chick. And I mean that as a compliment,' he adds, before I can give him any stick.

I smile wryly. 'I wish I wasn't. But even if my father hadn't interfered, it was time for me to do something different.'

'What about you, Hol?' Dan asks Holly. 'What are you going to do?'

My mind turns to other things, because we've had this conversation before.

I miss Luis. It's not the same without him here tonight. He's having dinner with his family, who are all staying in the city so they're close by for the race tomorrow. I really wish I were with him, right now.

Am I over Will? It's been four months since his death, and even when he was alive, I barely spent any time with him. It didn't feel like that when the accident happened, but now, looking back, my relationship with him is starting to seem quite surreal.

I go home early that night, while the others all head out to a bar in the Itaim area. The following morning I hide away in the kitchen again, poking my head out of the door to see if I can catch Luis when he arrives. I don't know what I'll say, but I'm hoping something will come to mind. When I finally do spot him, my heart flips and my spirits lift. I hurriedly wash my hands and go to walk out of the kitchen, but then I realise he has about ten members of his clan with him and my feet come to a stop. I turn around and hurry back to the worktop to continue with my chores. Hopefully I'll get a chance to catch him alone later.

But I don't. As the minutes turn into hours and the race draws nearer, I worry that I won't even get a chance to wish him good luck. Every time I see him, he's surrounded. Holly comes into the kitchen to ask if I'm going to watch the race.

'Are you kidding? I wouldn't miss it.'

'For the last time ever, girls,' Frederick says, a tinge of sadness in his voice. 'Can you take the tea, coffee and biscuits with you to the pits.'

'Yes, Chef!' we chorus, and he smiles at us.

'Ooh, I feel a bit sad, actually,' Holly says as we trek across the way to the garages.

'Me, too.'

'It's the end of an era. I'm going to really miss working with you.' She glances at me, tears in her eyes.

'Oh, don't, you'll make me cry, too,' I warn.

'Okay, okay, let's not get emotional,' she jokes. 'At least you're still living with me.'

'Not for long, I promise.'

'Take as long as you need,' she says. 'Although saying that, I might have to move into town if I'm going to be working for

Frederick and Ing
the sticks.'

'Yes, go on! T

'We'll see.'

Luis glance
immediately

'Daisy!'

I look o
platter do
ribly awk
since Fr
mother

'Hello!' She give
Luis's nearby presence as he tal

Luis doesn't make any effort to speak t
exchanged pleasantries with the rest of his family,
excuses about needing to get back to work. I return to the se
ing table and help Holly set up the coffee cups.

'Careful!' she warns, when I almost drop one.

'Sorry,' I murmur, looking over to see if Luis noticed. He has his back to me. *Cazzo*, I feel so on edge. What if this is it? What if I've missed my chance? What if I don't get to tell him that I care about him? What if he leaves the moment the race is over? No, I have to catch him alone. I'll confront him on the grid if I have to.

Oh, God. Luis confronted Will on the grid and then he crashed and killed himself. I put my hands on the table in front of me and take a few deep breaths.

'Are you alright?' Holly asks, all of a sudden realising I'm not in a good way.

mile. Perhaps I won't confront

and turn to see him standing there.
elf scarce.
flooding me.
and pokes at the platter of biscuits. 'Still no

I'm sorry!' I cover my mouth with my hands. 'I
tention of getting you some. I just forgot.'
kes his head at me, his face deadpan. 'How could you
omething so important?'
get you some when we get back to the UK, I promise.'
le folds his arms and stares at me. 'Are we going to see each
ther when we get back to the UK, then?'

'I'll come and camp on your doorstep, if you're not careful,' I tease.

'Luis!' We look over to see Dan calling him.

'I've got to go,' he says.

'Hey, good luck for the race.'

'See ya later.' He smiles and turns away.

'Bye,' I call, as a feeling of déjà vu overwhelms me.

Those were the last words I exchanged with Will on the morning of his death. A shiver goes through me and I feel like I'm freezing, despite the humidity.

Holly re-emerges. 'What did he say to you?' she asks, alarmed when she sees my face.

'Nothing.'

'You look like you've seen a ghost.'

'Oh, something he just said made me think of Will.'

'Aah, okay.' She pats my arm in sympathy. 'Do you want to

come outside to the grid? Maybe it'll take your mind off it.'

'No, I think I'll just stay here.'

It happens again. The exact same thing that used to happen when I watched Will race. When the red lights go out and Luis roars away from the starting grid, I start to feel dizzy almost immediately. It's the fear of losing him, the fear I had of losing Will.

Holly catches on quickly and leads me to the back of the garages before anyone notices. Luis's family are all too caught up in the action. He overtook Benni Fischer on the first lap and is now running second. Kit Bryson is first, but if Luis can beat him, he'll win the championship, so the pressure is on.

'I think you should return to the hospitality area, don't you?' Holly says.

'No. I can't. I have to watch this race.'

'Are you sure?' She looks concerned.

'Yes, I'm sure. I'll just stay here for a moment.'

'Okay, then.' She pulls up a chair beside me and we stare up at the television screens.

Fear clutches my stomach as Luis attempts to outbreak Kit into a corner. The cameras show spectators waving Brazilian flags in grandstands all around the circuit. There's so much support for him here. What if something happened to him at his home race? I start to feel light-headed again.

Is this how Laura used to feel? Is this why she didn't come to many of the races? She knew Will almost all her life and now he's gone forever. Someone help me. I'm finding it difficult to breathe.

Oh, Will, no, no, no. All the pain I felt at the time of his death violently overcomes me. I loved him and I lost him. I can't go through that again. I have to get as far away from here as possible.

To Holly's astonishment, I bolt out of the garage. I spot a team scooter parked up by one of our trucks and climb on and start it up, speeding away from the pits and paddock as I try to block my mind from my memories.

Tears fill my eyes and start pouring down my cheeks. And then, after threatening rain all weekend, the heavens finally open and it pours down. I try to wipe away my tears, because it's impossible to see, and then my wheel hits a pot hole and suddenly I'm flying through the air and crashing down on the road. I cry out with pain as the shock from the asphalt shoots all the way up my leg. And then I see the lights. An enormous truck is coming towards me and, as I try to get to my feet, I have a sense in that very moment of what it would feel like to know that I'm going to die.

I stagger backwards and the truck misses me by a few inches. I will never forget the feeling of its hot air rushing past and the tyres kicking out rain and mud onto my face. I make it to my feet and stumble off the road, collapsing onto the green grass nearby. And then I sob, and there's no one there to comfort me, no one there to pick up my scooter, no one there to check me for cuts and bruises. I'm all alone.

And then I think of Luis and his family and the warmth I felt at his house. I don't want to be alone anymore. I want to be with him.

In the far-off distance I see a big screen televising the race. The camera pans in on Luis. He's right behind Kit Bryson, and they're both lapping backmarkers.

I stand up and watch. Go on, Luis. You can do it. Win the championship. Do it for Will.

He pulls out from behind Kit and outbreaks him into the

corner. I scream for joy before the sound is ripped from my throat in horror as I watch a backmarker lose grip in the wet and crash into a wall. He spins back across the track and slams into Luis, whose car shatters as he hits a wall on the other side of the track. Kit makes it through the carnage unscathed.

In desperation I try to make out what's happening on the big screen through the rain and the mist, but I can't see if Luis is moving inside the cockpit. Oh, God, please, no, please, no. And then I'm running, as fast as my feet can take me, swiping my access-all-areas pass as I push through gates that allow me back to the pits, drenched, muddy, bleeding, but I don't care. Please don't take him from me, I beg. Please, no. He's mine. He's mine. He's mine to lose.

I run all the way down the paddock and burst into our garages. 'WHERE IS HE?' I scream. Everyone spins around to look at me, and then I hear Holly's words telling me it's okay. I look up at the television screens in a panic to see Luis walking down the pit lane and then I'm pushing through the crowd in the garages and running to him.

He's surrounded by camera crews and journalists, trying to catch a word from the guy who *almost* became world champion in his debut season. But there will be more races to win, more world championships to conquer, and I want to be here for Luis, by his side, supporting him so he'll never feel alone. Life can be snatched away from you in an instant, but if you don't give yourself up to love, even with all the risks of losing it, life isn't worth living.

I barge through the camera crews, ignoring the complaints, because I just want to hold him again, to check that he hasn't been hurt, to make sure he's real.

I reach him and fling my arms around his neck. And then he's holding me tightly, my face pressed into his racing overalls, as tears stream down my wet and muddy cheeks.

'Hey!' someone shouts. 'We're trying to conduct an interview here!'

'It's okay,' Luis tells the camera crews. 'It's my girl. My girl.'

Epilogue

I'm sitting on Luis's white designer chair in the bay window of his Hampstead home. Or should that be, *our* Hampstead home? I'm drinking a cup of espresso coffee and reading the Sunday papers, because they don't scare me anymore, even though I sometimes appear in them now with Luis by my side.

It's March, and the next racing season hasn't yet begun, but soon we'll be jetting off to Melbourne. I'm hoping my recent therapy sessions will help with my fears, but we'll see. I certainly won't be getting on any more scooters. I've promised that much to Luis, at least. Luckily Simon didn't make me pay for the last one I crashed. I guess he was still experiencing a guilt trip.

My tutors at catering college have agreed to let me have the time off to attend the races this year, due to my 'exceptional circumstances'. It's going to be hard juggling lessons with being a supportive girlfriend, but I'm up for the challenge. One day, Luis has promised me we'll open up our own restaurant, but first things, first. I need to get some proper hands-on experience before we think about taking that step.

Holly sold up her place in Berkshire and moved to Chiswick

in west London. We've seen a fair bit of each other since we quit the Grand Prix scene, but not as much as I'd like because she's been holed up in bed with the new man in her life. Pete's younger brother, of all people. Pete made the introductions. I kind of hoped she'd end up with Pete himself, but it wasn't to be, and Adam is definitely a cutie.

Catalina is pregnant with triplets, so she and Simon will both have their work cut out for them. I hope they make it. Perhaps their children will bring them closer together, but hmm, I don't know . . .

Luis and I spent Christmas with my nonna in the mountains and we fixed the walls for her ourselves. Luis is quite a handy man, even though he could have paid for someone to do the job several million times over, but we always knew Nonna would never have allowed that.

She passed away just after New Year and my mother and I attended her funeral together. She's promised me she'll go back to Italy with me to help me sort out Nonna's things. Nonna left her house to me. I still can't think of her without crying so I won't say any more about that.

Yesterday I bumped into Laura. I was tempted to put my head down and keep on walking, but I decided to stop and talk to her. She said she's doing well, but she still misses Will. The darkest part of me wanted to let her know that she wasn't the only one he left behind, but I could never do that to her. She told me that with blessing from his parents, she now heads a charitable foundation in Will's name which helps underprivileged children around the world. Later that day I arranged an anonymous bank transfer of 10 million dollars, plus all the interest that I've accrued over the last few years. I think that Will would have been proud of me.

I can see him clearly, now, and I know that's a good thing. It means that I'm over him. A part of me will always love him, but Luis owns my heart now.

Some might say that Luis and I have gone too fast by moving in together, but I believe life is too short to wait and see. He told me he fell for me the moment I shouted at him from across the street when he almost ran me off my scooter. I told him it took me longer than that. He doesn't care. I love him now, and that's all that matters.

Acknowledgements

Thank you first and foremost to my readers. Your Facebook messages, online reviews and overwhelming support are what make this already impossibly great job of mine even greater.

Thank you to my lovely, lovely editor Suzanne Baboneau for never dropping the ball, even though it's been really bloody heavy at times. You're nothing short of amazing. Thanks always to my friend and publicist Nigel Stoneman, who I still owe seven Bellinis to . . . And thank you to the rest of the team at Simon & Schuster – I appreciate your hard work and enthusiasm more than you will ever know.

A massive thank you to Rebecca Finn – one time 'waitress in a car park' (her words, but I stole them), for sharing her experiences of being a bun tart with me. Thank you to mechanic Alastair Roome for allowing me to run down the battery in his mobile phone while I picked his brains about all things F1. (I decided I'm allowed some artistic licence so any mistakes are absolutely, entirely, one hundred per cent intentional. That's my excuse and I'm sticking with it.) And thank you to Neil Trundle for taking my whole family on a tour around the ridiculously cool

McLaren Technology Centre – I borrowed only a little of the inspiration for my nowhere-near-as-good fictional team from it.

Thank you to the following friends for being fabulously foul-mouthed at my request: Giulia Cassini (grazie), João and Carol Bruno (obrigada), Blandine Jeunot (merci), and a big 'cheers' to Susan Rains for all her Americanisms.

Thank you to Ian and Helga Toon, Bridie Tonkin, Naomi Dean, Miranda Ramsay, Jane Hampton, Emma Guest, Tina Fox, Sarah Canning, Kath Moulds, Rachel Lissauer, Suzie Zuber and Ellie Samuels for their help and feedback on various things. And thank you to Kath Moulds for the proof reading, and Jassiara Sooma for sharing her knowledge about Brazil, and in particular, São Paulo.

Thank you – so much – to my mum, dad and brother, Jenny, Vern and Kerrin Schuppan, for giving me the best upbringing anyone could wish for. But it hasn't all been fun: the near-death accident story that Will recounts to Daisy is borrowed from my dad. I remember seeing his crash live on television when I was a little girl, and I'll never forget how my mum managed to stay so strong for us. I am overwhelmingly proud of both her *and* my dad, who, with all his success, is still the nicest person I've ever known.

Most of all, thank you to my gorgeous, super-talented husband Greg. From *Lucy in the Sky* ('*Another* lump in her throat? She should get checked out for cancer') to *Chasing Daisy* ('They could give Roger Moore a run for his money with all their raised eyebrows'), his often hilarious, sometimes annoying advice has without a doubt made my books better than they would have otherwise been. You're the best.

Last but not least, thank you to my son, Indy, who has done absolutely nothing to contribute to this book, but who makes me laugh my head off every single day. Love you, cutie.

Simon & Schuster and Pocket Books proudly present

Paige Toon's sensational novel

Available to buy in bookshops now!

ISBN 978-1-84739-044-8

Turn the page to read a sample chapter of
Johnny Be Good . . .

Prologue

'Sing! Sing! Sing!'

No. I can't.

'Sing! Sing! Sing!'

No! Stop it! And for God's sake, cut that bloody music!

'SING! SING! SING!'

Argh! My palms are so slippery I almost dropped the mic. I'm in bad shape. I can't sing. I can NOT sing. But they won't stop. I know they won't stop until I deliver. And I shouldn't disappoint my audience. Okay, I'm going to sing! Here comes the chorus . . .

I'm locked inside us
And I can't find the key
It was under the plant pot
That you nicked from me

That's not my song, by the way. And when I say I can't sing, I mean I *really* can't sing. When you're as drunk as I am, you could be forgiven for thinking that *if only* Simon Cowell were in the room, he would say, 'Girl, you've got the X Factor.' But I'm under no illusions. I know I'm, in his words, 'distinctly average'.

As for the audience . . . Well, I'm not singing to a 90,000-strong crowd at Wembley, but you've probably guessed that by now. I'm in the living room of my flatshare in London Bridge. And the music comes courtesy of my PlayStation SingStar.

The person who's just grabbed the mic from me is Bess. She's my flatmate and my best friend. She can't sing either. Jeez, she's hurting my ears! Next to her is Sara, a friend of mine from work. And then there are Jo, Jen and Alison, pals from university.

As for me? Well, I'm Meg Stiles. And this is my leaving party. And that song we're making a mockery of? That's written by one of the biggest rock stars on the planet. And I'm moving in with him tomorrow.

Seriously! I am not even joking.

Well, maybe I'm misleading you a little bit. You see, I haven't actually met him yet.

No, I'm not a stalker. I'm his new PA. His Personal Assistant. And I am off to La-La Land. Los Angeles. The City of Angels – whatever you want to call it – and I can't bloody believe it!

Chapter 1

Ouch. My head hurts. What sort of stupid person has a leaving party the night before starting a new job?

I'm not usually this disorganised. In fact, I'm probably the most organised person you're ever likely to meet. Having a leaving party the night before I had to board this plane to LA is very out of character. But then I didn't have much choice. I've only just got the job.

Seven days ago I was a PA at an architects' firm. My boss, Marie Sevenou (early fifties, French, very well-respected in the industry), called me into her office on Monday morning and asked me to shut the door and take a seat. This had never happened in the nine months I'd been working there and my initial reaction was to wonder if I'd done anything wrong. But I was pretty sure I hadn't so, above all, I was curious.

'Meg,' she said, her heavy French accent laced with despair, 'it pains me to tell you this.'

Shit, was she dying?

'I do not want to lose you.'

Shit, was *I* dying? Sorry, that was just me being ridiculous.

She continued, 'All of yesterday I toyed with my conscience. Should I tell her? Could I keep it from her? She is the best PA I have ever had. It would *devastate* me to let her go.'

I do love my boss, right, but she ain't half melodramatic.

'Marie,' I said, 'what are you talking about?'

She stared at me, her face bereft. 'But I said to myself, Marie, think of what you were like thirty years ago. You would have done anything for an opportunity like this. How could you keep it from her?'

What on earth was she going on about?

'On Saturday night I went to a dinner party at a very good friend of mine's. You remember Wendel Redgrove? High-powered solicitor – I designed his house in Hampstead a couple of years ago? Well, anyway, he was telling me how his biggest client had lost his personal assistant recently and was having a terrible time trying to find a new one. Of course I empathised. I told him about you and how I thought I might die if I ever lost you. Honestly, Meg, I don't know how I ever managed before . . .'

But she regained her composure, directing her cool blue eyes straight into my dark-brown ones as she said the words that would change my life forever.

'Meg, Johnny Jefferson needs a new personal assistant.'

Johnny Jefferson. Wild boy of rock. Piercing green eyes, dirty blond hair and a body Brad Pitt would have killed for fifteen years ago.

It was the chance of a lifetime, to go and work in Los Angeles for him and live in his mansion. To become his confidante, his number one, the person he relies on more than anyone else in the world. And my boss, in a moment of madness, had suggested me for the job.

That very afternoon I met up with Wendel Redgrove and Johnny Jefferson's manager, Bill Blakeley, a cockney geezer in his late forties who had managed Johnny's career since he split up with his band, Fence, seven years ago. Wendel drew up a contract, along with a strict confidentiality clause, and Bill asked me to start the following week.

Marie actually cried when I told her it was all done and dusted; they'd offered me the job and I had accepted. Wendel had already persuaded Marie to waive my one-month-notice period, but that left me only six days, which was daunting, to say the least. When I raised my concerns, Bill Blakeley put it bluntly: 'Sorry, love, but if you need time to sort your life out then you're not the right chick for the job. Just pack what you need. We'll cover your rent here for the first three months and after that, if it all works out, you can have some time off to come back and do whatever the hell it is that you need to do. But you've got to start immediately, because frankly, I'm sick to fucking death of buying Johnny's underpants since his last girl left.'

And so here I am, on this plane to LA, with a shocking hangover. I glance out of the window down at the city. Smog hangs over it like a thick black cloud as we fly towards the airport. The distinctive white structure of the Theme Building looks like a flying saucer or a white, four-legged spider. Marie told me to look out for it, and seeing it makes me feel even more spaced-out.

I clear Customs and head out towards the exit where I've been told there will be a driver waiting to collect me. Scanning the crowd, I find a placard with my name on it.

'Ms Stiles! Well! How do you do!' the driver says when I introduce myself. He shakes my hand vigorously as his face breaks out into a pearly white grin. 'Welcome to America! I'm Davey! Pleased to meet you! Here, let me take that bag for you, ma'am! Come on! We're this way!'

I'm not sure I can handle this many exclamation marks on a hangover, but you've got to admire his enthusiasm. Smiling, I follow him out of the terminal. The humidity immediately engulfs me and I start to feel a little faint so it's a relief to reach the car – a long black limo. Climbing into the back, I slump down into the cool, cream leather seats. The air-conditioning kicks in as we exit the car park and my faintness and nausea begin to subside. I put the window down.

Davey is rabbiting on about his lifelong ambition to meet the Queen. I breathe in the outside air, less humid now that we're on the move, and start to feel better. It smells of barbeques here. The tallest palm trees I've ever seen line the wide, wide roads and I'm amazed as I stick my head further out of the window and gaze up at them. I can't believe they haven't snapped in half – their proportions are skinnier than toothpicks. It's the middle of July, but some people still have sad little Christmas decorations hanging out in front of their tired-looking homes. They twinkle in the afternoon sun – no wonder they call this place Tinseltown. I look around but can't see the Hollywood sign.

Yet.

Oh God, how can this be happening to me?

None of my friends can believe it, because I've never been that fussed about Johnny Jefferson. Of course I think he's good-looking – who wouldn't? – but I don't *really* fancy him. And when it comes to rock music, well, I think Avril's pretty hardcore. Give me Take That any day of the week.

Everyone else I know would give their little toe to be in my position. In fact, make that their whole foot. Hell, throw in a hand, while you're at it.

Whereas *I* would struggle to give up more than my big toenail. I certainly wouldn't relinquish a whole digit.

That's not to say I'm not thrilled about this job. The fact that all my friends fancy Johnny like mad just makes it even more exciting.

Davey drives through the gates into Bel Air, the haven of the rich and famous.

'That's where Elvis used to live,' he points out, as we start to climb the hill via ever-more-impressive mansions. I try to catch a glimpse of the groomed gardens behind the high walls and hedges.

The ache in my head seems to have been replaced by butterflies in my stomach. I wipe the perspiration from my brow and tell myself it's just the side effects of too much alcohol.

We continue climbing upwards, then suddenly Davey is pulling up outside imposing wooden gates. Cameras point ominously down at us from steel pillars on either side of the car. I feel like I'm being watched and have a sudden urge to put my window back up. Davey announces our arrival into a speakerphone and a few seconds later the gates glide open. My hands feel clammy.

The driveway isn't long, but it feels like it goes on forever. Trees obscure the house at first, but then we turn a corner and it appears in front of us.

It's a modern architectural design: two storeys, white concrete, rectangular, structured lines.

Davey pulls up and gets out to open my door. I stand there, trying to control my nerves, as he lifts my suitcase out of the boot. The enormous and heavy wooden front door swings open and a short, plump, pleasantly smiling Hispanic-looking woman is standing beside it.

'Now then! Who have we got here?' She beams and I like her immediately. 'I'm Rosa,' she says, 'and you must be Meg.'

'Hello . . .'

'Come on in!'

Davey wishes me goodbye and good luck and I follow Rosa inside, to a large, bright hallway. We go through another door at the end and I stop in my tracks. Floor-to-ceiling glass looks out onto the most perfect view of the city, hazy in the afternoon sunshine. A swimming pool out on the terrace sparkles cool and blue.

'Pretty spectacular, ain't it?' Rosa smiles as she surveys my face.

'Amazing,' I agree.

I wonder where The Rock Star is.

'Johnny's away on an impromptu writing trip,' Rosa tells me.

Oh.

'He won't be back until tomorrow,' she continues, 'so you've got a little time to get yourself unpacked and settled in. Or even better, out there by the pool . . .' She nudges me conspiratorially.

I lift the handle on my suitcase and try to ignore my disappointment as Rosa leads me into the large, double-height open-plan room. The hi-tech stereo system and enormous flatscreen TV in the corner tell me it's the living room. Furniture is minimal, modern and super, super cool.

I'm impressed. In fact, I'm feeling less and less blasé about this job by the minute, and that's not helping my steadily swirling nerves.

'The kitchen is over there,' Rosa says, pointing it out behind a curved, frosted-glass wall. 'That's where I spend most of my time. I'm the cook,' she explains before I get the chance to ask.

'I try to feed that boy up. If I were a bartender I'd have a lot more joy. He likes his booze, that one.' She chuckles good-naturedly as we arrive at the foot of the polished-concrete staircase.

'Are you okay with that, honey?' She glances back over her shoulder at my suitcase.

'Yes, fine!'

'We should really have a butler here, but Johnny don't like a lot of staff,' she continues, as she climbs the stairs ahead of me. 'It's not that he's stingy, mind, he just likes us to be a tight-knit family.' She turns right. 'Your room is over here. Johnny's got the big one at the other end, and behind them doors there you've got your guest rooms and Johnny's music studio.' She points them out as we go past. 'Your offices are downstairs, in between the kitchen and the cinema.'

Sorry, did she just say cinema?

'I'll show you round later,' she adds, slightly out of breath now.

'Do you live here, too?' I ask.

'Oh no, honey, I got a family to go home to. Apart from the security staff, you're the only one who'll be here overnight. And Johnny, of course. Okay,' she says, clapping her hands together as we reach the door at the end. 'This is you.' She turns the stainless-steel knob and pushes the heavy metal door open, standing back to let me pass.'

My room is so bright and white that I want to put my shades on. Windows look out over the leafy trees at the back of the house and a giant super-king-size bed is in the centre, covered by a pure white bedspread. White-lacquer floor-to-ceiling wardrobes line one wall, and there are two doors on the other wall.

'Here you've got your kitchenette, where you can whip yourself up some food if mine ain't good enough for you.' From her jovial tone I'm guessing that's not likely to be the case. 'And here you've got your en-suite.'

Some en-suite. It's enormous, with dazzling white stone lining every surface. A huge stone spa is at the back, and a large open shower is to my right, opposite double basins on my left. White fluffy towels hang on heated chrome towel rails.

'Pretty nice, huh?' Rosa chuckles. She walks to the door. 'I'll leave you to settle in. Why don't you come on down to the kitchen when you're good and ready and I'll get you something to eat?'

As the door closes behind her, I start jumping on the spot like a mad woman, face stretched into a silent scream.

This place is mental! I've seen rock star mansions on *MTV Cribs*, but this is something else.

I kick off my shoes and throw myself onto the enormous bed, laughing as I look up at the ceiling.

If only Bess could see this place . . . It's such a far cry from our dingy flatshare back home. It's getting on for midnight now in England and she will have hit the sack long ago, sleeping off her hangover before work tomorrow. I decide to send her a text to wake up to in the morning. I climb off the bed, smiling at the feeling of the thick white shagpile carpet between my toes, and grab my phone from my bag.

Actually, I think I'll send her a picture. I slide open the camera lens instead, snapping the massive room with the (now slightly crumpled) bed in the middle. I punch out a message:

CHECK OUT MY BEDROOM! HAVEN'T MET HIM YET BUT HOUSE IS AMAZING! WISH YOU WERE HERE X

She is going to die when she sees the outside view. I'll have to send her that tomorrow.

I decide to unpack later and instead go and see Rosa downstairs. I find her in the kitchen, frying chicken, peppers and onions in a pan.

'Hey there! I was just preparing you a quesadilla. You must be starving.'

'Can I help?' I ask.

'No, no, no!' She shoos me away, minutes later delivering the finished product, cheese oozing out of the edges of the triangular-cut tortillas. She's right: I am starving.

'I would offer to make you a margarita, but I think you just need feeding up, judging by the state of those skinny arms.' She laughs and pulls up a chair.

My arms *are* skinny compared to hers. In fact, every part of me is skinny compared to Rosa. She's like a big Mexican momma away from home.

'Where do you live, then?' I ask, and discover that home is an hour's drive away, where she has three teenage sons, one ten-year-old daughter, and a husband who works like mad but loves her like crazy from the way she smiles when she speaks of him. It's a long way for her to travel, but she adores working for Johnny. Her only regret is that she's not often there to see him tuck into the meals she leaves for him. And it breaks her heart when she comes in the next morning and finds the food still in the refrigerator.

'You have got to make that boy eat!' she insists to me now. 'Johnny don't eat enough.'

Hearing her speak about 'Johnny' is strange. I keep thinking of him as 'Johnny Jefferson', but soon he'll just be Johnny to me as well.

I do already feel like I know him, though. It's impossible to live in the UK without knowing about Johnny Jefferson, and after a lunch break of Googling him when I worked at Marie's, I now know even more.

His mother died when he was thirteen so he moved from Newcastle to live with his father in London. He dropped out of school to concentrate on his music and formed a band in his late teens. They signed a record contract and were global superstars by the time Johnny was twenty. But he spiralled out of control at the age of twenty-three when the band broke up, before coming back almost two years later as a solo artist. Now thirty, he's one of the most successful rock stars in the world. Of course there are still rumours of his dodgy lifestyle. Drink, drugs, sex – you name it, Johnny's probably done it. I don't mind the odd drink, and I'm not a prude, even if I have had only three serious boyfriends, but I'm really not into the drug scene, and I've never been attracted to bad boys.

Rosa heads off at six-thirty and urges me to get outside by the pool. Ten minutes later I'm on the terrace, clad in the black bikini that I bought for my recent holiday in Italy with Bess. The sun is still baking hot so I stand on the steps in the shallow end and tilt my head back up to catch the rays. The glittering blue water is cool, but not cold, and I don't flinch as I immerse myself fully. I swim a few laps and decide then and there to swim fifty every morning. I did so much walking in London that keeping fit was effortless, but everybody drives cars here so I might need to work at it.

After a while I climb out and spread my towel on the hot paving stones beside the pool, forgoing the sunloungers so I can trail my fingers in the water. My hangover is long gone, and I lie there feeling blissfully happy, listening to the sound of the water filtering through the swimming pool and the cicadas chirping in the undergrowth. High overhead a distant aeroplane leaves a long white streak in the cloudless sky and out of the corner of my eye I can see little black birds swoop down to drink from the pool. I begin to feel dozy.

'Is this what I pay you for?'

I jolt awake to find a dark figure hovering above me, cutting out my sun. I'm so shocked I almost fall in the pool.

'Whoa, shit!'

I rummage around to try to pull my towel out from under my bum so I can cover myself up, but it drops in the water.

'Bollocks!'

I hastily scramble to my feet, realising all I've done in the last few seconds is curse at my new boss.

'Sorry,' I blurt. His eyes graze over my body and I feel like he's undressing me. Which isn't that difficult, because I've barely got anything on as it is. I cross my arms in front of my chest, desperately wanting to retrieve my soaking towel from the pool. Unfortunately, though, that would involve bending over, which is not something I feel comfortable doing right now. I look up.

He's actually quite tall – about six foot two, I estimate, compared to my five-foot-seven-inch frame – and is wearing skinny black jeans and a black T-shirt with a silver metal-studded belt. His dirty blond hair falls messily around his chin and his green eyes, with the light of the swimming pool reflected in them, look almost luminous.

Christ, he *is* gorgeous. Even more so in real life than in pictures.

'Sorry,' I say again, and his mouth curls up slightly as he

reaches down behind me to drag my sopping-wet towel out of the pool. I instinctively want to step away from him, but the only way is backwards and into the water, and I think I've made enough of a tit of myself as it is. He straightens himself back up and wrings the towel out, muscles on his bare arms flexing with the movement. I notice his famous tattoos and can't help but feel on edge.

I remember my sarong is hanging on one of the sunloungers behind him, but he makes no attempt to move for me as I awkwardly sidestep him before hurrying over to grab it. I quickly tie the still-way-too-small green piece of material around my waist.

'Meg, right?' he says.

'Yes, hi,' I reply, watching him while shading my eyes from the sun as he rolls the wet towel up into a ball and aims it at a basket six metres away. It goes straight in. 'And you, er, obviously, are Johnny Jefferson.'

He turns back to me. 'Johnny will do.' I note that he has a few freckles across his nose that I've never noticed in photographs.

'I was just, um, taking a break,' I stutter.

'So I figured,' he replies.

'I didn't think you'd be back until tomorrow.'

'I figured that also.' He raises an eyebrow and delves into his jeans pocket, pulling out a crumpled cigarette packet. Sitting down on one of the sunloungers, he lights up and casually pats the space next to him, but with the way my heart is beating, I figure I'd be safer on the sunlounger opposite instead.

'So, Meg . . .' he says, taking a long drag and looking across at me.

'Yes?'

'Do you smoke?' he asks, not offering me a cigarette.

'No.'

'Good.'

Hypocrite. I think it, but I don't have the guts to say it.

'How old are you?' he asks.

'Twenty-four,' I reply.

'You look older.'

'Do I?'

He flicks his ash into a two-foot-high stainless-steel ashtray and narrows his eyes at me. 'There's a lot of pressure with this job, you know.'

Oh, okay, not really a compliment, more a concern.

'I can handle it.' I try to inject some confidence into my voice.

'Bill and Wendel seem to think so.' He sounds quite American, which is surprising considering he spent the first twenty-five years of his life in England. 'Got a boyfriend?' he asks.

Hey, hang on a second . . . 'What's that got to do with anything?'

'Don't get touchy,' he says, looking amused. 'I just want to know what the chances are of you getting homesick and buggering off back to Old Blighty.' *Now* he sounds English . . .

His stare is making me feel uncomfortable so I hold his gaze for only a couple of seconds. He remains silent and I sure as hell don't know what to say to him.

'You haven't answered my question.'

Question? What question? Oh, boyfriend question . . . I'm finding it difficult to focus.

'No, I don't have a boyfriend.'

'Why not?' he bats back immediately, before taking another long drag on his cigarette.

'Er, well, I did have one but we broke up six months ago. Why?'

He grins, stubbing out his fag. 'Just curious.' He gets to his feet. 'Want a drink?'

I stand up quickly. 'I'll get it.'

He gives me a wry look over his shoulder as he wanders over to the other side of the terrace where there's an outdoor bar area. 'Chill out, chick, I'm perfectly capable of getting myself a drink. What are you having?'

I opt for a Diet Coke.

He returns with two large whiskies on the rocks and hands one over. I look down at it and back up at him. His expression is blank. Did he hear me?

'Um . . .' I say, but the next thing I know he's dragging his T-shirt over his head. Oh my God, I don't know where to look. I take a large gulp of whisky as he stretches out on a sunlounger.

Right then and there, the ridiculousness of the situation hits me. This is nuts. Johnny Jefferson – *the* Johnny Jefferson! – is here in front of me, so close that I could actually reach out and touch him. I could tweak his nipple, for crying out loud! Imagine if I sent Bess a picture of *this* view. A small snort escapes me at the thought.

'You alright?' He glances over at me.

'Yes,' I answer. But, embarrassingly, I start to giggle.

'What's so funny?'

'Nothing,' I quickly reply, but inside my head my mind is going into overdrive . . .

Nothing? A week ago I was working in an architects' studio in London and now I'm in LA, in a rock star mansion, sitting on a sunlounger next to a half-naked rock star! If that's not surreal, I don't know what is.

He knocks back his whisky in one and I hold out my hand for the glass.

'Another?'

He hesitates for a moment before offering it up. 'Why not.'

About time I start doing my job. I get up and hurry to the bar area, finishing the rest of my drink. I survey the bottles in the cupboard under the bar, searching for the whisky. I spot a can of Diet Coke and consider switching but think better of it. What I need right now is some Dutch courage. And a few shots of tequila wouldn't go amiss . . . Ooh, there *is* a bottle of tequila in here, actually. I glance over at Johnny Jefferson, sprawled out on a sunlounger and facing away from me, oblivious to my beverage dilemma.

No, Meg, no. No tequila for you.

Oh, bugger it, I'll just have one.

I take a quick swig from the bottle and almost spit the booze back out as it sears the back of my throat. I desperately, *desperately* want to cough. Instead I swallow furiously and choke back the tears.

I need water. Water!

Or perhaps another swig of tequila would help?

Oddly, it does.

'You know what you're doing over there?' Johnny calls out.

Whoops, I've been ages.

'Yes, just coming!'

I approach the sunloungers, trying not to get distracted by the sight in front of me.

'Cheers.' Johnny chinks my glass and takes a gulp as I sit down.

His chest is toned and smooth and he has a dark tan. There's a tattoo of some writing right across his trouser line. I can't read what it says, but *phwoar* . . .

Oi! Focus, Meg, focus!

'So Rosa said you were away on a writing trip?'

'Yeah. Trying to get everything together for next week.'

'What's happening next week?' I ask.

He looks a little surprised. 'The Whisky?' he replies.

'More whisky?' I ask. Jesus, he really *does* have a drink problem.

'No, *the* Whisky,' he says.

'I don't understand.' I look at him blankly.

'Girl,' he says, 'don't tell me you don't know about my comeback gig at the Whisky – you know, the *venue*?'

'No, sorry, I don't.' My face heats up. 'Should I have heard about it?'

He laughs in disbelief.

'Sorry,' I say, 'but I don't really know much about you.'

And then I begin to ramble like a lunatic . . .

'I mean, I'm not really a fan.'

Shut up, Meg.

'I don't mind some of your songs but, well, you know, I kind of prefer Kylie, to be honest.'

Why the bloody hell did I admit *that*?

'But at least you haven't ended up with a mad stalker,' I continue. 'I could know anything and everything there is to know about you. I could know your favourite colour, the brand of shampoo you use . . .'

Christ Almighty, ZIP IT! Nope. It just gets worse . . .

'At least I'm not a star-fucker.'

ARGH!

'I should hope not, Meg,' he says, stubbing out his second cigarette in five minutes. 'That would be going above and beyond the call of duty.'

'Another drink?' I offer weakly, the reality of everything I've just said starting to sink in. I'm going to lose my job. I'm going to lose my job before it's even started.

'Nah, I've got to shoot off.' He stands up. 'I'm going to hook up with some pals in town. Ring the Viper Room and reserve us a table for eight.'

'Sure. Er, where . . .'

'In the Rolodex in the office. You'll find all the numbers you'll need in there.'

'Is that eight people or eight p.m.?'

'Eight people. Get them to hold the table. I don't know what time we'll be there.'

So I'm still employed, then? I get up hastily and take his empty glass from him, unable to meet his eyes. I turn away and notice in the reflection of the glass window that he's watching his new PA's departing derrière as she makes her way inside to the office.

Half an hour later Johnny Jefferson comes downstairs and finds me tapping my fingers on one of the two big desks in the office. I'm still feeling nervy, despite the tequila, and I'm not quite sure what to do next.

'Table all booked?' he asks, hooking his thumb casually into his jeans pocket. They're the same ones he was wearing earlier, but he's changed into a fitted cream shirt with silver pinstripe.

'Yes, and champagne chilling on ice. I didn't know if you wanted the car so I called Davey just in case. He's waiting on the driveway.'

'Cool.' He nods. 'Thought I'd have to take the bike.'

At least I got that right.

He stays standing in the doorway for a moment, staring at me, his hair still damp from the shower.

'Right then, I'm off.' He pats the palm of his hand on the door with an air of finality.

I try to resist asking, but can't. 'When will you be back?'

'Tomorrow,' he answers. 'Probably.'

And then he's gone. And suddenly the house feels very empty indeed.

Paige Toon

Johnny Be Good

Lots of girls fall for their bosses . . . but how many work for the hottest rock star on the planet?

I'm Meg Stiles. This is my leaving party. And that song we're making a mockery of? That's written by one of the biggest rock stars in the world. And I'm moving in with him tomorrow. Seriously! I am not even kidding you. Well, maybe I'm misleading you a little bit. You see, I haven't actually met him yet . . .

No, I'm not a stalker. I'm his new PA. His Personal Assistant. And I am off to La-la Land. Los Angeles. The City Of Angels – whatever you want to call it – and I can't bloody believe it!

Celebrity PA to wild boy of rock Johnny Jefferson, Meg's glam new life in sun-drenched LA is a whirlwind of showbiz parties and backstage passes. Cool, calm Christian, in town to write his famous friend's biography, helps keep Meg's feet firmly on the ground. But with Johnny's piercing green eyes and a body Brad Pitt would kill for, how long will it be before she's swept right off them again?

'Wonderful, addictive, sharp and sexy' COSMOPOLITAN

ISBN 978-1-84739-044-8
PRICE £6.99

Paige Toon

Lucy in the Sky

A lawyer. A surfer. A 24-hour flight. The frequent liar points are clocking up and Lucy's got choices to make . . .

It's been nine years since Lucy left Australia. Nine years since she's seen her best friend Molly, and Sam, the one-time love of her life. Now her two friends are getting married. To each other. And Lucy is on her way to Sydney for their wedding.

Life for Lucy has moved on. She's happily settled with James, her gorgeous lawyer boyfriend, with their flat in London and her glamorous job in PR. Surely there's no reason to expect this two-week holiday in the sun will be anything out of the ordinary?

But just before take-off, Lucy receives a text from James's mobile. She can't resist taking a look . . . and, in one push of a button, her world comes crashing down . . .

'I loved it – I couldn't put it down!' MARIAN KEYES

ISBN 978-1-84739-043-1
PRICE £6.99

All of Paige Toon's books, as well as other **Pocket Books** titles, are available from your local bookshop or can be ordered direct from the publisher.

978-1-84739-044-8	**Johnny Be Good**	£6.99
978-1-84739-043-1	**Lucy in the Sky**	£6.99
978-1-84739-390-6	**Chasing Daisy**	£6.99

Free post and packing within the UK
Overseas customers please add £2 per paperback.
Telephone Simon & Schuster Cash Sales at Bookpost
on 01624 677237 with your credit or debit card number,
or send a cheque payable to Simon & Schuster Cash Sales to:
PO Box 29, Douglas, Isle of Man, IM99 1BQ
Fax: 01624 670923
Email: bookshop@enterprise.net
www.bookpost.co.uk

Please allow 14 days for delivery. Prices and availability are subject to change without notice.